CONCRETE EVIDENCE
EVIDENCE

RACHEL
GRANT

JANUS
PUBLISHING

For Dave,
Because you always believed in me.

Prologue

November 1952
US Army Garrison Fort Belmont, Maryland

*H*e arrived at Regina Guerrero's house at the usual time. As he walked up the front path, he waved to her son, Ricky, who played in the yard. The four-year-old grinned, his wide brown eyes the only part of his face not covered in dirt. Gina needed to take better care of that kid.

She met him at the door, then stumbled as she led him into the living room of her cramped army house. Dammit. She was already drunk. He'd wanted to talk to her about their future, but when she was drunk, the sex was quick and she usually passed out afterward.

Moving boxes were stacked against the wall. An agonizing surge of hope brought him to a dead stop. "You changed your mind. You're leaving Claudio and coming with me when my transfer goes through."

"You silly boy." She laughed, a cold, hard sound, and walked into the kitchen, probably to refill the empty glass in her hand.

He followed, his face burning at her insult.

She reached for the bottle of whiskey on the counter and filled her glass. Sipping her drink, she studied him over the rim, then reached for his pants. "We don't have much time. My sitter for Ricky canceled." She felt his hard-on and smiled. "Sometimes your age is an advantage."

He never should have told her he'd lied about his age to get into the army. Now that she knew he was only sixteen, she was always making cracks about his age, no matter what he did to prove he was a man. He pushed her away. "We need to talk."

"I didn't invite you here to talk." She reached for him again.

He closed his eyes as her hand cupped him. They could talk later…

No. Regina would pass out, and he'd end up babysitting Ricky. Again. He opened his eyes and stepped away from her. "Why are you packing?"

"We're going to live with my parents in Montreal while Claudio is in Korea."

Her words crushed his ridiculous hope. "But I'm being transferred to San Diego. I want you to come with me." Wanted. Needed. He was sick with the idea of being forced to live so far away from her.

"We're going to stay with my parents." She downed her drink in one long swallow.

"Please, Gina. I love you. I can take care of you and Ricky. You can get a divorce, marry me, and we'll be happy."

"Claudio will never let me take Ricky away from him. And he won't let me leave when he needs a mother to raise his son." Through the kitchen window, her gaze fixed on the boy. "As long as I have Ricky, I'm trapped." When she faced him again, her eyes were moist with tears. He pulled her into his arms.

Her kisses were as violent as her hands, and he wondered if sex was supposed to be so combative. She perched on the kitchen counter and bit down hard on his ear as she came, while her son played right outside the window.

After she finished, she pushed him away and slipped off the counter. "I need to lie down," she said and wobbled into the bedroom.

He zipped up his pants and stared though the window. The boy, completely covered in mud, played with the garden hose. He pushed up the pane of glass. "Ricky," he said. "You need to take a bath. Your mom wants me to take you to the movies."

Thirty minutes later, Ricky was clean, dressed, and on his way out to the truck while he looked in on Regina. She was sound asleep, her mouth wide open. He wrote a note saying they'd gone to see *Cinderella*.

"*Cine?*" Ricky said, after they'd been driving for a half hour.

It took him a moment to figure out what the boy was asking because he spoke Spanish and French better than English. "Instead of the movies, we're going someplace very special." He hoped the boy understood him, but it didn't matter.

They drove for another hour before he turned at the weathered sign that marked the driveway for the Carleton School for Indian Boys. He headed down the long drive and parked in front of the old building. The Pennsylvania boarding school was a dumping ground for Indian orphans and the perfect place for Ricky Guerrero. This way Gina could leave Claudio without fear, and they would no longer be stuck with a kid she didn't want.

The headmaster, a gaunt older white man, met them at the front door. "Is this a new student? I can't take boys younger than five."

"He's five," he lied. "He's small for his age." He held his breath, praying the boy wouldn't speak and ruin everything. But Ricky just looked confused.

He nudged the boy forward.

"Is he an orphan?"

"His parents died in a car accident two weeks ago."

The headmaster didn't bother to look at the boy again. "What's his name?"

His name? Shit. He needed something that sounded Indian and scanned the entryway. The school crest was mounted above the front door: an eagle ready to land, wings extended, talons out. "Talon," he said, then struggled for a first name. Who was that famous chief? Oh yeah. Joseph. "Joseph Talon."

The boy spoke in a combination of high-pitched Spanish and French.

The headmaster frowned. "We don't allow Indian languages to be spoken here."

"He seems to understand English but doesn't speak it."

"What tribe is he from?"

"Menanichoch," he said easily, naming the tribe that had once occupied Fort Belmont land.

The headmaster nodded. "Does he have a birth certificate?"

He shook his head. "He was born in a teepee. No papers."

The headmaster looked at him strangely, and he realized he'd made a mistake. Hell, should he have said wigwam? Igloo? Hut? What the hell did the Menanichoch live in? "He doesn't have any family, and the kids at the orphanage were picking on him for being Indian. The State of Maryland thought he'd be better off here, with his kind."

"No one called me."

He shrugged. "Someone screwed up. Look, I'm just the delivery guy. My instructions were to bring the kid here, and I did." He turned to leave.

"Wait. I'll take him, but I need you to sign a form

swearing he's Indian, or the government won't pay for his upkeep."

Another student meant a bigger budget to skim. He suppressed a smile. One of his fellow soldiers had escaped from the Carleton School; you never knew when information overheard in the mess hall would come in handy.

He filled out the form, then signed a fake name at the bottom. He'd given Joseph Talon a white mother and an Indian father to explain why he didn't look exactly Indian.

He patted the boy on the head and walked toward his truck, hardly able to believe it had gone so smoothly. Then the kid started to cry and ran after him. Ricky—Joseph now —wrapped his arms around his leg and clung to him. He pulled the boy's small hands apart, feeling sorry for him, but there wasn't any other way.

On the drive back, his mood lightened. Their problems were solved. Gina was better looking than Rita Hayworth and his sergeant's wife combined, and Gina would come with him to San Diego, and all the soldiers there would respect and admire him because she was his. He laughed out loud and wished he'd thought of taking Ricky to the school sooner. For weeks he'd been sick with anxiety over losing Gina.

She was kneeling in front of a cardboard box when he returned. Her dress was crisp, her hair and makeup perfect, the redness in her eyes the only sign she'd been drinking earlier. "Where's Ricky?" she asked idly, her attention on the books she was packing.

"Outside."

She stood and brushed wrinkles from her skirt. Not only did she look like a movie star, she moved like one.

"Good. I'll get you a drink." She headed into the kitchen.

He followed her, hardly able to believe she would be his forever.

She handed him a glass. He took a large gulp and nearly spit it out. It was straight booze and burned all the way down.

She grinned.

She was always doing shit like that, trying to make him feel like a kid. As if at twenty-three she was so much older and wiser. If she was so smart, how come he had to solve her problems for her?

He'd been tested his whole life by the meanest son of a bitch there was. Gina Guerrero was no match for his father. He chugged the drink and set his empty glass on the counter.

She laughed, and her eyes lit with admiration.

He felt a burst of pride, and the words he'd been dying to say came rushing out. "Your troubles are over. I've found a home for Ricky. You can come with me to San Diego."

"I told you, we're going to live with my parents."

She was so simple sometimes. So dense. "You don't need to worry about Ricky or Claudio." He spoke slowly so she'd understand. "I'm taking care of you now."

"You? You're just a boy. You can't take care of us."

He felt a flash of anger, the kind he'd worked so hard to control when his father told him he was stupid and useless. "Pigs are cleaner than your son."

She slapped him, a quick hard slash of her hand, just like his old man.

He raised his arm to strike her but checked his swing and shook his head, trying to force back memories of hard fists and leather belts. He would not become his father. He was a man now, a soldier. "You love me, Gina. I know you love me."

"For a whiz kid on the officer fast track, you sure are stupid. I don't love you. You're just a fuck while Claudio is away."

That had to be the booze talking.

"You fumble in bed and come too soon. You're not a man like Claudio."

You're not a man. He heard his father taunting him. Something inside snapped. He hit her, the entire weight of his body behind his fist when it slammed into her jaw.

She spun backward and crashed into the refrigerator. Her head hit the handle, and she slowly slid to the floor. A streak of blood ran from the silver handle, down the white door, ending where her head leaned against the refrigerator at an unnatural angle.

"Gina!" He touched her face, then straightened her slack neck as if that would fix her. "I'm sorry!"

Her eyes went blank.

A sob rose up in his chest. "I love you, Gina. I love you."

But he knew she couldn't hear him. Christ, what was he going to do?

Chapter One

July 2011
Bethesda, Maryland

usic pulsed through Erica Kesling's headphones as she thrust her foot high, hitting the hanging punching bag right where Jake Novak's face ought to be. Her gloved fists found the same spot, two blows in rapid succession, guaranteed to shatter Jake's imaginary nose. The next kick connected with his groin. In her mind, he doubled over and begged for mercy.

She showed him the same measure of mercy he had shown her. If this were real, the roundhouse kick would have finished him off.

The repeated kicks rubbed the skin on her foot raw until streaks of blood marred the blue bag. She ignored the pain. Each sore, each bruise, only made her stronger. She would be ready when she faced the thieving treasure hunter again.

As she abused the imaginary Jake, she felt real hope, a first since walking out of the jungle a year ago. She'd just kicked Jake in the stomach when the door opened and a very tall man in workout gear entered the room. He nodded to her and went straight for the free weights.

She acknowledged him with a tip of her head, annoyed her private workout time had ended. She'd never seen him in the company gym before, but Talon & Drake employed over two hundred people in Bethesda and several hundred more in other offices. He could be the hydrologist from the Boston office who was supposed to help out in Bethesda for a month. One of the chemists had told her the incoming hydrologist was hot and had called dibs.

She felt his eyes on her as he lifted weights. She waited until he looked away before she checked him out. Impressive delts and triceps, a nice complement to his handsome face. He hadn't shaved, and his short, light brown hair was mussed in a way that made her think he'd come here straight from bed. He had to be the hydrologist, because even his messy hair and stubbly jaw were sexy.

She looked back at the bag and planted another kick in Jake's abdomen. The guy might have a nice face and body, but she still wished she had the employee gym to herself.

She kicked and punched until she was dripping sweat and her breathing was ragged with exhaustion. From the corner of her eye, she saw the guy put away the weights and approach her. She twisted and kicked the bag from behind. He stopped on the opposite side of the bag and held it. He was imposing, even taller than she'd thought at first.

"You should take a break," he said.

With a gloved hand, she tapped her headphones and lied, "Can't hear you!" She kicked left, then spun around and kicked right, in the zone, her blood pumping, her aggression high. No one would tell her when she was done.

Her foot came dangerously close to him, but he didn't budge. "I'd like a turn with the bag," he shouted.

"I get the bag every morning until seven." Distracted, she missed her target and just glanced the slippery vinyl with her foot. Momentum sent her to the floor, hard. The headphones clattered to the mat next to her. *Crap. Could I look any more ridiculous?*

She caught her breath and winced, then tried to sweep her hair from her face, but the thick foam glove was awkward and made her feel even clumsier, answering her own question. Defeated, she blew her hair from her eyes and looked up at him. "And sometimes the bag gets me."

Warm hands encircled her wrists just below the gloves, and he pulled her to her feet, the light in his eyes hinting at a smile. "It's not your fault. The bag jumped out of the way."

"Damn thing has it in for me."

He picked up her fallen headset and used the cord to reel her to him. His actions were smooth, confident. She didn't hesitate to step closer and couldn't fathom why.

A scant foot separated them when he said, "You have a fantastic ass. It's a shame to see you fall on it." His eyes lit in playful challenge—*daring her to object?*—as he grinned, then placed the headphones over her ears and walked away.

Stunned, she stared after him. If it weren't for the teasing grin, she'd be offended. Turnabout was fair play, however, and she paused to admire his ass, which was damn fine in her estimation. She shook her head as if to clear it. She had artifacts to find, a reputation to redeem, and a treasure hunter to put in jail. Juvenile flirtation with the new hydrologist ranked dead last on her list of priorities.

She escaped to the shower. A half hour later, dressed and ready for work, she headed to the juice bar in the lobby of the large office building and treated herself to a smoothie. The five-dollar drink was extravagant, but today was special. Or at least it would be, if her boss gave her the Thermo-Con Environmental Assessment for the Menanichoch Tribe.

Drink in hand, she took the elevator to the eighth floor and headed straight to her boss's office. She paused in the open doorway and took a sip of the smoothie for courage.

"Oh, good, you're here," Janice Rabinowitz said. "We need to talk."

Janice's tone caused a surge of fear. If Janice had learned about the mistakes she'd made a year ago, she would fire Erica. She took a long, slow breath, forcing herself to appear calm. "What's going on?"

"A new archaeologist is starting today. Or tomorrow. To be honest, I'm not really sure."

Okay, Janice didn't want to talk about Mexico, but her relief was only marginal. Gossip on the archaeology grapevine was perpetuated by dig bums—archaeology's version of itinerant field-workers. A new archaeologist—especially if they were from the West Coast—could have heard Jake's twisted version of what happened in Mexico.

Jake couldn't tell the truth without implicating himself, but the truth would ruin her just as thoroughly as his lies had. So far, those lies hadn't crossed the Rockies and made it to Janice's ears. Thanks to the disconnect between coasts, and the fact that underwater archaeologists didn't play in the same sandbox with their land-based peers, Erica had lasted six months at Talon & Drake, and now, when the project she'd been waiting for was finally within her grasp, a new hire could get her fired. "You hired someone over the weekend?"

"He's being foisted on us by the home office. He's scheduled for a six-week internship. I want you to supervise him. He'll share your office."

An intern was unlikely to have field experience and probably wouldn't have heard of her. But sharing her office would seriously hamper her plans. "I don't have time to train a spoiled intern. I'm swamped with cell towers, and frankly, I was hoping you'd give me the Thermo-Con Environmental Assessment."

Janice adjusted her glasses. "That's why you need an assistant, Erica. I've been hesitant to give you the Menanichoch EA because of your workload. But the intern can help. Train him to take over the cell tower projects."

Erica groaned. "I'd rather chew aluminum foil than explain cell tower projects again."

Janice laughed. "Then I hope you don't have fillings."

"Do we really have to take this guy on?"

"He's been sent from the top—and I mean top, top. The call came from Joseph Talon, Jr.'s executive secretary. This kid happens to be some bigwig's cousin's nephew's next-door neighbor once removed."

Erica sighed. "Great. A pampered rich kid who's hoping to dig up treasure."

"That may be true, but we've got to take him. When someone from the home office asks for a favor and, more importantly, gives me the overhead to pay for it, I can't say no."

For the thousandth time, she wished she had the courage to tell Janice about Mexico. There was always a chance Janice would believe the truth: she had been trying to rescue the artifacts, not steal them.

The words formed in her throat, then lodged in a place that made breathing difficult. She'd been blackballed from underwater archaeology because of Jake. Erica was lucky archaeology was a field in which an extensive list of projects on her curriculum vitae was all she needed to show she knew her way around a trowel. In a pinch, employers rarely checked references, and Janice had been no different when she needed bodies in the field.

Erica had worked her butt off to parlay the field job into a full-time office position, and here she was. She couldn't risk being fired now, not when she almost had a Menanichoch project. "Okay," she said, consoling herself with the fact that an intern would be young, inexperienced, and pliable. "But unless he's good with computers, he won't touch the cell tower projects. It took me hours to fix the database after the biologists screwed it up."

"Then he can help you with the Menanichoch EA."

She sucked in a sharp breath. "You're giving me Thermo-Con?"

Janice smiled. "Yes. You need more environmental project experience if you're going to start grad school in September. But, here's the bad news: the EA is due a week from today."

Her heart beat faster than hummingbird wings, and she held back a smile that would reveal too much. But then the bad news sank in, and fighting a smile was no longer difficult. "The Scope of Work said we'd have a month to write the EA. What changed?"

"The left hand didn't know what the right was doing. The tribe's Environmental Compliance Officer called me late Friday with the change to the project timeline. I balked, and she said if we can't meet the deadline, they'll find someone who can." Janice handed her a manila file. "Here's all the information we have on Thermo-Con."

Seven days. Seven days to produce the best damned environmental assessment ever to bear the Talon & Drake logo and get her foot in the door with tribal chairman, Sam Riversong. Seven days to get a lead on the artifacts.

"Tomorrow, I want you to research Thermo-Con at the National Archives," Janice said.

"But tomorrow I'll need to train the intern. We should put off the new hire until after the EA is done." She smiled, having found the perfect argument to delay the intern.

"Or you can train the intern today and still go to the archives tomorrow," said a deep voice from the doorway.

She turned to see the man from the exercise room leaning against the doorjamb with relaxed grace, his tall form filling the opening. He'd cleaned up and shaved. Now his short brown hair stood up in damp disarray. His crisp shirt and slacks struck the perfect balance of business casual, which made him look authoritative in a sexy way. He pushed off the doorframe in a smooth motion that demonstrated comfort with his extra-long form, and she felt an unwelcome flutter in her belly.

This was no acne-laden college student.

"Lee Scott." He held out his hand to Janice. "Spoiled intern, pampered rich kid."

How long had he been standing there? She stiffened and thought of several more adjectives to apply to him.

He dropped into the chair next to her, his smile letting her know he enjoyed catching her off balance…again. "I'm sorry, I didn't catch your name."

"Erica Kesling." She braced for recognition but saw none in his intent green eyes.

"Now that you're here, Lee," Janice said. "Erica will bring you up to speed on our projects, and you both can dive into the Thermo-Con Environmental Assessment, which we're writing for the Menanichoch Tribe."

"I have no clue what Thermo-Con is," he said.

"Few people do," Janice said. "Thermo-Con was a type of concrete that rose like bread dough after the pour and would harden after it reached two and a half times its original size. The only known house made of Thermo-Con was built in the early fifties and is on land under tribal trust to the Menanichoch Nation. Erica will explain it all to you."

"I don't get how that relates to archaeology."

"Erica will explain that too. But first, tell us about yourself."

He shrugged. "I'm a student at Columbia. I'm an English major, but I've decided I want to study something more exciting. I figured it would be a good idea to see if archaeology is the right fit before I make another bad choice. I've already switched from premed to political science to English."

Great. A slacker career student and Indiana Jones wannabe. The changed majors explained his age, which had to be closer to thirty than twenty. The good news: he didn't know anything and probably wasn't connected to the dig-bum grapevine. The bad news: he didn't know anything and would be useless as an assistant. "So, what do you know about archaeology?" she asked. "Besides that you think dinosaurs are cool, I mean."

Amusement flashed in his eyes. "Nice try. I'm not inter-ested in *paleontology*—even though when I was six, I did think dinosaurs were cool."

Janice laughed.

Erica gave him a point for his smooth handling of her snide question. "What archaeology classes have you taken?"

"None so far, but I've been reading up on the subject. I'm interested in the intersection between archaeology and envi-ronmental law. I know the National Environmental Policy Act goes hand in hand with the National Historic Preservation Act, which has me wondering if I should consider a double major—biology and archaeology. I'm guessing expertise in both fields would make me most useful to potential employers."

"You have been reading." She felt strangely chilled. His words could have been taken directly from her application to American University's Environmental Science graduate program, which she was starting in September. Talon & Drake's continuing education program would pay her tuition, another reason she had to hold on to this job.

"That's an excellent plan, Lee," Janice said. "You were right to get an internship to see if you're making the right choice. You'll get some good experience with our cell tower projects. They're a perfect merge of environmental and historic preservation law."

"What do you do on the cell tower projects?" he asked.

"We make sure new towers are built without harming historic properties or the environment," Janice replied. "Erica, bright girl that she is, developed a database for managing the projects. Fill in the proper blanks in the database, and voilà, the report is generated."

"I'm not good with databases." His laugh turned into an embarrassed cough.

"How not good?" Erica asked.

"I accidentally deleted the last one I worked on."

A wave of horror passed through her. She couldn't let him near the database.

"I'm good with Word, though," he said. "Well, the old version. Before they made all those dumb changes."

"Erica can teach you all you need to know." Janice smiled at her with motherly pride. "You'll be sharing her office. I've already put in a request for a computer for you."

"I don't need a computer. I brought my own."

Janice paused. "You need to let tech support check it out and load the network firewall."

"I left it with them before I came here."

"Excellent. Erica can take you to human resources to get an ID badge. Tomorrow you'll both go to the National Archives. You're lucky, Lee. Research at the archives is a rare event and a good learning experience."

Erica stood, clutching the project file. "I want to go to the Thermo-Con house today—to take pictures."

"Take Lee with you." Janice waved them out of the room.

She had her project. At last. She held the file to her chest as she walked down the hall, Lee at her side. Feeling a bubble of hope, she laughed with relief.

"What's so funny?" he asked.

She stopped and turned to face him. He was at least a foot taller than she was. His sea-green eyes studied her. She felt his raw sex appeal and cursed him for planting that seed in the exercise room. Now it was hard to view him any other way. He was a coworker, her intern, and she'd given up on even making friends with coworkers, let alone developing a deeper involvement. Her grad school friends had all judged her harshly based on half-truths and outright lies. She wouldn't open herself up to that kind of rejection again.

He snapped his fingers in front of her face. "Hello?"

Embarrassed, she voiced the concern that nagged at her. "You aren't what I expected."

"What did you expect?"

"Someone younger. How old are you, anyway?"

He shrugged. "Does it matter?"

"It does if you think you're too old to do the lowly intern work."

"I'm twenty-five. As I said, I've changed my major a few times."

From his bearing, she'd have guessed he was closer to thirty, maybe even past that number. He must have been born confident. "You've been in college, what, seven years?"

He nodded.

"You could have three degrees by now." She had a Master's degree she couldn't use and was barely scraping by, while he'd enjoyed seven years as an *undergrad* at freaking *Columbia*.

"I like school. What's the rush to graduate?"

Spoiled didn't begin to describe him.

The man she'd met in the exercise room hadn't struck her as lazy. Even now he had an appealing energy which buzzed about him. What a waste.

His gaze moved down her body, and she shifted uncomfortably. She wished she didn't find him handsome. Attraction made her stupid.

He tilted his head and murmured, "This would be easier if you weren't so beautiful."

Oh. My.

She couldn't afford to be stupid right now.

Time to put him in his place. "You were a stranger back in the workout room, but now I'm your supervisor and expect to be treated with respect. If you can't do that, I can order you to attend human resources' sensitivity training."

She turned on her heel and headed toward her office. Their office. *Damn.* She reached the stuffy, windowless room and flung open the door. Today wasn't going at all as planned.

She pointed to the large lab table. "You can work there." After dropping her purse on her desk, she booted up her computer, ignoring the man who hovered in her peripheral vision, waiting for her to share with him everything she'd learned about archaeology through hard work and expensive schooling.

She clicked on the Talon & Drake email program, seeking distraction. He was spoiled, and she was jealous. She'd get over it; she just needed one minute to simmer.

She scanned the list of new emails as they downloaded from the server. One caught her eye, and her pique at him was forgotten. She placed her hands on either side of her keyboard to steady herself as her vision narrowed and cold sweat dotted her forehead.

Jake Novak had contacted her. The subject line was blank. She sank into her seat and clicked on the email with trembling fingers.

His message appeared in stark black and white: *You have a good job at Talon & Drake, but I can take it away.*

Chapter Two

*L*ee ran through his list of required personality traits: flaky, check; Indiana Jones wannabe, check; annoying to his new supervisor, check twice. Not bad for his first hour in the office. His cover story was in place, and Janice and Erica had accepted him at face value.

Erica didn't miss much. That would be a problem. She'd zeroed in on his age immediately. He'd started to duck the question, then decided that could make her suspicious. Subtracting seven years from his age had been a necessary improvisation. A flaky twenty-five-year-old was believable, and she had no reason to question his cover story, for now.

He leaned against the break room counter. She gave him a rundown of what she expected from him while they waited for the coffee to finish brewing.

She cleaned up well. He'd said she was beautiful to rankle her, but he still meant it. Even the harsh, fluorescent light of the break room couldn't diminish her high cheekbones, slim nose, and smooth pale skin. And he could get lost in those large, wintry gray eyes. In the workout room, he'd been transfixed by her glossy, dark hair, then confined to a sweaty ponytail; now pulled back into a bun so tight he wondered if it hurt whenever she moved her head. If he hadn't watched her while she exercised, then her clothing, her hair, and her demeanor would all make him believe she was repression personified.

Earlier, he'd been caught off guard by the instant attraction he'd felt for the woman who let loose on the heavy bag with ferocious energy. Now he wondered where she hid the fire beneath this icy exterior of hers, and the thought of trying to find out held a masochistic appeal.

An older man with silver hair and sharp blue eyes walked into the break room. "I've been looking all over for you," he said to Erica.

She looked startled. "For me? Why?"

"Janice told me she gave you the Thermo-Con Environmental Assessment."

She pushed away from the counter and straightened her shoulders. "I may not be an architectural historian, but I've read up on International Style structures and—"

The man cut her off with a sharp wave of his hand. "My only concern is the project timeline. Sam Riversong called me this morning. The tribe screwed up, and they need a fast turnaround on the EA. He asked me to make sure you stay on schedule."

"So what do you want from us?" Lee asked to inject himself into the conversation.

The man turned his sharp gaze to Lee. "Who are you?"

"Sorry," Erica said. "Rob Anderson, this is our new intern, Lee Scott."

Rob Anderson. The project manager overseeing all the Iraq contracts. The man was second on his list of suspects and one of the reasons Lee was here, pretending to be an archaeological intern.

Erica turned back to Rob, dismissing Lee from the

conversation. "Why would Riversong call you when you're not even part of the environmental team?"

"Sam and I go way back."

From his research, Lee knew Rob had served in the army with Sam Riversong and Edward Drake decades ago.

"I want daily updates on your progress," Rob said. "Starting today."

"Today we're going to the house, tomorrow the National Archives," she said.

"Good." He turned to leave but paused in the doorway. "As an archaeologist, what's your take on Ed Drake's plan to submit a proposal to bring up the historic navy airplane from the Chesapeake?"

Alarm flashed across her face. "This is the first I've heard of it, but I think it's a terrible idea. Underwater work is incredibly dangerous and expensive, and we don't have anyone on staff with underwater archaeology expertise."

Now Erica had Lee's attention. She was lying.

Yesterday he'd hacked into her application to American University. Her file included a transcript from the University of Hawaii, where she'd earned a Master's degree in under-water archaeology and had been working on her PhD when she left the program. The woman qualified as resident expert on the subject, yet he'd found no mention of her graduate degree in her curriculum vitae, and now she said nothing to tout her expertise to one of Talon & Drake's most senior engineers. Interesting.

"That's what I was afraid of, but Ed is determined to pursue it." Rob ran a hand through his thinning gray hair. "I'll talk to him. Get to work on Thermo-Con. Email me with your progress when you get back from the house." He left the room.

Lee smiled. Rob had completely ignored him. It was as if the title "intern" was an invisibility cloak. Maybe he could actually pull this off. He poured the freshly brewed coffee into two mugs and handed her one. "Who was that?"

"He's an engineer. He manages our Iraq projects."

Just the segue he was aiming for. "Talon & Drake has projects in Iraq?"

She looked at him quizzically. "Don't you read the paper?"

"I'm a student. I don't have time to read."

"Didn't you even google Talon & Drake before you accepted the internship?"

Excellent. Nothing said incompetent quite like the inability to use Google. "It didn't occur to me."

She rolled her eyes in exasperation. "Talon & Drake has been in the news a lot lately. For several reasons, but mostly because Senator Joseph Talon—you do know who Senator Talon is, don't you?"

Better than you'd imagine. "Yes." He put insult and exasperation into the single word.

"Then you know he's all but announced he's running for president."

"Is he a Democrat or a Republican?" Playing dumb was easy. Too easy.

"And to think your uninformed vote is worth the same as mine," she muttered.

He wondered how she'd react if she knew he could recite the senator's voting record.

She took a sip of coffee, then cradled her mug in her hands and stared at him over the rim. "If you're going to work here, there are a few basic facts you should know. Starting with, one: Senator Talon owns Talon & Drake."

The exact ownership and management of Talon & Drake had been combed through and nitpicked by pundits for weeks, and her one-sentence summation was vastly inadequate. "What about Drake?" he asked, just to needle her.

Her brow furrowed in exasperation. Mission accomplished.

"Correction," she said, "Edward Drake owns a portion of the company, but Senator Talon is the *majority* shareholder." She held up two fingers. "Two: the senator doesn't run the company. Joseph Talon, Jr., has been running the company since his father became senator."

"JT," Lee said, deciding to raise his IQ by a few points.

"What?"

"Joseph Talon, Jr., goes by JT."

She cocked her head to the side in question.

He grinned and pointed to the ten-year-old *TIME* magazine cover that had been enlarged and mounted on the break room wall. JT smiled with confidence next to a headline that read: MEET JT TALON, THE 27-YEAR-OLD WUNDERKIND CEO WHO TRANSFORMED HIS FATHER'S COMPANY.

Erica's lips quirked in the smallest of smiles. He felt a miniscule thawing of the frost that had formed when he'd called her beautiful. "Which takes me to item three." She held up three fingers and continued ticking off the facts. "Because *JT* runs the company, the senator hasn't made a management decision at Talon & Drake in twelve years."

He wasn't surprised that fact was important enough to earn a spot on her list. It had been hashed over by the media ad nauseam. If the senator were involved with running the international engineering firm, he'd be in violation of Senate ethics.

"Four: the company holds several Department of Defense contracts for work in Iraq and Afghanistan. Five: the senator's rivals for his party's presidential nomination are comparing Talon & Drake to Halliburton and saying he voted to invade Iraq so he could profit from the war."

Her voice dropped to a less teacherly, more solemn tone. "And the last reason Talon & Drake has been on the news lately: one of our employees was killed in Baghdad last week by an IED."

And there it was—his real reason for being here. JT Talon had received an email claiming Talon & Drake employees were smuggling something—probably artifacts—out of Iraq. The informant died an hour later. Lee needed to find the smugglers and expose the killer. And he needed to do it before it became a scandal that would ruin Joseph Talon's presidential campaign.

*A*s Erica drove her old Honda wagon down the road that marked the boundary of the Menanichoch Reservation, she ignored both her disturbingly handsome passenger and the pressing fear Jake's email had caused. Instead she focused on the remnants that indicated the land had been owned and occupied by the US Army until the mid-1990s. Hidden by the roadside was an old sign covered with vines and shot with bullet holes; the faded lettering announced the main entrance to Fort Belmont was a quarter mile ahead.

She knew Sam Riversong and Joseph Talon had struggled for years to get the federal government to recognize the Menanichoch Tribe. Five years after that success, they convinced the army to close Fort Belmont and return the land to the tribe.

Erica parked on the street in front of the house that represented the first step in her plan to rescue the artifacts and return them to the Mexican government. She looked past Lee and stared at the house, excitement coursing through her. "This is it," she said softly.

Lee's profile was all she could see as he gazed at the house, and she wondered what he thought of it. Finally, he let out a low whistle and said, "Whoa."

She smiled. "Not what you expected?" She loved everything about the funky two-story, flat-roofed, box-shaped home. She handed him the photolog and got out of the car. "Write down what I tell you." Camera in hand, she snapped a picture and then checked the image. "Photo 26: Thermo-Con house south façade. Don't forget to include the date."

They moved to the west façade, and she took another picture.

"Which side is the front?" he asked.

"All of them. Or none, I suppose." Each side of the house contained a door and small porch, making it look as if there were four front sides. In addition, the structure had off-kilter windows of different sizes. Nothing was symmetrical or balanced, giving an almost deranged appearance.

"*This* was built by the military?" he said with disbelief.

"That's one of the questions we need to answer." She smiled, strangely pleased by his reaction to the house. "We have two newspaper articles, both published in 1952, but neither article says who developed Thermo-Con, or why. All we know is this house was supposed to be a prototype for military housing."

"So what, exactly, is our job?"

"We need to answer several research questions. For starters, we want to find out who built the house on Fort Belmont, and why."

"I don't get the connection between Fort Belmont and the Menanichoch Tribe."

"This land belonged to the Menanichoch Tribe until 1935, when the tribe lost federal recognition and the army took the land and built Fort Belmont. Ten years ago, the base was shut down through the Base Realignment and Closure program—BRAC for short—and the Menanichoch got their land back."

"Why are we writing an environmental assessment?"

"The house is eligible for listing in the National Register

of Historic Places and needs major repairs. Under BRAC, environmental and historic preservation laws kick in, and they require an EA before the work can be completed."

He stared at the house, and she had the sense he was taking in much more than the structure before him; then his mouth curved in a warm, full smile that lit his green eyes. "The house is cool."

Her belly fluttered, and she didn't know if the sensation was caused by his smile or the fact that he appreciated the house as much as she did. She turned away. She needed to work without escaping into girlish fantasies based on magnificent pecs and a shared taste in architecture.

His good looks explained his lack of direction. Wealthy pretty boys like him had everything handed to them and didn't know how to work for a living. He was the opposite of everything that was important to her. "Yes, well, archaeologists research quirky houses. We rarely travel to exotic places. And we never look for treasure or get shot at by bad guys." *Except for the one time in which I did all of those things.*

His smile faded. "Damn, I wish you'd told me that before I bought my whip and fedora." He rounded the corner of the house, anger showing in his quick stride.

Guilt swept her for insulting him when he'd done nothing but show enthusiasm for the project. She hurried after him, intending to apologize, but after turning the corner, she saw a plumber's truck and came to a dead stop. "They're not supposed to be working yet." She walked briskly toward the nearest door and entered the kitchen. "Hello? Is there someone here?" If they'd started work on the house without a signed EA, she would have the perfect excuse to complain to the tribal office and Sam Riversong.

She glanced at Lee, who'd followed her inside. His mouth was set in a firm line.

"I'm sorry I was bitchy," she said.

He shrugged. "Don't worry about it."

A voice called out from the basement. At the top of the basement staircase, the smell of something rotten made her gag. Lee made a face and covered his mouth, then said, "By all means, ladies first." She saw the smile behind his hand.

She smiled back, accepting her penance, and led the way. In the basement, two men in dirty coveralls were bent over an opening in a corner. "Are you here for the house rehabilitation project?" she asked. "Work isn't supposed to begin until next week. The EA has to be signed first."

One of the men glanced over his shoulder at her; his dark beard was shot with the same gray that covered his head. "Don't know what you're talking about. We were called here to fix the broken sump."

"Smells like something died in here," Lee said.

"Rats," the younger plumber responded. "The sump was broken for weeks before anyone noticed, and rats were floating in the muck we pumped out this morning."

Her excuse to complain to the tribe suffered the same fate as the rats; no one could blame them for fixing a flooded basement before the EA was signed. "We're from Talon & Drake, the engineering firm handling the rehab on the building. We're here to photograph the house."

The bearded plumber scanned her from head to foot. "You're an engineer?" His disbelief was evident.

What decade did this guy live in? "No. I'm an archaeologist."

"So you're the engineer," the man said to Lee, obviously relieved natural order wasn't in jeopardy.

"Me?" Lee squeaked out the word like a timid mouse, making it hard for her to keep a straight face. "No. I'm her lackey."

They headed back up the stairs, and when they were out of earshot, she said, "Thanks."

He grinned. "You owe me. When do I get to collect?"

She rolled her eyes. "When you're my boss."

His grin widened. "With my connections, two weeks should do it."

"With my luck, you'll be like JT Talon and get the job because you're somebody's son."

He stopped. "You don't think he deserved the job?"

"He was twenty-five—your age—when he became head of the company. You can't convince me that decision was anything but nepotism." She opened a cupboard but saw nothing of interest in the decaying wood. "It doesn't matter, really. By all accounts, JT's done a great job." She paused, then added, "I guess I don't like nepotism because I'm not in a position to benefit from it."

"So what now?" he asked, glancing around the kitchen.

"Aside from taking pictures, we're here to poke around. I'm looking for anything we can google to find out more about the house. Names, dates. Scraps of paper left behind the stove. Nobody knows anything about this house."

They wandered through the rooms, peeking in closets, looking in drawers. She took pictures, all the while hoping to find something—anything—she could use to ask for access to the tribal archives. All she found was disappointment.

They were getting ready to leave when one of the plumbers called out, "Yo! Archaeologist-Lady. Got an artifact for you."

"Great," she said. "Just watch. He's going to show me a rock and claim it must be a tool because it fits in his hand so well."

Lee touched her arm. "If I have to demean myself to make you look good again, my price will go up."

"Eh. You're cheap."

He laughed. "How can you be so sure?"

She smiled. "You're a guy." She descended the stairs.

The bearded plumber held something brown and sodden out to her. "Check this out."

At first she thought it was a piece of wood, but the way

the wet lump disintegrated in her fingers made her examine it more closely. "It's bone." A bubble of hope built inside her. This she could use. "Where did you find it?"

"Beneath the old pump. There's more down there."

She bent over the hole in the floor and saw a pile of friable material poking out of the saturated soil. The bubble expanded, near to bursting. "Lee, can you get my dig kit, please? It's in the car, the blue backpack."

She reached down and touched a visible bone fragment. It could be very old. Being buried below the water table, the preservation would be excellent as long as it wasn't removed from the wet soil conditions that had preserved it for so long.

Lee returned. She grabbed her trowel and scraped the sidewall to get a clean view of the drained soil. No sign of a burial pit, but the fluctuating water level could have wiped away evidence of a pit centuries ago.

"What kind of bone is it?" Lee asked.

She turned over another clump of soil, popping out a bone. "Could be anything from canine to human. Hand me a ziplock. They're in the front pocket."

"What's a ziplock?"

"A plastic bag."

"Oh. Thaaat ziplock."

The plumbers snickered, and Lee winked at her. She turned back to the pit to hide her smile. He was quick—and funny. There might be more to Lee Scott than her initial assessment of pretty-boy career student.

She dropped the one-inch segment of bone inside the bag, packed damp soil around it, and turned to the plumbers. "Can you fix the sump without disturbing the bones?"

"I think so. The new pump is smaller than the old one."

"You can dig deeper and try to find an identifiable piece," Lee said.

"We don't have an excavation permit, and this could be a prehistoric Native American burial. We need to check with the tribe and see how they want to handle this." She faced the plumbers. "Please leave the bones alone, in case they're human."

Finally she had what she wanted: an excuse to meet with tribal chairman Sam Riversong.

Chapter Three

$\mathcal{L}$ ee wiped sweaty palms on his pants as he sat next to Erica in the waiting room. One question haunted him: would the Menanichoch chairman recognize him?

He'd met Riversong once, twenty years ago, when he was twelve years old, leaving a minute but devastating possibility Riversong would remember him and blow his cover.

He looked around the deluxe waiting room. In the years since their last meeting, the tribe had changed. They now had land and a casino, and Riversong's success as tribal chairman was visible in his designer office suite, which combined the posh of Wall Street with the playful perks of a late-nineties dot-com. The room was filled with ping-pong, air hockey, and pool tables, which seemed disturbingly quiet to Lee as he waited and worried.

Erica tapped her foot and clutched the zipper-topped bag in a tight fist. She was anxious too, and he wanted to know why. Maybe if he got her to relax, she'd tell him why the bone was so important to her. Air hockey or pool? He'd enjoyed watching the way she moved in the gym. Pool, definitely.

He stood and grabbed a triangle, racked the balls, and selected a cue. "Nice," he said as he admired the expensive stick. With a smooth, swift shot, he started the game. A solid went into the corner pocket. The cue ball rolled into position, and he sank a second solid. Next he winged a ball so it would leave the cue behind a striped ball in perfect alignment for the side pocket. No one could resist the call of that easy shot. "Your turn."

She looked uncertain for a moment, then set the bag on a table and grabbed a stick. "I haven't played in a long time."

"Aim low."

She looked at him, her mouth curved in a playful smile. "I know. I went to college—not as long as you, of course—but I know how to play pool." She made the shot, aiming low to create backspin so the cue didn't follow the nine into the pocket. She sank three more balls before her turn ended with the cue ball the length of the table away from a good shot at a solid.

"Damn. You're good." He studied the table. He knew exactly where he wanted to leave the cue ball to force her to attempt a behind-the-back shot. He missed his long shot on purpose and placed the ball strategically.

She went for the tricky shot and looked good with her back arched over the cue. But her next shot was even better. She leaned across the table, hips pressed to the rail, ass angled upward as she rose on her toes. He became instantly hard.

Damn. He was a fool playing with fire.

Movement caught his eye, and Sam Riversong entered the room. He must have witnessed Lee's gaze transfixed on Erica's ass, because a knowing smile spread across the chairman's face. *Busted.*

She sank her ball.

"Nice shot," Riversong said.

Erica whirled in surprise. "Mr. Riversong. I'm sorry, I

didn't know you were here." She returned her cue stick to the wall rack.

"No, finish your game," the elderly tribal member said. "We can talk here. Looks like you're about to wipe the table with this man's ego anyway."

On Lee's turn, he sank one to save his pride, but the stick slipped on the ball when Erica introduced him using his full name.

Would his last name jog the man's memory? His mother's last name had been Scott for only two years before changing to husband number two's name. The man would only recognize the name if he had a long memory for details.

But the moment passed without incident, and Erica took her turn. She sank the eight ball and won. The chairman challenged Erica to a game. Lee did his best to fade into the background while they played and discussed the Thermo-Con house.

Riversong lined up a shot and said, "Why should I care about the bones under the sump?"

"I suspect they're human. They could be a prehistoric burial."

"They won't be disturbed anymore. The pump is fixed."

"From what I've read of the rehabilitation plan, the basement is going to be revamped. The sump fix is a temporary measure to end the flooding, but what if you want to make more dramatic changes? The fact that there could be a burial there would severely limit what you could do, unless you plan ahead. It's possible the army placed the house in the middle of a prehistoric burial ground. In the fifties, everyone would have looked the other way."

"So what do you propose?"

"I'd like to have the bone tested to determine the age and if it is human or not."

"And if the bone isn't human?"

"Then we assume we found the remains of a prehistoric dinner."

"And if it is human?"

"We'll dig shovel tests in the yard to determine if there are other burials in the vicinity."

Riversong was silent for a moment, considering. Finally, he said, "No. There's no need for that."

Erica lined up the cue and the eight ball. "I've read the tribe's agreement with the government, which requires you to develop management plans for all Menanichoch trust lands," she said. "You need to know where your cultural resources—including burials—are. Your land wasn't set aside by a treaty, so it isn't a reservation and protected from seizure as such. The government could use any perceived mismanagement to nullify your agreement and take the land back." She paused, never taking her eyes off the table. "The tribe would lose everything, including the casino."

Shock kicked Lee in the gut as Riversong's jaw clenched and eyes hardened. Erica had just threatened a man who ate shortcake like her for breakfast.

Holy crap. She'd just threatened the casino. The meeting was not following the script Erica had envisioned. He wasn't swayed by her reasonable argument, so she'd had to pull out a cannon. She was shocked by her own nerve.

She had good reason to suspect someone high up in the tribe. Sam Riversong, a former museum curator who knew all the players, remained her top suspect. For a year now she'd wondered if a tribal elder would buy stolen artifacts—trafficking in artifacts was so far outside the value system of every Native American she'd ever known—but now, after finally meeting the man face-to-face, she believed he might.

While the bones were a curious find, she wasn't pushing for the tests out of concern they were human. No, her motives were self-serving, and she would add the guilt this triggered to the load she'd amassed over the last year. Someday her conscience would demand deep reckoning, but for now she just wanted to know what really mattered to Sam Riversong: bones, house, tribe, or casino?

She focused on the table and took her shot. The cue ball smacked into the eight, which obediently slid into the corner pocket but was followed by the white cue. She swallowed a lump of dread. On the most important shot of the game, she'd forgotten to aim low.

"You lost." Riversong's voice was frigid, the look in his eyes even colder. "You might think my win due to your scratch isn't a real victory for me, but I like to win, and I don't care how I do it."

"I was careless." She met his eyes without flinching. "And lost fair and square."

Riversong's cold brown eyes pierced her; then suddenly he smiled. "Good." He snatched a ball out of the nearest pocket. "Let's place a wager on this game."

"Great." Lee grabbed a cue. "If I win, then Shortcake gets her tests to determine the species and age of the bone."

"Shortcake?" she asked, bristling at the nickname.

"And if I win?" Riversong asked.

"We return the bone to the hole and forget about it," Lee said.

"Lee, this isn't how archaeology is done!" Panic jolted through her. Lee sucked at pool. Would she lose this opportunity to work with Riversong?

The chairman grinned. "I like it. Rack 'em up. I break."

She squirmed as Riversong sank three balls before relinquishing the table. "Don't go for the long shot, go for the corner," she said. She felt sick. "You're lousy at long shots."

Lee turned to her. His green eyes swept her from head to

toe in a blatant caress. "I can sink long with my eyes closed. Earlier I missed on purpose. You looked great, by the way, with your back arched over your stick and your butt up on the table."

The sonofabitch had just reduced her to a sex object in front of a client. She would maim him. At the first opportunity. "Just take the shot," she said through gritted teeth.

Lee leaned down, lined up the ball, and closed his eyes.

"With your eyes open!"

He winked at her and made the shot. Riversong never got another turn.

Chapter Four

With Sam Riversong's permission, Erica returned to the Thermo-Con house to collect bones for the species and carbon-14 tests. Kneeling over the hole in the floor, she studied a fragment that was the right size and shape to be a human carpal bone. She smiled. This was almost certainly human; the expert might not even need to run a genetic test. If this turned out to be a burial, then Riversong would have to meet with her again, and more than anything, she wanted access to the chairman.

She packed the bones inside another bag, said good-bye to the plumbers, and left the house. At her car, she slid into the driver's seat and faced Lee, who'd been waiting while she collected the samples. She still hadn't figured out how she was going to murder him without being arrested. She faced forward and twisted the key in the ignition.

"Stop brooding and say it," he said.

She glared at him. "You're a pig."

He smiled. "See, was that so hard?"

She put the car in drive, but his hand covered hers on the gearshift. "You're pissed, but the truth is, by diminishing you,

I made it hard for Riversong to take you or your threats seriously. I saved your ass."

The look in his eyes said he was serious. The hand covering hers squeezed slightly, and she had the insane notion he was soothing her in the same way he'd calm a riled cat.

Who is this man?

"Did you really do it on purpose?" she asked.

"I just said I did."

"No, I mean miss your shot. Did you set me up for the behind-the-back-shot?"

He looked at her incredulously, then laughed. "*That's* what you're upset about?"

She jerked her hand away from his and pulled onto the road, disgusted with herself for asking such a revealing question.

"Okay, I admit it," he said. "Yes. And it was worth it."

Ignoring the miniscule ripple of pleasure his words caused, she fixated on the tidal wave of frustration. "You are my intern. I am your boss. This stops here. Now."

"Okay, *Boss*, as your intern, I'm trying to learn about archaeology and want to know why those bones are so important you threatened the casino to get authorization for the tests."

"I wasn't *threatening*. I was *explaining* why my client needs to comply with environmental law."

"If Riversong thinks you're a threat to the casino, he'll have your perfect ass fired."

Her grip on the steering wheel tightened. "I told you to stop."

"I wasn't hitting on you. I was merely stating a fact: your ass is perfect."

She jabbed at the buttons on the car stereo and turned up the volume until a lovesick girl singing about a boy she'd lost prevented further conversation. Too bad the music couldn't make her stop worrying about the disturbing pleasure she took from Lee's callous compliment.

Back at Talon & Drake, she wrapped the bones for testing, then dropped them in the overnight mail bin. She returned to their office and studied Lee, who was filling out paperwork for personnel. Maybe if she bored him to tears, he'd leave her alone.

She cleared her throat to get his attention. "I've got a cell tower site to visit. While I'm gone, I want you to read the regs that govern our work. Look them up online. Start with the National Historic Preservation Act of 1966, as amended. Focus on Section 106—it's the primary driver for the work we do. When you're done with that, read the Native American Graves Protection and Repatriation Act—NAGPRA; and the Archaeological Resources Protection Act—known as ARPA." She held back a smile. He'd be asleep before he got through Section 106.

Lee turned back to his paperwork, dismissing her. "Fine. See you tomorrow."

Tomorrow. The National Archives. Lee was connected to a bigwig, and it was her job to train him. Bad enough she was ditching him now; Janice would be angry if she ditched him all day tomorrow as well. She couldn't screw up her job, not now. "We'll meet at the Archives as soon as it opens. I want you to look up their research protocol online."

"What do you mean?"

"I've never been there before. Find out what time they open and what we can bring with us—computers, papers, pencils, purses, that sort of thing. Call me on my cell and let me know what you find out." She gave him her number.

"Tech support still has my laptop, and I need a network ID to access the internet."

She hesitated, but really, she had no choice. "Use my computer." She pulled her company ID card from the lanyard around her neck. "This plugs into the card slot and will give you access to the network." She placed a hand on the table and leaned over him. "If you lose my ID, you'll be my new workout bag."

The warm glint in his eye said he had already begun to fantasize. "Yes, ma'am."

He moved to her desk and inserted the card while she gathered her purse and project files.

"What's your password?" he asked.

Oh damn!

He was looking at her, waiting.

"Riversong. One word, lowercase." She turned on her heel and left before he could ask any questions.

Chapter Five

$\mathcal{T}$uesday morning, Lee stood in front of the National Archives building in College Park, Maryland, and watched Erica's car pull into the lot. He braced himself for the coming day and wished he'd taken acting classes. Maybe then he'd do a better job of staying in character.

At least yesterday had been successful. After she'd left the office, he'd used her ID to hack into the Bethesda server and create a network client that couldn't be traced to him. He hadn't been able to access the Iraq project files, but he'd evaluated the security. It would take him a few days to break through the firewall. Less if Erica would stop dragging him along on these annoying field trips.

Erica's dark sandals made a steady tapping sound as she crossed the parking lot. He liked the way her knee-length black skirt and tight-fitting burgundy blouse clung to her hips and breasts. Too bad she hadn't been wearing this outfit when she draped herself over the pool table. He could appreciate her looks and enjoy their verbal sparring, but he couldn't let himself lose sight of the fact that his sexy supervisor was a prime suspect for stateside conspirator in an international artifact smuggling ring.

Questions simmered in his mind, but he'd pushed his cover to the limit yesterday and knew it would be a serious mistake to ask her about her password today. She was only a few feet away, so he started their first argument of the day. "You're late."

Her tentative smile was replaced by a look of annoyance and she glanced at her watch. "It's nine thirty. I'm right on time."

"The archives opened at eight forty-five."

"You told me the archives opened at nine thirty."

"No, I said the *first pull* was at nine thirty." What he'd really said was a very carefully phrased, *"We can begin researching at nine thirty,"* because arriving ahead of her gave him a chance to show his ID and get his researcher badge without her seeing his driver's license and discovering his real age.

"What does 'first pull' mean?"

"The archivists only pull records at certain times. If you'd been here on time, we could have submitted our records requests for the first pull. Since you're late, we won't be able to get any documents until the next pull, which is at ten thirty."

"Dammit, Lee! You didn't say anything about pull times. And what the hell have you been doing since eight forty-five? You could have submitted a records request without me."

"I don't know what records you want to request."

She stared at him in obvious frustration but didn't say a word. Instead, she grabbed a bottle of Mylanta from her purse and popped two tablets into her mouth.

Each time her teeth crunched on the antacid tablets, guilt stabbed him in the gut.

She sighed. "Let's go. We've got a lot of work to do."

Guilt was the last thing he felt after hours of sitting in the bright, climate-controlled, camera-monitored room, surrounded by dozens of silent researchers hunkered over boxes. Next to their table was the last cartload of Fort Belmont archive boxes. Another hour and they'd be done. He opened yet another box full of brittle, musty papers and muttered under his breath, "This is the most boring day of my life."

Erica glanced at him over her shoulder and gave him a half smile. "Not Indiana Jones enough for you?"

He bit his cheek to keep from smiling. "Indy never spent hours in an archive getting paper cuts."

"He did. It just happened off scene."

"Do you really do this kind of thing all the time?"

"No. Today is special."

He expected to see a teasing smile, but she was serious. "You're *enjoying* this?"

"This is my first time at the National Archives, and we're looking through boxes that were classified until a few years ago. Who knows what we'll find?" Her eyes revealed enthusiasm that told him much about her. He had to respect her dedication to her work.

"*I* know what we'll find. Papers that are old, musty, and full of military acronyms." He decided to mess with her. "What's the acronym we're supposed to be looking for, again?"

She glanced at the half-dozen boxes he'd just gone through, her eyes wide with alarm. "It's called ERDL, Lee. E-R-D-L. It stands for Engineer Research and Development Laboratory."

He kept his face blank. "And why do we care about them, again?"

"The lab was on Fort Belmont, and Thermo-Con might have been invented by ERDL engineers." She spoke to him as if he were slow, which he totally deserved. Her voice went up an octave. "Do I need to go through those boxes again?"

A woman two tables away made a shushing sound.

He grinned and whispered, "Gotcha."

She dropped her head into her hands. "I so do not deserve this."

He spoke in a quiet voice. "True. But teasing you is more fun than looking through box after box of ERDL research papers. As far as I've seen, ERDL engineers only worked on camouflage and amphibious vessels."

"Have you seen anything to indicate they experimented with concrete?" she asked.

"No. Have you?"

"No." She shook her head, clearly disappointed, and he knew one thing about Erica Kesling for certain: she did want to find out the history of the Thermo-Con house. He didn't know if her drive came from her desire to please her client, or if she was really intrigued by the house's mysterious origins.

Hell, it was just a house. Odd looking and made out of yeasty concrete, but still, a house.

Her neatly printed list of research questions lay on the table next to a sharpened orange No. 2 pencil. Neither the pencil nor the paper had been touched since they cracked open the first box several hours ago. The day was a total bust for them both. He should be in the office hacking into the network, not here. Tomorrow, he decided, he'd act completely incompetent so she wouldn't take him along on any more field trips.

"This is strange," she said.

"Did you find something?"

"Not about Thermo-Con. But look." She handed him a notebook. "That's the 1952 logbook for Fort Belmont. Someone recorded every event on the army post—ice-cream socials, softball games, that sort of thing—but look at November twenty-eighth."

Lee read aloud, "'Mrs. Claudio Guerrero and son, Ricky, were reported missing today.' So?"

"It's just odd. A missing woman and child got the same one-sentence treatment as the colonel's luau-themed birthday party," she said. "Why not include a note about where they might have gone or if the police were investigating? And where was the husband, Claudio Guerrero? Was he a soldier stationed at Fort Belmont?"

"I know Thermo-Con is boring, but I think we should finish that research before you go off on some mystery-solving tangent."

"I said I thought it was odd, not that I was going to try to solve it."

She reached for the book, but he held it away from her, reading some of the log entries. He turned the page, and a word jumped out at him. "I found Thermo-Con!"

Several people shushed him while Erica tried to snatch the book from his hand. He used the need for quiet as an excuse to scoot closer to her, then wondered if that was a mistake. Her subtle, sexy perfume had been tormenting him all day.

He held the book between them so she could see the important log entry. "*November 29, 1952: Construction of a Higgins Thermo-Con house was begun today.*"

"One page," she muttered. "After spending six hours looking for the words 'Thermo-Con,' I handed the book to you one page—one log entry—too soon."

She was cute when frustrated.

"Well, it's not like we learned anything. It's only one sentence."

She playfully punched him in the arm. "Don't try to placate me. First you make me late, then you steal my moment of discovery. You owe me."

His lips tickled her ear as he whispered, "Shortcake, anytime you want to collect, I'm ready." *Shit.* Yesterday, he'd hit on her to annoy her, but this…this he'd done without thought or intention. This had come naturally, a teasing flirtation because he'd enjoyed her wit and company. This was a complication he didn't need.

Her pupils dilated, and he felt the shiver that ran through her. She was interested too, which only compounded the problem.

She scooted away. "Behave," she said. That she didn't react with outrage after her intern hit on her—again—was telling. She dropped her gaze to the book and cleared her throat. "Look at this: Higgins. I wonder if Higgins is a style or manufacturer?" She picked up the pencil and wrote the logbook's exact entry on the notepaper. If she were a computer, he'd say she was running in Safe Mode.

She finished reading the logbook and replaced it in the archive box. They went through the remaining boxes and found no more mention of Thermo-Con. At six o'clock, they left the archives. All they had to show for their day was one sentence that linked Thermo-Con with the name Higgins.

He stuck his hands in his pockets as they crossed the lot. "Can I buy you dinner?"

She stopped midstride and faced him. "That isn't a good idea."

"Why?"

"You're an intern and only here for six weeks. Let's keep things simple."

"Friendship isn't simple?"

"For me it's not." She looked away and sighed. "I've had a long day, and I'm tired. I'm going home."

Where had her sudden melancholy come from? He had the urge to press her against her car and kiss her. If he did that, would he find himself in the sexual-harassment workshop she'd threatened yesterday, or would she open up and let him meet the woman she'd locked inside?

He let the urge pass and instead watched as she climbed into her car.

The hot, summer-evening air did nothing to cool his mind, so he used logic instead. For unknown reasons, Erica had lied about her credentials as an underwater archaeologist

and had threatened the Menanichoch tribal chairman yesterday. She wasn't his friend. She wasn't his supervisor. She was
a suspect.

He hurried to his car. He would follow and find out if she
was really headed home. She was a suspect, he repeated to
himself. He had to question everything she did.

He'd been following her for a few minutes when she
surprised him by exiting the beltway. She was headed for the
heart of the Menanichoch Nation's trust land.

Yes, Erica Kesling was definitely a suspect.

Chapter Six

One year earlier
Off the coast of Oaxaca, Mexico

The merciless noonday sun beat down on the boat deck, draining color from everything but the vibrant blue water. In the distance, Erica could see a yacht anchored above a coral reef, where vacationers probably drank piña coladas while listening to salsa music. Here, on Jake's boat, the *Andvari*, the crew of six men passed around stolen artifacts and wondered aloud how much they'd get for the exquisitely carved obsidian jaguar, the large jadeite monkey, and the onyx rabbit-motif *pulque* jar.

In spite of the heat, she felt cold and somehow hollow as she stood on the periphery. Jake had looted the shipwreck, and she'd made it possible.

"You didn't bring up the necklaces," Marco, Jake's second in command, said as he placed the *pulque* jar in the conservation tub that would keep the artifact from drying out.

Jake ran his fingers through his short, sun-lightened hair, shaking off water and spraying her with a few drops in the process. "I was on the bottom too long. I'll bring them up this afternoon, after I've had a chance to off-gas."

The distancing chill vanished. In a flash, she felt the sweltering heat; with it came equally hot anger. "Yeah, it would be a crying shame if you got bent while looting the site."

Jake laughed. "Still pouting, Erica? I thought you were more pragmatic than that."

"Make Erica retrieve the necklaces," one of the crew suggested. "Then the ice bitch can't pretend she's innocent anymore."

But she was already as guilty as the rest of them. She was the one who'd found the cache of Aztec artifacts and foolishly told Jake, expecting him to honor the excavation permit, which gave him the right to sell Spanish and Asian artifacts recovered from the shipwreck but specifically forbade the removal and sale of pre-Columbian Mexican artifacts. She had believed him when he said she needed to excavate around the artifacts so they could be photographed in situ. The photos were supposed to go to the Mexican government so they could decide how to handle the incredible find.

But Jake had lied, and she'd bought his story, hook, line, and diving weights. Now he'd taken the artifacts she'd conveniently excavated for him, violating the permit, her trust, and jeopardizing her reputation as an archaeologist. And, trapped on his boat a mile and a half from shore, there was nothing she could do about it.

"Yeah. Send her down, Jake," Marco said. "Put the bitch in her place." His glare said her place was seventy-five feet deep.

"Leave us," Jake said to the crew. As the men disappeared through the hatch, Jake pulled off his wet suit, revealing a muscular swimmer's body. Weeks ago, she'd found his physique appealing, but now his muscles only served to intimidate her, an effect she suspected he'd been aiming for. Stripped down to his wet swim trunks and deep tan, he put on his sunglasses and stared at her. "What am I going to do with you, Cream Puff?"

When she'd accepted his job offer, she warned him, *"If you're looking for some cream puff to rubber-stamp your decisions, hire someone else."* He'd laughed, and Cream Puff became his nickname for her.

She looked unflinchingly at his sunglasses but wished she could see his eyes. "Take my advice as a professional underwater archaeologist and return those artifacts to the shipwreck."

"No. But I do give you credit for trying." He fondled the five-hundred-year-old jaguar. "You knew when you took the job, we planned to sell any artifacts we found."

"I'm not stupid. I did my research before signing your damn contract. This Manila galleon sank en route to Acapulco. The ship's cargo was supposed to be trade goods from the Philippines—ivory, porcelain, mercury, perhaps even gems and gold—not cultural relics from Mexico. Trade goods are all you are permitted to sell." She pointed to the conservation tubs. "Those Aztec artifacts date back to the time when Spanish conquistadors destroyed Aztec art because they considered it the Devil's work. They represent a destroyed culture."

"And they're worth a lot of money."

From the moment she took the job, she had stood precariously close to an ethical line, one she'd had no intention of crossing. "You're violating the permit—a permit *I* got for you."

"And quadrupling my take for the summer." He lifted the jadeite monkey from the tub.

Sunlight passed through the jade. The sculpture glowed like sea-green fire, a sight both beautiful and disturbing because transparent jadeite was the most valuable of all. "This little fellow will sell for a million alone—and the necklaces are worth twice that."

Her hands fisted. "They belong to the people of Mexico."

He placed the monkey back in the tub and took a step closer. "You really believe that, don't you?" He cupped her jaw and ran a thumb over her lips. "How far are you willing to go to convince me?"

She jerked away from him. "I'm not a whore."

"Could have fooled me. You sold your credentials readily enough."

"You bought my credentials, yes. Not my ethics. Those you stole."

"Either way, your ethics are gone. So what's wrong with a fuck between partners in crime?"

"Marco's your partner. Fuck him."

He laughed. "I've got a contract with your signature on it. You're in this up to your beautiful gray eyes, Cream Puff. Seems to me you have two choices: shut up and you'll get your big paycheck as promised; or turn me in and your repu-tation as an archaeologist will be destroyed, because I'll send copies of the contract to your graduate advisor at the Univer-sity of Hawaii. First you'll be kicked out of the PhD program; then you'll be blackballed from the profession."

She felt sick. "You used me." She'd left her summer field project after her mother's sudden death only to discover her mom had stolen her identity and had run up a massive debt in her name. Then Jake showed up with a devil's bargain.

"You chose to work for me."

"I was desperate." Her words sounded hollow, and she could no longer justify her choices, even to herself. When he offered her the job, the money had been too good to be true, but she'd ignored her doubts, and now guilt sat in her belly like a lead weight.

"You needed money. I needed an underwater archaeolo-gist to get the permit. Win-win."

There are two career-ending taboos in archaeology: do not desecrate a grave, and do not buy, steal, or traffic in artifacts. She had been convinced she could maneuver around the taboo by writing about this job for her dissertation—an academic attempt to bridge the chasm that separated treasure hunters from underwater archaeologists. Her goal had been to ensure Jake's excavators collected archaeological data instead of just plundering the ship for trade goods. If the excavation was conducted ethically, she'd believed she'd be able to keep her reputation and earn the money she desperately needed for school.

Her fingernails dug into her palms. "You can't do this. You're destroying my career!"

He took her clenched fist, pried open her fingers, then placed three four-hundred-year-old Spanish doubloons in her palm. He closed her fingers around the coins, pressing to the point of pain. "Only if you force the issue," he said, his voice low. "If you keep quiet, no one will ever know you worked for me." Jake walked away. Just before stepping through the hatch, he turned and faced her. "The doubloons are a bonus —payment for your precious ethics."

Then he was gone, and she was alone on the deck, holding in her hand shameful compensation for every bad choice she'd ever made.

She saw now, when it was far too late, that no matter how good her intentions, taking a paycheck from him was the same as taking the doubloons. She wanted to chuck the coins in the ocean, but the archaeologist in her couldn't cast away an artifact.

Across the turquoise water, the Oaxaca coast was only a mile and a half away. A long swim, but possible with careful planning. If she made a break for it, Jake would probably let her go, but he would still sell the Aztec artifacts. She couldn't let that happen.

She'd been on her own for much of her life, but she'd never felt as alone as she did now. She stood by the railing for a long time, then felt someone behind her and turned to face

Marco, who stood only inches away. His cold dark eyes gave her the chills as they swept her from head to toe. He scared her more than anyone else on the crew.

He reached out and grabbed the long braid she wore to fight the heat, and twisted it around his fist. "You aren't Jake's pet anymore, *puta*."

Stomach-dropping fear erased all traces of self-pity. She tried to jerk away, but his firm grip tugged the roots of her hair. Pain burned across her scalp.

"He can't protect you."

Her frantic gaze traveled over the deck behind him, seeking a weapon, help, anything. She spotted Javier, the only crew member who seemed to like her. His eyes went wide with shock. He turned and bolted through the hatch, leaving her alone with Marco in the blistering heat.

She grabbed the hand that held her braid and dug in with her nails while glaring at him.

He swatted her hand. A sharp sting raced up her arm, and she dropped his hand with a convulsive jolt.

He laughed. "You fight like a girl." He twisted her braid tighter.

Her eyes teared with the pain.

Jake emerged through the hatch "Marco! Leave her alone."

He released her braid, and she slumped against the railing, giving thanks for Javier—assuming he'd alerted Jake.

Marco swung around to face Jake, puffed up like he wanted to fight. While Jake was taller and more muscular, she didn't doubt Marco's wiry strength. Cold fear shot through her. If he chose to fight his boss for the right to rape her, the outcome was questionable.

Jake stared him down. "Take the tender and pick up the mail. Visit a fucking whore if you need to, but leave Erica alone." Then he turned his angry eyes on her and barked, "Get in your cabin, now!"

She fled, her heart pounding as she ran below. She had to get the hell off this boat.

❁

*E*rica was in her cabin, quietly packing her gear, when she glanced through the porthole and saw Marco returning from the marina in the tender. Minutes later, he knocked on Jake's cabin door. She pressed her ear to the wall and could just make out his words.

"…wants to display the Aztec artifacts in a tribal casino in Maryland."

Oh Christ. They had a buyer already.

"We'd have to forge provenance documents if they go on display in the States," Jake said. "The papers would need to be impeccable."

Marco laughed. "You can forge the papers to say some Spaniard found the artifacts in his attic. No one will know they were pulled from this site."

She felt sick. With the right paperwork, no one would know the casino had bought the artifacts illegally. No one—except Erica—would even know a crime had been committed.

"What's the offer?"

"He wants to trade some hot artifacts. I have photos."

She could hear movement but no words. Then Jake said, "Christ! We're supposed to find a buyer for these?"

"With our connections, we can sell them, easy. And we'll get a better price for them than he could."

"Maybe."

"There's more where these came from. A shitload more."

Jake whistled. "Tell him it's a deal."

She sat back on her bunk. She didn't have much time if she wanted to save the Aztec artifacts.

*E*rica waited until Jake went diving for the necklaces, then slipped inside his cabin. Jake didn't have internet on the boat. He was paranoid other treasure hunters—or, she now realized, federal investigators—would hack his Geographic Information System database and see the inventory of the artifacts they'd retrieved, which were all keyed into the shipwreck map she'd created for him. Jake was similarly paranoid about smartphones. No one on the crew was allowed to have one—not that they'd have coverage out here anyway—so if Marco had photos, they must have arrived in the mail.

In Jake's desk, she found an envelope addressed to Marco Garcia care of the marina, with a postmark from Menanichoch, Maryland. Inside the envelope was a thick stack of photographs. She gripped the edge of the desk when she saw the photos. Years ago, she'd attended special lectures and participated in online forums discussing the disastrous chain of events which led to the loss of all the artifacts shown in the stack of pictures.

Jake planned to trade the Aztec artifacts for relics that had been looted from the Iraq Museum in April of 2003.

She pocketed the envelope with the Maryland postmark and fled back to her cabin. After locking the door, she leaned against it. Her mind raced; fear made her entire body tremble.

How did a tribal casino in Maryland end up with a large stash of Iraqi artifacts? And worse, what would happen after Jake got them?

What a fool she was to think Jake Novak was merely an unethical treasure hunter. He was a high-end dealer in black market antiquities. Her employer was a very dangerous man, and she was stuck on a boat with him. Worse, no one knew where she was.

Chapter Seven

July 2011
Menanichoch, Maryland

*E*rica had intended to go home. She was tired and bothered by her reaction to Lee's dinner invitation. She'd enjoyed the research and his company. He'd made her laugh. For the first time in a year—maybe more—she hadn't felt alone. So why did the idea of dinner strike such fear in her? The answer was simple, the problem complex. She was scared of her attraction to him.

She'd paid dearly the last time she let attraction cloud her judgment.

She exited the beltway almost without thinking. She'd driven this road so many times. It was almost as if the casino were a siren, calling to her.

Each room of the Menanichoch Casino celebrated a different native culture. There was no Aztec Room, but a new room would be opening soon. She would bet all her meager possessions the room would have an Aztec theme.

When the Aztec artifacts went on exhibition for the whole world to see, and it was too late for Sam Riversong—or whoever had purchased them—to hide them or alter them, she would use the photographs she'd taken of the excavation to prove they'd been found in the Manila galleon and not in some Spaniard's attic. In Mexico, Jake would be charged with theft and smuggling. She smiled tightly and wondered how he would like being locked in a stinking Mexican jail cell.

In the parking lot, she rested her arms on the steering wheel and stared at the stylish casino. The building had presence—its own offbeat charisma. Before her stood a glass-and-metal structure that looked like a Frank Gehry design with modernized art deco touches that managed to incorporate a Native American aesthetic. The digital marquee screen said the progressive slot machine jackpot was up to ten million dollars. She checked the ashtray and came up with twenty-four cents—a penny shy of being able to try her luck. She scrabbled under the passenger seat and came up with four pennies.

It was time to make another attempt to find out when the artifacts would go on display. She opened a button on her blouse and smoothed her skirt as she entered the lobby. Cold air hit her in a frigid wave, and she took a deep breath of relief from the outside heat. Noise and lights from the gaming rooms carried across the foyer and assaulted her senses.

The foyer opened in three different directions: to the left was a corridor that led to the Inuit and Great Basin Rooms. Straight ahead was the Pueblo Room, and to the right was a grand archway currently hidden behind thick canvas and plastic, covering the entrance to the new addition, what she was certain would be the Aztec Room.

As usual, ceiling-mounted security cameras were trained on the canvas covering, but this was the first time a security guard was stationed at the opening. Did the security guard mean the artifacts were in the display cases? One thing was certain: with a guard in place, she wouldn't be able to look behind the canvas tonight.

With twenty-eight cents burning a hole in her pocket, she headed to the Pueblo Room. The young bartender she'd been flirting with for the last two months worked on Tuesday nights, so she made her way to the bar on the far side of the room.

"Hello, gorgeous," he said.

"Hi, Tommy." She slid onto a barstool.

"I've been waiting for you to show up. I've got news for you on that manager job."

Weeks ago she'd told him she was hoping to get the position of manager of archaeological collections, which would open up when the current manager went on maternity leave. "Are they getting ready to advertise?"

"No. Word is the current manager is going to quit once her baby is born. They're looking for a permanent replacement." He placed a white napkin with extra limes in front of her along with a tall mojito. "On me."

"Thanks. You're a sweetheart." She tried to put as much flirt into her smile as she could, but the idea of flirting with him for information made her feel sleazy tonight.

Still, the end was in sight. All these months… She couldn't let a moment of conscience destroy everything she'd worked for. "I hope I have the right experience. I've only worked with Meso-American collections. You know"—she paused and leaned closer—"it would help if I knew what the theme of the new room will be. Then I'll know what to highlight on my résumé."

Tommy looked around and whispered, "Do you want to see the room tonight?"

Her heart skipped a beat. "Absolutely."

He grinned. "I get a break in fifteen minutes. Meet me in the corridor that leads to the Great Basin Room, and I can get you in through the back way." His expression told her exactly what the price of admission would be.

She'd brought this on herself by flirting with a young man

she wasn't interested in. This was wrong. She'd reached a new low.

"Riversong, I don't care what your last name is. If you don't restock the bar for the next shift again, you're fired."

Erica whirled around and saw a dark-skinned man. His name badge identified him as a tribal member and one of the casino managers.

"I know," Tommy said, bristling. The manager walked away, and Tommy flipped him off behind his back. "Jerk-off."

"Riversong," she murmured. "You're related to the chairman?"

"He's my uncle."

She glanced around the room, seeing the lights of the slot machines, hearing the bells and chimes, but the details were a blur as she processed this information.

"Meet me in fifteen minutes?" he asked.

She picked up her drink and slid off the barstool. "I'll be there."

After trading her nickels and pennies for a quarter, she found an open classic-style slot machine. She dropped the coin in the slot. *If I win, it's a sign I should go through with it. If I lose, I'll just go home.*

Three cherries came up. She leaned her head against the machine and closed her eyes. She'd won two dollars and fifty cents but feared she'd lost her last shred of self-respect.

"I guess we can have dinner together after all."

Lee? She spun around. "What the hell are you doing here?" Had he followed her? She shook her head. The idea was ridiculous. He had no reason to follow her. But still, she couldn't quite let the suspicion go.

He loomed above her and placed his hand against the slot machine, looking all too casual and appealing. She'd enjoyed her day with him at the Archives more than any day at work since before she'd stepped aboard *Andvari*. "I saw the sign for the casino from the beltway and thought it would be fun to check out, especially after meeting the chairman yesterday. Why are *you* here?"

She scooped her winnings from the mouth of the machine and picked up her drink. "The food is cheap and the drinks even cheaper." She took a large swallow. Liquid courage.

He touched her arm, then nodded toward the steak house. "Let's get a bite to eat."

"Sorry. I've got plans. See you tomorrow." She walked away and took refuge in the ladies' room. Coward that she was, she stayed there until it was time to meet Tommy.

She didn't see Lee as she crossed the foyer and entered the wide hallway that led to the Great Basin Room. She waited next to a display of Menanichoch artifacts. The wall-mounted signs gave a detailed history of the Menanichoch Nation. She stared long and hard at a photo of Senator Joseph Talon with Sam Riversong.

Tommy was late. Where was he?

At last, she heard footsteps behind her but didn't turn. She felt hands at her waist. Tommy's hands. *Close your eyes and think of England.* Lips pressed against the nape of her neck. She closed her eyes but didn't think of England. Instead she thought of Lee.

Self-loathing slid up her spine. Like she'd told Jake a year ago, she wasn't a whore. "I can't do this."

"Do what, Shortcake?"

She whirled to face Lee. She couldn't speak. Couldn't think.

"Do what?" he asked again.

She had to say *something*, but confessing that her intern's kiss was welcome in a way that Tommy Riversong's was not was a bad idea. A very bad idea. She found her voice. "Get involved with you," she said and slipped out of his arms.

You are here to find the artifacts. Lee Scott is a distraction you don't need.

She was halfway down the hall when an alarm sounded. *Oh God. They know why I'm here.* The thought was as irrational as the sharp jolt of fear that accompanied it. She really was losing her mind.

She reached the foyer as four security guards ran out of the Pueblo Room and headed in her direction. Without a second look, they passed her on their way out the front door. Her relief was short-lived as Lee came up beside her. His hand found the small of her back. He steered her toward the security guard stationed in front of the concealing canvas.

The guard muttered something into his headset, then listened.

"What's going on?" Lee asked him.

"An employee was just found in the bushes outside. Looks like he was stabbed."

Her stomach churned, but still, she had to know. "Who is it?"

"A bartender, Tommy Riversong."

"Is he—will he be okay?"

"He's dead."

Chapter Eight

*E*rica arrived in the workout room at her usual time, determined to work and live as though the day were like any other. She stretched the same way. Kicked the bag with the same fury. Listened to the same music on her cheap MP3 player.

But nothing was the same. She'd told herself once she found the artifacts and Jake went to jail, her life would return to normal. But there was no going back. For her, there was no longer any such thing as normal.

A kid she'd flirted with for information had been murdered. Did his death have anything to do with her? What sort of world had she immersed herself in? She couldn't live this life—or these lies—anymore.

She needed to tell Janice. Everything. She'd kept silent out of fear. Fear of being fired. Fear of Jake. Fear of Marco. She was done living in fear.

She kicked the bag, punctuation to her decision. She'd tell Janice. Today. This morning.

The door opened and Lee entered. He stood in the doorway, silent, his eyes questioning. He was so tall, so strong. So very masculine. At the Thermo-Con house and again at the archives he'd shown a rascal charm she found terribly appealing.

He'd unknowingly witnessed her shameful decision last night. But he'd also been the reason she'd decided not to go through with it. She hadn't put him in his place when he'd kissed her neck, then Tommy…happened…and dealing with Lee's inappropriate advance seemed petty. The police had questioned them separately. When her interview was over, she'd bolted rather than wait for Lee. She hadn't wanted to face him then, and she didn't want to talk to him now.

She turned up the volume on her music and faced the bag. In her peripheral vision, she saw him head to the free weights across the room. She shifted so her back was to him and finished her workout.

After showering, she reached their office ahead of Lee but knew he would be up shortly. A strange calm descended upon her as she dialed Janice's extension. Soon it would all be behind her. Voice mail picked up, and Janice's recorded message informed her that her boss had a meeting with a client in Virginia and would be in the office after eleven a.m. Dammit. She left a message telling Janice, "We need to talk. It's urgent."

Lee arrived. She murmured, "Good morning," then turned her chair to face her computer. She had work to do.

She heard him setting up his laptop and tried to block him out of her mind. She opened the first of several cell tower reports she needed to finish and got to work. Prickling along the back of her neck alerted her to the fact that Lee stood directly behind her. Longing mixed with fear coursed through her, the same feeling she'd had last night when she realized it was Lee, not Tommy, who had kissed her.

She swiveled around and faced him. Might as well get this over with.

He half sat, half leaned against the worktable and studied her, his face showing his concern. "Did you sleep okay?" he finally said.

She cleared her throat around a sudden tightness. "No. You?"

He shook his head. "I barely slept at all." He paused. "You were waiting for Tommy Riversong in the hallway."

It was a statement, but she knew he wanted an answer. She shrugged. Last night she'd told the police the truth—mostly—and after she talked to Janice, what she told Lee would no longer matter. "He asked me to meet him."

"Why did you agree to meet a twenty-two-year-old drug dealer?"

"He was only twenty-two?" Jesus, he was just a boy. And now he was dead.

"Yes. Why were you meeting him?"

"I didn't know he was a drug dealer." She looked at him sharply. "Who told you that?"

"My family is connected. They asked questions and got answers. Tommy Riversong was a low-level dealer. He'd been arrested several times and pleaded no contest to a drug charge three years ago. After his probation ended, he got the job at the casino."

"But he didn't stop dealing," she said.

"It doesn't look like he did. My understanding is there were drugs on him. He was probably killed in a deal gone bad."

Tommy's death had nothing to do with her. She wanted to believe that. Desperately.

Lee took her hands and cupped them between his own. "Why were you waiting for Tommy in the hallway?"

"I wasn't going to buy drugs from him, if that's what you're asking." Dammit, she sounded defensive—guilty. She slid her hands from between his. "He was going on break. We were going to look at the archaeology exhibits together." It was close enough to the truth, and more than her intern needed to know.

He reached for her chin, but she pulled away. She was losing her grip on their roles. She didn't need to answer to Lee Scott. "It's time we got to work. I need you to do internet searches on Thermo-Con and Higgins."

The morning dragged on. After checking all the usual internet sites to see if anyone was selling Aztec artifacts, she called Janice's cell again. She wanted to make her confession and be done, but her call went straight to voice mail.

Lee was useless. Now she understood how he'd coasted in college for the last seven years: he knew how to look busy without doing any actual work.

She hit the print button on a cell tower report, quietly crossed the room to stand behind him, and nearly choked on aggravation. The slacker was playing Tetris and had completed 428 rows. Clearly he'd been playing for a long time. She placed her hands on his shoulders, and he jolted, causing his finger to hit the wrong button. In seconds the Tetris cubes piled on top of each other, ending his game.

Her fingers tightened on his shoulders as she leaned down and said next to his ear, "I was going to ask you to make copies of a cell tower report, but I see you're busy." She marched out of the room, expecting—wanting—him to follow and apologize. But he didn't.

"Don't hold your breath," she muttered as she shoved open the copy-room door. She hit the door too hard, as evidenced by the loud bang, shaking walls, and four men in suits inside the room who stared at her in shock.

With alarm, she recognized JT Talon standing with Edward Drake, Rob Anderson, and a senior engineer named Arnie Ross. She'd never seen any of these men in the copy room before, let alone trying to work a binding machine.

"Sorry," she said, deciding not to turn tail and run or

make excuses. Hell, she could end up fired after she talked to Janice today anyway. She grabbed her papers from the shared laser printer and made a beeline for the industrial copier.

"How's the Thermo-Con EA coming, Erica?" Rob Anderson asked.

Crap. She hadn't sent him an update on the project since Monday afternoon. "Yesterday we went to the National Archives and found a name, Higgins. We just have to figure out how that name is connected to the house."

"Thermo-Con?" said a voice she didn't recognize, which could only be JT.

She placed her originals in the document feeder, hit the green button, then turned to face the head of the company. "It's a project for the Menanichoch Tribe." Remembering the man was one-quarter Menanichoch, she added, "There's a house on tribal land—it was built on the military base in fifty-two—made out of concrete called Thermo-Con."

"I know. I love that crazy house. I've been nagging Sam to have it repaired for years."

The copy room door opened, and Lee entered. "Erica, did you want me to copy something?" he asked, completely oblivious to the power players in the room.

"Don't trouble yourself, Lee. Your Tetris game won't play itself."

JT looked at Lee, and a flicker of amusement entered his eyes. Dread, which had been second only to fear on her current playlist of emotions, surged to the top of the charts. She suddenly knew with horrible certainty that JT's executive secretary had set up the internship because JT knew Lee. Well.

"Arnie, Ed, have either of you ever heard of Thermo-Con?" Rob Anderson asked.

As if she didn't already feel like crap, now she wanted to smack herself. She'd never thought to ask either man about the historic concrete, but both had been concrete engineers since sometime before the late-Paleolithic era.

Arnie, a balding man who had to stretch if he wanted to pass for five-foot-two, looked up from the papers he'd been reading, then did a double take when he saw Lee. "Good Lord! It's Bigfoot!"

Lee laughed and introduced himself to the elderly concrete engineer, then asked the man again about Thermo-Con. Arnie's wild silver eyebrows, which could have been drawn by Dr. Seuss, rose toward the ceiling. "Sounds interesting, but no, I haven't heard of it. How about you, Ed?"

"No." Drake checked his watch. "Gentlemen, we've only got twenty minutes until the colonel gets here, and the comb binder is clearly broken."

JT's gaze returned to her. "Erica…Kesling, right?"

"Yes, Mr. Talon." He knew her last name. Had he learned it from Lee? Or worse, had Sam Riversong told him about their meeting on Monday?

"We need help," he said. "We need to replace incorrect pages in a proposal package, but none of us has been able to figure out how to work the binding machine." He held up a booklet. The comb-cut holes had been shredded by the machine because they'd misaligned the pages when they tried to take the booklet apart.

The greatest minds in the company—these four men designed bridges, skyscrapers, oil wells, and managed millions of dollars in projects—couldn't work the manual comb binder. She smiled and felt some of her apprehension dissolve. "No problem." She brushed JT aside and quickly disassembled a booklet and replaced the pages.

The copy room door opened, and Janice entered. "I've been looking all over for you."

Erica's stomach dropped. She'd been waiting for this moment all morning. In truth, from the moment she started working for Talon & Drake. But she couldn't talk to Janice here and now. Not in front of JT Talon. "Did you get my message?" she asked, her voice cracking on the last word.

"Message? No. My cell's dead." Janice held up a piece of paper. "I just received an email from an ethnozoology lab giving a preliminary evaluation for the Thermo-Con EA."

She felt a surge of relief. This they could talk about. "Wow, the lab was fast."

"I don't remember authorizing osteological analysis for Thermo-Con," Janice said in her rarely used I'm-disappointed-in-you tone. "Erica. This is your first EA. You need to check in with me every step of the way."

"Did I forget to mention the bones?" In spite of her best efforts, she let out a sharp, nervous laugh. "This was a test for some bones we found under the sump of the Thermo-Con house. Sam Riversong wanted an expert to determine if the bones are human or not."

Janice was silent, then nodded. "That's exactly the sort of thing you need to tell me." Then she smiled. "But you did well, sending it in right away. Especially since, the expert believes the bone is human. He still needs to run the definitive species test, but knowing our tight schedule and the delicacy of dealing with human remains, he wanted to give us the heads-up."

"Riversong also authorized a C-14 test so we'll know how old the remains are. We should get the results on that in the next few days." Her mind raced. Could she use this to push for a meeting with Sam this afternoon?

Then reality hit her. The man's nephew had been murdered last night. She couldn't disturb him now. Besides, in a few minutes, she would have a conversation with Janice that could change everything.

Janice set the email printout on the table. "When you're finished here, come to my office."

After the corrections were made, the men headed to their meeting, while Erica and Lee copied the cell tower report.

That done, she headed for the door, then remembered the email. "Lee, will you grab the email for me, please? It's next to the binding machine."

"It's not here."

She returned to the table. He was right. "It must have gotten mixed in with the proposal papers," she said. "I'll ask Janice to print another copy."

In the corridor heading toward their office, anxiety slowed her pace. She wasn't sure if she was nervous about her upcoming confession to Janice or what she wanted to ask Lee, but she brushed her fear aside. "You know JT Talon," she said, keeping her voice casual.

"We've met."

"You know him better than that."

He shrugged.

Dammit, she wanted to know how well he knew the man. "Do we have more nepotism?"

"Is it really nepotism when you're given the lowest job with the lowest pay?" he asked.

"It is when you're getting paid to play Tetris."

"The Thermo-Con searches were boring."

She turned on her heel to face him. He stopped just short of crashing into her, and she patted his cheek. "Poor baby," she said in a sarcastic imitation of a motherly voice. "I'm sorry your work was so taxing. Maybe after you finish your computer game, you should take a nap."

He covered her hand with his own, rubbing her palm against the stubble he hadn't bothered to shave. His green eyes fixed on hers, and his mouth curved in an alluring half smile. "Only if you take one with me."

She rolled her eyes. She'd give him grief for hitting on her again, but she was the one who'd stepped close and touched him. The air thickened as his intense gaze ensnared her. Gone was the feckless intern; in his place was a compelling man she wanted to know.

She heard footsteps, breaking the spell. She tried to pull her hand away, but Lee gripped her fingers tighter.

"Well, well, well," a familiar voice said. "If it isn't my favorite...Cream Puff."

She ripped her hand from Lee's and whipped around. The last time she'd seen Jake, she'd been locked in a stinking Mexican jail cell.

Chapter Nine

One year earlier
Oaxaca, Mexico

Erica sat on the dirt floor of the jail cell. The cell had no window, no bunk, no plumbing, and the air was hot and stagnant. She'd tried breathing through her mouth to avoid the putrid stench, but had given up on that hours ago. She pressed herself against the bars and tried to get comfortable in the least filthy spot. Previous prisoners had peed on the floor and used their own feces to write Spanish and English swear words on the concrete walls. Flies coated the curse words, giving the letters both motion and sound. A high-end art gallery might appreciate the display, but she didn't.

She had to get out of here.

Before he locked her inside the cell, the officer made her take off the wet suit she'd donned over her shorts and T-shirt. Her clothes had long since dried. The salt on her skin made her feel itchy and twitchy, and she was sick to her stomach with fear. What the hell was going to happen to her?

She'd asked in both English and Spanish to speak with

someone from the *Instituto Nacional de Antropología e Historia*. She needed to convince an INAH official that Jake meant to steal from the Mexican government. She wasn't the criminal. She'd been trying to save the artifacts when she took them and fled. But the officers ignored her.

The arresting officer pulled a chair into the corridor outside the cell. A fat burrito dripped juice onto his pant leg. The aroma of spices and beans masked the stench of the cell for a brief moment. She guessed it was early evening, which meant she hadn't eaten in about twenty-four hours. She'd give anything for a bite of that burrito. "Are you finally going to question me?"

"No."

"They know everything they need to, Cream Puff." Jake walked into the corridor carrying another burrito. "Leave us alone," he said to the officer. The man stood up and left.

Shit. "The cops are on your payroll," she said bitterly.

"Of course. I have a very large payroll. But then, I have a very large income. Which you are jeopardizing." He sat down in the vacated chair and ate a bite, making a show of savoring the food. His smile was predatory. "Hungry?"

She changed her mind. There were several things she wouldn't do for a meal, and they all involved Jake.

"Tell me where the artifacts are, and I'll let you go."

"No."

"You can't win, sweetheart."

"You'll never find the artifacts. *You* need to cooperate with *me*."

"You've got spunk, that's for sure. But that's all you've got." He dumped the food on the floor, just out of her reach. "See you tomorrow."

She repeatedly called out to the officers, demanding they contact INAH. At last an officer entered the hallway and said, "If you don't shut up, we'll stop giving you water."

She shut up.

Sleep came with great difficulty but was the only way to pass the time, the only way to escape the hunger that gnawed at her from the inside.

Jake returned the following day. From the slanting light in the hallway, she guessed it was evening and she'd been in the cell for about thirty-six hours. This time he had a steak that smelled so good it brought tears to her eyes.

"You look terrible," he said. "But don't worry, Marco would still fuck you."

She turned and faced the flies on the wall. The words shimmered as the angled sunlight caught their shiny backs and fluttering wings. Mesmerizing but grotesque. Just like Jake.

She had been attracted to him. The idea seemed ludicrous now. But she had, and for that she was ashamed.

"All you have to do is talk, Erica." He said the words kindly, as if he cared about her.

She stared at the flies. "Go away, Jake."

He left, and the police officers went with him. She was alone, locked in a cell without food, and they hadn't given her water since midday. The Mexican summer heat was unbearable. She no longer cared about food. She just wanted water.

It was a relief when Jake came back the following evening. She'd begun to believe she would be left there to rot. Fly food.

He gave her a sip of water. But the paltry swallow wasn't enough.

"Where are the artifacts?" he asked.

"In the jungle. Near where my car broke down." She'd been so close to freedom when the engine quit.

"I knew that. Where in the jungle?" He held the water glass just out of her reach.

"I just hid them and ran."

Jake dumped the water on the ground and walked away.

She escaped into sleep, curled up on the hard dirt floor. In her feverish dreams, she was hot, thirsty, and alone. Sleep wasn't an escape after all.

She opened her eyes to see a murky light shining down the hallway. By her estimation, that was morning light. How long had she been here? Four days without food, two without water? More? Less? She couldn't be certain.

She drifted off to sleep again. This time she dreamed of her mother. "Why?" she asked her mother. "Why?" But her mother was dead and would never explain herself.

She had no idea how much time had passed when she heard Jake say, "Cream Puff, I brought visitors." Had it been less than a day? It could have been more. It seemed like forever.

She opened her eyes. Her vision was blurry, and the dim light from the hallway hurt. She couldn't help it, she let out a whimper of pain, hating the fact that Jake knew he'd beaten her. Her vision gradually cleared, dark shapes became people, and she realized the crew of the *Andvari*—all but Javier— stood in the narrow hallway in front of her cell. That her one potential ally was absent didn't bode well.

"Your choice is simple. Tell me where the artifacts are, or Marco and the others take turns raping you." Jake's voice was so casual, as if he were reciting lunch options. He tossed a key into the air and caught it, then slid the key into the cell lock.

The men leered at her with malevolence.

She'd thought hiding the artifacts would protect her. She'd believed he wouldn't let her die of dehydration or star- vation because he was eager to find the Aztec relics so he could trade them for Middle Eastern ones.

She'd forgotten he could make her sorry she was alive.

"You're mine now, *puta*," Marco said.

A crew member grabbed her arms. She struggled against him. His grip tightened. Pain shot through her wrists. She felt dizzy, nauseated. Marco grabbed her shorts and pulled on the waistband. She bucked and kicked. He jumped backward.

"Dammit! Hold her."

The man holding her wrenched her arms back. Searing pain burned her shoulders. Marco pulled down her shorts, then unzipped his pants. He was hard and ready.

The metallic taste of fear filled her mouth. Her throat seized. She couldn't breathe. This was really happening. She was about to be raped by Marco. Then the others.

"Tell me now, Cream Puff. In another ten seconds, I won't be able to stop him."

"Enter the jungle due east of where my car was parked." Her voice cracked and she tried to swallow, but her mouth was too dry. "Walk five hundred steps southeast, fifty steps east, then two hundred steps south."

"That's where you buried it?"

"No," she rasped. Marco stood with his hard prick in his hand. Would he rape her anyway? "Repeat that pattern three times. It was dark, so I took small steps. If a tree blocks the way, veer to the left. The artifacts are buried under a downed tree."

"Find the artifacts," Jake said to the crew. "I'll stay here with Erica. Call me when you've got them."

The grip on her arms loosened. She would have felt relieved, except Marco looked angry and disappointed. "What if she's lying?"

"Then you get to rape her."

"If she's telling the truth, will you let her go?"

Jake didn't answer.

She doubled over and began to heave.

The crew left. She pulled up her shorts, then curled into a ball. After a few minutes, Jake dropped next to her and rolled her onto her back, then pulled her into an upright position. Cupping her head with one hand, he pressed a cold, clean, clear glass of water to her lips. She opened her mouth and drank.

He shifted her so her head and shoulders lay across his

lap. She wanted to resist, but he held the water. Jake Novak was always in control.

He caressed her forehead, then traced her nose and cheekbones like a lover. He poured another sip in her mouth. "The Aztec artifacts don't exist, Erica. No one knows about them. The police here only care about the money I paid them. You have no proof we excavated the artifacts."

He didn't know about the photos she'd taken. "What artifacts?" she croaked.

"Good girl." He gave her another sip of water and petted her head.

She'd become his fucking lapdog.

"Your car is fixed. You can drive away a free woman—"

"What was wrong with it?" She'd wondered for days why her car broke down.

"Marco tampered with the gas line when he went to the marina for the mail drop, just in case you decided to do something stupid."

Yes, Jake Novak was always in control.

"I hated being forced to break you," he said softly. He set the water glass aside, then traced the column of her throat. "Every time I look at you, I wonder how in hell you have skin so pale after living on a boat in Mexico for five weeks. But then, I've watched you apply sunblock a hundred times. And a hundred times, I've had to stop myself from grabbing the damn lotion and rubbing it in for you. And then there's your wet suit and the way you shimmy into it. I could come just watching you. Every time I watched, I hoped you wouldn't be able to get your D-cup tits into the tight suit." He slid his hand under her T-shirt and squeezed her breast.

To save herself, she had given up the only advantage she had, and now she would still be raped on the dirt floor of a fetid jail cell. With the last of her strength, she pushed his hand away.

"Easy, Erica. I won't do anything you don't want." He pulled her back onto his lap.

"Then stop."

"Think about it. You can come back to the boat, share my cabin. I'll double your pay—you'll get a hundred and fifty grand for two months' work." He pressed her hand against his erection. "I'll make you come so hard you'll forget the last few days even happened."

She shoved at his chest. "You couldn't find a clitoris with a compass."

He laughed and touched her breast, her side, then her crotch. "It's right here. Waiting. For me." He slid his hand inside her shorts. "Admit it. You're as turned on as I am."

She shuddered at the assault. This nightmare was never-ending.

Then all at once, she knew what to do. The man wanted the ultimate power trip—her broken, beaten, and living with him as his prisoner. He wanted to own her. His trophy. His hand in her shorts was repulsive, but she willed her body to relax. She bit her lip and made her eyes say yes while her mouth said, "No."

She slid off his lap, dislodging his hand, and scooted back to lean against the bars. "No," she said again. This time she made her voice breathy, aroused. She reached down and touched her nipple, squeezed her breast.

His eyes widened; then he slowly smiled. "I knew you'd see things my way."

She could beat him.

He pressed her into the bars as his mouth covered hers. She kissed him enthusiastically, as if he were the water she'd been deprived of. He groaned, then lifted her shirt and pulled her bra aside. His mouth locked on her nipple.

She grabbed the forgotten water glass and smashed it against the bars, breaking the top. He jolted backward, but she caught his cheek with the jagged edge.

He lashed out, knocking the broken glass from her hand. He was too fast; she was too weak.

Her wrist throbbed. She pulled down her shirt and felt her body begin to shake.

Blood made dark tracks on his cheek and pooled in the hollow of his neck. "You'll regret that, Erica."

He pulled her to her feet. Holding her in a viselike grip, he called for an officer. The man came running, eager to do his bidding.

"Clean up the broken glass while I hold her," he said in Spanish. He kicked the heavy broken base of the glass toward the bars. "When you're done, get a doctor. I need stitches."

She wondered how he would punish her and struggled against him. His arms might as well have been bands of steel. The officer finished picking up the broken glass, and Jake let her go. She dropped to the ground.

"If you lied and the boys don't find the artifacts, then you're going to find out what it's like to get fucked in your mouth, ass, and cunt all at the same time. A true cluster fuck." He left, locking the cell behind him.

She hated him. She hated the crew. She hated the police who were so easily bribed. But most of all, she hated herself.

He returned much later, sporting a fresh white bandage on his cheek. "They found the artifacts." He unlocked the cell. "Your car is parked out front, loaded with everything you left behind on the *Andvari*. I'm giving you enough pesos to buy food and gas to get home."

She paused, hardly able to believe he was really letting her go. She wanted to ask him why, but that would be stupid, which she was trying very hard not to be. Not anymore.

He flashed the Jake grin, the one that was so warm, so appealing, the dimples alone had convinced her to work for him. "You're wondering why I'm letting you go." He lifted her chin and ran the pad of his thumb over her lips. "You're mine. You have no idea how hard I've worked to protect you these last five weeks. It would be a shame to waste all that effort, and if you're here when Marco gets back…" His voice trailed off. "But you stole from us. For that, there is a price. You're never working as an underwater archaeologist again."

He held her passport and keys just out of reach. "If you even *think* about contacting INAH or tell anyone what happened here, I'll let Marco have you. What's left of you after that will go to the crew."

She took her passport and keys and staggered for the door. She could barely walk, but dammit, she would find the strength to drive.

She was certain of one thing: she wouldn't be safe until Jake and Marco were behind bars. She could make that happen, as long as the Aztec artifacts didn't disappear into some unknown buyer's private collection. If they went on display in that tribal casino in Maryland, she could take her photos to the FBI and show them her proof that a crime had been committed.

Chapter Ten

July 2011
Bethesda, Maryland

The metallic taste of fear filled Erica's mouth, and again, her throat seized. Blood rushed from her arms and legs, and she swayed on her feet. Jake Novak was here. Standing in front of her. She felt Lee's hands on her hips as he steadied her. She leaned against him, the back of her head resting against his chest, grateful he was there.

Jake wore his predatory smile. His eyes raked her possessively, and Lee tightened his grip on her hips. This was wrong. Terribly, horribly wrong. She didn't want anyone to know her past with Jake Novak, and yet here she stood, weak-kneed, facing Jake in the hallway while Lee held her protectively.

"Erica?" Lee whispered in her ear.

If Jake misread her relationship with Lee, then her foolish intern could be in danger.

She shook herself, pulled away from him, and found her voice. "Sorry. All that coffee without eating caught up with

me, I guess. Caffeine and low blood sugar don't mix."
Breathing became easier. Not natural, but easier.

"You were starving the last time I saw you too," Jake said.
"You really need to take better care of yourself."

White-hot anger evaporated her fear. She straightened
her spine and fixed her gaze on the inch-long scar on his left
cheek. "Nice scar. Looks like it must've hurt."

"Chicks love it."

"Why are you here?" She heard the brittleness in her
voice and worried Lee could too.

"I was going to ask you the same thing," Jake said.

What sort of game was he playing? He'd emailed her at
work; he knew about her job. But with Lee watching, she had
to play along. "I work here."

"Wonderful." His eyes were as cold as his voice. "I'm
teaming with Talon & Drake on a proposal."

"The navy project," she said with deep dread. When Rob
Anderson first mentioned the underwater salvage project,
she'd felt a rush of panic, knowing Talon & Drake would
team with an underwater archaeologist who knew her past—
they all knew her past—but she'd never, ever, considered the
nightmare scenario of Talon & Drake teaming with Jake.

"That's the one."

Lee slipped an arm around her waist as he held out his
other hand. "We haven't been introduced. I'm Lee Scott."

She caught the steely look in Lee's eye and could feel the
tension in his body. He'd picked up on her fear. As repugnant
as the idea was, she needed to talk to her old boss alone. She
stepped forward, away from Lee's protective arm, and pushed
Jake in the chest, forcing him backward. "In there," she said,
pointing toward the vacant conference room across the hall.

Jake tossed a look over his shoulder at Lee and slid a
possessive arm around her shoulders. She itched to shove him
away but needed to lose Lee first. At the doorway, she nudged
Jake into the room with a sharp jab of her elbow, then turned

and said, "Sorry, this conversation is private," and shut the door in Lee's face.

She whirled to face Jake, knowing better than to turn her back on him for long. "What the hell are you doing here?"

"What? No kiss hello?"

"Pucker up while I bend over."

He laughed. "I've missed you, Cream Puff. Life on the boat was dull after you left."

"You can't team with Talon & Drake."

He held up a manila envelope. "But I am. This is my qualifications package for the team. I was hoping to talk to Edward Drake, but I hear he's in a meeting." He took a step toward her and lifted her chin with his forefinger. "Don't fuck this up for me, sweetheart." He leaned into her. "I mean it. You've been blackballed on the West Coast. Breathe one word of our past association to anyone here, and the rumors about you will finally make it to DC." His lips were within an inch of hers. "You do want Talon & Drake to pay your tuition for grad school, don't you?"

Her stomach lurched. She'd finally begun to hope. She couldn't be an underwater archaeologist, but she still had a future as an environmental scientist.

He smiled. "You have no proof of what happened in Mexico. Nothing. So let it go. You so much as mention the word 'Aztec' to anyone and not only will you lose grad school, but Marco will pay you a visit. Understand?"

She could not show fear or weakness. She'd trained until she was bruised and bleeding, knowing she'd face him again someday. "I'm not a prisoner on your boat anymore, and the cops here can't all be on your payroll. Leave me alone." She turned and grabbed the doorknob.

Jake reached over her shoulder and held the door closed. "Listen closely, because your life depends on it. I know why you took the job at Talon & Drake, and you need to let it go. You have no proof. Now, I need your word that you won't tell anyone about the Aztec artifacts. You won't tell anyone about Marco."

"Fine," she said.

"If you break your word, there is no way I'll be able to protect you." He released the door.

She jerked the door open and came face-to-face with Lee. She grabbed his arm, dragging him toward their office. "C'mon," she said sharply. "We've got work to do." As much as she wanted time to think, she couldn't leave Lee alone with Jake.

Only one thing was certain. She couldn't tell Janice the truth.

Not today.

Not ever.

Chapter Eleven

After witnessing Erica's reaction to the stranger in the hallway, Lee knew he'd finally caught a break. At last, he had something tangible to investigate. Erica didn't say a word as she steered him back to their office, and her shuttered expression only raised more questions. She'd seemed frightened of the mystery man, yet she'd faced him head-on and taken complete control of the situation. Her fear triggered Lee's protective instincts, while her steel nerves impressed the hell out of him.

He had a path to follow, a code to break. All he needed was to identify the man who frightened Erica. He settled in front of his computer and searched the company network for references to a navy project. There were several, but none were in the proposal stage. JT should know. He'd ask him when the meeting with the colonel was finished. Across the room, Erica shifted in her seat. He couldn't let her see what he was doing. With the touch of a button, he brought up the Tetris game and pretended to play.

He glanced in her direction. She looked calm. He would even say serene. "Who was that guy?" he asked.

She startled, proving her serenity was a façade. "Nobody."

"I don't get it. First you swooned, then you acted like you don't like him. Which is it?"

"I didn't swoon. I was hungry and surprised, is all."

"So you don't like him."

"No. I don't." Her words were clipped.

"Is he an ex-boyfriend?"

"God, no." The words came out harsh, laced with disgust.

The amount of relief he felt worried him.

She closed her eyes for a second and breathed slowly. Then she met his gaze. "Thank you. For helping me. When I nearly fainted."

"No problem, *Cream Puff*."

She stood abruptly. Her chair crashed into the table behind her desk. "Don't *ever* call me Cream Puff." She bolted from the room.

He sat in stunned silence. In the last three days, he'd said and done several things he should have regretted, but his mission was paramount. This time, however, in crushing her sincere thank-you with a taunt, he'd gone too far.

He closed his laptop and picked up the Thermo-Con file, mindful of the fact that he needed to look like he was working if he wanted to blend into the background as he wandered the maze of offices. Over two hundred people worked in the Bethesda office, and so far all but Erica had paid him no mind. Which was exactly what he wanted.

He tried to look clueless and lost, but in truth he'd memorized the Talon & Drake floor plan. Nameplates on doors and cubicles aided his sense of direction as he looked for Erica. She wasn't in the break room or any of the empty conference rooms.

He approached the main conference room where JT and his top engineers were meeting to hammer out a contract for work in Afghanistan. The conference room door opened, and Edward Drake stepped out.

JT's prime suspect looked anxious. Lee paused by a water fountain. Drake headed for the stairwell. Lee followed. Making up with Erica would have to wait.

Drake used his ID card to unlock the door at the top of the stairs. He stepped into the ninth-floor corridor and turned right just before the door swung closed.

When he reached the top, Lee turned left. He could circle back behind the center cubicles and not look like he was following Drake. He walked with purpose, holding the file as though he were making an important delivery. Rounding the corner, he entered Drake's office hallway from the far end and stopped at a shared printer and fax station. He flipped through the papers in the printer tray as though he were looking for a printout. At the other end of the hall, Drake entered his corner office.

The words "Request for Proposals from the United States Navy" caught his eye on one of the pages. He felt a rush of excitement as he read the page. He'd found the navy project Erica had mentioned to the mystery man.

The navy wanted to hire a salvage expert to pull up a Douglas TBD-1 Devastator Torpedo Bomber from the bottom of Chesapeake Bay. This had to be the same aircraft project Rob Anderson had asked Erica about in the break room just before she denied her background in under-water archaeology. He slipped the RFP into the Thermo-Con file.

At the far end of the hall, Drake's administrative assistant opened the man's door. "Here's the qualifications package you were waiting for, Ed."

He couldn't hear the response, but the door started to close. The woman's voice rose. "JT has already called—"

"Edward Drake, line one," the front-desk receptionist said over the loudspeaker. "Edward Drake, line one."

Drake's assistant pointed up at the commanding speakers. "He wants you in the meeting."

Lee heard Drake clearly this time. "Answer the page and tell the interfering prick I'll be back in five minutes!" The door slammed.

Lee waited another minute, then headed toward Drake's office. He paused when he reached Drake's assistant at the corner. "Which way is Arnie Ross's office?" he asked.

She pointed in the direction he'd been heading. "He's at the end of the hall, near the stairwell."

Drake's office door opened a crack. Drake was speaking to someone inside. "I appreciate you stopping by on your way to the senator's."

"I'll talk to Joe, but I don't think it'll make much difference. Per Senate ethics rules, JT's in charge." Lee recognized both the cadence and the voice. Sam Riversong was inside Drake's office. Drake was trying to use Riversong to override JT.

The door opened another inch. So far, the one thing Lee had going for him was his intern status, which made him invisible to the powers-that-be in the office—a difficult feat for a six-foot five-inch man. But Riversong had *seen* him. And he'd certainly notice Lee now and likely say something that would make Drake take notice. He had to get out of there. Fast.

Lee hurried to Arnie Ross's office and twisted the knob. The door was locked. Crap!

Days ago, he'd made a copy of JT's ID card, which opened every office door but left an electronic trail that couldn't be erased. He had no choice. He slid his magic card in the slot and entered. Thank goodness the concrete engineer was in the meeting with JT.

He stood by the window that faced the hall. After setting the Thermo-Con file on a shelf, he closed the blinds, then held up one slat a fraction of an inch and watched Drake and Riversong pass by.

Exactly which of JT's plans did Drake want to override? And why hadn't JT told Lee he was rattling Drake's cage? Was JT holding out on him?

Lee waited a few minutes, then reopened Arnie's blinds and slipped into the hallway. After using his card to relock the door, he casually strolled down the corridor.

He was safely back at his desk, wondering where Erica was, when he realized he'd left the Thermo-Con file inside Arnie's locked office.

Chapter Twelve

*E*rica sat at her desk and simmered. She was supposed to be working, but in her mind she heard Jake's threats, while in her office she heard Lee's incessant questions.

She'd given him an environmental assessment template and asked him to use it to create the Thermo-Con report. All he had to do was adapt the headings to this particular project and paste in the sections that had already been written. He cooperated by asking her to explain every aspect of the task.

"I don't get it," he said. "If the appendices aren't paginated with the rest of the report, how do we show them on the table of contents?"

She was too frazzled after seeing Jake. She couldn't take his incompetence for another second. She growled and said, "Give me the Thermo-Con file. I'll do it later."

"But I need to know——"

"Play Tetris and leave me alone!"

She hit the print button for another cell tower report. The blue screen of death flashed on her computer. "Nooooo!" she wailed. Not today. She couldn't take this today.

It took ten minutes to reboot her computer, and when she

got back into the cell tower database, her worst fear was confirmed. The crash had corrupted the file. Even the backup contained the damaged data. As if today wasn't already on her top-ten list of most rotten days ever.

She glanced at Lee, wondering if he could help. But when she'd explained how to cross-reference the Thermo-Con photo captions, he'd accidentally deleted the photos.

He was hopeless with computers.

Unless he was playing Tetris, which he was doing now. She smiled grimly. This was the first time all day he'd done as instructed.

After cursing and sighing, she started copying the data one record at a time and pasting it into a clean, bug-free file. The task would take hours. Hours in which she wouldn't be working on Thermo-Con, but it was the only way to rescue the database. And no matter what happened, she needed this job, needed to keep her annoying cell tower clients happy.

She would never be safe. Not unless Jake, Marco, and the crew were locked up. Several times over the last year, she'd considered going to the FBI with her photographs of the artifacts, but she'd chickened out every time.

Without the actual artifacts, the photos proved nothing. The photos were meaningless as long as there was no record of the artifacts' existence.

Lee left the office at five o'clock, triggering envy that he was done for the day and a surprising disappointment at his absence. He might be useless as an assistant, but she didn't feel lonely with him in the room. She worked into the night, afraid to go home, afraid Marco would be waiting for her.

She'd come face-to-face with Jake and was such a wimp that she'd almost fainted. Pathetic.

At nine fifteen, she finished and shut down her computer. She stretched her neck and rolled her knotted shoulders. Her body ached from sitting and staring at the screen. She grabbed her purse and heard the rattle of antacid tablets.

Some people salivated at the smell of steak, but for her it was antacids, the one thing she ate on a regular basis. She popped two into her mouth and called it dinner. Her experience in Mexico had taught her what true hunger was. This was nothing compared to that.

She heard the click of a door closing in the hallway and jumped. Another person working late? "Is anyone there?" she called out.

Silence was the only answer.

What if Jake was still here? This time of night, even the cleaning crew had gone home. The building was empty. Chills raced up her spine.

She leaned through her open door into the hallway. The lights were on. The motion detector switches had been triggered by someone. "Hello? Who's here?"

Cold sweat broke out on her brow. A fellow employee would have answered. She reached into her purse and grabbed her pepper spray. What if both Jake and Marco were here? She felt her knees tremble and placed her hands on a file cabinet to steady herself. Dammit. How could she be so weak?

Because Jake broke my will with dehydration, starvation, and the threat of gang rape. Then he assaulted me.

Yeah, but what has he done to you lately?

She let out a small, bitter laugh.

"What's so funny?"

She jumped and faced the door. JT Talon stood before her, a wry smile on his handsome face. "Jesus! You scared the crap out of me!" Her hand went to her racing heart, and she realized she still clutched her pepper spray. "You're lucky I didn't use this." She held up the spray, and they both could see how badly her hand shook. He was even luckier she hadn't launched into a roundhouse kick.

"Sorry. I didn't realize anyone was here."

"I called out."

"I must've been in the stairwell. I came down, then realized I forgot something and went back up."

She felt tension release by slow degrees and tucked the pepper spray inside her purse. "Sorry I snapped at you."

"You shouldn't be here so late by yourself."

"If I had a better computer, I'd have left hours ago."

He laughed. "Point taken. Will you be here much longer?"

"I just finished."

"I'll walk you to your car."

"I'm taking the Metro."

"You're riding the subway this late? Alone?"

She shrugged. "I do it all the time."

"Not tonight you're not. I need five minutes; then I'll give you a ride home."

"The Metro is perfectly safe—"

"If you argue with me, you're fired."

She laughed, surprised at the relief she felt. Someone was looking out for her.

"I'll be right back." He disappeared down the hall. The stairway door closed, echoing in the silent building, and she recognized the sound that had alerted her earlier. He'd been telling the truth about being in the stairway.

She grabbed her purse. Maybe during the drive she could get him to talk about the new room at the casino. Did he know she'd been there last night? The last thing she wanted to talk about was Tommy Riversong.

He'd said he loved the Thermo-Con house. That was a safer subject. She reached for the project file to act as a prop to get the conversation going, but the folder wasn't where it belonged.

She searched her desk and Lee's. The file was gone. Could Lee have taken it home? Why would Mr. Incompetent do that?

"Ready?" JT asked from the doorway.

"I can't find a project file I was hoping to work on tonight."

He smiled. "Next you'll be wanting a better computer for your home too."

"A laptop would work for both."

"Nice try."

She gave up on the file and followed him out the door.

JT drove a bright orange, foreign, and obviously expensive convertible sports car. The low car hugged the road as they sped along the George Washington Parkway with the top down. She knew a large percentage of the single women—and even a few of the married ones—who worked for Talon & Drake would envy her right now. The man was more handsome in person than in his publicity shots, a feat that shouldn't be possible. Wealthy and credited with a genius IQ, he had been photographed several times escorting beautiful women to newsworthy functions. She'd been prepared to dislike him, but he seemed rather personable over a binding machine and was kind to give a lowly employee a ride home.

Young, handsome, rich, successful, and son of a presidential contender, JT Talon was the object of many women's fantasies. But not hers.

She would never get involved with anyone who held so much power over her.

As the miles sped by, she knew she was wasting her opportunity but had no idea how to open the conversation. At last, inspiration struck, and she spoke. "Is your father going to make his announcement soon?"

He smiled but kept his eyes on the road. "Yes."

His frank answer surprised her. "He's really going to run," she murmured. She'd thought about the senator running for president on an abstract level, of course, but her focus during the last year had been so narrow, she'd missed the broader view. "He really could win," she said, and heard the awe and excitement in her own voice.

His grip tightened on the steering wheel. "Yeah. Kind of crazy, isn't it?"

Here was her opening. "He'd have a huge advantage if casino profits could fund the campaign."

He glanced sideways at her. She knew the statement was odd for a casual conversation. *So I'm not normal. Get over it and tell me something I can use. Please.*

"It's complicated," he said finally. "We're our own nation, so some rules don't apply."

"Will tribal gaming be a negative for him? Many people are against gambling."

"The casino is a mixed bag," he said. "It'll turn off some voters for sure, but the senator is prepared for that. And Sam Riversong has worked hard to make sure our casino is better than the rest. The museum component is key. We're not just making money off gambling, we're educating people on tribal issues, history, and prehistory. As an archaeologist, you must appreciate that."

She felt the solid thud of her pulse all the way to her fingertips—much as she'd felt last night when Tommy offered to show her the room. This was her chance. "I do. I've been to the casino several times just to see the exhibits. I can't wait to see the new room. I'm dying to know what the theme will be."

He smiled. "You're going to love it."

That was it? "C'mon. What is it?"

He shook his head. "It's a secret."

"At least tell me when it's going to open."

"Nope. All I can say is the displays will be top-notch. I can't believe the stuff Sam managed to procure."

A translucent jadeite monkey, perhaps? A cast-gold skull necklace?

She gave him directions to her apartment, and minutes later, they pulled up in front of her building in Southwest DC. She climbed out of the flashy car and leaned over the closed passenger door to shake his hand. "Thanks for the ride."

He gave her hand a gentle squeeze. "Glad to do it."

She began to pull away, but his fingers hooked around hers in a manner that was anything but casual. He glanced up at her building. "If you invite me up for a drink, we could talk about your need for a new work computer."

Damn. She hadn't seen that coming. How in hell did she keep winding up in this situation? She cleared her throat and said, "I'm sorry, but I can't."

※

*J*T watched Erica Kesling as she hurried inside her apartment building. His lawyer would have his ass if he knew he'd just come on to an employee. Even worse, he'd botched it. But then, he wasn't the least bit interested in her, so he could hardly be expected to bring his A-game.

The building was nice. Not deluxe or anything, but with twenty-four-hour concierge and security, it couldn't be cheap either, and Lee's hacking hadn't revealed any roommates. A steady income from artifact trafficking might be the only way she could afford to live here.

He'd had the perfect opportunity to try to earn her trust and blew it by waiting too long and then coming on too strong. He should have chatted her up from the moment she climbed into his car, but he'd held back. Because Lee had a thing for her.

Lee needed to understand the simple truth: Erica was a suspect or tool for gaining information. Nothing more, nothing less. JT didn't know if his former stepbrother had the stomach to be so manipulative, but he suffered no such qualms.

Erica had been a suspect even before he decided to ask

Lee to work undercover. As an archaeologist, she was in a key position to know the other players. Then Lee's hacking had revealed her shockingly bad credit history, including allegations of fraud. She'd moved closer to the top of the list, and they'd decided to place Lee in her office. The woman had motive and means. Had she seized an opportunity?

He picked up his cell and called Lee. "You still at the office?"

"Yes."

"If you've already grabbed that file from Arnie's office, you need to take it home with you. Erica noticed it was missing."

"Will do," Lee said. "I just finished rewiring my Ethernet jack so I can connect to the protected Iraq LAN."

"You know I have no idea what that means, right?"

"Sometimes I can't believe you're an engineer," Lee said.

"I don't need to know how a computer works to use it."

"Basically, I have access to the secure Iraq project network without anyone in Bethesda knowing."

Finally. "Did you get ahold of Dominick?"

"Just got off the phone with him."

"What did he say? If you find something we can use, will it be admissible in court?"

"According to him, I'm not a federal law enforcement agent, so I don't need a subpoena or warrant. And since you —the CEO—gave me permission, legally, I'm not hacking. We're good."

JT had been worried about Lee talking to his longtime friend, Curt Dominick, the US Attorney for the District of Columbia, about their investigation. He didn't want the feds to open their own investigation. To avert scandal, JT wanted to find the guilty parties and hand them over to the feds with a red bow—a display that corruption wasn't tolerated at Talon & Drake. After debating the issue for a week, he finally gave in to Lee's request to consult with Dominick. They needed to be certain anything Lee found could and would be used against the bastards who were using *his* company to smuggle. "Good. Now find the sons of bitches. This is taking too long."

"I've only had a day and a half in the office, I have to hide what I'm really doing, and I have a supervisor who expects me to work on her projects."

"I told you to be inept so she'd give up on you and do the work herself."

"You told me to be an incompetent, indecisive, Indiana Jones wannabe," Lee said. "I'm the intern from hell. I *hate* me."

JT laughed. "I'll meet you at your apartment in a half hour." He hung up, glad Lee had conquered the network-access problem. Lee was relentless when trying to solve a problem or master a task. That was why he'd earned his fifth-degree black belt before he turned thirty, could play pool blindfolded, and had never met a computer system he couldn't hack. If there were clues in the Bethesda network files, Lee would find them.

The problem now was Erica. JT stared into the lobby of her building. He'd seen the way Lee's eyes had followed her in the copy room. He'd heard it in Lee's voice. Lee was taken with her.

Regret twisted JT's gut. If Lee's infatuation stopped him from pursuing every lead, JT would have to intervene. There was too much at stake to worry about Lee's—or Erica's —feelings.

Chapter Thirteen

*L*ee made a point of arriving in the exercise room before Erica on Thursday and was working out with the bag when she arrived.

She shook her head. "Are you trying to annoy me, or does it just come naturally?"

"Use the treadmill," he said, knowing that would irk her even more.

She rolled her eyes and instead chose the free weights. For work, she always wore her hair in a thick twist at the nape of her neck, but for exercising, she always tied her hair in a ponytail that reached her lower back. The silky dark strands tantalized him, and he wondered what her hair looked like loose and free. She weight-lifted with the same intensity she worked the bag, constantly pushing herself harder. The bruise she'd gotten when she fell on Monday was visible below the hem of her shorts, a vivid purple mark on otherwise perfect skin, but he was more interested in the way her tight tank top hugged her chest as she strained and flexed.

"If you're not going to work out, let me use the bag," she said.

He shook himself, realizing he'd been staring. "Want to spar?"

She set down the hand weight and studied him. "We don't have pads," she said finally.

"I'll be gentle with you." He tightened the Velcro straps on his foam gloves.

She smirked and pulled her gloves from her workout bag. "I make no such promises."

She circled him on the mat, clearly not wanting to waste time with trivial things like rules. Of course, he'd been doing his best to piss her off since they met, so he had it coming.

She kept her eyes on his and feinted left, then kicked high to the right. He blocked the kick and punched, checking his swing so his glove merely kissed her shoulder.

As she kicked and punched, her face became flushed, her eyes bright. He caught her in a clinch hold to halt a blow and felt the burn of her vibrant energy. She kicked high, and his block knocked them both off-balance. They hit the mat with arms and legs entangled, her body pinned beneath his. She laughed, full, loud, exuberant.

He propped himself on an elbow as his own laughter subsided, then looked down on her. His breath caught. She was so damn beautiful…but it was more than that. It was her brains, her drive, the way she'd faced down a man who obviously scared her. And his reaction to her was a problem. But right now, he just wished he weren't wearing the damn gloves. He wanted to run his fingers through her hair.

She pushed against his chest. "Let me up."

Remember your role. "What are you afraid of?" he asked.

"I'm not afraid." She pushed again.

"Liar. Let me take you out. Dinner, tonight."

"You aren't my type. I like men who can earn a degree in less than seven years."

He held back a grin. She didn't like his character. He

could live with that. He didn't like the intern either. "And I like a challenge."

This time when she pushed, he rolled back and she got to her feet. "Then go challenge yourself with the weights, Romeo. We're done sparring. I get the bag now."

He chuckled and gave her what she wanted. After he'd showered and dressed, he timed his exit from the locker room to match hers. "I was going to get a smoothie. Join me?"

She hesitated, then said, "I can't."

"C'mon. My treat." He took her arm and pulled her toward the juice bar. He bought her a drink and breakfast sandwich, and they settled into a table in the corner. "Since I paid, we can consider this our first date."

She shook her head but smiled and thanked him, then took a bite of the egg-and-cheese sandwich. The look of pleasure on her face was out of scope with the rubbery food.

The only thing he'd seen her eat all week had been antacid tablets. He knew about her financial troubles from hacking into her credit report. Was she so broke she was skipping meals? He felt a rush of something he didn't want to name.

She was a suspect, but her outward poverty indicated innocence. Was she really as impoverished as she seemed? He had an idea for another way to get close to her. "You've taken some karate. Do you have a dojo in town?"

"Not anymore. I can't afford it. But the company gym is free."

"I can teach you. I'm a fifth-degree black belt in Kenpo." It was refreshing to tell her the truth for a change.

"You've worked that hard at one thing? You didn't switch to yoga, then Tae Kwon Do? You're destroying my slacker image of you."

He smiled. When he was twelve, after a CIA hacking incident that nearly landed him in jail, Joe had been determined to find Lee a safer hobby. Being a sly bastard, Joe convinced

JT to take up karate. Private lessons with the stepbrother he worshiped was all the incentive Lee needed to make karate the focus of his teen years. He shook off the feeling the memory stirred and focused on the woman who had begun to wreak havoc with his mind. "When do you want to start your private lessons?"

"Never. And I won't spar with you again." She set down her drink. "Lee, I'm your supervisor—"

"So? We're both adults."

"Really?" she said, cocking her head to the side. "Are we both adults?"

If only she knew. He'd never been fond of his intern persona, but in that moment he really hated the bratty prick. "It's not like this is a real job. I'm only here for six weeks."

"That's the problem. For you, this isn't a real job. For me, it's my whole life."

"That's…pathetic. We need to find a way to entertain you outside of work." He grinned. "I have an idea…"

She sat back in her chair and crossed her arms. "You are the most exasperating—"

"—charming—"

"—frustrating man I've ever met."

He leaned to whisper in her ear and inhaled her heady scent. "And you're as turned on by me as I am by you." He stood and headed for the elevator, secure in the knowledge she was staring after him, probably annoyed by the truth of his words.

He found the truth damned inconvenient himself. He didn't want to be attracted to her, but as long as he was, he'd use it.

She joined him as he waited for the elevator. Like her tightly coiled hair, her face was all business. The workday had begun.

When they reached their eighth-floor office, he pushed

open the door and came to a dead stop. Their office had been ransacked.

Chapter Fourteen

*T*he following morning, Lee faked running internet searches on Thermo-Con and Higgins while Erica sat at her computer and quietly muttered curses directed at the room, the computer, the project, and herself. If he'd made progress yesterday during their sparring match, it had been undermined by the vandalism, and she'd been remote for the last twenty-four hours.

Other offices had been trashed on Wednesday night: Rob Anderson's, a chemist's, and accounting. Now he was left wondering which office was the real target?

His Ethernet rewiring hadn't been discovered—he currently had unfettered access to the Iraq network. But there could be other reasons to target the archaeology lab he shared with Erica. On Monday he'd used Erica's log-in to hack into other secure areas of the network, to familiarize himself with the system. Had he made a mistake and left tracks? Had someone targeted their office because he'd screwed up and directed suspicion to Erica?

She let out a stream of curses that would make a Teamster proud.

"What's wrong?" he asked.

She leaned back in her chair and rubbed her temples. "We've got seventy-two hours until the Thermo-Con EA is due, and we've found exactly nothing about the history of the house. We haven't answered a single research question."

He tried to think of something encouraging to say but was distracted by the way her blouse stretched taut across her breasts, one button threatening to give way. Christ, he was thinking like a damn teenager. He turned back to his computer.

He was losing sight of what mattered.

She might have turned to trafficking Iraqi artifacts because she needed money. The theory was solid. The only problem was Erica. He couldn't reconcile the woman sitting across the room with those actions.

She was a puzzle he didn't need. He had bigger mysteries to solve. He opened the email that had started this foolish quest, hoping to see a piece of information he'd missed the first five hundred times he'd read it.

JT—

Talon & Drake employees are smuggling something out of Iraq. I don't know for certain what is being smuggled, but I suspect artifacts.

Talon & Drake equipment is being shipped back to the US via military transport. Because the military is involved, security is tight and transport information is classified. I don't know what is being shipped or when it will arrive, but I believe the smuggled goods will be hidden inside the equipment and a Bethesda office employee will know how to retrieve them. I am gathering proof and will keep you informed.

—Matt Weber

On the surface, the email was short on substance and details. It lacked names and specifics but was full of unsubstantiated accusations and excuses for being vague. It could have been a hoax. Lee *wanted* it to be a hoax. But the damning fact was Matt Weber had been killed by an IED an hour after sending this. Just another contractor caught in the cross fire.

JT didn't believe it, and neither did Lee.

JT's request for an inventory and status of equipment in Iraq revealed nothing. Officially, Talon & Drake had no equipment en route from Iraq via military transport. But JT hadn't been satisfied with that and had asked Lee to hack the network to see if shipping data had been buried on purpose. Lee's job was to search without tipping off the conspirators. JT wanted to catch them red-handed. So here he was, scouring the internal network to determine what piece of Talon & Drake equipment was being returned, how it was being shipped, and when it would arrive. Once he had a lead, they'd use the information to catch the smugglers in the act with the help of the FBI. By rooting out the bastards internally and making an example of them, JT hoped to protect Joe's campaign from being tainted with scandal.

But figuring out who in Bethesda was involved wasn't so simple. Because of the need for security on the defense contracts, the Bethesda network at Talon & Drake was extremely secure, and the computers used for the Iraq project had their own separate network. Until Lee spliced the cable Wednesday night, all the computers with access to the Iraq project files had no online access at all. The only way in was for Lee to rewire the system so his Ethernet jack had access to the internal Iraq project LAN.

Between the necessary rewiring, copying all emails sent to and from Talon & Drake employees, and setting up a trap to capture every cell phone call made within the building—and then matching cell phone numbers to known users, to weed out all but the anonymous prepaid phones favored by criminals—he'd been very busy as he pretended to be the ultimate slacker.

Time wasn't on their side. In a little more than a week,

Joe would officially announce he was running for president, and Lee's cover was sure to be blown. Lee's mother had divorced the senator twenty years ago. Right now, no one cared about or remembered their five-year marriage. When Joe ran for the Senate the first time, Lee had been a twenty-year-old junior at Columbia. Living in New York and busy with school, he hadn't been part of the campaign and was just a footnote in Joe's biography. Six years later, Joe's reelection had been a walk, and there'd been no reason for Lee to get involved. But presidential politics were on a different scale, and after Joe made his announcement, the press would scour Joe's history, and it would be impossible for Lee to keep his identity secret. He needed a break. And he needed it soon.

***

*L*ate Friday afternoon, Erica sat at her desk, flipping through the Thermo-Con file. Lee was doing Lord knew what at his computer, but she'd bet good money —if she had any—it wasn't the research she'd asked him to do.

She'd get on his case, but she didn't have the energy to argue. More than a day had gone by since someone had destroyed her office. Someone. Who was she kidding? It had to be Jake. But why? Was it a warning? Had he been looking for something? If he knew about the photos she'd taken of the artifacts… She didn't want to think about what he was capable of.

But she couldn't stop thinking about what Jake was capable of.

She could contact the FBI, but it wasn't that simple. Artifact theft didn't rank with drug trafficking or mob violence. It wasn't like the FBI would place her in the witness protection program. Hell, given her credit history, they'd probably assume she wanted to be in the program to escape her debt.

She would never be safe from Jake and Marco.

And now the project she'd demanded so she could have an in with the tribe was a bust. The draft EA was due on Monday, and she had no new information on Thermo-Con except for the paltry sentence they'd found at the National Archives that included the name Higgins. She'd spent hours yesterday at the Library of Congress and come back with nothing.

She'd managed to leave Lee behind, but this morning Janice sent her a stern email saying she wasn't supposed to go on research excursions without her intern.

She studied the bad photocopy of the front page of the Fort Belmont newspaper, the *Citadel*, from early 1953. She'd read the article several times. She'd even read the neighboring columns, in hopes they would contain a kernel of information. One of the headlines said, FORT BELMONT SOLDIER DIES IN KOREA, WIFE'S AND SON'S WHEREABOUTS STILL UNKNOWN, and told about the missing mother and son mentioned in the journal they'd read at the archives.

But she was wasting time wondering if the Guerreros had ever been found. She needed more information on Thermo-Con. Something that would get Riversong's attention. In hopes of gleaning something useful, she read the article that concerned the Thermo-Con project again.

NEW BUILDING MATERIAL AROUSES KEEN INTEREST

> *The prototype house completed in November is one of the most interesting projects at Fort Belmont. Several generals, a lieutenant colonel, and even a bishop from the Republic of Nicaragua have all visited the house.*
>
> *What makes the building so interesting might well be answered by*

one word, "Thermo-Con": the new type of building material creating such a stir in the construction field. Its qualities are almost legendary —it floats, can be sawed with an ordinary carpenter's handsaw, and drilled with a brace and bit; it holds nails and common wood screws, and its heat-resistance and insulating qualities defy belief.

Ordinary cement, water, and a patented formula of mineral origin are mixed in a "Thermo-Con Generator" to a thick paste called slurry. It is then pumped into building forms through a flexible hose to a predetermined depth. As the Thermo-Con sets, it begins to expand until, after about forty-five minutes, it reaches proper volume. Closer examination reveals the finished Thermo-Con is impregnated with tiny cells. Thus it gets its excellent insulating properties and light weight. The expansion that takes place actually increases the volume of the mass two and a half times.

She stared at the page until it was blurry, willing some bit of information to break loose.

And then it did.

One word. A word she'd read many times in the last five days but had never once considered important: *patented*.

Excitement blossomed. She took a shallow breath. She didn't know if it was instinct or foolish hope that made her belly flutter. "Lee, I think I found something."

He grunted in disinterest.

She was too excited to care about his lack of reaction. "I think I know where we can find information on Thermo-Con."

"Hmmm?"

She stood. "Thermo-Con was patented. The patent office will have information that could answer our research questions." A visceral déjà vu-like certainty enveloped her. She was on the right track. "Let's go tell Janice."

"One minute," he said.

He probably wanted to finish his computer game. Lazy and incompetent. Lee Scott was driving her nuts.

"Now, Lee!" Her voice projected anger in a way even he couldn't miss. She turned and hurried into the hall.

"I'm coming," he said, sounding like a put-upon teenager. He quickly caught up to her with his long-legged stride, and together they barged into Janice's office.

"I have a great idea!" she announced, trying to recapture the excited feeling she'd had about the patent office. She stopped short. Edward Drake was seated in Janice's guest chair. "I'm sorry. I didn't mean to interrupt."

"No problem," Janice said. "Ed and I were just discussing the navy aircraft project."

Her stomach lurched. Dammit, just when things were feeling…*right*. "I thought we decided not to bid on that."

"We're still considering," Janice said. "Now, tell me this idea you're all fired up about."

She quickly described her plan, and Janice grinned. "Excellent. How late is the patent office open today?"

"I haven't checked yet."

"I'll look." Janice swiveled to her computer and launched the internet browser.

Ed Drake let out a heavy sigh. "We're not finished, Janice. Jake thinks we can raise the airplane for less than you estimated, and he's the expert. This project is an excellent opportunity to get our foot in the door with the navy. Admiral Redmond is overseeing it personally, and no other engineering firm in the area has the right expertise."

"*We* don't have the right expertise, Ed," Janice said. "If I had one underwater archaeologist on staff, someone I trusted, I'd feel differently. But I don't. And frankly, I'm concerned about teaming with Jake Novak. He's more treasure hunter than salvage expert, which may sound fine to you, but in my line of work, that's a big, fat no."

"His work is perfectly legal," Drake said.

"He's no Bob Ballard. He's not a scientist. He's after the loot and to hell with the context, to hell with the resource.

Now, give me a minute to look up the patent office information for Erica."

Erica prayed Janice would hold firm. If Jake managed to team with Talon & Drake, she'd quit, even though that meant giving up graduate school and leaving archaeology for good.

Janice's fingers tapped at her keyboard. She stared at her monitor, then smiled. "The US Patent and Trademark Office Public Search Facility is open until eight." She tapped a few more keys. "I've printed the address and directions. It's in Alexandria, so you'd better get going. If you find anything new, write it up over the weekend."

Erica was almost out the door when Janice said, "Erica, I almost forgot, here's the reprint of the bone analysis." She waved a piece of paper. "Have you contacted Sam Riversong about the human remains yet?"

She took the letter from Janice. "No." Each time she'd reached for the phone, Tommy Riversong's face had come to mind, stopping her cold. "I'll call him after I get the carbon-14 results." There wasn't anything she could do before she got the carbon date anyway.

"Fine," Janice said.

"Can we get back to this proposal now, Janice?" Drake asked. "I'm meeting with the senator in an hour, and I happen to know the admiral is meeting with Joe before me. I should have a chance to talk to him on his way out."

Damn, damn, *damn*! Drake wanted the aircraft project and had used the senator to arrange a backdoor meeting. Her days at Talon & Drake were numbered unless she could expose Jake before they won the contract.

Feeling sick, she left Janice's office with Lee in tow. She picked up the patent office information from the printer, then hurried down the hall. She was preoccupied, looking down, and didn't see Rob Anderson until she almost crashed into him.

"Sam's been on my case about Thermo-Con," Rob said, an edge in his voice.

"We're about to leave for the patent office," she said. "We're going to try to find the Thermo-Con patent in hopes it will tell us something about the inventor."

He fixed her with a steady gaze. "I want to see the EA before it goes out on Monday." Rob turned on his heel and disappeared around the corner.

"What's his problem?" Lee asked.

Erica shrugged. "He's usually friendly. I don't know what it is about Thermo-Con that has him on edge."

"Maybe Sam told him about your threat."

She picked up her pace, part of her wishing she could lose him in the maze-like corridors. Then she could go to the patent office alone. Back in their office, she slipped the osteological report into the slowly thickening project file. How could she use the remains to her advantage? She was playing chess without a board, pieces, or rules, but still needed to predict ten moves ahead to decide her current move.

She gathered what she'd need to write the Thermo-Con EA from home over the weekend, then checked her email one last time.

Her stomach churned. She had an email from Jake. The subject: *Don't forget our deal.*

Chapter Fifteen

"Patents aren't issued in the name of the item being patented," the clerk said. "They're issued in the name of the inventor."

Lee almost felt sorry for Erica as her excitement evaporated. She looked crestfallen. "But I don't know the inventor's name."

"What about Higgins?" he said. "For all we know, that could be the inventor."

"It's worth a try," she said and turned back to the clerk. "The patent was issued around 1950. Does that help?"

The man frowned. "Not all the old patents have been scanned into the database yet. Your best bet is the card catalog." He circled the counter. "Follow me."

Lee lagged behind Erica and the clerk as they climbed a narrow staircase. He berated himself for not getting out of this research expedition. This was a ridiculous wild-goose chase. He had more important work to do.

At the top of the stairs, they entered a storage room where excess chairs, tables, and desks were stacked together and blocked the light cast by bare bulbs. The resulting patches of darkness gave the musty room an eerie atmosphere. They walked down the narrow aisle to the back, where hundreds of card catalog drawers spanned the wall.

"These are arranged alphabetically by the inventor's last name. If you find anything, copy the patent number, and bring it to me." The clerk left them alone.

Erica looked around. "This room's creepy."

Lee smiled. At least this field trip could serve a purpose. He'd exhausted his ability to learn about her through hacking. To learn more, he needed to spend time with her. Earn her trust. This was a start. "I'll protect you," he said. "Unless there are spiders. I hate spiders."

Her lips quirked. "My hero." She turned to the rows of cabinets. "Get to work, Romeo, and find the H drawer. I'm going to look up 'Thermo-Con' just for jazz." She pulled open the "Th" drawer and started flipping through cards.

A few minutes later, she returned to his side. "How're you doing?"

"This drawer is full of patents issued to one Higgins or another. No concrete yet."

With only one name to search for, they went through the cards together. Bent over the drawer as they were, her head was below his. He breathed in the fresh, clean smell of her glossy dark hair, which was—as usual—in a knot at the nape of her neck. He fought the urge to pluck out the hairpins.

She stopped his hand as he started to flip another card. "Wait," she said, her voice brimming with excitement.

He reread the card. "Amphibious Vehicle Propulsion System. It's not concrete."

"No, but have you noticed what all the Higgins Industries patents are for?"

Lee flipped though several of the cards. "Amphibious vessels, amphibious craft, amphibious shallow draft engine."

"Exactly. Just like Tuesday, at the archives—file after file detailed ERDL's work on amphibious this or that—you'd think they were studying frogs."

"So Higgins and ERDL were both working on amphibious vehicles."

"Yes." She held up her notebook. "Read research question number three."

She was playing school teacher. He had to admit, he liked it. He read aloud, "'If the engineers at the Engineer Research and Development Laboratory on Fort Belmont didn't invent Thermo-Con, then why was the house built on the post?'" He knew where she was leading him, but she was having fun, so he let her continue. "So?"

"Assuming Higgins Industries invented Thermo-Con, maybe ERDL and Higgins Industries worked *together* on amphibious projects. Maybe the ERDL engineers asked Higgins to build the house because they knew about Thermo-Con from their joint research."

"Or Higgins Industries wanted to show off their new invention to ERDL engineers." Her excitement was infectious; he felt his own buzz as he considered the possibilities. "What better way to impress the military than to wow their engineers with a prototype self-rising house."

She gasped and grabbed his wrist. "Lee, remember what the newspaper article said about Thermo-Con? It floats!"

"So it may have been developed by Higgins for boat building," he said, liking her theory more and more.

"Exactly!"

Together and with deliberate slowness, they flipped through the Higgins cards, pausing on each one to carefully read the patent description before going to the next. She let out a soft squeal every time the patent described another amphibious invention. Erica excited was a definite turn-on.

Anticipation built with each flip of the cards. Finally they came to patent number 2,560,871: *Method of Mixing Cement Composition.* Erica sucked in a sharp breath that in a different situation would have pushed him over the edge.

"I don't believe it," he said. "We found the Thermo-Con

patent." In that moment, he made another connection. "Higgins…amphibious…boats…Higgins Boats. Of course. It's so obvious—I can't believe I missed that."

"What are you talking about?"

"The Thermo-Con house was built by the guy who invented Higgins Boats."

"Um, what are Higgins Boats?"

Miss Smarty-Pants didn't know. He grinned. "Higgins boats were used in every major allied invasion in World War II. The Germans didn't believe boats existed that could deliver our troops to Normandy, and so the Normandy beaches were less defended. Without Higgins Boats, D-Day couldn't—wouldn't—have happened."

Her jaw dropped. "How do you know all this?"

He felt sufficiently mollified that after being a slacker piece of shit all week, he could show he wasn't a complete idiot. "I like military history." He paused, realizing he had a perfect opportunity. "Tonight we're going to watch *Saving Private Ryan*."

"That's the movie that opens with D-Day, right? I've heard it's pretty graphic."

"You haven't seen it?"

"Never got around to it."

"Then you need to watch it. Tonight." He paused. "With me."

"I've got to work on Thermo-Con tonight."

"Your Friday nights sound enthralling."

"Some of us have to work for a living."

He used his most cajoling smile. "So tonight you'll watch a movie and still be working."

She chewed on her bottom lip, then said, "Okay. But I don't have a decent TV. We need to watch the movie at your place."

Damn. He wanted to see her apartment. Fortunately, he was prepared. Yesterday he'd taken down all his photos and scoured each room in his condo of everything that indicated the place was his. He'd even tossed clothes into a suitcase and changed the address on the luggage tag. It was safe to invite her over. "Okay."

"Where are you living, anyway?" she asked.

"A friend is letting me stay at his place."

"Figures you'd have a free place to stay. Some people get all the breaks." But she said the words with a smile. Maybe she could forgive his fake self for having opportunities she so obviously envied.

He wondered if he could make her forget the role he'd been playing. Earning her respect would be even harder than earning her trust. She worked long hours every day, each minute an exercise in efficiency and dedication. All while he cultivated a slacker façade that drove them both crazy. His ability to act like a dickhead had exceeded even his own expectations.

It was time for the intern to evolve. Tonight was the perfect opportunity.

With the tip of her finger, she caressed the file card. "We need to go through the rest of the Higgins cards first, to see if there are any others that could be Thermo-Con."

Again, they flipped through the cards, now lacking the anticipation of before, but with a companionable silence. It felt strangely like cuddling after sex, when the actions were often the same, but it was the wind down, not the windup. A dozen or so cards later, he touched her hand, preventing her from flipping to the next one. "This mixing-machine patent could be the Thermo-Con Generator the newspaper article referred to."

She paused and studied the card. "I think you're right."

After copying the information from the two cards, they returned to the information desk. The man who'd helped them earlier grinned broadly when Erica produced the patent numbers. "Let me see if we have it here." He typed the information into his computer and frowned at the results. "These files are in our storage facility. I'll have to order them for you. It should take a few days. Fill out this form, and I'll call you when the patents arrive."

Lee tucked the Thermo-Con file into his laptop case while she filled out the form; then they headed to the Metro station. "Let's go to your apartment first," he said, "so you can change into something more comfortable."

"You don't mind? These shoes always hurt by the end of the day."

No, he didn't mind at all.

After a short Metro ride and walk, he stepped inside her top-floor apartment five blocks south of the Mall in the southwest part of DC, and his jaw dropped with awe at the stunning view. The west wall of the living room was entirely made up of windows, from the sloped twelve-foot ceiling to the parquet flooring. "This place is amazing," he said.

"Thanks. I do love it here." Her voice was filled with pride.

He opened the sliding-glass balcony door. An intense wall of heat struck him as he stepped out onto the sun-drenched white trapezoid-shaped balcony and looked out across the Potomac River. Directly west sat the Jefferson Memorial and the vast hillside of Arlington National Cemetery. The Pentagon sat to the right, while planes landed at National Airport to the left. He took a deep breath of the muggy air, enjoying the scent of the thriving tomato plants that flanked the balcony.

She joined him outside and handed him a cold bottle of beer. She clinked her bottle against his and said, "Happy Friday. The end of the first week of your internship."

As far as she knew, he'd been a lazy jerk the last few days, and here she was drinking a toast to him as though he'd reached a real milestone. He squelched his guilt with the knowledge he'd been putting in eighteen-hour days. Every waking hour and even a few of the sleeping ones had been devoted to hacking into the network and narrowing down his list of suspects.

"Thanks," he said. The icy drink slid down his throat and revived the part of him that had been flattened on the hot walk from the Metro station. "That's just what I needed. This heat is killing me." He watched traffic move slowly over the I-395 bridge.

He turned his back on the view and studied her large, starkly furnished living room. Her building had a twenty-four-hour manned security desk. It wasn't a luxury develop-ment, but still, the rent had to put her at the edge of her financial limits, and she didn't have a credit card to help make ends meet. Was security more important to her than food? "How on earth did you find this place?"

"This condo is owned by a friend of Janice's. When she heard I needed a place to live, she made some calls. It's just outside my budget, but living alone, security was important, so it's worth it." She led him back into the air-conditioned room and closed the balcony door. "You complained about the heat. Doesn't it get this hot in New York City?"

"Yeah. As soon as I'm done with school, I'm leaving."

She smiled. "It must not be so bad. After all, you could have finished three years ago."

He laughed. "But then I wouldn't have met you."

Her eyes lit with surprising warmth; then she spun on her heel and spread her arms to indicate the room. "So, this is the living room," she said in a blatant change of subject.

The couch was a notch above junk but draped with a clean quilt and matching throw pillows. He suspected the end tables were cardboard boxes covered with sheets. But most startling was her dining set: an expanding oval table surrounded by six chairs. Made from a rich, red wood, with clean, modern lines, the table surface was smooth and pristine.

She could have purchased the table with the proceeds from selling Iraqi artifacts.

"Nice table," he said.

Her face lit up. She touched a ladder-back chair with reverence. "Thanks. I just bought it. I saved for months."

He considered her work attire: clean, functional, appropriate. Her plain skirts, slacks, and blouses were, in a word, cheap. But her frugal lifestyle could be a façade. If he stripped her down, would he find her wearing designer lingerie?

She was a smart woman who worked hard. She had a BA and a Master's degree. A bad credit report didn't fully explain why she appeared so destitute or why she was so *alone*.

He waited in the living room while she changed clothes in the bedroom, wondering if he should make a move to find out how expensive her lingerie was. His instincts told him he needed to build trust between them, but he was short on time. In one week, his cover would be blown.

He studied a photo of her underwater in full scuba gear with three other divers. Her face was hidden behind a mask and regulator, but her gray eyes penetrated the glass shield, clearly identifying her among the women in the photo. The air bubbles that surrounded the group and the light in their eyes made him conclude they all laughed behind their regulators. He couldn't imagine the Erica he knew that happy.

She entered the room dressed in shorts and a tight V-neck T-shirt that showed off her cleavage and wouldn't cover her midriff if she raised her arms. She looked sexy and warm and very different from the woman he'd worked with all week. He couldn't help but hope she'd chosen the outfit for him. Perhaps he was making better progress than he thought.

He pointed to the photo. "You're a diver," he said. "Have you ever done underwater archaeology?"

She met his gaze without flinching. "No. I haven't."

Erica might be sexy as hell, but she was still a liar.

Chapter Sixteen

*T*he Watergate. Of course. Her rich, pretty-boy intern was staying—*for free*—at the Watergate. Erica wandered through the gigantic living room, looking for clues as to the condo's owner.

She'd accepted Lee's invitation for one purpose, and it wasn't to watch a movie or learn more about Higgins Boats. She wanted to know if Lee could be working for Jake. They'd both invaded her life this week. Her office had been trashed. And, for an eager intern, Lee showed shockingly little interest in archaeology.

Could this be Jake's apartment?

Jake knew her job at Talon & Drake—a company owned by a Menanichoch tribal member—was no coincidence. He knew she was looking for the artifacts and the new casino room was opening soon. Had Jake hired Lee to watch over her?

She circled the room. There wasn't a photograph in sight; nothing to tell her who owned this place. Yet it looked lived-in, not like an apartment used only part-time. The only thing she knew for certain was the owner was a man. The furnishings, the organization, even the colors all indicated the place was inhabited by a bachelor.

In the guest bathroom, she searched the medicine chest, looking for prescription bottles with the owner's name, knowing it was more likely they would be in the master bathroom. She wasn't willing to jump into bed with Lee just to get access to that room.

She returned to the living room. Where was the owner? Why was he gone for the summer? And why hadn't Lee mentioned his name?

Initially, she'd questioned the wisdom of coming here—if he really worked for Jake, she could be walking into a trap—but playing it safe was getting her nowhere. And Lee didn't have any reason to think she was suspicious of him.

Then there was the fact that she didn't *want* to be suspicious of him. He was frustrating, immature, and a complete slacker, but he was also funny, charming, and, well, enticing.

He walked down the hall toward her. He'd changed into shorts and a bright Aloha shirt decorated with vertical ribbons of red ginger flowers. All those years of karate had given his extra-long legs well-defined muscles. He strode with an easy, masculine grace.

He's twenty-five and a shiftless career student, she reminded herself.

Or he's not.

His gaze swept her from head to toe, and his eyes lit with appreciation. She'd seen that look a dozen times and it still caused a flutter in her belly. She acknowledged there were other reasons she might end up in bed with Lee.

If only she could be certain he wasn't working for Jake.

"Let's eat out, then rent the movie," he said.

"I'm not hungry."

"There's this great restaurant right around the corner."

He wouldn't take no for an answer, and minutes later, she was being seated inside a casual restaurant with a cozy, romantic ambience. One look at the menu and she began to panic. She had eighty-six dollars until next payday, and there was nothing on the menu less than twenty bucks.

The waiter arrived, and she started to order water, but Lee interrupted. "We'll have a bottle of pinot noir and the crab appetizer."

He and the waiter discussed the wine choice while she took an anxious look at the menu. The cheapest pinot noir was forty bucks a bottle, and the appetizer cost half that. The waiter left.

"Don't worry," Lee said, a cocky smile on his handsome face. "I'm buying."

She gave him a stern look. "This isn't a date."

"Yes. It is." The confident look in his green eyes caused another flutter, and she wondered how this Tetris champion managed to tempt her.

The answer came readily enough: dinner with Lee was more fun than any evening since she'd learned of her mother's betrayal. Intelligent, funny, interesting; take away the slacker, and he was the full package. She sipped her wine, enjoying the warm buzz of good food and conversation. It had been far too long since she'd gone out for dinner with a friend. Then she wondered if Lee was a friend and honestly had no idea.

But he made it clear he wanted to be more, and she was dangerously interested. "Just because you paid doesn't make this a date," she said stubbornly as he signed the credit card slip.

He stood, stepped behind her, pulled her chair back, and bent low so his lips touched her ear, sending a shiver down her spine. "You know, 'Thank you for dinner, Lee, I had a lovely time,' is the standard polite response."

She stood and grabbed her purse, disconcerted to find he'd positioned himself expertly behind her so she brushed against him and then had to crane her neck to look up at him. "That's the kind of thing one says when fishing for a good-night kiss."

"Try it later, and we'll see if it works."

Oh God, she feared she'd do exactly that. Instead, she beckoned him with a curled finger to bend low and whispered in his ear, "Thank you for dinner, Lee, I had a lovely…meal." The sexy, masculine scent of his cologne filled her with longing. She wanted to bite his earlobe. "And, just so you know, you're not getting on base tonight. You're not even at bat."

"Dinner was just the first inning of a nine-inning game."

She'd thrown down the gauntlet, and the determined glint in his eye caused a frisson of excitement to run through her. She should put a stop to this dangerous flirtation now, but instead enjoyed the tingle caused by the slight pressure of his hand on the small of her back as he guided her out of the restaurant.

When she settled on his couch half an hour later, she made sure she sat tucked into the corner, giving him as much space as possible. He, of course, sat right next to her.

On the screen, boats landed amidst gunfire and blood. The front panel of the boat dropped, and the occupants had no choice but to move forward, off the boat, marching up the beach without any sort of cover from the rain of bullets and explosives.

"That's an LCVP. A Higgins Boat."

She smiled. He didn't care about the acronyms that governed their work on a daily basis but knew the obscure acronym for a World War II boat. "What does LCVP stand for?"

"Landing Craft, Vehicle, Personnel."

"Oh. Of course. It was obvious."

She knew from the media attention when *Saving Private Ryan* was first released that the invasion depiction was accurate. She tried not to cover her eyes from the carnage on the screen. This wasn't violence for violence's sake. This was a recreation of an actual historic event. She flinched as bullets rained down, and Lee gave her leg a comforting squeeze.

The overactive air-conditioning and the intense action on the screen combined to give her goose bumps. One degree colder and she'd be shivering. She fought the urge to shift her position and lean against him for warmth.

He could be working for Jake.

Yet, she didn't believe it. Jake's style was direct. Threatening. His crew was the same. Lee was nothing like them.

She grabbed a throw pillow and hugged it to her chest. Lee paused the movie and fetched a blanket, which he spread over both of them, then pulled her against his side.

"You could just turn off the air-conditioning," she said.

"Are you kidding? I'm thinking of turning it down to fifty." He draped his arm around her, pressing her snug against him, then dropped a light kiss on her forehead. "Now hush and watch the movie."

Warmth from his body seeped in, and a brief, sharp pain pulsed through her, as though she were sitting next to a hot fire after suffering frostbite. She'd missed this casual intimacy. For the first time since she'd walked out of that awful cell, she felt safe. Cared for.

When the movie ended, she extricated herself from his side, and stood and stretched. She caught the heat in his eyes as her shirt rode up to her ribs and immediately dropped her arms. It wouldn't take much persuasion to get her into bed, but that would be a mistake.

"I should get home," she said.

He stood and towered over her. "I'll walk you."

Relief mixed with a hint of disappointment. "Thanks."

When they stepped out into the muggy night, warm air enveloped her but was a poor replacement for Lee's body heat. It was at least eighty degrees at eleven p.m. She doubted she'd ever get used to the East Coast summer heat.

"We can take the long way home and walk through the

Roosevelt Memorial," he said. Perhaps it was the serious nature of the movie or his face half-hidden in shadow, but he seemed much older to her. And more appealing than ever.

She should refuse and suggest they take the Metro. Every minute they were together, she was playing with fire. But instead the truth slipped out. "I've never been to the FDR Memorial at night." She was embarrassed to admit that in her months in DC, she'd made no friends to hang out with in the city at night, and the dark paths around the tidal basin weren't safe for a woman walking alone.

He took her hand in a casual gesture and pulled her in the direction of the Kennedy Center. After a few steps, she tried to pull her hand away, but his grip tightened.

"Better hold on," he said. "I have a long stride and forget to walk slower for shorties like you. Tug on my hand when I start going too fast."

He sounded reasonable, but she didn't buy his excuse. She faltered, and he gave her hand a comforting squeeze. She relaxed her shoulders and allowed herself to enjoy the simple pleasure of a hand to hold in the darkness.

❖

The Franklin Delano Roosevelt Memorial was divided into four outdoor rooms, one for each term the man served as president. They entered the memorial from the first-term side and moved through the rooms in chronological order. Even though it was eleven fifteen at night, the park was full of visitors. Perhaps it was the isolation darkness provided or the controlled light and shadow, but whatever the reason, Lee had always felt this memorial was best viewed after the sun went down.

He watched Erica in profile as she studied the breadline sculpture, and saw the raw vulnerability she usually kept hidden behind an icy façade, a reminder that darkness could expose as much as it hid. He wondered if she had faced hunger or homelessness in the wake of her credit nightmare and wanted to hold her, to protect her. He forced the feeling down, crushing it with the suspicion he needed to keep in the forefront of his mind.

He walked away from her into the next section of the memorial, then waited for her to join him. They meandered through, talking about the quotes inscribed in stone, sharing their reactions. When they reached the World War II part of the exhibit they talked about the movie they'd just watched, Higgins Boats, and Thermo-Con. Once again her keen mind dampened his suspicions. He *liked* her. A lot.

She paused in front of the statue of Eleanor Roosevelt. "I love it that she's here." She looked at him. "Quick, what was Eleanor's maiden name?"

She did love to test him. "Roosevelt," he answered.

"Very good. Most men don't know Eleanor's history."

"I'm a history buff."

"I've seen little sign of that at work." She said it saucily.

"I want to dig, not sit at a desk and work on boring reports."

"I don't care if JT Talon is your long-lost twin brother, you've still got to do the scut work, just like the rest of us."

He nearly choked and was glad she didn't seem to notice. He imagined a future where he could remind her of this moment when she'd come so dangerously close to the truth, but his stomach clenched as he recognized Erica would never forgive his lies.

She walked to the statue of FDR. "Want to know why I think they only made him slightly larger than life?"

"He looks big to me."

"Yes, but Lincoln, Jefferson—their statues are huge. FDR is only a little bit big. I think it's because of the way people remember him. He was approachable. Fireside chats and all that. He's not a monolithic figure. He was great, but human."

"You could be right. It also could be that this memorial is less formal than the others. No columns here."

"But that too is a product of who he was. He would look odd in a Grecian temple."

"The dog wouldn't match," he said, indicating the Scottish terrier who sat at the president's feet.

She giggled.

He couldn't believe it. Erica Kesling had actually *giggled*.

"No," she said. "Fala isn't dignified enough for Ionic, let alone Corinthian, columns."

They wandered over to an area where lighted waterfalls splashed over flat rocks in a shallow pool. The muggy heat pressed down on him as he looked at the water. "God, I'd love to go swimming right now."

She grinned. "There's always the tidal basin."

He faced the basin and laughed. "No, thank you."

Water splashed across his legs, and he turned to see she had slipped off her sandals and stood on one of the low, submerged stones. She kicked, and a spray of water hit his legs again.

He lunged for her in one broad step. Her eyes widened, and she stepped backward, slipping on the wet rock. He caught her waist and pulled her against him, stopping her fall. "I shouldn't have done that," he said. "You'd look damn good in a wet T-shirt."

Her gray eyes matched the water that rushed over the stones. With a hand on the smooth, bare skin of her waist, he held her against him, while his other hand caressed her butt. "Bottom of the ninth and finally at bat," he said and lowered his mouth to hers.

He expected her to protest. She didn't.

He expected her to pull away. She didn't.

He brushed his lips across hers, softly at first; then she slid her arms around his neck and opened her mouth to initiate a deeper kiss. Her fingers threaded through his hair as her tongue entwined with his, and she let out a soft hum that ran through him like fire. He pulled her snug against him and explored her mouth slowly. Thoroughly. For the first time, he enjoyed every facet of this undercover job.

"Mommy, can I play in the water too?" a young voice asked excitedly.

"No, honey. They're being naughty," a stern voice responded.

Lee managed to open one eye and saw the woman and her child walk away.

Erica broke the kiss and tucked her head against his chest. He could feel her body shaking with silent laughter.

He whispered in her ear, "Not nearly as naughty as I want to be."

She looked up at him, laughter in eyes so bright they were almost blue. "And what kind of mother is she, letting her kid stay up this late?"

"We should report her to Child Protective Services, preferably before she sics the park police on us."

She stepped out of his arms and leaped back to solid, dry concrete. He waited while she slipped on her sandals, then reached for her hand.

She glanced around, her eyes pausing on several tourists before returning to his. "Lee, this isn't—"

"You're not going to go all Queen Frostine on me now, are you?"

"Queen Frostine?"

He paused. Where did the name come from? Then he remembered. "Queen Frostine is from the game Candy Land."

Her eyes widened. "Surely you're not *that* young?"

"I told you. I'm twenty-five." He hated the lie. He considered what he could tell her and decided the truth was safe enough. "A friend of mine has a five-year-old daughter who loves Candy Land. I'm an expert at letting her win the game. Queen Frostine is the key."

"And you think of me as Queen Frostine." She sounded hurt.

"No, I think of you as Shortcake."

"Why Shortcake?"

"Because you're short—"

"I'm not short, you're just tall."

"—and I want to taste you with strawberries and whipped cream."

Her breath caught. Good. "This really isn't a good idea," she said.

He reached for her hand again, and this time she allowed it. They walked in darkness around the basin. She managed to drop his hand before they reached the Jefferson Memorial, and he could feel her build a barrier between them until it was as solid as the marble columns surrounding the statue of the nation's third president.

Damn JT. Damn the senator. Damn the campaign. Wasn't there a better way? But with each step, he considered their options. There were few, and none had the same chance of success as the current plan.

"I'll walk you up," he said as they neared her building. He didn't believe for a moment she would invite him to stay, but he wanted a few more minutes with her.

They arrived at the secure doorway to her apartment building. Erica waved her keychain in front of the sensor until it beeped, and she opened the door. He walked beside her as she nodded to the concierge, who called out, "Good evening, Miss Kesling."

Inside the elevator, the barrier she'd built was a tangible presence. "Why?" he asked, breaking the tension-filled silence.

"We've got to work together for five more weeks. Let's not make it complicated, okay?"

"And when the five weeks are up?"

"You'll be gone," she said softly.

The elevator doors opened, and he followed her down the dimly lit hallway. She stopped abruptly a few feet from her door. He bumped into her and saw why she'd halted. Her apartment door was ajar. They had closed and locked it when they left hours ago.

He pushed open the door. The entryway closet was open, the contents scattered on the foyer floor. The word WHORE dripped in long red streaks on the opposite wall.

Chapter Seventeen

*N*early an hour passed before the police allowed Erica and Lee to enter the apartment. On leaden legs, she walked through her home, astounded by the extent of the destruction. A nauseating jumble of odors permeated the rooms, but above all other smells was the stench of wet paint.

The contents of her refrigerator had been spilled across the kitchen floor. She'd had precious little food, but her paltry eggs, mustard, and relish had been dumped out and stepped on. Her mattress, pillows, cushions, and clothing had all been slashed, painted, gouged, and ripped.

"The damage appears to have been done in a way that minimized noise, so your neighbors wouldn't be alerted while the suspect was still here," a police officer said.

She nodded numbly. Her apartment looked like the site of a massacre, with red paint splashed over furniture, across the walls, dousing everything. Her few photographs and fewer electronic items had been dunked in a bathtub full of bloodred water.

Quiet, yet thorough.

The odor of fresh paint indicated the red splatters weren't

blood, but she couldn't ignore the implied threat. Jake intended to finish the destruction of her life he'd started a year ago.

She shuddered as nausea, revulsion, and shame washed through her. The one thing she didn't feel was surprise. She'd expected Jake to do something. Just because he could.

The vandal had left behind a gallon-size canister of red paint. "How could one gallon coat so many surfaces?" she asked.

"The suspect was methodical. He or she cut the paint with water in the bathtub, and then poured the diluted mixture over everything," the cop answered.

She took a deep breath and inhaled the sickening odor. A headache grabbed hold.

Both cops circled the room, taking photos, writing notes, and dusting for fingerprints. Lee stood by, watching everything, saying nothing.

She wouldn't cry. Jake wasn't there to witness her emotional state, but still, she didn't want him to have another victory over her.

Her eyes strayed to her dining set—the one place she'd refused to look—and in that moment, he won. He'd found her vulnerability and ripped it wide open. She walked to the table, ran her fingers over the deep gouges, and a sob escaped.

From behind, Lee wrapped his arms around her. She turned, collapsed against him, and cried. "It'll be okay," he murmured. "The wood can be sanded and refinished. I can restore it."

He didn't understand. She'd been trying for the last year to restore her life. No amount of sanding would take away the shame or the guilt.

Even if the deep grooves were sanded away, she would never be able to sit at that table—which had been her pride and joy when she paid cash for it a month ago—without seeing the insult etched into its surface. She'd always be reminded of Jake, Mexico, and the jail cell. She'd see the void in Marco's eyes where a soul should be and remember the sound of his fly unzipping as he prepared to rape her.

So she shook her head and cried into the ginger flowers that decorated Lee's shirt while he held her and an officer paced, waiting to question her.

Finally, she calmed, and the questioning began. "Does anyone have a grudge against you?"

She took a deep breath. "No," she said with as much earnestness in her voice as she could muster. "I can't think of anyone who would do this." She pulled on her bottom lip with her thumb and forefinger, then remembered reading in a psychology book that people often touched their face when they lied. She dropped her hand.

"Someone trashed our office at work this week too," Lee said.

The cop raised an eyebrow.

She felt her face heat. She should have told the police about that sooner. The cop stared at her, waiting. Lee pulled her close against his side and explained the situation to the officer.

"You share the office," the cop said. "Where were you, Mr. Scott, while Ms. Kesling's apartment was being destroyed?"

She cleared her throat. "He was with me. On a date."

Lee lifted her chin to catch her gaze. "I knew you'd come around."

In spite of everything, she found a weak smile. He kissed her temple.

After the cops finished taking their notes, they told them it was okay to clean up, and left. She picked up the blanket she'd used to cover her beat-up couch. The quilt had been a particularly good thrift-store find but was now garbage. She dumped the shredded fabric in a corner and sorted through other items in the living room on automatic pilot.

Her rent ate up most of her budget, but she'd paid it because the building had good security. As she worked, she couldn't, wouldn't look at the table. The table she couldn't afford but couldn't resist. She'd scraped and saved for months to buy it. The table where she'd hoped to entertain friends and have a dinner party like the old days, before she accepted the job from Jake Novak that not only ended her career but caused every friend she had to treat her like a pariah.

A dinner party that would fill her empty apartment with warmth, love, and laughter.

But it was just another fucking pipe dream.

"I think that cushion has been mangled enough, don't you?" Lee said.

She glanced down at her hands and realized she had taken a ripped cushion and thoroughly gutted it. She faced Lee again and tried to think of something to say. But she was empty. She had nothing. Was nothing.

"C'mon," he said. "Let's clean the kitchen floor so the food doesn't rot. Then we're leaving. You're staying with me tonight."

The incredible kiss they'd shared earlier flashed through her mind, and the idea of finding oblivion in sex was enticing. She could wrap her legs around his hips, take him deep inside, and escape the reality of her rotten life.

"You'll stay in the guest bedroom," he said as if he'd read her thoughts. "I won't take advantage of you right now."

Then maybe she should take advantage of him.

Chapter Eighteen

*L*ee awoke to the sound of the front door closing. It took several seconds for his eyes to focus on the clock. Seven a.m. What was Erica doing up this early? They hadn't gone to sleep until after three in the morning.

He slipped out of bed and pulled sweatpants on over the hard-on he'd gotten while dreaming of her, while the fog in his mind began to clear. Had she left? He felt a ripple of fear for her safety. Her apartment had been brutally trashed last night. She shouldn't go out alone.

He entered the hallway, stopped at Erica's door, and silently opened it. She lay in bed, sound asleep.

Crap! JT must have arrived. He bolted for the living room.

He was there. "You're up," he said, his voice sounding like a bellow in the quiet apartment.

Lee launched himself toward JT, but he continued talking, oblivious. "I'm anxious to hear what you found out about Er—"

Skidding into the couch, he slapped his hand over JT's mouth just in time. "Quiet," he hissed, then straightened and rubbed his aching shin, which had hit the coffee table.

Erica stumbled into the room, more asleep than awake. "Lee, what's going on?"

His breath came out in a rush at the sight of her. The threadbare T-shirt he'd loaned her reached her knees, and now he realized it was alarmingly sheer. More enticing than a teddy, it draped her full breasts and left nothing to the imagination. But most stunning was her hair, which fell past her waist in a tousled curtain of shimmering black.

She was a vision that would feed his fantasies for days, weeks—hell, probably years—to come. But this wasn't the time. He scooped up the blanket they'd snuggled under while watching the movie, crossed the room, and wrapped it around her.

She rubbed her still-unfocused eyes. "I heard a noise. What's going on?" she asked again.

"JT is here," he said softly.

Shock lit her face. She glanced down at the blanket and T-shirt, made a sound that was part yelp, part curse, part muffled groan, and fled the room. Her door slammed closed.

"Damn. I'm impressed." JT spoke softly so his voice wouldn't carry. "She turned me down cold."

He swung to face JT, also keeping his voice low. "You hit on her?"

"She's a suspect. I wanted to get to know her."

Lee ran his fingers through his hair. Part of him wanted to throttle JT; another part understood. Hell, he'd been doing the same thing. "Don't hit on her again."

"It's obvious she made her choice. Good work."

Dammit, he wanted to go after her, but he needed to talk to JT first. With a sigh, he plopped down on the couch. "We need to get our story straight."

*E*rica frantically pulled on the shorts and T-shirt she'd worn last night. She cursed the vanity that made her select her smallest, tightest, most cleavage-showing, V-neck shirt to wear for Lee. What had she been thinking? As if it wasn't bad enough she'd just appeared practically naked in front of the company CEO, now she had to go out and talk to him wearing the sexiest clothing she owned—which, thanks to Jake, was now the only clothing she owned.

She twisted her hair into a tight knot and began ramming pins into the heavy mass. At least she could make her hair look professional. She was going to hurt Lee. Badly. He could have told her JT would be here. Hair restrained, she reached for the doorknob, intending to hold her head high as she marched into the living room.

She faltered. What the hell was JT doing here? What was his relationship to Lee?

The man had hit on her the other night. But it had seemed like an afterthought, like he suddenly realized he had an itch she could scratch.

He must think she'd slept with Lee. Would he be jealous? She didn't think for a moment JT had actually been interested in her, but when egos became involved, anything was possible.

Another worry came to mind. Company policy allowed coworkers to date, but Lee was her subordinate. Could she be fired for sleeping with her intern?

I didn't sleep with him.

But she'd wanted to. Lee had been a perfect gentleman last night—this morning—hell, a few hours ago. He'd tucked her into bed, and when she tried to turn his platonic good-night kiss into something more, he'd pulled back and cupped her face in his hands. *"I want you,"* he'd said. *"But not like this."* Then he kissed her forehead and left her alone.

She leaned against the closed door, fighting the urge to

bang her head against it. As if she didn't have enough to worry about. Last night Jake had destroyed everything she owned. She bit on a knuckle to keep from sobbing.

"Erica?" Lee said from the opposite side of the door.

She jumped back as though she'd received an electric shock. She needed to compose herself. She squared her shoulders, took a deep breath, and opened the door.

Lee stepped inside, shut the door, and leaned against it. His gaze raked her from head to toe, a lopsided grin warming his chiseled features.

"I was just coming out," she said hoarsely. She cleared her throat. "I think you should open the door."

"JT's gone. He went to get coffee and won't be back for at least an hour." A frown marred his handsome face. "Why did you put up your hair?"

She ignored the question. "Is he going to fire me?"

"For putting up your hair? I doubt it, but it's worth considering."

The knot in her belly tightened. "Dammit, Lee, I'm serious!" She took a deep breath. She would act calm. Dignified. If nothing else, it was practice for when she faced JT. "What did you tell him?" She enunciated each syllable with precision.

"Your hair is beautiful. You should wear it down." His voice was low, husky.

Heat slid down her spine. "You didn't tell him that."

"I didn't need to. He'd have to be blind not to notice for himself."

Her nipples hardened. How could he do that—in this situation—with just words? He wore nothing but a pair of sweatpants. She kept her gaze fixed on his eyes, willing herself to ignore his muscular torso. She would not think about how much she enjoyed snuggling against him last night, or how safe she'd felt with those thick arms wrapped around her.

He plucked out one of her hairpins, and the heavy mass loosened but didn't fall. She crossed her arms and took a step backward, but his feet moved forward, in sync with hers.

"I want to know why JT Talon was in the living room," she said, but her voice came out huskier than she'd intended. "And I want to know what you told him about me."

"This is JT's condo. He's letting me stay here during my internship because he's only in DC periodically. He lives in New York City." He stepped closer, his gaze locked on her mouth. "I convinced JT there's nothing going on between us. Not that he'd care, by the way, but I figured you would." He reached around her and pulled her to him. His other hand removed another hairpin, and several strands fell. "Want to make a liar out of me?"

Foolish laughter bubbled up inside her, and she tucked her head on his chest. Was this what it felt like to be on the edge of hysterics?

A pleasing truth penetrated her jumbled thoughts. JT had given Lee the job and apartment. Lee couldn't be working for Jake.

She pushed him away and stepped back. "Why didn't you tell me this is JT's place?"

"JT and I didn't want anyone to know we're acquainted."

"You're staying in his apartment. You're more than acquainted."

"His family and my family go way back. He's helping me out."

"So why the big secret?"

"I'm an intern, and I've got to do the scut work, just like everyone else. If you'd known I was staying at JT's place, would you have treated me the same?"

"Yes."

He arched an eyebrow. "Really?"

She hesitated, admitting to herself that if she'd known his connection to JT, she'd have tried to figure out a way to use that to her advantage. JT was Menanichoch, after all. "You should have told me JT would show up."

"I didn't know he was coming. I'm sorry."

She was slightly mollified. "Does he know why I'm here?"

"Yes. He also knows we've only gotten four hours sleep." He took her in his arms again. "I'm going back to bed. You're more than welcome to join me."

"That's not a good idea."

"It's a spectacular idea." His lips traced her hairline as he removed the last of her hairpins. "I knew I shouldn't have listened to my conscience last night."

She rose on tiptoes and kissed his cheek. "Thank you for that."

"I won't be so noble next time." His fingers threaded through her hair; then he leaned down and dropped a kiss on her collarbone. His tongue traced the line of her V-neck, and she felt goose bumps form.

She gently pushed him away, fighting the reckless urge to pull him to the bed and forget everything in a rousing romp of mindless sex. She couldn't give in to the wild impulse. She'd known him all of five days, and in that time, her carefully constructed life had collapsed.

"JT will be around all weekend. Get some sleep. Later you can tell him I keep trying to seduce you. You might get lucky and he'll fire me for sexually harassing you."

"I know how men are—he'd probably give you a raise."

"The only person giving me a raise, Shortcake, is you." He left the room, closing the door behind him.

She collapsed on the bed and picked up his T-shirt, the one she'd slept in. She lifted it to her nose, but it smelled of her, not him. After pulling off her clothing and donning the T-shirt, she slipped back under the covers and mentally listed her troubles. Jake was back. Her job was in jeopardy. And she had the hots for her intern.

Wanting Lee was the least of her problems, but with his

current proximity, the sexual hunger between them loomed large and dangerous.

Was four years that big an age difference? Probably. She was a few years away from her biological clock going off, and he was barely old enough to rent a car.

⚜

*L*ee needed a cold shower after leaving Erica's room. He'd used the attraction between Erica and him as a tool to deliberately rattle and confuse her, and his conscience needled him. His words and actions were accurate —hell, yes, he wanted her—but he'd behaved like a rutting fool to downplay the significance of JT being here.

She couldn't examine his relationship with JT. A simple Google search would turn up the facts of Joe's life, including the long-ago marriage, and his mother's Facebook page, which contained pictures of all of them.

He'd begged his mother to remove the photos, but with Joe's impending campaign, she was angling for her fifteen minutes. He'd crashed her page and put off her pleas for her techno-wizard son to fix it, and the woman had stunned him by hiring someone to restore her page within a few days.

He returned to the kitchen to face another blatant lie. JT sat at the table in front of his open laptop. Lee had known JT hadn't left. He'd lied because Erica would've insisted on talking to him, and he and JT needed more time to figure out how to handle her presence in his apartment. "She's going back to sleep."

He searched through the playlist on his iPod and found a Beethoven symphony. He aimed the speakers toward the entry, then spoke softly, under the music. "I think her apartment was destroyed because of me. I may have tripped a trap in the network."

JT just looked at him.

"Damn it, JT, that first day, I used her ID. Someone noticed."

"You're too good to be caught."

"I'd like to think so, but I've never seen a network this tight. If everyone had systems that secure, I'd have no clients."

"So you think you screwed up and put Erica in the crosshairs?"

"It's possible."

"I don't think so. I think she's part of it. And you do too."

He closed his eyes and could see Erica struggling with her desires and her fears. He knew how important his job was. He understood what was at stake.

"You told me days ago she's afraid and is hiding something. And we know she's lied to you and Rob Anderson. Lee, I'm sure she's a superb piece of ass, but don't let that fuck with your brain. I need you to focus."

"I am focused."

"I don't think it's on the job I've asked you to do."

He took a deep breath. This was JT he was talking to. His brother in all but blood. "I am focused," he said again. "I'm not blinded by Erica's ass or any other part of her anatomy. I spent time with her last night to learn more about her. I know this: she doesn't live like someone who's got another source of income."

He rubbed his eyes. He felt like hell. Four hours sleep. Sexual frustration. And his closest friend in the world wanted to pin treasonous smuggling on a woman he'd begun to feel protective of—*when the hell had that happened?*—and the theory had merit.

He left the room without a word and retrieved his own laptop, then set it on the kitchen table across from JT's. "I think I know what—or rather who—we're looking for." He'd been itching to google Jake Novak since he'd heard Drake say the name. Google had an answer for him in .26 seconds.

Third on the results list was the website for Novak Underwater Salvage and Treasure.

He followed the link. The homepage featured a photo of Jake Novak on the deck of his boat, *Andvari*.

"JT, meet Jake Novak. He's teaming with Ed Drake on a proposal, and Erica is terrified of him."

Chapter Nineteen

*E*rica stood in the hallway, just around the corner from the kitchen, gathering her courage. After sleeping a few hours, she'd sat in her room for a long time, dreading facing JT. She glanced down at her clothing. It was skimpy, but at least she wasn't braless and wearing a sheer T-shirt. She should have throttled Lee for not warning her that JT could show up.

Taking a deep breath and squaring her shoulders, she entered the kitchen. JT sat at the table, sipping coffee while marking papers with a red pen. "JT, thank you for letting me stay here last night." She'd considered calling him "Mr. Talon," but since he'd hit on her *and* inadvertently seen her nearly naked, she decided they should be on a first-name basis.

"I'm glad Lee brought you here after what happened."

She let out a breath, willing the knots of tension to go away, and cast about the room, seeking something to do, to say, and spied the coffeemaker. JT noticed. He stood, fetched a mug from the cupboard, and poured a cup. "Cream or sugar?" he asked.

"Cream, please," she said with a genuine smile. The CEO

had just gotten her coffee. She thanked him and sat at the table, wrapping her hands around the warm mug, feeling the raw edges of her nerves begin to smooth. So far, so good. She breathed in the calming aroma. If only she could forget their earlier encounter.

"I'm sorry about your apartment," he said.

"Thanks." She bit her lip. She'd crossed her first hurdle and faced JT, but her apartment would require a pole vault. With a twenty-dollar air mattress and a thrift-store plastic garden chair, she supposed she could live there, but she'd have to stare at walls that called her a bitch and a whore in bloodred paint. It wasn't all that different from her cell in Mexico, where shimmering flies fed on fecal curse words. Her apartment now had the stink of the cell, but she had nowhere else to go. Maybe she should just disappear, start someplace fresh. Would anyone even notice?

No. She would not wallow in self-pity. That was the road her mother had traveled.

She'd come here to make amends and restore her reputation. She couldn't give up. Hell, right now she was sitting with JT Talon, drinking coffee. She might not like how she ended up here, but she could use this turn of events. She just needed a plan.

She felt his stare and realized she'd been sitting in self-absorbed silence for too long. "Sorry," she said. "I'm feeling a little overwhelmed."

"No need to apologize." He cocked his head to the side. "In fact, I should be apologizing to you. The other night——"

She cut him off with her hand. "Don't worry about it."

"I shouldn't have come on to you. I put you in an awkward position, and for that I'm sorry." He brushed his thick dark curls out of his eyes in a gesture that seemed almost nervous, and she marveled at the idea that *she* worried *him.* Of course, he feared a lawsuit, but still, it felt strange to have even that small bit of power.

He hadn't shaved, and the dark stubble on his jaw combined with a scar that bisected one eyebrow gave him a sexy, dangerous look. He exuded masculinity, power, and confidence.

"Thank you," she said. "Apology accepted."

He smiled and leaned back in his chair, and she wondered if he'd later place a check mark on a to-do list. He looked like a to-do list sort of man.

"You've been in the Bethesda office a lot lately," she said, hoping to put the awkward moment behind them.

"Bethesda has several military contracts I need to oversee."

"Because Drake's more interested in the campaign than managing the projects himself." She felt her face turn red and couldn't believe she'd actually said that aloud. She was just a step above intern, after all. She didn't have enough fingers to count the layers of management that separated her from the man she'd just dissed.

But JT laughed. "Exactly. I didn't realize he was so obvious."

Her cheeks began to cool. "There've been rumors he's angling to be vice president."

"Campaigns are...big." His expression said he knew the word was grossly inadequate. "And this is the biggest prize of all. We're all obsessed with the senator's campaign these days."

Joseph Talon had been in office for twelve years, and his own son had just referred to him not as "Dad" but as "the senator." Had politics consumed Joseph Talon's identity, even to the people who mattered most in his life?

"How is Lee doing? Is he working hard?"

If she'd been asked that question yesterday morning, she'd have said he was a waste of time and money. But now she felt differently. It wasn't because he'd rocked her world with one knee-weakening kiss, but because he'd been there for her when her life was ripped apart as easily as her mattress.

"He's helping me with Thermo-Con and has provided an interesting lead." She saw her escape and glanced at her watch, not faking her dismay when she saw it was noon. "Speaking of which, I should head to the office."

"It's Saturday," he reminded her.

She inclined her head toward the papers spread across the table. "You're working."

"I'm always working. It's the nature of my job. But your apartment was vandalized. You have other priorities."

She shrugged as coolly as she could manage. She couldn't let him know how afraid she was. He needed to believe it was a random act of violence. "My apartment is a total loss," she said, a break in her voice telling them both she wasn't as cool as she wanted to be. "I can't face it yet, but I have a report due on Monday, so I need to go to the office."

She felt Lee's presence as a tingle in the back of her neck even before he entered the room and wondered when exactly she'd developed a Lee radar, or Lee-dar, as her grad school friends would have called it.

"I thought you were planning to work from home this weekend," Lee said.

"I was, until my computer was dropped in a bathtub full of water."

"You can work from here," Lee said.

Feeling uncomfortable that Lee had just offered up JT's apartment, she looked to the CEO.

He nodded. "You can stay here as long as you need."

She looked again at Lee, who relaxed against the counter, still wearing only sweatpants. He turned and reached into the cupboard for a coffee mug, and the fabric stretched across his perfect butt. He poured himself a cup of coffee, then turned back so she could appreciate his sculpted abs. Like JT, Lee hadn't shaved, and his jaw was covered in attractive stubble.

She wondered if he'd entered the room half-dressed in an attempt to out-masculine JT. Frankly, it worked.

Lee had a spectacular physique. She'd always known lust made her stupid, and she could feel IQ points slipping away just looking at him. Could she stay here without sleeping with Lee? While JT was here, certainly. But what about after JT returned to New York and they were alone?

The truth was, she had nowhere else to go. She had no one.

This half-dressed man she'd met six days ago was the closest thing to a friend she had in DC.

She straightened her spine. She'd survive. That was the one thing she knew how to do. She also knew when to accept help. "Thanks, I'd like to stay."

"Good," JT said. "There's a desktop computer in the den you can use."

"I've got to go back to my apartment to get the Thermo-Con file. Hopefully it wasn't destroyed. I didn't think to check last night."

"I forgot to take it out of my laptop bag," Lee said. "I've got the file here."

At least one thing had gone right in the last twenty-four hours. "I should get to work, then." She stood up.

"No," Lee and JT said simultaneously.

"You need to eat first," JT said.

Lee pulled a carton of eggs from the refrigerator. "I make a killer spinach omelet."

She felt her throat close up. These men acted as though they cared.

❦

*L*ee listened for the sound of the shower then reentered the kitchen. "She can't hear us."

"What did you find out?" JT asked.

"Novak is primarily a treasure hunter, although he does do some salvage work. He usually operates out of California. He has a permanent help-wanted ad on his website. He wants to hire an underwater archaeologist so he can get excavation permits from foreign governments for shipwreck excavations."

"So?" JT asked, leaning back in his chair.

"I called the archaeologist from the university—the one I spoke to last weekend to prepare for the job. He said it's career suicide for an underwater archaeologist to work for a treasure hunter. It's not illegal, mind you, but it's the sort of thing that would get a person quietly blackballed. As in nothing would be in writing, but word would spread.

"The university archaeologist said Novak's excavations are anything but archaeological—he takes the goods and destroys the resource. Novak has never published a report and provides no data on his finds. These are the cardinal sins of archaeology."

"And you think she worked for him."

"Yes. It all makes sense. I couldn't find anything official. I'd wondered why she had perfect grades, then withdrew from the University of Hawaii." It had been a big red flag when he realized she was enrolling in another Master's program. Why drop one grad program after the coursework was complete, then start another? She owed thousands in student loans for the UH classes.

He continued. "I bet she was told her transcript would remain clean if she left quietly. As far as work goes, no one gave her a recommendation at all—good or bad. But that's standard practice these days, due to companies' fear of being sued. I think she moved here because her reputation in the West was shot."

"Why would she work for a man like Novak in the first place?"

Lee pulled out a chair and sat down. "I've already told

you about her credit problems. She's broke. My guess is Novak promised her the moon."

"What did she do with the money?" JT asked.

"I don't know. I think something bad happened between them."

"Did he trash her apartment?"

"I think she thinks it was him," Lee said. But she hadn't said a word. Her silence didn't sit well with him.

"Why didn't she tell the police about him?"

"I'm not a mind reader."

"Then we need to get her to talk. Is the den computer safe for her to use?"

"I switched to a blank hard disk while she was sleeping. And I've installed a program that will record every keystroke."

"Good. Keeping your cover while she's living here will be difficult but worth it."

"I've set it so calls to the land line will roll to my office phone. The last thing we need is Erica answering a call from my mother or Joe. If you need to reach me, call the cell."

"I want to keep her here as long as possible." JT paused. "Her walls need painting; that'll get us a few days."

Uneasiness spread through Lee. "I'll pay for it."

"It might be easier if I make her my new pet charity case." JT sat back, a speculative gleam in his eyes, and Lee's unease built.

"No."

"Look, she's keeping secrets. One of us needs to win her trust if we want to find out why she's afraid of Novak. I'm perfectly content to let you be the one to wine and dine her, but I'm worried you aren't objective where she's concerned."

"I said no." Lee sat forward, not bothering to hide his anger. "For all we know, Novak took advantage of her when she was vulnerable. I won't let you do the same thing."

JT's eyes took on a cold look, every inch the powerful

CEO who negotiated with presidents and generals. Once upon a time, this man had been his brother. He'd always been his best friend. "I'll do whatever is necessary. Someone is using *my* company to smuggle artifacts out of Iraq. I need to find out who and hand them over to the Feds with a big red bow before the press gets wind of what's going on and the scandal ruins the campaign." His voice hardened. "Erica is either actively involved or she knows something. Her office and home have been trashed. And don't forget what happened to Tommy Riversong."

"I haven't forgotten, but I won't let you toy with her emotions. If you do, I'll tell her everything."

"You wouldn't do that. You owe me, Lee."

The reminder was a cheap shot. Lee's mother had dissolved her marriage to Joseph Talon without a second thought and dragged Lee along through more nightmare relationships until he was old enough to choose his own home. There weren't many twenty-one-year-olds who would provide a home to a damaged sixteen-year-old kid who wasn't even related to him anymore.

"I'm not your spy because I owe you or Joe. I'm doing it because I believe in Joe. I want to see him win, but not at any price. I won't let you use her. She's a person, JT, and she may be innocent. Would you screw me over if you thought I was a liability for the campaign?"

"That's a pretty speech. But the truth is you're only objecting because you want her."

Lee choked on his answer.

"Fuck her if you want to, but don't fuck up the investigation because you're thinking with your dick."

"I'm not thinking with my dick." But he was afraid he was.

"Christ. I can't believe this. You've never fallen for anyone. Why Erica? Why now?"

Lee was silent. Memory of the warm light in Erica's eyes

when he held her at the FDR memorial came to mind. Finally he said, "I don't know. So what are you going to do?"

JT leaned back in his chair and relaxed as though their confrontation was of no consequence, while Lee struggled to maintain his calm.

A wicked grin played across JT's features. "She believes you're twenty-five and a lazy intern, right?"

Lee nodded.

JT snickered. "Good luck, Skippy."

Chapter Twenty

*E*rica rested her head on the desk. She could feel the clock ticking away the minutes until the environmental assessment was due, but the report had large gaps. It was Sunday afternoon, and all she had was speculation. She needed to *prove* Andrew Jackson Higgins's company had invented Thermo-Con.

If she could do that, the historic value of the house would increase, and therefore, the human bones in the basement would be more troubling for Sam Riversong. He couldn't ignore it; he'd have to investigate. Which meant he'd have to meet with her again.

Unfortunately, the Higgins name on the patent card wasn't Andrew Jackson Higgins. She reread the book description online. The book was a biography, titled *Andrew Jackson Higgins and the Boats that Won World War II*. She'd called every bookstore in DC and none had the title in stock. She would call the publisher first thing tomorrow morning. If she could speak to the author, maybe he could confirm her theories about Thermo-Con and Higgins.

She clicked on a search-engine icon and followed the link to people search, finding nothing promising when she typed in the author's name. She studied her notes from the patent office. The patent had been filed under two names: Johnson and Higgins. On a whim, she typed in the full Higgins name, giving Louisiana, where Higgins Industries had been located, as the state.

She felt a flutter in her belly as one listing appeared. She shrugged it off. It wasn't possible. The patent was over fifty years old.

She went back to the report and read through what she'd written. It was fairly good, but it would be better if all the supposition and theory could be replaced with fact.

The result of the people search nagged at her. What did she have to lose? She picked up the phone and dialed. A young man answered the phone, and she asked to speak with the man named on the patent.

"He doesn't live here anymore, but I can give you his number."

"Maybe you can tell me if he's the person I'm looking for. I'm trying to find a man who worked for Higgins Industries just after World War II? He's named on a patent for what I think is a type of concrete known as Thermo-Con."

"Oh, you're talking about my grandpa, he worked for Higgins Industries. I thought you were asking for my dad, who has the same name, but is junior. My grandpa worked on Thermo-Con. He died a long time ago, but you can call my dad. He can tell you all about grandpa."

She could feel her pulse in the fingers that gripped the phone. "So you're saying Higgins Industries—the company that built Higgins boats—did invent a type of concrete called Thermo-Con?"

"Yeah. That's right. Andrew Jackson Higgins—AJ—is my great-grandpa. My grandpa worked for him on the Thermo-Con team. My dad knows all about AJ and the company. You should call him." He rattled off the number.

Erica's hands shook as she wrote down the phone

number. She thanked the young man, hung up the phone, and let out a loud yelp.

Lee came running into the den. "Erica? Are you okay?"

Thrilled to have someone to share her excitement with, she launched herself at him. He caught her with an oof as she wrapped her arms around his neck and her legs around his waist.

"I did it!" she exclaimed, then kissed him with all the exuberance she felt. Her tongue slid into his mouth as she threaded her fingers through his hair, and he kissed her back with equal enthusiasm. Damn, he was a good kisser.

She pulled back and grinned. "Aren't you going to ask me what I did?"

"I don't care what you did," he said, taking a step toward the extended sofa bed.

She laughed. She didn't know what had come over her but didn't care. She gripped his hair and pulled his mouth to hers again. After another interval, she leaned back and said, "We don't have time for this now. I've got a phone call to make."

"You started it," he said. They'd reached the foot of the bed, and he dropped kisses along her throat as she arched backward to give him better access.

"Oh God, Lee. I'm so excited," she said breathlessly. He plucked out her hairpins one by one. Her hair tumbled down her back.

"So am I, Shortcake." He nibbled her neck as his fingers threaded through her hair.

She laughed. "No. No. I'm excited about Thermo-Con."

He stopped. "You're hell on my ego."

"You'll survive." She kissed him again, then wriggled until he set her down.

"So what, besides me, are you all excited about?"

"You were right about the connection between Higgins Boats and Thermo-Con. I just spoke with Andrew Jackson

Higgins's great-grandson. He said Higgins Industries did invent Thermo-Con. We may not have the patent file, but we did find the patent!"

"That's great," he said without enthusiasm.

She laughed. "Aren't you excited?"

"I was excited about getting you naked."

"But we've found the inventor, and now we have a solid theory for why the Thermo-Con house was built for ERDL. We can connect the house to a bona fide historical figure who was directly involved in the project. We're talking about a person who Dwight D. Eisenhower referred to as 'the man who won the war for us.'" She pushed Lee away from her. "Now shoo. I've got to call AJ's grandson—the son of the man named on the patent."

He pulled her against him, and she felt his arousal against her belly. His voice deepened as he said, "I think we should celebrate with sex first." His mouth captured hers in a kiss that blew their earlier efforts out of the water.

He had a good point. No, scratch that. A hard point. Her fingers wandered to the buttons on his shirt as the mattress pressed against the back of her knees. All she had to do was lean backward and she'd be on the bed with Lee tumbling on top of her.

The front door opened, then closed with a bang. "Honey, I'm home," JT called out.

"Damn," Lee muttered, releasing her.

She laughed. "Another time, maybe." She reached for the telephone.

※

"So, after I got off the phone with AJ's grandson," Erica said, "I called his aunt. She and I had the loveliest conversation." She grinned at her dinner companions—her temporary roommates. They sat in the dining area, eating delivered Chinese food and drinking wine JT had opened to celebrate her success with Thermo-Con. She knew little about wine but suspected this bottle sold for three figures.

She swirled the liquid in her glass and admired the deep garnet color, feeling a hum of satisfaction with both the company and her progress on the report. JT reached for the rice. While he was distracted, Lee shot her a heated look, causing a sensuous flame to slither through her, adding a certain naughty pleasure to her already giddy mood.

JT's eyes crinkled indulgently. "What did the aunt tell you?"

She swallowed a bite of mu shoo pork before answering, "She was married to the guy who ran the Thermo-Con development team. He died about twenty years ago, but she knew all about his work. She told me how Higgins tried to market Thermo-Con. She doesn't know anything about the house built on Fort Belmont, but she agreed with our theory that Higgins was trying to sell Thermo-Con to the US Army. He probably had the house built for ERDL, hoping army engineers would love it so much they'd build Higgins Thermo-Con homes on bases all over the world."

She wondered if she was babbling and worried her social demeanor had grown rusty with disuse. JT had been nothing but kind to her and treated her like a kid sister, but still, she couldn't help feeling uneasy around him. The man was way out of her league. He was tennis to her ping-pong.

Then there was Lee. She didn't know how or why, but he'd gotten under her skin. She felt his presence on a cellular level and craved his company like fine chocolate. But Lee wasn't ping-pong either. No. Rugby came to mind: foreign and unfamiliar, but rowdy, fun, and blatantly physical.

"So what does all this mean for the house?" JT asked.

"Well, for one thing, we meet our deadline. I finished the report. But mostly it means the house is historically significant and should be protected as such. It looks like there is at least one burial beneath the basement, and there might be more, so protecting the burials versus the house could get tricky. In most cases, the burials would trump the historic property." Belatedly, she remembered she was speaking to a man who was one-quarter Menanichoch. "As well it should. Human remains are much more important than structures, even when the structure is connected to an historical figure."

JT shrugged. "It's important, I know, but in this situation, I run the company doing the work, and I'm looking out for Talon & Drake's interest, not the tribe's. Will the tribe be happy with your work?"

"The house is in poor shape. Letting it slide into further disrepair would be an adverse effect to what is clearly an historic property. The remains are tricky, though, and will require consultation, mitigation, and management." This opportunity was too good to let slide by, and she gave the big boss a sweet smile. "I'd like to be the Talon & Drake point person. I know the issues; I know the project."

JT cocked his head. "But you don't have an MA. Based on the Secretary of the Interior Standards, you aren't qualified."

She strained to maintain her smile. She had a perfectly good MA, which she was still paying for. "I would work under Janice's supervision, of course."

"Then I'm sure the tribe would be satisfied if you were selected."

Dammit. She was as qualified as anyone to run this project. In her pre-Jake life, she'd written several EAs and had run a few sensitive burial excavations. "It might be a good opportunity for Lee. He could learn about the process."

"Actually, I've got other plans for Lee. I need him elsewhere for the next week or so." He looked at Lee. "The New York office is having problems with a database you created.

Since you've wrapped up Thermo-Con, you can take a break from helping Erica and fix it."

Lee's eyes flashed with alarm.

She set down her chopsticks. "Lee created a database for the New York office?"

Worry faded, and Lee's expression turned blank.

"Yes," JT said.

Lee didn't flinch or look away. He just gazed steadily at Erica, neither confirming nor denying JT's statement.

She looked from Lee to JT. "But he's incompetent with computers. Especially databases."

Surprise crossed JT's face; then some sort of understanding registered. He took a deep breath and spoke as though resigned. "He's been programming since he was a kid."

"Is this true?" She wanted to skewer Lee with a chopstick.

He nodded, but his expression remained blank.

Hurt was followed by rage. She held Lee's gaze but spoke to JT. "He's still a kid."

Lee inclined his head in agreement.

"Why did you lie?"

"I'm working at Talon & Drake to learn about archaeology." His voice was cold and steady. "I'm not there to work on your cell tower database. I already know about databases. I get paid much more than minimum wage to work on databases. It seemed prudent to lie."

He obviously didn't care about the hours she'd spent fixing the damn database while he played computer games. "But you haven't shown the slightest interest in archaeology or anything we do at Talon & Drake. The only thing I've seen you work on with any kind of dedication is improving your Tetris score." Appetite gone, she stood and left the room.

*E*rica's door slammed, rattling the dishes on the dining room table. Alone with JT, Lee took another sip of wine and set his glass down with extreme care, determined not to take his anger out on the fragile crystal. No, he had a better target. He glared at JT. "Nice job."

"I was trying to give you an outside job so you could hack without looking like a slacker in her eyes. I didn't know you'd lied about your skills."

"Dipshit move. I've lied to her about *everything*. You told me to be incompetent. So I am."

"I told you to be incompetent about *archaeology*. Not computers."

"It's not like we're on some sort of dig. We're in the office. All the work is on the computer. Hence, I've been a techno-logical nightmare pretending to play ancient computer games."

JT smiled slightly. "Damn, she's pissed."

"You have no idea what she went through with her cell tower database. That's why she worked late Wednesday night."

"But you could have fixed it for her."

"Hell, I'm the one who broke it. I'd left the Thermo-Con file in Arnie's office and couldn't get it back because your meeting ended. I had to give her something to do so she wouldn't notice the file was missing."

How on earth could he repair the rift between them?

He closed his eyes and thought about how she'd felt in his arms today. Wild and wanton, she'd kissed him with abandon while her thick hair draped over his arm. All he'd wanted to do was toss her on the bed and slide slowly into her, gazing into her warm gray eyes as he discovered the secrets of her body.

He opened his eyes, letting go of the fantasy. "I've got a lot of cell phone calls and emails to sort through at the office.

Pretending to play computer games was wearing thin. Your idea of giving me a fake programming task was a good one. I just wish you'd warned me. But, even if you had, her anger was inevitable."

JT nodded. "We'll have to ask her to keep the fact that you're working for me a secret."

"I think she'll go along."

"Unless she's involved. Then she might guess what you're doing."

"She's not," Lee said. He didn't know where this conviction came from, but he didn't doubt it.

"Find out everything you can about Novak. My gut says he's involved with the smuggling, and if we get something solid, I can stop Drake from teaming with him. But we have to do it in a way that doesn't tip them off that we're on to them."

"I know. I'm on it."

Chapter Twenty-One

*J*T faced Erica across the breakfast table. He had to deal with his screwup now, before she went to the office and ruined the perfect cover he'd created for Lee. "I have a favor to ask."

She cocked her head, inviting him to speak. Her hair captured the early morning sun. Her beauty today was remote, reserved, a far cry from the relaxed, warm woman he'd had dinner with last night. She was a puzzle, and he worried that Lee, the most cool-headed and rational man he knew, was preoccupied with solving her.

"I don't want you to tell anyone at the office Lee is staying in my apartment. And, of course, it'd be best if you don't mention you're here either."

"I understand what people would think if they knew about me, but why Lee?"

"He needs to make his own name for himself at Talon & Drake."

She scoffed. "He doesn't stand a chance."

"I know you're pissed right now, and I don't blame you. But he's a good kid with a good mind—when he chooses to use it." He smiled, knowing how his words would grate on Lee.

"Why is he working for Talon & Drake?" she asked. "He doesn't really have a burning interest in archaeology. None that I've seen, anyway."

Shit. She'd asked the one question they'd hoped to avoid. Why couldn't Lee have been paired with a flake who didn't give a crap? Weren't archaeologists supposed to be crystal-hugging Indian-wannabes? As one-quarter Menanichoch, he'd met his share of wannabes and suffered through their thoughtless questions and bizarre adulation of a genetic heritage they couldn't claim. None of those people would have noticed Lee's lack of interest.

He sighed in a heavy but not overblown manner. "I wanted to place him with technical support, but he refused. We compromised on archaeology."

"I don't get it. Why did you give him a job at all?"

"His mother asked me to. She's hoping—and I am too—the experience of working in a professional office will help him to find his focus." *Good luck getting into her pants now, Lee.*

He wasn't *trying* to sabotage Lee's chances with the potential artifact thief; it was just a side benefit of this cover story. He cleared his throat and added, "His mother told him if he doesn't complete the internship, she won't pay his tuition in the fall."

"So he can't quit."

"No, he can't. And I won't fire him." *So don't even try, sweetheart.* "It sounds like he hasn't been much help to you, and the database needs a major overhaul, so for the next week, he's going to work on that."

"You're going to pay him minimum wage to do technical work worth several times that?"

He smiled at her obvious glee. "Yup."

"I hope it's a task he hates."

"Don't worry, he hates everything about this job."

That was the truest thing he'd said to her since they'd met.

*

*E*rica took the Metro to her apartment and picked up her car, which she'd left there because she had an underground, secure parking space included with her monthly rent, and it was impossible to find parking by the Watergate. The drive to the office was maddening, and she cursed the stop-and-go traffic as she inched up Wisconsin Avenue. She much preferred the Metro, but today she needed the car.

Traffic only soured an already poor mood. She alternated between anger and disappointment. The ridiculous way she'd thrown herself at Lee yesterday nagged at her. Why had she kissed him like that? Worse, she'd lain awake half the night wishing he'd come to her room to apologize. And make amends.

He was an irresponsible, immature pretty boy who showed no sign of growing up. Except for the rest of the time…when he was the exact opposite.

He was a distraction she didn't want or need. Her week was up, and Thermo-Con was due. She would deliver the report to the tribe today and hopefully find an excuse to see Riversong.

Lee had the good sense to skip his morning workout. Alone with the bag, she opened a new sore on her foot, but her imaginary Jake and Marco were broken, bleeding messes by the time she finished. After she showered and changed into clothes she'd purchased at a thrift store on Saturday evening, she headed to her office. Within an hour, she had the Thermo-Con EA polished and ready for printing. She emailed the document to Rob Anderson, marked for urgent review.

Now what? It was a rare moment when she had downtime before she needed to jump to the next project, and she couldn't deliver the report until after Rob and Janice approved the draft. She turned her chair and watched Lee, who had arrived a half hour ago. They hadn't spoken since she'd left the table last night.

He caught her gaze, and, instead of looking contrite, he gave her a heated look worthy of yesterday, pre-argument. His glance raked the length of her with appreciation; then his bright green eyes returned to hers. His eyebrow rose in a suggestive way, and she felt instant and unwelcome desire. Damn him.

"Give it up," she said.

"Never."

She was saved from responding by a knock on their open office door. She looked up to see Lily Davenport standing in the doorway. "I've got a FedEx for you, Erica," the buxom blonde chemist said.

Since when did chemists deliver FedEx packages?

The woman's eyes fixed on Lee, and Erica understood her sudden desire to play receptionist. Lily had called dibs on the hydrologist from Boston, and now she wanted to check out the good-looking archaeological intern. She'd never once stepped foot in the archaeology lab, but now she breezed into the room and dropped the envelope on Lee's desk. She then sat on the worktable and expertly flaunted her cleavage, miniskirt, and heels, all of which were more appropriate for a Friday night on the town than a Monday morning at the office.

The fact that Lee appeared to enjoy the display irked Erica. She supposed Lily was pretty—if one liked cougars. The meow that accompanied catty comments rang through her mind, and she acknowledged that even though she didn't want Lee for herself, she didn't enjoy watching him admire someone else.

"What is it?" she asked Lee, drawing his attention away from Lily's cleavage.

He ripped off the strip on the cardboard envelope and pulled out the single sheet. "It's the radiocarbon test result for the bone from the Thermo-Con sump."

"How old is the bone?"

He studied the page. "It's unclear."

"I don't understand most of the technical data either, but there's always a line that gives the conventional age and another that gives the calibrated age—that's where they adjust for carbon fluctuations due to nuclear testing or something like that. What's the calibrated age?"

"Like I said, it's unclear."

She sighed and crossed the room to read over his shoulder. The conventional age was -2 ± 3 BP, but next to calibrated age it said, "Some probability for 19th or 20th century antiquity."

"You're right," she said. "It *is* unclear."

He smiled. "Yeah, one thing I learned in all my years of college is how to read. I can recognize numbers too."

Lily snickered.

"Smart-ass," Erica said. She pointed to the conventional age. "Nineteen fifty is the baseline year for all radiocarbon dates. Every date before present—which is what BP stands for—is a calculation from AD 1950. So the uncalibrated test indicated the bones date between 1949 and 1955. But when they adjusted for the extra carbon in the atmosphere due to nuclear testing, they couldn't narrow it down beyond a two-hundred-year range." She glanced at Lily. "Does that sound right to you?"

The chemist shrugged. "Not my field."

"I need to call the lab." She nearly tripped over Lily's legs as she made her way back to her desk. "Thanks for delivering the envelope." Her voice was polite but dismissive.

"No problem." She glanced at Lee. "You taking your morning break soon?"

"We've got to deal with this," Erica said, waving the paper and hating herself for jumping in because she didn't want Lee to take a break with Lily.

Lee's grin was self-satisfied. To Lily, he said, "She's the boss."

"Well, I should go, then." She stood up and smoothed her skirt in a way that practically waved her butt in Lee's face, then left.

The room was silent for a minute. Finally Erica said, "Need a cold shower, Romeo?"

"She doesn't turn me on nearly as much as you do."

The memory of exactly how much she'd turned him on caused her breath to catch.

"I love it when you make that sound. *Now* I need a cold shower."

She shook her head and reached for her phone, smiling slightly. He did have a certain relentless charm.

Ten minutes later, she hung up the phone, exhilarated. "We've got a problem. We can't say with certainty whether the bones are prehistoric or not, and if they aren't prehistoric, then this would require a criminal investigation."

"You think if the bone really dates from 1952, then it could be the remains of a body that was hidden there," Lee said.

"Most likely the bones are prehistoric, but we can't ignore the fact that the house was built in 1952 and the uncalibrated test came up with that year, plus or minus three. I don't believe the army would have built the house over a recent grave, but after I deliver the report, I'm going to check the tribal archives and see what information they have on how the land was used by the military, on the off chance there was a cemetery and they missed moving a grave."

"If that was the case, shouldn't the bones have been inside a coffin?"

"Good point. Another reason to think the date is wrong and the bones are prehistoric."

"I'm going with you."

"You've got work to do for JT."

"Your job will go faster if I help you search the archives."

Now he was willing to do some work? She didn't want to bring him along. She intended to finagle a meeting with Riversong over this issue and wanted to talk to the chairman alone.

But then again, she might need him. Lee could beat Riversong at pool with a broken cue and one arm behind his back, and she wanted the chairman to authorize another DNA test for these bones. And, more than anything, she wanted Sam's DNA for the comparative sample.

Chapter Twenty-Two

*L*ee's code-breaking program flashed on his laptop screen. He'd finally unlocked the last of the Iraq project files. He clicked on the icon and the list of files loaded. Several files had an unfamiliar extension. A quick search told him the files were blueprint documents. He opened the readable text files and learned the blueprints were for something called SARAC.

He felt a jolt of recognition and went to his databank of captured messages to search for a text he'd read last Friday. He found it immediately. A text message, sent from a prepaid cell phone from inside the building, to a prepaid cell phone located in Menanichoch, Maryland when the text was received. The text was short and sweet: *Sara C will be back a week from today.* He'd flagged the message, but it could have been innocent, referring to Sarah Castleberry, a Talon & Drake structural engineer, and Talon & Drake had several tribal projects; any number of employees could be on the reservation or communicating with a client.

Sara C had to be SARAC, and whatever the equipment was, it was being shipped back. From Iraq. Probably with one of the many drawdown shipments. Matt Weber's email to JT had said, *Broken Talon & Drake equipment is being shipped back to the US via military transport*. Lee was certain whatever was being smuggled would be hidden inside SARAC.

But even more important, he'd identified the cell phones of two conspirators.

Lee was anxious to tell JT, but knew he was meeting with Joe. The campaign was only days away from becoming official.

An hour later, the Thermo-Con EA was approved, printed, and bound. Lee hadn't gotten hold of JT, but as he climbed into Erica's car, he was still flying high from his discovery. If all went well, he'd be done with this spying job by Friday. He looked over at Erica as she fastened her seat belt. When she was cleared, he could take her out to a fancy dinner, convince her to forgive his lies, then take her home and prove he was neither lazy nor a kid.

First they delivered the EA to the environmental compliance officer, a sixty-something tribal member with a warm smile. She was thrilled with the information Erica had gathered on Thermo-Con. The odd radiocarbon date was a concern, and she immediately led them to the room where all the land records, both military and tribal, were stored.

They spent an hour poring over old maps and ethno-graphic data and found nothing to indicate the property had ever been a cemetery or prehistoric burial ground. "We need to talk to Sam Riversong about this," Erica said.

Lee's mood took a nosedive. The radiocarbon date didn't warrant a meeting with the tribal chairman. At best, she should follow up with the environmental compliance officer. But Erica was pushing this to the top, and Lee wanted to know why. He knew in his gut she wasn't acting out of concern for the bones.

Once again they found themselves waiting in the game room in the shiny new tribal office building. Lee went straight to the pool table and racked the balls. He would distract Erica with the game and try to find out what her agenda was.

The problem was, she distracted him. Every time she leaned over the table, he felt a stirring in his gut that told him this was no ordinary attraction. There was something about her that touched him in a primal way. He'd known he wanted her from the first, but what he wanted scared him: he wanted to break through the shields she'd constructed around herself. He'd only seen glimpses of her relaxed and happy. He wanted more.

One thing was certain, she didn't like to lose, and she focused on the game with fierce concentration, determined not to make any mistakes.

She leaned down for another shot, and he wished she were wearing the tight V-neck T-shirt she'd worn all weekend. She'd gone shopping Saturday evening and managed to find a cheap but respectable outfit, but the clothes were large and ill-fitting.

He decided to rattle her. Leaning against her back, he slid his arms along hers and repositioned her cue. "You're too far to the left for that bank shot."

She pulled back the stick in a fast, hard jab, ramming the butt end into his ribs. The cue ball hit the rail, where it bounced wildly and missed the striped ball that had been her target.

Lee rubbed his side. "Damn. You're as good with a cue as you are at the bag."

"Consider yourself lucky—I didn't want to hurt you…too much."

He backed her into the table and dropped his voice so it wouldn't go farther than her ears. "Sounds kinky. We should come up with a safe word." His lips hovered above hers.

She snickered, then, rolling her eyes, she pushed at his chest and leaned away from him. "Please. You've got trouble written all over you. You're too young, immature, and spoiled. And lack of finesse leads to boring sex."

He choked on her assertion. "What do you mean, lack of finesse?"

"College boys are all grope and hurry with no understanding of foreplay."

"Sounds like a challenge to me."

Her gaze raked him from head to foot. Assessing. Admiring. Hot. But she shook her head. "You'd just be yet another disappointment." He could see from the blue in her eyes and the quirk of her lips she was both amused and turned on.

She pushed on his chest again.

He covered her hand with his. "I'm determined to redeem your opinion of me. Come to my room tonight." Somewhere in this game, he'd lost sight of what was real and what was acting, but his plea did sound like a college boy, so at least he was in character.

"Not a chance. Now are you going to take your shot?"

"If you think I handle this stick well, wait until you see—"

She cut him off. "Shoot, before I use my stick to whack your balls."

"Ouch, I hope we're still talking about the game. Let's see, you missed your shot entirely, so it's ball-in-hand for me."

"And that's no different from how it will be tonight, tomorrow night, and the rest of your nights until you go back to school—your stick, your balls, your hand. Alone."

He laughed then picked up the cue ball and used it to line up an easy shot at the corner pocket. "Why do you want to talk to Riversong?"

She looked like she was about to speak, then stopped, and he knew he'd startled her with the change of subject after the playful conversation.

He took his shot, sinking the last of his solids. He knew it wouldn't be possible to get her to suddenly confess her agenda, but he thought she *wanted* to tell him. She wanted to trust him.

He'd never used sex for anything other than sharing pleasure with someone he wanted to be with, but sleeping with Erica as a shortcut to earning her trust remained on the table. He needed to know why Novak was sniffing around the Bethesda office. Now.

He sank the eight ball. "Was it worth sacrificing your shot to jab me with your cue?"

"Yes. Retaliation is better than winning."

Riversong walked into the room. "No, Ms. Kesling. Nothing is better than winning." Another man followed the chairman into the room. Riversong turned to the man, whom Lee had seen once before. "Don't you agree, Jake?"

Chapter Twenty-Three

Lee watched through narrowed eyes as Novak crossed the room and stopped in front of Erica. He took her hand and brought it to his lips. "Erica, my dear, it's good to see you again."

Her skin was pale, and she looked frightened for a moment before her eyes turned the coldest shade of gray he'd ever seen. She jerked her hand away, straightened her spine, and turned to the chairman. "Mr. Riversong, I see you're busy. We can meet later." She took a step toward the door.

Novak grabbed her arm, halting her. "Erica, when will you learn running doesn't work?"

Adrenaline pulsed through Lee. He wanted to rip the man's hand off her.

She yanked her arm out of Novak's grasp. "I'm not running, Jake. I just don't think it's proper to negotiate with a client in front of an uninvolved third party."

"Oh, but darling, I am involved. I'm teaming with Talon & Drake. You and I are going to work together." Novak looked at her possessively.

Jealousy stabbed Lee. He fought the urge to put Novak in his place. With fists. He settled for the crappy-intern equivalent. "Won't that be fun?" He draped an arm around her shoulders. "The three of us, working together."

"You're the intern, right? Make yourself useful and get us coffee. Sam, Erica, and I need to talk."

"Jake, shut up or leave," Riversong said. "You aren't in charge of this meeting." He glanced at his watch. "I don't have much time. I understand there's a problem with the Thermo-Con house." He looked expectantly at Erica.

She wriggled her shoulders, and Lee dropped his arm. Novak had rattled her—again. She gathered her composure. "The bones we found are human," she said. "Today I got the radiocarbon date, which was unclear. It's possible the bones are a hundred and fifty years old, but there is an equal likelihood they were buried there in 1952."

Riversong raised a brow. "The year the house was built?"

"Yes."

"Interesting." Riversong paused. "If the radiocarbon date indicates the bones could be a hundred and fifty years old, then this is a tribal matter, and your input is no longer necessary."

"But your BRAC agreement with the government—"

"Is none of your concern," Riversong said with sharp finality. The man was done playing with Erica, and from the look on her face, she knew it.

She closed her eyes briefly, and Lee had a sense she was gathering her courage. "Whenever human remains are discovered, I am required to notify the Maryland State Police, the State's Attorney's office, and the Maryland Historical Trust, which I have yet to do."

Riversong's mouth flattened to a thin line, but Lee had read enough to know Erica spoke the truth.

"Given the lack of clarity on the age of the remains," she continued, her voice now stronger, "it is possible the State Police or the State's Attorney will want to pursue a criminal investigation, which will halt all work on the Thermo-Con house indefinitely. But there is a test that would indicate whether or not the 1952 date was erroneous. If that's the case, then it's highly likely all parties would agree that this is a tribal matter, and you can deal with the remains as you see fit."

"What test do you propose?"

"A comparative DNA test. We can compare the bones to Menanichoch DNA. Even if the bones are a thousand years old, there'll be a match in the DNA, telling us the bones are from a tribal member who was buried long before the army took the land and built Fort Belmont."

Riversong physically recoiled. "No."

"I know many tribal members are worried about DNA testing because genetic mapping undermines the foundation of your religion. I promise, this DNA test wouldn't be used for that."

"My people have been hearing promises for centuries. We've been betrayed every time."

Tension arced between Erica and the tribal chairman, while Jake Novak leaned against the pool table and stared at her with a predatory grin. The man was enjoying this exchange.

"I'll have the lab send the results directly to me. Our contract will forbid the entry of the DNA into a database. They won't even know what ethnic group is being mapped."

Lee decided his role of ignorant intern was useful. "Why is this a problem, when you authorized testing of the bones last week?"

Riversong poured himself a glass of water and took a long drink before answering. "The first test determined the bone was human. Genetic sequencing wasn't necessary. This test requires genetic sequencing—meaning Menanichoch DNA would be isolated and defined."

"And you don't want that?"

He set the glass down. "No, we don't. Our DNA, our

heritage, is all we have left. Pharmaceutical companies want to steal our DNA. They want to use our genes to create pills and vaccines to protect others against diseases to which we are naturally immune. They want to use the core of our existence to save those who stole from us, to save the very people who sent us to boarding schools to make us forget who we are. Others wish to use our DNA to destroy all we have left by undermining our religion and taking away the foundation of our belief system with the claim our ancestors migrated here from the Old World." He paused. "I don't like this proposal of yours, Ms. Kesling."

"This is the quickest way to determine if the bones are Menanichoch or not. If the DNA isn't a match, then we know the remains are probably that of someone associated with the Army base. Keep in mind, the police could push for the same test, for the same reason, without the same guarantee of privacy for the results," she said.

"That would only be an issue if *I* choose to notify the police," Riversong said.

Erica started to speak, but the chairman put out a hand to stop her.

"You forget, you are on tribal land. We are our own nation, and that means we don't always have to follow state law."

Erica straightened her shoulders. "But you must comply with your BRAC agreement, which clearly outlines the protocol for dealing with unintentional discoveries of human remains."

Riversong's eyes narrowed.

Lee held his breath and felt sweat form on his brow. Erica was right about the BRAC agreement, but still, she was crazy to keep pushing the man this way.

Riversong finally spoke. "Fine. Run the test."

Her eyes lit up. "I'll need a DNA sample from a tribal member. Will you give it to me?"

"No. Find someone else."

Her jaw clenched tight.

"Good luck finding a tribal member who's willing, Cream Puff."

She shot Novak a glare, then turned to the chairman. "I'll need another bone fragment."

Riversong wandered over to the pool table and picked up a cue. "I was told just this morning the new sump failed and shorted out the electrical system. The sump has been removed for repairs, so you shouldn't have a problem collecting the bone." Riversong paused. "You have two days to find a tribal member to give you a sample, or I handle this my way."

She smiled tightly, and Lee wondered if she would ask JT.

Chapter Twenty-Four

"$\mathcal{D}$o you mind if I wait in the car?" Lee asked Erica as she parked in front of the Thermo-Con house.

"You just want to avoid the smelly basement."

He opened his laptop. "I've got a lot of work to do on JT's database." After a few rapid clicks, a screen full of code appeared. He scrolled down the list and typed something that looked like gibberish to her and another, smaller, window opened, this one running what she thought might be a database simulation.

She felt a pleasant jolt of surprise. He really was working. "I don't know why you rejected the job with Tech Support. You obviously like programming much more than archaeology."

"Yes, but then I'd be working with a bunch of computer geeks, not a dark-haired beauty who turns me on just by breathing."

She rolled her eyes and started to climb out of the car. He caught her hand. "I didn't like the way Jake Novak looked at you. If he does that again, I'll have to break his face."

He sounded macho, Neanderthal even. But she liked it and smiled. "I'll help you."

She grabbed a plastic bag and entered the Thermo-Con house. She hadn't thought it possible, but the house smelled worse today than it did a week ago. At the top of the stairs, she hit the wall switch, and nothing happened. She remembered what Riversong had said about the power and returned to her car to grab a flashlight.

Lee murmured something absentmindedly, clearly engrossed in his work. She didn't think he'd notice if she flashed him. Who would have thought he was a computer nerd?

Back inside, she heard a humming noise she hadn't noticed before and followed the sound outside, where it became much louder. She rounded to the back and found a generator hooked up next to one of two narrow, ground-level basement windows. Power cords and a hose ran through the window, and she realized the plumbers must have set up a portable pump to drain the basement. A quick glance around told her the plumbers must have left for the day, as their truck was nowhere in sight.

She returned to the staircase, switched on her flashlight, and descended into the dark, rank room. The dead-rat smell was minor compared to the thick odor of exhaust and singed electronics. The new sump must have fried the fuse box.

The open basement door shed a small amount of light on the top steps. The lower half of the staircase was cloaked in darkness. She grimaced when she realized an inch of water covered the floor. Why hadn't she sent her intern to do this task?

Her shoes weren't waterproof, and she had precious little clothing to waste, so she sat on the stairs, pulled off her shoes and stockings, and rolled up her slacks. Breathing through her mouth, she placed her foot in the murky water, in her mind chanting the phrase, *I will find a way to get Sam's DNA. I will find a way…*

The stairs landed in the middle of the basement, with the

sump located in an alcove tucked next to the coal room. Dirt and shrubs diminished the light from the two narrow windows, and once she rounded the bend behind the staircase, her flashlight provided the only illumination.

She tucked the flashlight under her chin and squatted as best she could before she reached down into the muddy sump pit. Her arm was in up to her elbow, and she nearly pitched forward into the hole before she felt a piece of bone. Again she asked herself why she'd let Lee stay in the clean car with its pine-scented air freshener.

She examined the bone fragment in the beam of the flashlight. There was plenty of saturated spongy marrow, making the piece a good candidate for a DNA test. After bagging it, she reached for another bone, but a tickle in the back of her throat caused a coughing spasm, and the flashlight slipped from under her chin and dropped into the mucky water.

"Shit!" Coughing and cursing, she reached for the light, which glowed dimly as it sank in the brown water. The light extinguished just as she caught it.

Still coughing, she stood and held her wet arm out from her body, hoping she hadn't ruined the one work-appropriate outfit she had.

Giving up on gathering a second fragment, she caught her breath, then carefully made her way out of the alcove in the pitch-darkness. In the main room, only the tiniest sliver of light from the windows guided her toward the staircase. Clutching the bone bag and dead flashlight in one hand, she climbed the stairs and picked up her shoes. She was almost out of this foul, dark hellhole.

Another coughing spasm hit her just as she noticed the door was closed. No wonder it was so dark. Rocked by violent coughing, she dropped her shoes and clutched the railing with a slippery, wet hand. Finally recovered, she grasped the knob.

It wouldn't budge.

"Lee. This isn't funny. Open the door."

She waited.

"Lee?"

She tucked the bone in her pocket and set down the flashlight, then tried the knob with both hands, but it was jammed. A wave of dizziness swept through her. She took a deep breath to steady herself on the steep staircase and realized the exhaust smell couldn't be a remnant from the sump fiasco, because the smell had gotten worse.

Her eyes flew to the window. The small crack of daylight confirmed her worst fear.

The generator spewed exhaust directly through the open window.

Oh God. She was trapped inside a basement that was rapidly filling with carbon monoxide.

Chapter Twenty-Five

*A*s soon as Erica disappeared inside the Thermo-Con house after retrieving a flashlight, Lee called JT. "I just saw Jake Novak."

"He's at the office?"

"No. He was with Sam Riversong, at the tribal head-quarters."

"I hope Riversong isn't doing anything on the edge of legal," JT said.

"I'm worried about full-blown illegal. The casino makes a nice money laundry."

"Shit, Novak is suddenly popping up everywhere, and the timing couldn't be worse. Get her to talk."

"It'd go faster if you'd leave us alone."

"Hey, I left you last night," JT said.

"After you screwed up, and she was pissed at me. Where did you go last night, anyway?"

"To see Alexandra."

"God, are you still stringing her along?"

"She dumped me. And we're still friends."

"Who have sex occasionally?" Lee asked.

"That's the best kind of friend."

"One of these days, one of you is going to get serious about someone else, and the other one will be hurt."

"That'll be me, little brother. That'll be me."

"Listen, Erica will be back soon, and I need to know what SARAC is."

"That's our primo, high-tech crane."

"What does the name stand for?"

"Stationary Armored Radial Arm Crane," JT answered. "Sara's special because of the radial arm—which twists in addition to pivoting. It's like having a giant robot to lift and position construction materials. No other crane in the world can do the things Sara can. It's armored because we've used it in war zones."

Lee watched the door of the Thermo-Con house. Erica could return at any moment. "I intercepted a text message that indicated the crane is coming back. On Friday."

JT let out a string of curses. "Sara wasn't supposed to come back. She's supposed to be on the way to Afghanistan."

"It looks like she's coming stateside. Why send it back?"

"Either because someone made a massive mistake or because the arm mechanism broke. That happened a year ago, and the arm had to be shipped back here for repairs. The equipment is proprietary, and the technology, the engineers, they're all here."

"How would it be sent?" Lee asked.

"Most likely a ship."

"Where would it go once stateside?"

"Menanichoch," JT said. "The wharf has a fifty-ton gantry crane and deep-water moorage. We have a shop there with the technology to make repairs. Motherfucker, if it's broken and Rob didn't tell me, I'm going to fire his ass. I don't care how long he's worked for Talon & Drake. We need that crane in Afghanistan, ASAP. The shit of it is, I can't question Rob without tipping him off that I know Sara is coming back."

"We need to know how it's being shipped."

"There's a chance Rob doesn't even know that detail."

"Why wouldn't he know?"

"To prevent terrorists from knowing the transport routes or hiding bombs inside civilian equipment being transported on military ships or aircraft, there are crazy layers of secrecy. I try to avoid military transport for that reason, but sometimes it's necessary. I'll do what I can from my end to find out. You said the message was a text. Can you find out who sent it and who received it?"

"Working on it. Disposable cell phones, but now that I have the numbers, I can lock onto the signals when the phones are turned on. Right now, both phones are off."

"We finally caught a break." The relief in JT's voice was palpable. "Focus on that. And Erica."

Lee stared at the house. "I wonder what's taking her so long?"

"What's she doing?"

"She's made another deal with Riversong and is collecting some bones for DNA testing. I think she's going to hit you up for the comparative sample." He briefly told JT about the meeting with Sam.

"Should I give her the sample?"

"Depends. Sam's dead set against giving her Menani-choch DNA. Are you concerned about DNA mapping?"

"No. It's inevitable. Frankly, I'm sure we've been mapped already. Instead of fighting it, I think it's better to seize control. Own the data ourselves."

"If you aren't worried, then give it to her. From my reading of the regs, Erica's right that human remains must be dealt with. Not to mention that it would hardly look good for Talon & Drake if the tribe desecrated a burial ground thanks to a botched EA."

"You really read all those archaeology regs?"

"Of course."

"Fine. If she asks, I'll give it to her." JT hung up.

Lee closed the phone and slipped it back into his pocket. He stared at the house, wondering if he should go inside and help her. She probably needed someone to hold the flashlight while she collected the sample.

He shrugged off the concern. She'd be out in a minute, and he needed to appear engrossed in the database.

❀

*E*rica pounded on the door. "Help! Lee! Help!"

Another wave of wooziness swept through her. She clutched the railing, barely keeping her feet under her. Nauseous and dizzy, she knew she had to get out of this basement before she passed out, or she'd never wake up.

Pulling the collar of her shirt over her mouth and nose, she hurried down the stairs, letting her pants trail in the water as she made her way to the window. Closer inspection revealed there was no pane of glass—she couldn't close the window to cut off the flow of exhaust.

Holding her breath, she tried to reach the generator, but she was too short and could barely get her fingers over the window ledge. She looked for something to climb on. Maybe she could escape through this or the other window. But she couldn't see any promising shapes in the darkness and didn't remember seeing any furniture down here last week.

"Lee! Help!" she yelled through the window, but the generator covered the sound, even to her own ears.

She tried to breathe as little as possible as she made her way through the dark room, trying to find a pocket of breathable air. The air was marginally better in the coal room. She took several deep breaths, then returned to the stairs.

At the top, she pounded on the door, no longer yelling because she was saving her breath. She was a scuba diver. She knew how to conserve air. The problem was it wouldn't buy her much time.

Please, Lee. Save me.

❋

*W*hat the hell was taking Erica so long?

Lee set the laptop on the driver's seat and climbed out of the car. He stared at the house for a moment. The house had two exterior doors that weren't visible from where he'd sat in the car, and Novak knew they were coming here after their meeting with Riversong. Lee broke into a jog, remembering the man had swept Erica with a possessive leer.

He pushed open the door and stepped inside. "Erica?"

"Lee! Help!" Her voice came from the basement.

He raced through the living room to the kitchen and tried the basement doorknob. "What's going on?" The knob wouldn't move. He studied the mechanism. There was no lock.

"Help! I'm trapped!" Her voice was laced with hysteria. She began to cough.

"Don't worry, sweetheart," he said, hoping to soothe her. "The latch must be stuck, but I'll get you out." She must be afraid, being trapped in the dark. He didn't blame her; that basement was rancid.

"Hurry! The basement—" Her words were cut off by more violent coughing.

"I'll just run out to the car and grab the tools in your dig kit."

"No! Don't leave!" she screamed between coughs. He could hear her gasping for air. "The basement is full of carbon monoxide." Her voice dropped. "And I'm feeling sick and dizzy."

Adrenaline shot through him. "Move back from the door!"

He kicked next to the knob once, twice, three times, then took a few steps backward and used momentum to put force behind his heel.

The wood cracked. Another kick and half the door swung out over the stairs. The other half splintered and fell.

Erica clung to the railing several steps below, coughing and shielding her face from the raining wood fragments. He ran down the stairs, scooped her into his arms, then carried her up and outside the house.

He dropped to his knees on the lawn while cradling her against his chest.

She sucked in great, gasping breaths of air, then leaned away from him and vomited.

He yanked his cell phone from his pocket and dialed 911.

Chapter Twenty-Six

The ambulance pulled away with sirens blaring. A helicopter was waiting on the fire station landing pad to airlift Erica to a Baltimore hospital equipped with a hyperbaric pressure chamber. A paramedic told Lee her prognosis was good, but the faster she got to the hyperbaric chamber, the better her chances for full recovery.

He didn't ask, and the paramedic didn't mention it, but he knew there was a chance Erica could have permanent brain damage.

Twenty minutes before she'd been trapped in the basement, Jake Novak had looked at her with predation. Lee wanted to kill the man with his bare hands.

He swiveled and faced the Menanichoch police officer who was investigating the incident. He was a tribal member and the same cop who had interviewed him the night Tommy Riversong was murdered. "Check Jake Novak's alibi."

The man cocked his head. "You don't think this was an accident?"

"Of course not. Someone jammed the door and turned the generator so it vented through the window."

"The door is old and could have merely stuck, and the

plumbers could have made a mistake when they positioned the generator."

The plumbers were called, and the younger one Lee had met last week returned to the scene twenty minutes later. The man studied the position of the generator. "I don't know," he said at last. "I don't think we would have set it up this way, but I can't be certain. I wasn't thinking about the exhaust. I was more concerned with the hose, which was barely long enough."

"What happened to the pump you installed last week?" Lee asked.

The man looked from Lee to the cop, clearly wondering if he had to answer the question.

The cop shrugged. "Tell us."

"We did a good install last week, but the electrical system failed and fried the pump and the fuse box at the same time. The wiring is old."

"Why did the basement flood again?" Lee asked. "It hasn't rained in over a week."

"The main water line to the house had been shut off for months—maybe years. While we were here, we opened the valve to test the rest of the plumbing. Near as I can tell, late last week a damn pipe burst and might be what caused the electrical to go out in the first place."

No wonder he wasn't eager to answer Lee's questions. He might have caused both the flooding and the electrical damage.

"Did you run the generator while you were in the basement?" the cop asked.

The man shook his head. "We checked to make sure the pump was working; then we left. An electrician is supposed to fix the wiring tomorrow; then we're going to reinstall the sump."

Lee left the cop to finish the interview and stepped back

inside the house. He stood at the top of the stairs, studying the broken door. How had it been jammed?

He circled the kitchen, and something on the floor caught his eye. A penny. The old dorm room prank came to mind, and he suddenly understood.

"What the hell are you doing messing with my crime scene?" the cop asked.

Lee turned to face him. "I thought you didn't think this was a crime."

"I'm examining every possibility. Now get out of there."

He pointed to the penny. "That's how the door was jammed. She was pennied in."

"What?"

"Pennies were jammed into the frame until the latch was so tight against the metal plate it wouldn't retract."

The cop looked down at the penny. "With one penny?"

"I bet you'll find more in the basement. When I kicked the door in, they must've gone flying."

He studied Lee, and his eyes took on a hard edge. "You're full of answers. I think I should take you in for questioning."

"I'm the one who saved her."

"Hoping she'll be grateful to her hero?"

"That's ridiculous."

"You were with her the night Tommy was killed. Were you jealous of the poor kid?"

Lee's frustration reached new heights. First the man wanted to write this off; now he considered Lee a suspect. "I don't have time for this. I'm going to the hospital. If you need to know anything else, you can call me."

"I don't think so, Mr. Scott. I'd like to interview you back at the station."

*E*rica barely remembered the helicopter ride to the hospital. She didn't fully come to awareness of her surroundings until she'd been in the hyperbaric pressure chamber for what she assumed was a long time. She felt pressure in her ears, had a pounding headache, and fought nausea, but the sweet, cool air soothed her raw and aching lungs.

She lay in the chamber, a long, coffin-like glass tube, and tried to think about her father and a time when her life had been simple and happy. It was getting harder and harder to recall his face. But she saw his eyes every time she looked into the mirror and knew she had his smile.

She and her mother had both worshipped him, and when he died, her mother didn't just fall apart, she shattered. They then suffered an abrupt and astonishing role reversal, and their relationship never recovered. She never forgave her mother for being weak, and her mother never forgave her for looking and being so much like the man she'd loved and lost.

Was that why her mother had stolen her identity? To punish her? To destroy her one remaining connection with her father, her pursuit of a PhD in archaeology, just like dad?

Erica had learned to walk and talk on archaeological sites. Literally. Pictures of her first steps showed Yosemite Valley in the background, and her first word was "dirt." Her father finished his PhD at the same time she started kindergarten, and from that point he left academia behind and established his own business in the emerging discipline known as cultural resource management.

Dr. Peter Kesling was a respected man in his field, known mostly for his efforts to establish ethical standards for CRM archaeologists. And she'd violated those very same ethics, placing a black mark next to the Kesling name.

A nurse came in to check on her. The chamber was

equipped with an intercom. "How much longer will I be in here?" Erica asked.

"You're halfway finished. You've got two more hours."

She nodded and closed her eyes. She had plenty of time to think. Too much time.

Jake had destroyed everything she'd worked for, and now he'd tried to kill her.

And he'd come damn close to succeeding.

◉

*L*ee watched the grainy footage from the casino's security camera. He easily recognized himself as he stepped out of the building a few minutes prior to Tommy's death and returned seven minutes later. He probably should have demanded to have a lawyer present for this interview but didn't want to waste time. He needed to get to the hospital. "I told you then the same thing I'm telling you now. I stepped outside to make a phone call. It was too loud on the casino floor."

"Who did you call?"

Lee looked the officer in the eye. "JT Talon."

The man looked slightly taken aback. Only two names were more powerful in this tiny nation within Maryland's borders: Joseph Talon and Sam Riversong. "Can you prove it?"

"Of course." Lee pulled out his cell phone, speed-dialed JT, and handed the phone to the cop.

The man asked JT several questions, then hung up. "Mr. Talon is on his way here."

"I gathered as much."

After JT arrived, Lee was free to go, but the officer was still suspicious. "I just hope he puts this much effort into nailing Novak for trying to kill Erica," Lee said to JT.

"I made some calls on my way here. Novak's got an airtight alibi."

"Who?"

"Sam Riversong."

He swore and climbed into JT's ridiculously expensive Lotus. "Still driving the midlife-crisis mobile, I see."

"Fuck you."

"How many days after Alexandra called off the wedding did you buy this piece of crap?"

JT's mouth was a rigid line. "Two."

"Next time get a puppy. You'll pick up just as many women but get fewer speeding tickets." The seat was so small his knees were practically next to his ears. "Take me to Erica's car."

Ten minutes later, he was in the driver's seat of Erica's old Honda and finally on his way to the hospital. He tightened his fingers on the wheel, thinking of the crease she got just above her nose when she drove through stop-and-go traffic. The woman didn't have an ounce of patience.

She could have died.

A well of fear opened up inside him, the one he'd kept locked tight for the last two hours as he dealt with the cops.

He was falling for her. He couldn't lie to himself about that any longer. Somewhere in this ridiculous charade, he'd let real emotions develop to supplement the fake ones he'd been using to manipulate her.

And now he was afraid those emotions would manipulate him.

When JT recruited him for this job, Erica Kesling was just a name. He'd tried to find out everything he could about her, but reading her résumé and hacking into her college transcripts and applications didn't prepare him for the woman she was.

Erica, whose stare could form frost in the midst of a summer heat wave. Erica, who had a sharp mind, a strong sense of loyalty, and a desperation for affection that blew him away. Erica, who had a sultry beauty she kept hidden behind an icy façade, burned like fire in his arms, and who aroused a protectiveness he didn't want to feel.

No, no words on paper, no list of classes, jobs, and accomplishments could possibly have prepared him for who she was.

And he still didn't know if he could trust her.

Chapter Twenty-Seven

The dark hospital room slowly came into focus. A glance at the clock told Erica it was two a.m. She'd drifted to sleep in the hyperbaric chamber and only dimly remembered being transferred to this room.

She rolled over, and her hair fell across her face. She shuddered at the strong stench of exhaust and brushed the loose strands away from her nose. She desperately needed a shampoo.

A shadowed form moved in the chair next to her bed, and she let out a soft gasp.

"Shhh. I didn't mean to scare you, Shortcake."

Lee. She breathed deeply and settled back into her pillow.

He lifted her hand to his lips. "How do you feel?"

"Better." Sleep pressed on heavy eyes. She turned her fingers and traced his mouth. "Thank you. For saving me."

She felt his smile. He kissed her fingertips.

"You should be home, sleeping," she murmured.

"No. I'm right where I belong."

She wanted to smile but was unsure if it made it to her face as she dropped back to sleep.

He was gone when she woke in the morning. A note on

the bedside table said he'd gone to work and to call when she was released. Her car keys sat next to the parking garage receipt, which gave the floor and number of the space. A quick search of the closet and she found her shorts and V-neck T-shirt with her purse. Lee had thought of everything.

The closet also held a large plastic bag marked with the hospital logo, which contained the clothes she'd ruined yesterday. She opened the bag, and the smell of exhaust wafted out, causing an instant headache. From her pants pocket, she extracted the bag that held the bone fragment she'd nearly died collecting, then tossed the clothing in the garbage.

A hearty breakfast was delivered at eight a.m. After that she took a long, hot shower and washed her hair several times, then waited for the doctor to make her rounds. The exam was brief. Erica's oxygen level was normal, her prognosis good. She could leave after the last of her paperwork was signed.

She felt good. Strangely good. New-lease-on-life good.

She was still waiting for the paperwork when Jake entered her room and closed the door. "Your pet intern told the cops I tried to kill you."

"Get out." She backed around to the opposite side of the hospital bed and braced her hands on it. She'd shove the heavy piece of furniture into him if he took one step closer.

"I want to know what you told him."

She got her breathing under control. "Get out now."

"You better not have told him about the artifacts."

A steely calm enveloped her. She stood up straight and walked around the bed, reminding herself she'd prepared to face him every day for the last year. She didn't need to hide behind the bed. She stopped two feet in front of him and crossed her arms. "What do you want, Jake?"

"I warned you not to tell anyone. Ever."

"I didn't tell him anything. I have no idea why he suspects you. Maybe because you were an asshole yesterday."

"What happened to you in that basement must have been an accident. You need to convince the cops of that."

The attempt on her life was an accident. The artifacts didn't exist. Her mother hadn't stolen her identity.

These were the lies Jake and the credit card companies had demanded of her. The credit card companies had urged —and now were trying to force—her to declare bankruptcy because it was better for their balance sheet to write off the debt than to admit being complicit with fraud, whereas Jake's motive was pure, simple greed.

She didn't want to repeat his lies, but now wasn't the time to stand up to him. The artifacts had to go on display first. "Get out."

"You're running out of options. I've protected you as much as I can."

She let out an incredulous laugh.

He stepped closer to her. "I have. I've been protecting you from Marco since the first day you stepped on my boat. If he believes you told anyone about him or what happened in Mexico, he'll come after you, and I won't be able to stop him."

"Right. You're merely his boss."

"The only way I can ensure your safety is if you're with me. Only then will Marco trust you to keep your mouth shut."

Jake's fixation on her made no sense. "Why, Jake? Why me?"

He took another step toward her and ran a finger down the side of her face. "You've fascinated me from the moment you joined the crew." He let out a derisive laugh. "You, with your ridiculous morals. Maybe it's because you're the first honest person I've ever worked with." He shrugged. "I brought you on board, so it was my responsibility to protect such innocence from the likes of Marco."

He sounded like he really believed that.

"You think you're so superior to Marco, but you're worse. Marco owns his awfulness. He doesn't pretend he's heroic. Of the two of you, you're the one who sexually assaulted me."

He flinched. "You wanted me."

"Not then. Not now. Not ever. Let me be clear: you are repulsive."

"But still, I'm your only hope for staying alive if Marco thinks you've squawked."

"You keep threatening me with Marco. We both know who the real villain is here."

"It's not a threat, Erica." He turned on his heel and left the room.

She peeked out the door and watched Jake saunter down the hall like he didn't have a care in the world. He turned left, so she grabbed her purse and car keys and headed right. To hell with the paperwork. She was getting out of here.

She hurried past the nurses' station, rounded the corner, and came face-to-face with the Menanichoch police officer she'd met the night Tommy was killed.

His face showed his surprise. "Leaving, Ms. Kesling?"

"Yes. The doctor said it was okay."

"I have a few questions for you."

"No problem. You can walk me to my car." Jake wouldn't accost her in the parking garage if the officer was with her.

"Your intern believes Jake Novak tried to kill you yesterday."

"Jake Novak? That's not possible." She had no choice but to give Jake what he wanted. In spite of her bravado in calling him out for his delusions of heroism, she still feared Marco coming after her. "What happened in the basement was an accident."

"Novak doesn't have a grudge against you?"

"No. Of course not. Why would he?"

"Who do you believe destroyed your office and apartment?"

Shit. "I have no idea. I guess I'm just having a bad week." She found the elevator and pushed the call button.

"A bad week?" The cop laughed but looked at her like she was nuts. "Do you include Tommy Riversong's murder as part of your 'bad week'?"

"I'd consider that the kickoff. Yeah."

"You have a remarkably blasé attitude."

The elevator doors opened, and they stepped inside. She hit the button for her parking level. "I'm hanging by a thread. It's either that or fall apart."

The cop inclined his head in acknowledgment. "So you believe you were stuck in the basement of the Thermo-Con house by accident?"

She looked him square in the eye. "Yes." She realized her hand had strayed to her bottom lip and dropped it.

"Did you close the door at the top of the stairs?"

It would be stupid to shut out the main source of light from a pitch-dark basement. "No. It must have drifted closed."

"It drifted closed, then jammed?"

"I was coughing so hard at the top of the stairs, maybe I somehow jammed it when I grabbed the knob."

The elevator doors opened, and he walked her to her car. He pulled out a card. "Thank you for your time, Ms. Kesling. Please call me if you think of anything else."

"Of course."

The officer headed back toward the elevator.

She locked her doors, started the engine, and headed to her apartment. She needed to find out if the camera disk and envelope were still safe in their hiding place.

*E*rica hesitated outside the door to her apartment, bracing herself to face the mess, the painted insults. She unlocked the door, stepped inside, and was immediately stunned. The crimson slur still adorned the wall, but the mess on the floor was gone.

Friday night, she and Lee hadn't bothered to clean anything but the food that would rot if left on the kitchen floor.

In a daze, she wandered into the living room. A well of emotion swirled inside her. The room was spotless and cleared of destroyed furnishings. Her sandals slapped loudly on the parquet flooring, and her breathing echoed off the walls in the vast, empty space. The only visible sign of damage was the splatters of red paint.

In the center of the floor was a receipt from the cleaning service, addressed to Lee Scott and marked paid. She leaned on the wall and took several deep breaths, shaken by a rush of emotion.

She collected herself and wandered down the hall. Her bedroom was empty except for a few items of paint-stained clothing, which would be useful for workouts or fieldwork. The bathroom was scrubbed clean, no paint stains in the bathtub. Back in the hall, she opened the linen closet and was surprised to see the vandal had missed this space. She still had towels and a few blankets. Her scuba gear was stored on the floor beneath the towels. She checked the hose and regulator. They were intact. She might be able to make a few bucks by selling the tank on eBay and could use the money to buy clothes.

She closed the closet door. She was stalling and couldn't put it off any longer.

She headed to the kitchen. Her dishes had survived, probably because smashing them would have alerted her neighbors, but her toaster and coffeemaker had been submerged in the bathtub. Her heart beat heavily and her stomach lurched as she reached for the lower cupboard door. Time to find out if Jake and Marco had found her hiding place.

She said a small silent prayer, pushed aside a can of beans and a bag of flour, and sucked in a shallow breath when she saw the box of cherry-flavored Jell-O. Her only hope of living a life without fear of Jake and Marco was sealed inside this box.

She closed the cabinet door and stood up, clutching the box, feeling the knot in her stomach loosen. The weight felt right—the doubloons gave it extra heft—and the glue seal on the thin cardboard didn't appear to have been broken.

She slipped a nail under the end flap. There was no other way to be certain.

"I thought I'd find you here."

Her heart leapt out of her chest, and the box flew out of her hands. She turned abruptly to see Lee standing in her kitchen doorway.

"Good Lord. You scared the hell out of me!" She placed her hands over her heart and felt the frantic beating. Her eyes followed him as he picked up the box of Jell-O, which had landed at his feet. She took a deep breath and exhaled slowly.

"Sorry," he said. "I didn't mean to scare you. You left the front door wide open."

"I did?" God, how could she be so careless? "I was surprised the place had been cleaned. I guess I walked in without paying attention."

He studied the box for a moment, then tossed it into the air and caught it with the same hand. "I've been worried about you." The box flew up again. "How are you feeling?" He caught it and tossed it again.

She was hypnotized by the motion. Every cell of her being screamed for her to grab the box midflight. She put her hands behind her back and leaned against the counter, trapping her itchy fingers. It took her a moment to comprehend his words, caught up as she was in the rhythmic game. That box contained her salvation.

"I'm fine," she managed, her throat dry. Jesus, she was so distracted, she hadn't thanked him for staying with her at the hospital or having her apartment cleaned. "Thank you." She cleared her throat. "For everything you've done for me. I'm overwhelmed." The box flew up again, and she searched for something to say. "How much do I owe you?"

He missed the box; it bounced off his arm and hit the floor.

She did not race him to retrieve it. She could not, would not, let him see any glimmer of its importance.

He looked at her, his eyes showing a mixture of anger and hurt. "You don't owe me a thing."

She'd hurt him. Dammit, this wasn't how she'd imagined seeing him for the first time since he'd saved her life and spent the night at her bedside. And she had imagined it. In the shower, on the long drive here, even when she'd faced Jake, Lee had been in her thoughts.

But now the Jell-O box lay at her feet, clouding her mind, destroying her ability to talk, to act. Had she waited long enough to casually pick it up now?

She bent down, but again he beat her to it.

"You having a craving for more hospital food?" he asked, handing the box to her.

"I was just going through the cupboards to see what food I have left."

He raised an eyebrow and looked at the cabinets. She instantly realized her mistake: all the doors were closed.

"It's expired." She tossed the box in the garbage, thankful the can was lined with a clean, empty bag.

Finding her focus, she pulled him out of the kitchen, away from the box and questions she didn't want to answer. They stopped in the center of her hollow living room. "What are you doing here?"

"I was worried. The hospital said you'd been released, but JT said you weren't at the Watergate, and you weren't answering your cell. I guessed you might have come here." His mouth was a firm line. "You should have called me."

"I'm sorry."

He touched her cheek. "Don't scare me like that."

She leaned against him, but he was stiff, still angry. She needed to get his mind away from the Jell-O. She stretched up on her toes to gain a few inches in height, but she still came up short. She grasped the front of his shirt to pull him down so his lips could meet hers. Whatever works, she thought, hating the reason for the mercenary action but still anticipating the kiss.

He hesitated. His green eyes bore into hers, questioning, hurt, mad. Dammit, he could see right through her, knew she was hiding something.

His height meant she couldn't kiss him if he wouldn't bend. Mortified he'd leave her there, lips poised for a kiss that wasn't coming, she dropped back to her heels. Suddenly his arms clamped around her waist, locking her in place, and his mouth descended on hers.

The kiss was pure heat. Thoughts receded as sensation ran through her like fire.

His mouth left hers to explore the column of her throat. Her eyes remained closed as each touch sent shock waves of desire through her. He pulled back, and she opened her eyes and stared into his.

His arms tightened, and his mouth returned, but softly this time, with tenderness in addition to passion.

His fingers slipped beneath the waistband of her shorts, and a shiver of anticipation ran through her. His hands cupped her butt and squeezed, pressing her hips against his. Want—no *need*—coursed through her, and she moaned against his mouth. She'd started this to distract him but was caught in her own trap.

His hand slid up her side, under her top and cupped her breast. Her hardened nipple ached as he brushed aside the cup of her bra. He bent her over his arm, and his teeth grazed her nipple through the fabric of her T-shirt, sending jolts of pleasure straight to her core.

This man had enticed her from the first moment they met. He'd been sweet and tender, hot and passionate, silly and sexy. He'd comforted her after her apartment was destroyed and had saved her life. These thoughts combined as his searing kisses drove her into a frenzied arousal.

She felt wild, ravenous and fumbled with the top button of his shirt. She needed to touch his skin.

He let go of her with an abruptness that left her off-balance. She stumbled backward, and he caught her before she hit the wall.

"Did I do something wrong?" she whispered, feeling completely vulnerable, lost.

His eyes conveyed nothing but fury. "I wouldn't say no to a fuck right now, but I'm still going to ask about the box of Jell-O."

Chapter Twenty-Eight

Lee was stunned by his own reaction. His last thought before he shoved Erica away had been that she would have sex with him, not because she ached for him like he did her, but because she wanted him to forget he found her clutching a too-heavy box of Jell-O as though it were her only friend in the world.

Ironic that she'd merely done what he'd been doing to her from the start: using the attraction between them to redirect attention. It was his comeuppance that he detested having her use the same technique to manipulate him.

Her eyes narrowed. She straightened her spine and transformed from sensual woman to angry ice queen.

"Good. Now you're as pissed as I am," he said. "Don't *ever* use what's between us as a weapon." Hands on her hips, he pulled her back against him and locked his arms around her waist. "Don't demean this—us—by making it a tool." He was the worst sort of hypocrite. Someday she'd know it and hate him.

And then he'd lose her.

She shoved at his chest. "I wasn't using you—this—us—"

"Then what were you doing?" He let her go, and she stumbled again.

"I wanted to kiss you. You saved my life, and I'm grateful."

Her words were a kick in the gut. "You kissed me because you're *grateful*."

"No. That didn't come out right."

"I'm sick of your lies," he said.

She jerked and looked him in the eye. "What lies?"

"Do you know who destroyed your apartment?"

"No!"

"Let me rephrase that. Do you *think* you know who destroyed your apartment?"

"No." Her mouth was a thin line, so different from a moment ago when her hot kisses had him seconds away from pulling down her shorts.

"Who do you think tried to kill you?" he persisted.

She flinched but said, "No one. I think it was an accident."

"Dammit, Erica, I want to help you!"

Her harsh, brittle laugh echoed through the empty room, filling the air with grief. "No. You just want to fuck me."

A new wave of anger washed through him. "That's only part of what I want from you," he said, his voice low and tight with barely controlled temper.

Her gray eyes lit with cold contempt. "Yeah, I know the rest. You need me to sign off on your internship or Mommy won't pay tuition in the fall. Since you suck at the job, you're trying to screw your way to a pass."

It took Lee a moment to understand; in the midst of the argument, he had forgotten his role. She had no clue who he was, what he was doing. She was so focused on her own deceptions, it hadn't occurred to her that he had his own agenda.

When her words did sink in, his anger peaked. He had to

marvel at her methods. She'd managed to neatly turn the tables, charging him with the exact same thing he'd accused her of moments before. The shit of it was he couldn't demand the truth from her without tipping her off that he was more than an idle intern.

"Guilty," he said, his voice dropping to silken tones. He decided to go for blood. "You won't believe how relieved I was that first day when I saw you and knew screwing you wouldn't be a chore."

A stricken expression flashed across her features.

Shortcake, that's the least of my lies. Or yours, for that matter. Hell, if she couldn't figure out that he'd been drawn to her from their first encounter in the company gym, that was her problem.

There was a knock on the still-open front door. JT entered without waiting for a response. "Oh, good," he said. "You're here." Lee was certain he'd been listening the whole time, waiting for an opportunity to enter.

Several emotions—none of them good—crossed Erica's face before she said, "JT. I had no idea you were here."

"Lee got me worried when he couldn't reach you, so we agreed to meet here before we called the police."

She looked down at the floor, wiped a cheek, and looked up again. "I'm sorry. I didn't mean to worry you or Lee."

Was she crying?

"Excuse me," she said and disappeared down the hall.

He wanted to chase after her.

"You blew it," JT said in a quiet voice as soon as they were alone. "You had her right where we want her, and you let ego take over instead of sealing the deal."

"Screw you."

"Do your job."

"Go back to New York."

"I'm leaving tomorrow."

"Good."

She returned a minute later with clear, dry eyes and gave no excuse for bolting. Instead, she said, "From the look of things, I can move back in here. Thanks to Lee."

"The walls need to be painted," JT said.

"I can't afford that."

"I'm paying," Lee said. "The painters start tomorrow."

"You can't afford tuition, but you can pay to have my apartment painted?"

Dammit. The lies were piling up and negating each other. He shrugged. "I have money, just not enough for tuition at Columbia. I found someone cheap who can start tomorrow. He said he's got another job scheduled after he does the first coat, so it'll take him at least a week to finish." He congratulated himself for thinking fast and securing her presence in his apartment for another week.

Her eyes were unreadable. Finally she nodded. "Thank you. I'll pay you back, when I can." She wrapped her arms around herself, like she was cold or needed a hug, but he just stood there, hating himself, hating the situation.

JT turned to Lee. "Now that we know she's okay, I need you back at the office. That database is vital, and we need it by Friday." He pulled out his wallet, took out two hundred dollars, then turned to Erica. "You're taking the rest of the day off." He pressed the money into her hand. "Go clothes shopping. If you wear that outfit to the office, then Skippy here will never get any work done."

Her face reddened. "I can't accept this." She held the money out to JT.

"You can and will, and it's not a loan." He headed for the door. "If you don't buy yourself some decent clothing, you're fired." The front door closed, and they were alone again.

"Is he mad at me?" she asked.

"No. He was just making it impossible for you to refuse."

"Are you mad at me?"

He looked into her eyes and could see the pain she tried so hard to hide.

"I don't know," he said. He headed for the door but stopped at the entryway. With his back to her, he said, "Don't take off without telling me again. Someone tried to kill you. I can't protect you if I don't know where you are."

"Okay." She paused. "Lee?" Her voice cracked.

He turned.

"Thank you. For saving me."

He walked back to her and cupped her face in his hands. "Stay safe. Keep your cell phone on you at all times and go directly to the Watergate when you're done shopping." He kissed her firmly and left.

He was in the elevator when he realized he'd forgotten to grab the Jell-O box from the garbage.

Chapter Twenty-Nine

$\mathcal{J}$T glanced up from the TV when Erica entered Lee's kitchen at six fifteen the following morning. She clutched her gym bag and wore one of Lee's old T-shirts and a pair of paint-splattered sweatpants. Shadows under her eyes told him she wasn't as chipper as her smile tried to appear. He held up a hand to stop her from speaking, as the news segment he'd been waiting for was just about to start.

She poured herself a cup of coffee, then leaned against the counter.

Lee entered the room. "Is it on?" he asked.

"Just starting," JT answered. It was too early for the national morning programs. Local news would have to do.

The reporter stood in front of the casino, microphone in hand, looking eager and excited, knowing the story could be picked up by the network. "The Menanichoch Tribe is hosting a gala reception Saturday night for the grand opening of the newest room at the casino. Sources say Senator Joseph Talon himself will cut the ribbon at the ceremony and will use the occasion to make a big announcement." She grinned. "One we've all been waiting for." She winked in an exaggerated manner, completely upping the cheesy factor.

JT shook his head. "She just lost her shot at the network. Now they'll send their own political reporter to stand in front of the casino to say the same thing, rather than use this footage."

"They could cut off that last bit," Lee suggested.

"Not if they want to include this part." He turned up the volume.

"…revealed the new room will have an Aztec theme. Tribal Chairman Sam Riversong promises the room will be chock full of Aztec art and history."

A crash startled him. Erica cursed as she bent to clean up a shattered coffee mug. "Sorry, I missed the counter."

He grabbed a towel and bent to help her, but she shooed him away. "Watch the segment."

The broadcast switched to stock footage of the casino. Artwork and signage befitting a museum surrounded gamblers sitting at baize tables, oblivious to the cultural experience around them, as the chipper reporter described the themes of the other rooms: the Inuit people of the Arctic, the Great Basin cultures of Utah and Nevada, the Pueblo people of the Southwest, the Cherokee Tribe of the East and Southeast. At least thirty seconds of precious airtime was spent describing the casino's practice of having a table in each room at which gamblers could try their luck at the designated culture's own historic or prehistoric game of chance.

The Indian games had been Joe's idea. It had always amused Joe that every culture gambled. "We couldn't buy advertising like this. Too bad the reporter screwed up, because the networks might've replayed the whole piece, including that last bit."

"Is that why the senator is making the announcement at the casino?" Lee asked.

"Yeah, plus it ties him to his cultural heritage. He's

decided that if he's going to run on Indian heritage, he's got to run on all of it, including Indian gaming." The segment was over, and he shut off the television. "I'm heading back to New York after meeting with Dad." Crap, he'd forgotten to say, *my* dad and now wondered if he should say the next bit in front of Erica. But then, she must have figured out Lee was a closer family friend than they'd let on. "Lee, he'd like to see you too. Old Ebbitt Grill. One o'clock."

Erica glanced at her watch. "I'm heading to the office. You ready, Lee?"

"I need to talk to Lee about the database. You go on ahead," JT said before Lee could jump up and follow her.

After she left, he said, "I won't be at lunch. I'm meeting the senator earlier so I can get back to New York. I want to warn you, he's going to ask you to replace Drake."

"Drake's leaving Talon & Drake?"

"Even if he's not involved with the smuggling, he's a liability. He wants to use Dad to get more government contracts and I suspect he's set his sights on becoming a key player on the campaign team. He's finished at T&D."

"He knows this?"

"I'm sure he suspects."

Lee nodded. "That's why he met with Riversong. Why he's so pissed with you." He met JT's gaze. "I don't want to run the Bethesda office."

"I need you. You aren't intimidated by me and won't push me to take the company public so you can make a killing in stock options."

"I've got my own business to run."

"It won't be forever, just until we find the right person to take over."

"Have you told Joe that I'm working undercover in Bethesda?"

"No. He doesn't know you're in the Bethesda office at all."

"I'm sick of lying, JT."

"You can't tell him. The press will scream cover-up if he knows anything—even after the fact. He knows nothing until the smugglers are caught."

"He's going to ask me to run the very office I've been spying on, and I'm going to have to play dumb? JT, this sucks."

"You've only got a few more days. Sara C comes back Friday, and in all likelihood, your cover will be shot Saturday night." JT stared into his coffee mug. The situation was rotten. Worse even than Lee realized. "I have no idea how Dad will react if we find out Sam's in on the smuggling." Sam. His father's best friend and mentor.

Lee flopped back in his chair. "The deeper I look, the worse it gets for Sam." He paused. "I think I've isolated who received the text message."

"Sam?"

"No. It was Sam and Drake's new buddy, Jake Novak."

Chapter Thirty

*J*oseph Talon was about to make the biggest announcement of his political career in front of Aztec artifacts Erica intended to prove were stolen. Her actions could damage his reputation and that of his tribe. She could destroy his campaign just as it was getting started.

Could she do that?

It was either expose the artifacts or live life fearing the day when Jake would decide to stop toying with her and move in for the kill.

She had to meet the senator. Then she could decide what to do.

But timing was critical. Lee had just left the office to meet JT and the senator for lunch. She intended to wait twenty minutes, then join them. The minutes inched by as she rehearsed what she would say, praying they would accept her reason for crashing their lunch.

She was about to leave when Janice entered the room. "How are you feeling, Erica?"

She was so nervous it took her a moment to comprehend her boss's question. Janice had been gone all morning, and she hadn't seen her since Monday. Oh, yeah. The near-death thing.

"I feel fine."

"I've been so worried. I talked with Sam Riversong. He feels just awful about what happened, and the plumbers have been fired. I can't believe anyone would be so stupid as to set up a generator with the exhaust aimed at an open window."

So the accident story had taken root. She didn't find that comforting. Her throat felt dry. She forced a response. "The doctor told me it happens with alarming frequency."

Janice pulled out a deck of cards, decorated on the back with an historic tablet of Arabic writing. "I have something cool to show you." She laid the cards faceup in different patterns on the lab table.

"A card trick?"

"No. A deck of playing cards that was made for the troops in Iraq and Afghanistan by the Department of Defense's Heritage Resource Preservation program."

"Like the deck they gave soldiers to identify the Most Wanted people in Iraq?"

"Yes. These cards show some of Iraq's and Afghanistan's most precious archaeological sites. They were made to educate the troops about protecting sites and artifacts." She held up the seven of clubs. "This one's my favorite."

The card had a picture of the ruins of an ancient arched building with the caption: *This site has survived for seventeen centuries. Will it and others survive* you?

"It's brilliant," Erica said, touching the cards. "I'm glad the DoD is taking cultural history in the Middle East seriously." She picked up the queen of clubs, which had a picture of an artifact with the caption: *Remember! The buying and selling of antiquities is illegal and punishable under the Uniform Code of Military Justice.*

She stopped when she came to the nine of diamonds, which depicted a mask that had been looted from the Iraq

Museum, and thought of the artifacts Jake had acquired by trading the Aztec pieces. "How did you get the deck?"

"A friend in the heritage program."

She'd had a year to wonder how Sam Riversong—if it was indeed Sam—had gotten the Iraqi artifacts he traded with Jake. The logical conclusion was he'd somehow gotten them through Talon & Drake. She'd worked that angle as much as she could, but security being what it was, she'd gotten nowhere.

Janice finished laying out the cards, and Erica saw that when arranged properly, the background of each card created a bigger picture, one puzzle for each suit. Clubs was a famous monument, diamonds a gold artifact.

"These are amazing," she said, wondering if she should skip the FBI and go straight to the Department of Defense with her photos of the Aztec artifacts. The DoD was dealing with the looting problem and had a vested interest in correcting the situation. But her proof was Aztec, not Iraqi. She doubted she'd be able to connect Jake to the Iraq artifacts. Her biggest fear, though, was that she would end up being prosecuted with Jake and the crew. After all, her name was on the excavation permit.

Janice set down the cards. "Have you put together a budget for the navy proposal?"

Her belly twisted. Janice had asked her to do that on Monday, before she delivered the Thermo-Con EA. "I haven't had a moment to look at it. I really think it's a bad idea, Janice. Jake Novak strikes me as unethical."

"My hands are tied. Ed wants to bid, and he wants to team with Jake." She glanced at her watch. "Do you have time? I want to talk about how to organize the project."

The knot in her stomach tightened as they discussed a project she would never work on, fully aware her chance to catch the senator was slipping away.

Finally, Janice left, and Erica slid the Thermo-Con file

into her bag and headed to the Metro station, hoping and praying she wasn't too late.

⬖

*J*oe was already seated in a booth when Lee arrived at the restaurant. He greeted his former stepfather with a firm handshake and a politically expedient man hug, well aware that these days Joe was under constant media surveillance. Lee had always lived on the edge of Joe's inner circle. As an adult, he appreciated the anonymity of life at the fringe, but as a kid, he'd resented the hell out of it.

He slid into the seat across from Joe. No matter where he was positioned in Joe's public life, privately, they were close. Lee would always be grateful for the many times—even long after the divorce—Joe stepped in and was a father to him when both of Lee's biological parents failed miserably. He respected the man's integrity, knew he'd make a spectacular president, and would do anything to help him get elected. Hell, he'd proved that when he took on the intern role.

"It's been a while since I've seen you." Joe's eyes held a subtle reprimand.

"I've been busy with a client." That was true enough.

"Not so busy you won't be there when I make my announcement, I hope."

"I wouldn't miss it."

"Good." Joe paused. "Did JT mention why I wanted to talk to you?" The man was never one to waste time.

"You want me to run the Bethesda office."

Joe's grim smile reminded Lee of the time he'd switched his high school's computer-synchronized clocks to run on metric time, and Joe's intervention saved Lee from expulsion.

"Ed has become a liability," Joe said. "He's getting older and slipping, but he owns a third of Talon & Drake, so it's going to be tricky. But Ed's eager to work for the campaign, and I can placate him by giving him an important-sounding job until the transition is done. Then I'll have to let him go." He studied Lee. "But this is a sensitive situation. We can't have just anyone in charge at the second largest office of T&D while I'm running for president. We're going to have to maneuver around some very complex issues, not the least of which is adhering to the Senate Ethics Manual. We need someone we can trust completely. I need you, son."

Lee had waited a lifetime to hear those words from Joe, and if what he suspected about Ed Drake was true, then it was vital they remove him from the company.

But Lee didn't want the job.

The waiter arrived. He ordered the special, too preoccupied to give the food any consideration. How would Erica react? When she realized the extent of his lies, she'd hate him.

And when he became her boss?

If he couldn't explain the lies, she'd never forgive him.

But if he ran the office, he could get rid of Novak. He could protect her.

"What's her name?"

Lee startled. "What?"

"You've got the same look in your eye you used to get when you were sixteen and full of hormones."

He laughed and considered his answer. The truth? "Her name is Erica."

"Is it serious?"

"I don't know." He paused. "But I hope so." The words slipped out, an uncontrollable urge to be honest. With Joe, with himself.

"Promise me she isn't another reporter hoping to capitalize on your connection to me."

Damn, he'd thought Joe had let that go. "She's an archaeologist. Actually, she works for Talon & Drake—Bethesda." *Crap, he'll want to know how we met.* "JT introduced us." Sweat formed on his brow. JT *never* socialized with employees. And Joe knew it.

"You'll be her boss. Is that a problem?"

"She'll freak. And not in a good way." That was an understatement.

"Work it out. I need you to start on Monday."

Typical Joe. He'd embraced the idea and moved on it with hurricane force, not even waiting for Lee to agree. The man was short on patience and had absolute confidence in his abilities. This attitude sometimes led to spectacular failures, but Joe didn't shirk from his mistakes any more than he'd deny his successes. Lee had learned much from him over the years, and owning faults was paramount.

"I'll do it," Lee said. "But when the campaign ends, I'm gone."

Joe grinned and relaxed back in the booth seat. "Deal."

Christ, what had he just agreed to? Now it would be *his* employees who were stealing from Iraq. Firing those involved would be easy enough, but finding replacements to finish the contract while making Joe look good to the voting public would be a nightmare.

By taking this job, he ensured he'd be as thoroughly scrutinized as JT by the press. Everything he did would reflect on Joe and could become a campaign issue. And even if he could persuade Erica to forgive him, her murky past would be a liability.

Not that it mattered. Odds were they wouldn't be on speaking terms come Monday.

Their meal was winding down when the woman who dominated his fantasies entered the restaurant and walked with purpose toward him. He sprang from the booth seat. *What the hell is she doing here?*

Erica reached his side. "Lee, I'm sorry to barge in like this—"

He cut off her words with a fierce kiss. When he pulled

back, her eyes held confusion and a smoky passion. He felt a jolt of male satisfaction followed by a stab of guilt. The kiss was the only way to silence her before she said something he didn't want Joe to hear.

Her gaze cleared, and her face slowly turned red.

He was a dead man.

Joe slid out of the booth, and gave Erica a warm, expectant, even indulgent smile.

Lee draped an arm around her shoulders. "Joe, meet my girlfriend, Erica Kesling."

If he could get through the next several minutes without her calling him on this lie and mentioning he was her intern, or Joe revealing Lee had been his stepson, it would be a miracle.

Chapter Thirty-One

$\mathcal{M}$ ortification, anger, lust, and confusion all jockeyed for position in Erica's racing mind. Lee's kiss had been intense, hard, arousing, and so very *public*. And why the hell had he called her his girlfriend? Worse, why did she get a little giddy thrill from the title? *Get a grip, girl. There are so many more important things going on.*

He smiled in a way that begged her to play along and kissed her temple. Hell. She didn't have a choice. She'd come here to meet Joseph Talon and wasn't going to blow her chance by pointing out the man who made the meeting possible was a skilled liar.

She felt the senator's assessing gaze as he invited her to sit. "I'm sorry to intrude, but I was hoping to catch JT." She glanced around the room, wondering where the senator's son was.

"JT is on his way back to New York," Senator Talon said.

She hesitated. JT wasn't here? *Damn.* She'd planned to ask JT for a DNA sample. She smiled tentatively at the senator. Without JT, the senator was her only hope.

Lee nudged her toward the bench, and she slid into the

seat. He sat next to her and again draped his arm around her. "Why are you looking for JT?"

His ardent gaze caused her belly to flip. If she didn't know better, she could believe she was the center of his universe. The idea filled her with longing, which she ruthlessly brushed aside. She was weak and a fool.

She sucked in a shallow breath and closed her eyes for a brief moment to get her bearings and remember her objective. She'd wanted to meet Joseph Talon to decide if she should tell him about the stolen Aztec artifacts, but first she needed to justify her intrusion. She reached into her bag and pulled out the kit she'd picked up from a pharmacy yesterday. "I need to ask JT if he'll give me a DNA sample for comparison to the bones from the Thermo-Con basement. Today is my last day to get a sample. I'd hoped to catch him before he left for New York."

She'd intended to ask JT yesterday, but he hadn't returned to the Watergate last night until after she was asleep. Then this morning, they watched the news, and she decided to use this as her excuse to crash their lunch with the senator so she could meet the man. But JT wasn't here.

Joseph Talon straightened in his seat across from her. "Thermo-Con? Wait a minute. You're the woman Sam told me about who was trapped in the basement a few days ago."

She nodded.

"I can't begin to say how sorry I am about what happened. You're feeling fine now?"

"Yes." She glanced at the man by her side. "Lee saved me."

The senator looked at Lee curiously. "I didn't know you were there."

Lee shrugged, then picked up the DNA collection kit. "You could give Erica a sample."

She wanted to kiss him for making the suggestion. She

looked eagerly at the senator, but he was studying Lee. "I'm not sure if I should."

Lee signaled to the waiter. The man hurried to the table and asked for her lunch order, but she declined. She wanted the freedom to bolt if the conversation didn't go well.

She studied Joseph Talon and wondered what to do. He was handsome, possibly even more so than JT, who bore a strong resemblance to his father. His dusky complexion showed minimal lines to give away his sixty-plus years of age. He had a full head of dark hair with only a smattering of gray at the temples, which lent him the perfect weight of authority. His hair and facial features weren't so much defin-able as Native American as they could be described as "ethnic."

She remembered seeing an interview with the Filipino American actor, Lou Diamond Phillips, in which he discussed being cast in a range of different ethnic roles. If Joseph Talon had pursued acting, she imagined he'd have been given similar options.

She wanted to know what made this man tick. How would he react if she told him the truth? Sam Riversong was his friend.

She decided to let the DNA test drop for now and gath-ered her courage to steer the conversation toward the real reason she'd wanted to meet the senator. "According to the news, you'll be making your announcement at the casino."

"Yes. I will."

Lee's hand dropped to her knee. The senator couldn't see his warm touch, but she was aware of him as if each indi-vidual nerve ending were sending a separate message to her brain.

"You aren't concerned the casino backdrop will hinder your campaign?" she asked.

"Every major news organization will be there. I can't pass up the opportunity for free publicity for the casino."

"But won't the fact that you're in a casino turn off some voters?"

"I owe the tribe everything I have, everything I am. I'm not going to shy away from what my people need for fear of losing a few votes."

She'd always admired him for his forthrightness. He exhibited an integrity that was hard to find in politicians, and she wondered if he was genuine. "What if it's more than a few?"

"It's a risk I'm willing to take. When I was thirteen, my boarding school burned down, and I ran away from the social worker who was determined to place all the kids who'd been dumped in that school in juvenile hall, as if we were criminals just because we were Indian. I showed up in the town outside what was then Fort Belmont—the only place where a few dozen Menanichoch tribal members still lived. There I met and was taken in by Sam Riversong."

Erica had seen photos of him, taken right after the fire. He'd been so young, so sweet-looking, and his eyes had been filled with sadness and loss. She knew something about isolation and loss at the age of thirteen but still couldn't begin to imagine Joseph Talon's journey.

"I lived with Sam for five years, worked at the local diner, and went to school," he continued. "I learned about my heritage as Menanichoch—something that had been forbidden at the boarding school. The tribe claimed me. When I was accepted at the university, the community pooled their money and paid my tuition." His expressive face conveyed his every emotion, as though he were reliving his transformation as he told the story. Sitting across from him in a crowded DC restaurant, she realized that, if anything, televised news clips didn't convey half of this man's true charisma.

"I look at my accomplishments and see my tribe holding me up, giving me the support that made me who I am. In return, I do everything I can for them. I worked my ass off for federal recognition. After we got that, I worked to have the Fort Belmont land returned to the tribe and then raised money to build the casino. Now I do what I can to promote it. My candidacy may flounder, I may be out of the race in a month's time, but by making my announcement at the casino, the tribe will benefit from my run for office."

She made her decision. She would tell him and hope he would believe her and help her use the artifacts to convict Jake. She took a deep breath. "You can't make your announcement in the Aztec room. If you do, your backdrop will be stolen artifacts."

As she said the words, a man in the booth on the other side of the wooden partition stood and made a show of trying to get the waiter's attention. Strategically placed plants had obscured him, but now she saw the soulless brown eyes which had filled her nightmares for the last year, and cold, metallic fear filled her mouth and spread through her body.

Marco Garcia had followed her to the restaurant.

Chapter Thirty-Two

$\mathcal{L}$ ee's grip on Erica's knee tightened as shock and disbelief spread through him. She had just revealed her secret. Chief among his emotions was overwhelming relief. Erica wasn't the crook he was looking for.

Joe's eyes narrowed. "What are you talking about?"

She shrank into her seat and transformed in a heartbeat. Her eyes filled with the fear that always lurked beneath her surface. Joe's tone had been sharp, but her reaction was extreme.

She cleared her throat. "I'm sorry, I misspoke—or, overstated, really. I meant to say cultural art is a source of communal pride, and permanent exhibition in a foreign country can feel like theft of culture. Some people believe any artifact removed from its country of origin is stolen—even if the artifacts were legally acquired. Aztec art comes from Mexico. Wouldn't it be wiser to make your announcement in the Pueblo or Cherokee room?"

Her answer was smooth. Joe might even buy it, but Lee didn't.

"You aren't the first person to wonder if I should make

my announcement in a more 'American' setting, but I don't need to wrap myself in an American flag.

"When the Birthers came after me last year, demanding proof I'm an American because I don't have a birth certificate, I showed them the scars I got at my Indian boarding school when the headmaster tried to beat the Indian out of me. I'm a Native American and therefore more American than ninety-eight point five percent of this country. I don't need a piece of paper to prove that, and I'll stand with pride in front of the Aztec Room. The Menanichoch casino is classier than most, the architecture is superb, and the artifacts and historical displays are breathtaking. It's the perfect backdrop for the launch of my multicultural campaign."

"I still think you're making a mistake."

Joe smiled. "You'll keep Lee on his toes, which is good. His last girlfriend was a twit."

She glanced sideways at Lee, but her attempt at an amused smile was clouded by a wariness she couldn't hide.

"Yes, well, twit is the last word I'd use to describe Erica," he said, squeezing her thigh. Liar was the first word, followed by alluring, beautiful, and then secretive.

"After Sam told me what happened to you in the Thermo-Con house," Joe said, "I'd planned to invite you to the ribbon cutting on Saturday—a small apology from both the tribe and the company. But this is perfect. You'll be Lee's date."

She looked at Lee questioningly.

Now it was his turn to lie. "I was going to tell you about it tonight, Shortcake."

"Thank you," she said to Joe. "I'd love to go."

"The party is black tie. Make my son buy you a dress."

"JT?" she asked.

"He means the company," Lee said quickly, catching Joe's gaze. "As a representative of Talon & Drake, you need to shine. JT will authorize the purchase."

Joe leaned back against the booth cushion. "You're right, Lee. Given the changes that are happening in Bethesda and that she's your date, her gown will be important…" His voice trailed off. *Thank God.* Still, Lee's heart beat a rapid tempo.

He had to end this hellish conversation and get her away from Joe.

"You're quite pretty," Joe murmured. "Your work is intriguing, even exotic-sounding." He smiled in a way that told Lee he was calculating her campaign value, and she'd garnered a high rating. "You're perfect to play the role of a Talon & Drake non-management representative." His gaze met Lee's. "Go designer. Pick out a dress that will stand out in a roomful of peacocks. I want her noticed."

Erica's eyes widened, visibly appalled at Joe's edict. "I don't want to stand out." Her gaze darted from Lee to Joe before fixing on the booth partition.

"Too bad," Joe said.

If the conversation weren't so stressful, Lee would be amused. No one said no to Joe, and Lee would ensure Erica was no exception. He wanted her to shine at the party too.

"I'll take her shopping." He picked up the DNA test kit again and shoved it toward Joe. Maybe if Erica got what she came here for, they could get the hell out of here. "You should give her a sample. The tribe needs the test to determine if the bones are Menanichoch or not."

Joe took the box and read the label. "You promise Menanichoch DNA won't go into any genetic mapping database?"

"Yes," Erica said.

"I'll make sure of it," Lee added. He'd promise anything to get out of this meeting.

"No one will know you provided the sample, Senator," Erica added.

Joe shrugged. "If Talon & Drake and the tribe needs this, then fine." He opened the kit and swabbed the inside of his cheek, then dropped the swab into the protective plastic vial and gave the kit back to her.

At last, the perfect moment to escape with Erica. Lee grabbed her hand and slid toward the end of the booth. "We've taken enough of your time today, Senator."

She said a hasty good-bye as he dragged her away from the table.

"Good to see you, son. And Erica, it was delightful to meet you."

She clung to his arm as they hurried from the restaurant. Outside, he walked with purpose, pulling her with him, away from the door, away from any further contact with Joe. He slipped a hand into his pocket and clenched it into a fist. Had she caught that last "son"? Did she write it off as a figure of speech, or had she guessed at their relationship?

She glanced back toward the restaurant several times.

What was she expecting to see? He had no idea what was going on in that beautiful head of hers. All he knew was he had to go on the attack before she had a chance to question everything that had just transpired. When they were a block away, he rounded the corner and stopped. "Did Jake Novak steal the artifacts about to be displayed in the Aztec Room?"

Her gaze darted back and forth down the street; then her eyebrows drew together in what could only be false confusion. "What do you mean?"

He pushed her against the building and cradled her chin. In spite of all the anger and suspicion, he couldn't resist, and his mouth captured hers. She gasped softly and locked her arms around his neck. He lost himself for a moment; then sanity returned, and he broke the kiss.

She released him and pressed her palms flat against the wall while she caught her breath. A dozen emotions crossed her face, and her eyes held a heart-wrenching vulnerability. He couldn't let that sway him. "You're such a beautiful liar. I think the senator believed you. But I didn't."

She jerked away from him. Traffic flowed by on the busy city street. The noise of the stream of pedestrians and cars cloaked them in anonymity.

He touched her arm. "Dammit, Erica. When are you going to tell me what's going on?"

"There's nothing going on, Lee. You've got a wild imagination, that's all."

"So I imagined what happened to our office. To your apartment. To you in the basement of the Thermo-Con house."

She didn't answer.

"Why did Jake Novak trash your apartment? Was he looking for Aztec artifacts?"

"No!"

"When are you going to admit you worked for him?"

Blood drained from her face. She jerked her arm away, turned, and flat-out ran.

Chapter Thirty-Three

After running several blocks, Erica slowed to a walk and crossed Constitution Avenue, wishing she could disappear among the people strolling the National Mall. She carefully scanned the crowds and didn't see Marco's wiry form skulking amongst the tourists. She hadn't seen him after Lee dragged her from the restaurant, but if he had followed her, hopefully she lost him in her mad dash.

Lee had guessed she worked for Jake. She shouldn't be surprised. He must have realized days ago she was hiding something. She'd been acting like a freak ever since they met, and the first time she saw Jake, she'd nearly fainted. A part of her had been aware she'd been falling apart from the moment she started to cry in front of Lee and JT yesterday. And now, after seeing Marco, she felt so fragile a strong breeze would shatter her.

She wished she could return to her own apartment. And yet being alone was scarier than facing Lee. She really had no choice. She would have to answer his questions. Later.

Her cell phone rang. She let it roll to voice mail, then a minute later checked her message. But the call hadn't come from Lee. It had been the clerk at the patent office. The files had arrived. Going to the patent office would save her from facing Lee for a few hours.

Knowing a FedEx drop box was in the Promenade area, she headed to the L'Enfant Plaza Metro station. She found a bench and pulled out the DNA kit. After wrapping the swab and bone, she took the box of Jell-O from her purse and pulled out the empty envelope she'd taken from Jake's cabin on the *Andvari*. The envelope that had contained photos of Iraqi artifacts.

She studied the ripped flap. Had Sam licked the glue to seal the envelope?

She slipped the envelope into the padded mailer with the other two samples. DNA from the envelope would be compared to the senator's DNA. She hadn't gotten a sample from Sam, but at least this was Menanichoch DNA. She'd know for certain if the person who licked the envelope was a tribal member. It was a start.

Later she'd try again to get a sample from Sam, but at least she'd found a way to have the envelope tested for DNA —and she didn't even have to pay for it. The tribe was picking up the tab. Fortunate, because there was no way she could have afforded the test herself.

She smiled grimly and dropped the package into the FedEx bin, saying a heartfelt prayer she'd be able to use the results, then headed to the patent office.

Thirty minutes later, she opened the first of the two patent files. At the top of the thick stack of papers was a brochure with the words: *Higgins Homes Presents Thermo-Con*. Even though she'd already confirmed their theories, she still felt a rush of excitement when she saw the words "Thermo-Con" in print in association with Higgins Industries.

She studied the brochure before making photocopies, proud that she'd connected bits of information in a way no one had done before. She felt bad Lee wasn't there to enjoy the moment. He'd been an integral part of the project; it didn't feel right that he wasn't with her.

How was she going to face him tonight? What would she say?

Did Marco know where she was staying, or was she safe at the Watergate? These thoughts swirled through her mind as she made copies.

In spite of his accusation, she felt safe with Lee. She would never forget the moment he kicked through the basement door. Lit from behind and clouded by exhaust, he was haloed. Her own personal savior.

But her feelings for him were far from saintly. She felt a bone-deep hum whenever he was near. Just thinking about him, about the way his mouth felt on hers, she found herself short of breath and aroused. But she was a walking time bomb. To save herself, she would undermine—possibly even destroy—Joseph Talon's campaign. When Lee learned the truth, he'd distance himself from her so fast he'd set a new land-speed record.

The copy machine ran smoothly as she carefully placed one document after another on the glass. She worked methodically, paying little attention to the pages in front of her.

Her cell phone rang again. This time it was Lee. "We need to talk," he said.

"I know."

"Meet me at the Watergate. Six o'clock."

"Fine," she said and hung up, feeling sick to her stomach. Part of her desperately wanted to tell him everything. The rest of her was terrified.

She continued copying the patent documents, then switched to the file for the mixing machine, which, as Lee had guessed, was the Thermo-Con generator described in the newspaper article. The letterhead indicated the DC law firm of Morton, Fairfield, and Lawson had handled the patent for

Higgins. Was the firm still in existence? Would they have files for patents they'd handled over fifty years ago? The patent hadn't been officially granted until after the Thermo-Con house was built. Could the law firm have specific information related to the construction of that particular house?

While the draft Environmental Assessment was done and filed, the bones meant the project was still active, and the tribe had requested she follow up on any new leads the patent information provided. This was a solid lead, and it could give her another reason to meet with Sam. A meeting in which she could somehow collect a hair follicle from him.

Good Lord, she was considering tackling an elderly man and yanking out his hair. But what else could she do?

At the counter, she paid for her copies and asked for a phone book. In minutes, she had the phone number for Morton, Fairfield, and Lawson programmed into her cheap, pay-as-you-go Blackberry-type cell phone. She left a message as she headed toward the Metro. She slipped her phone into her purse and stepped onto the escalator to descend into the station, a sinking sensation in her stomach.

It was time to face Lee.

◈

*L*ee heard the key in the lock and met Erica at the door. He didn't say a word as he closed the door behind her and threw the dead bolt. Nothing would interrupt them this time.

Before she could speak, he kissed her. She was stiff, almost rigid at first, but he was determined, and deepened the kiss.

Her arms slid around his neck, and her body melted against his as she kissed him back with a passion that rocked him. He lost himself in the moment but then remembered his purpose. Raising his head, he looked into her gray eyes, faltering when he saw unguarded desire.

She opened her mouth to speak. He covered her lips with his fingertips. "Don't talk," he said. "I don't want to hear any lies." He kissed her again, pressing her into the closed door, trying to lose himself again, trying to forget the real reason he was seducing her at last.

He pulled the ever-present hairpins from the knot at the base of her neck and ran his fingers through her silky hair, smoothing and separating the glossy strands that had fueled his fantasies for days. He felt her shiver as he trailed kisses up her neck, stopping at her earlobe.

She pushed against his chest. "We need to talk."

He returned to her lips, silencing her as he opened the buttons of her blouse one by one. "The only thing I'm willing to talk about right now is baseball." He slid her top over her shoulders and let it drop to the floor.

"Baseball?"

"It's taken me a week and a half to get past first, but tonight I'm going to round every damn base—slowly." His fingers worked the clasp on her bra. In seconds, the lacy garment landed on top of her shirt. His mouth captured one nipple while his hand caressed the other.

She let out a soft moan. The sound ran like electricity through his system, every nerve ending on fire as he pulled her closer.

He released her from his mouth, then scooped her up and carried her from the entryway into the master bedroom. His room. He dropped her on his high four-poster king-size bed, completing the picture he'd had in his mind for days.

"This is JT's room. We can't—"

He silenced her with a kiss, hating that even this was a lie. "JT's not here. I refuse to make love to you on the sofa bed in the den, and the bed in your room is too small for what I have in mind."

"Lee—"

"If it's not about baseball, I don't want to hear it."

She sat up and looked around the room. She didn't know she was getting her first glimpse of his world. He was suddenly nervous, wondering what she thought of the paintings that faced the bed, ones he'd spent far too much money on because they touched his soul.

Her shoulders relaxed, and she smiled.

It was the sexiest, most earth-shatteringly seductive smile he'd ever seen. She crawled toward him across the big bed. "Why are you still dressed?"

Damn, if only this moment could have come about without being paved by lies—on both their parts. But he refused to entertain those regrets and began to unbutton his shirt.

She tugged his shirt from his pants. "Since you're only twenty-five, I expect a high-scoring game."

There it was, another lie, this one his. "You can count on it." That, at least, was true.

She unbuckled his belt, then reached for his fly.

He sucked in a breath. "Damn, you don't waste time when you make up your mind."

She kissed him while tracing the outline of his erection. Intense pleasure rippled through him. She freed him from his pants and briefs and her cool fingers closed around his hard penis.

He closed his eyes and sucked air through his teeth. He was so turned on, he was liable to embarrass himself. Only a young, inexperienced man would bunt at this point in the game.

He reluctantly scooted off the bed, and she let out a feral groan as she let him go. He quickly shucked his clothing, then grabbed her foot and dragged her to the edge of the mattress. He undid her slacks and slid them off, tossing them over his shoulder. Her skimpy underwear was all that remained.

She rose to her knees on the edge of the bed. The longest strands of her hair reached her butt. She far exceeded his fantasies with her smooth skin, full breasts, trim waist, and curvy hips. He cupped her ass, pressing the length of her against him as he stood on the floor. His mouth covered hers as he willed his resisting mind to forget the lies.

Later she would realize making love had been a means to an end, but he'd deal with her fury when the time came. Whatever deceptions lay between them, the one truth was he wanted her. Desperately.

He tugged on the thin elastic of her underwear. "Why are you still wearing this?" he murmured against her lips, then ripped the panties apart.

"Lee! I only have ten items of clothing to my name, and that includes underwear!"

"And then there were nine." He ripped apart the other side and tossed the satin fabric behind him. "I'll buy you more." He dropped kisses along her perfect body as he descended to his knees. "I won't be able to concentrate tomorrow, knowing you're going commando." He kissed her center. "Do you like this?" His tongue found her clitoris.

She arched backward and gave vocal praise to God.

He took that as a yes and continued to explore her with his mouth and hands. Her fingers twined in his hair while she whimpered his name. He slid a finger deep inside while he tasted her. God, she was magnificent as she arched against him and made a sexy mewing sound that turned him on as much as the scent and taste of her arousal.

What was happening to him? As much as this moment was what he wanted, he feared making love to her now would make it impossible for her to forgive him later. But he couldn't stop, even if he wanted to.

He brought her to the edge of orgasm. "Do you want to come now?"

"No. Yes. No." She leaned away and tugged at his shoulders. "I want you inside me."

He stood up and leaned into her, tipping her backward.

Lying next to her, he dragged her into his arms and kissed her deeply, then looked into her eyes. He'd pushed her to the brink, then stopped, and she squirmed against him, anxious for him to be inside her, but he wanted to savor this moment. What was to come might ensure this was all they would ever have.

He'd spent hours wondering if her slate eyes would take on more blue when aroused. His grin started dangerously close to his heart as he gazed into smoky blue irises.

"What?" she asked.

"You're breathtaking."

She smiled. "Do I turn you on?"

He slid a hand down her side, resting it on her luscious hip while he sucked on a nipple. "So much I'm in pain right now, Shortcake."

"Poor baby." She rose on all fours and kissed him as she slid down his body. She stopped, her head level with his erection. She teased him cruelly, licking and nibbling the inside of his thighs, touching everything except his hard cock. She finally showed mercy and took him into her mouth.

She was an erotic vision with her ass in the air as she knelt over him. Her shimmering hair pooled over his legs while his hard prick disappeared inside the velvet softness of her mouth. He'd lost sleep imagining her silky hair draped over his thighs. He had a good, healthy imagination, but he hadn't done the moment justice.

"Oh God. Erica. Stop." He gasped. "I want to be inside you."

She massaged him with her hand. "We need a condom."

He reached for the nightstand and pulled a box from the drawer. "This should last us tonight, at least."

She laughed and grabbed a strip of condoms. She ripped one off, removed the wrapper, and slid it over him.

Sheathed, he took over, flipping her onto her back and moving on top of her, settling between her thighs. "You said something once about lack of finesse." He slid two fingers deep inside her. "You're ready now, but I'm tempted to make you pay for those words by torturing you with endless foreplay."

She grasped his penis and guided him toward her opening. "Don't even think about it. You've hit an inside-the-park homer, but you've got to run the bases to score. A cocky walk now, and you might get stopped at third, or worse, get tagged out."

He pressed against her. "No chance you'd tag me out now." But she should. If she knew what was good for her, she would.

She cupped his face between her hands. "I want you inside me, Lee. Now."

"We're playing for the same team then, 'cause we're both about to score." He slid inside her.

Her eyes closed, and she let out a sharp breath and clutched him tightly to her.

"Open your eyes," he said against her lips.

She shook her head.

"I won't move, then."

She scoffed. "As if you could stop now."

He laughed and pulled back slowly, nearly pulling out of her.

Her eyes flew open. She locked her legs tightly behind him and grabbed his butt.

He kissed her and thrust deeply. Pleasure rippled through him. "Thank you," he murmured as her eyes drifted closed again. "Your eyes"—he moved in a slow, even rhythm as she clung to him—"are so damn sexy."

She let out a low moan. "Oh God, Lee. I was so close before…I'm going to come already." She kissed him, her mouth clinging to his with the same ferocity as her legs wrapped around his hips.

He wanted to slow down, but his own orgasm slammed

into him. He captured her moans in his mouth as their bodies shuddered together.

Spent, he lowered himself and rolled to the side, bringing her with him. Still inside her. Her eyes fluttered open and she smiled and stroked his cheek.

She was relaxed and happy. He'd given her that peace. That pleasure.

He wanted this moment to last forever.

He kissed her softly as he slid from her body, then he released her mouth and held her tight to his side. She snuggled against him and let out a happy sigh.

"That was a good idea," she said.

He laughed. "One of my better ones, I think."

"I'm sorry I bolted—"

He placed a finger over her lips. "I want to talk. But let me get rid of this condom first."

She nodded and he slipped from the bed. He disposed of the condom in the bathroom then returned, stretched out beside her again, and pulled her to his chest.

Tension had returned to her body now that the time to talk had arrived. Did she plan to lie to him again?

He needed to cut off that path before she started on it. He didn't want to entertain more of her lies.

Jake had tried to kill her, and she'd protected the sonofabitch.

There was one thing he could say that would let her know in no uncertain terms he wouldn't be fooled. He would accept nothing but the truth. "So, is the proof the Aztec artifacts were stolen inside the box of Jell-O?"

Chapter Thirty-Four

Shock and disbelief spread through Erica. Had Lee really asked her about the Jell-O box? *Now?*

He looked down at her, expectant, waiting for her answer.

Horror surged past shock, and she shoved at him, wanting to escape the bed. Escape the room.

His arms locked tight around her. "Don't you dare run again. You promised we'd talk."

She had. But now…she had no idea what to say. "I changed my mind."

"Answer my question."

How could she have been so stupid as to end up here, now? She pushed on his chest again. "Let me go."

He released her and she scooted back.

He reached for her hip. "Please, Erica. Stay. I want to help you."

She evaded his hand and managed to rise to her knees. She waved in a gesture that encompassed both their nude bodies and the rumpled bedspread. "How is this *helping*? If anything, what you did was help yourself to my body before you blindsided me."

Pain swamped her, causing her to tremble.

Who is this man?

She crossed her arms over her bare breasts. "What do you want from me?" Her words sounded like a pained whisper, even to her own ears.

"What I've always wanted. The truth."

She didn't even know what the truth was anymore. Would he condemn her because she'd violated her own ethics and taken a job from Jake? This situation was her own doing.

Stupid, stupid Erica for trusting Jake.

Stupid, stupid daughter for feeling a rush of needy joy when her mother suggested Erica use her apartment as a permanent address while she was in school. *"You'll be traveling so much doing fieldwork. I can handle your bills for you."*

Stupid, foolish child, so pleased her mom was acting like she loved her, at last. She'd never know if stealing her credit had been her mother's intention from the start, or if the preapproved credit card mailings were too good for a financially strapped drunk to resist. She felt the tingling sensation that preceded tears and took a deep breath. She'd never cried over her mother's betrayal and wasn't about to start now.

No. She had a whole new betrayal to deal with.

Stupid, foolish woman for opening her body and mind to Lee. He'd given her an incredible orgasm, yes, but all she'd gotten was screwed.

He spoke, his voice soft but carrying a note of anger. "You have a history of bolting. You tell me your password is Riversong, and you're out the door before I can form a question. I call you Cream Puff, and you storm away. I ask you about Novak, and you take off down the street. I had no choice but to wait and ask you when fleeing wouldn't be easy."

"Why do you even care? You're a frigging intern, for Chrissakes!"

"Whatever is going on with you could hurt the company and the campaign."

"What makes you think that?"

"Shortcake, since I've met you, you've twice gone to see Sam Riversong. The first time you threatened to force an issue that would put the tribe's land in jeopardy. The second time we met with Riversong, he was with Novak, a treasure hunter you're terrified of who is also trying to team with Talon & Drake. I know treasure hunting is bad news in your line of work. Then there's the fact that your office and apartment were trashed, and someone tried to kill you. It doesn't take a brain trust to deduce something is up, and it involves you, the company, Novak, and the tribe. Joseph Talon's tribe and Joseph Talon's company. You bet I'm worried."

She'd been so transparent, taking comfort in the fact he was an intern, hoping he wouldn't clue in to her abnormal handling of the Thermo-Con project. But he'd seen it all, put it all together, all while flirting and touching, enticing her into his bed. "So you fucked me so you could question me."

He rose to his knees and cupped her cheek in one large palm. She should recoil, but she couldn't help herself and leaned in to his touch. She was pathetic.

And desperate for one person to be on her side for a change.

His voice was soft and seductive as he said, "I made love to you because you're all I've been able to think about since the first moment we met." His eyes were earnest. "I wanted you then. I want you now. I can't explain why I want you so badly. It just is. Like the need to breathe."

Her breath hitched as her nipples hardened and her pelvis clenched. Hurt. Anger. Desire. They all boiled inside her until something snapped. Tears broke free and slid down her cheeks.

She swiped at the tears and pulled herself together, halting both the tears and accompanying sobs. Jake had broken her with torture and threats. But Lee had broken her using her own fragile need for affection, her unfathomable but undeniable attraction to him.

He wrapped her in his arms. "Sweetheart. Tell me the truth. Please."

"I can't." He might be friends with the Talons, but he was still just an intern, a twenty-five-year-old career student. He couldn't protect her from Marco.

"You need to tell me what's going on."

She began to shiver uncontrollably. He scooped her up and pulled back the covers. He set her down again and slid under the duvet, pulling her into the circle of his arms. She didn't protest. His body was a warm comfort and it wasn't like there was anywhere else she could go.

"Tell me why you worked for Novak." He caressed her back, then slid his hand along her shoulder and behind her head, where he threaded his fingers through her hair. Here at last was the affection she'd craved, the postcoital tenderness she deserved.

She pulled away from him and met his gaze. Was that compassion she saw in his eyes?

"Tell me," he whispered.

She didn't really have a choice. He knew about the Jell-O box. She would tell him as much of the truth as possible. "Fifteen months ago, I was in graduate school at the University of Hawaii, working towards a PhD in underwater archaeology, when my mother died."

She saw relief and something else in his expression. He cupped her face and kissed her cheeks; then his lips found hers, and she couldn't resist him. She needed his comfort, his affection. She must be a glutton for pain.

He whispered against her lips, "Thank you."

She took a deep breath and found the tightness in her chest had loosened. The truth was surprisingly freeing. "I had some grant money, which I used to pay for my mother's burial. It was too late to apply for a student loan to replace the money, so I applied for a consumer loan and was stunned when I was denied. I checked my credit report and discovered someone had stolen my identity. It was easy to trace who did it. She hadn't even tried to hide what she'd done. The bills were mailed to her address. Before she died, my mother racked up over a hundred thousand dollars in debt in my name. She'd—she—" She stopped. She didn't want to admit her own mother hadn't given a damn about her.

Lee's arms tightened. His lips found her forehead, then traced her hairline. "I'm sorry."

She cleared her throat. "She'd taken out seven credit cards and maxed out every one. I found dozens of collection agency notices—all sent to me at her address. I'm still fighting the credit card companies. The people at the credit bureaus didn't believe a mother would do that to her child. They said my mother's inability to defend herself was 'too convenient.'"

"How did your mother die?"

"She was drunk and wrapped her car around a tree." She paused, then added, "I feel bad for the tree."

"Oh, Erica, honey…"

The way he held her told her he understood her bitterness, and she wondered about his relationship with his parents. She'd learned long ago—when she was a teenager and her mother was still alive, and still, supposedly, taking care of her—people didn't understand. Mothers were to be worshiped. Mother's Day was a sacred holiday, and any deviation from that line was a sign she was a bad daughter and a terrible person.

She snuggled against his warmth, wondering how big a mistake she was making. But she needed him, needed this. She needed one damn person to care about her. Just one.

"Have you declared bankruptcy?"

"That would be an admission of guilt, but I'm innocent. I'm a victim of fraud, but because my own mother stole from me, I'm supposed to suck it up."

"Do you have a lawyer?"

"Oh, yeah, they're just lining up to take me on credit." She lifted her chin. She hated the pity she could see in his eyes. "The debt is frozen, pending investigation. The problem is, so many things depend on credit. I wouldn't have gotten a lease if Janice hadn't known my landlord. I can't afford the place, but I had no choice—with my credit, the only apartments available were scary. I can't get a credit card. Can't get a cell phone beyond a pay-as-you-go plan. Right now I've got exactly twenty-seven dollars until next payday—five days from now. If I don't drive or eat, I might make it."

He rested his lips against her temple. "And so you took a job from Novak."

"I didn't have a dime for tuition, and my student loans would come due if I dropped out. I was reeling from my mother's death, from what she'd done, when Jake—who knew my financial situation—offered me a job. For one summer's work, he said he'd pay me enough to get me through two years of school. I knew I was risking my reputation, but he promised me—I was so fucking stupid—analysis would take precedence on the excavation. Salvage and profit were supposed to be secondary."

"But he didn't keep his promise. What happened?"

"We had a disagreement and I didn't complete my contract, so he refused to pay me. He told my professor I'd worked for him, and I was politely instructed to withdraw from school. Within weeks, I couldn't get a job in California. Within a few months, the entire West Coast was out. So I moved here and got the job with Talon & Drake. The rumors haven't reached Janice yet. I've lived in fear she'd hear about me every day since."

"What was your disagreement with Jake about?"

If she told him the truth, he might make the artifacts discreetly disappear—before they could harm Joe's campaign —and without the artifacts, there was no evidence a crime had been committed. There would be nothing for the FBI to investigate. She'd live the rest of her life in fear of Jake and Marco. And the rest of her life probably wouldn't be very long.

It might not play out that way, but could she really take that chance? "He was gutting the shipwreck, destroying the data to get to the artifacts."

"Why did you warn Joe about Aztec artifacts?"

For a moment, she'd hoped the senator would be able to help her, but Marco was there to remind her she couldn't admit to having proof without endangering herself. Until the artifacts were made public, she was on her own. "For exactly the reason I said. There are people who feel like Aztec artifacts belong to the people of Mexico, not some casino in Maryland."

"Did Jake find artifacts on the shipwreck? Could he have sold them to the casino?"

"I wouldn't know. I left the project early." *Please let this drop.*

"Why did you run from me today?"

"I don't want anyone to know I worked for Jake. If Janice finds out, she'll fire me. I was scared. I'm still scared."

"And the box of Jell-O?"

She couldn't flinch, couldn't give him any reason to doubt her. "It's where I kept my savings."

His voice hardened. "Try again."

"Fuck you if you don't believe me."

"Been there, done that." His sudden anger spoke volumes. This man—who didn't care about archaeology, history, or culture half as much as she did—had the gall to condemn her.

"I'm leaving." It took her a minute to get free of the blanket. She gathered her clothes from the floor and stopped when she found her torn underwear. How many minutes ago had he ripped her panties from her? A wave of pain slammed into her, and she dropped to her knees on the carpeting. "Damn you," she whispered.

She had to get away. She hugged the clothes to her chest and started to stand but felt a hand on her shoulder. His arms came around her, pulling her against his chest. His lips pressed her hair. "If you don't want to see me again, I'd understand."

Damn right she never wanted to see him again. The sonofabitch had used sex to get her to spill her secrets—not because he was worried for her, but because he was concerned about a campaign.

"I don't want to hurt you."

She let out a bitter laugh. "Too late."

"I'm sorry." His cheek rested on her hair. "I'm angry. I thought you decided to trust me. Then you lied again."

"Why should I trust you? I don't even know you. And what I do know, I don't like." She felt him stiffen and knew her words had hurt him. Good.

"I had that coming." He turned her to face him. She saw pain and anger in his deep green eyes. "Regardless of what you think of me, I care about you and want to help you."

His hands dropped away; she could bolt if she wanted. She hesitated and then asked herself why.

"We're good together, Erica. Really good."

She pulled on her pants and wished her shirt wasn't by the front door. She needed clothing, protection. She needed to get away from him while she still had a shred of sanity. "I'm leaving."

"Don't!" He reached for her but then dropped his hands. "I'm sorry. Please stay."

"Why?"

"If you leave now, you're running away. Again. I didn't take you for a quitter."

"Please, you're going to have to come up with something better than that tired line."

"How about I want you; I'm falling for you."

"That's two. Three clichés and you're out." She picked up his shirt and slipped it on.

He grabbed her shoulders. "Dammit, Erica! I'm crazy about you. So crazy I'm angry you don't trust me—and lash out and say stupid things. I'm so damn wild for you that I want to toss you on the bed and make love to you until you can't think, can't walk." The turmoil in his eyes cut into her. "Can't leave me."

She caught her breath. The anguish in his voice was real. This was Lee, telling her he cared about her. That he needed her. And she believed him.

She found a shred of resistance. "What do you want from me this time?"

He kissed her, then spoke against her lips. "Nothing more than to look into your eyes as I make you come, repeatedly." His kiss was hot, sensual, like a drug, and she wanted another hit. "To make you forget what a jerk I am."

She threaded her fingers through his hair and captured his mouth with hers. She felt the tension in his body, his fear she would leave. She deepened her kiss, and he melted against her, relief spreading from his body to hers.

She tightened her fingers, pulled his hair. "No more questions. One more strike and you're out—out of the inning, out of the game."

His sexy smile was her undoing. "Shortcake, I'm about to hit it out of the park."

For her, all that mattered was tonight she wouldn't be alone.

Chapter Thirty-Five

$\mathcal{L}$ ee woke long before Erica did. He watched her sleep and breathed in her scent. Sex, shampoo, and Erica's own personal essence. He was addicted to the fragrance. Addicted to her.

He wasn't proud of the way he'd questioned her, of the anger he'd exhibited at her lies. She was lonely and hurt, and he'd caused her even more pain.

Afterward, he'd been terrified she'd leave. But she hadn't, and they'd made love until they were both sated and exhausted. And then, because he couldn't get enough of her, he'd made love to her again in the shower. Hot water poured down his back, she panted his name, and he came with a powerful, mind blowing orgasm. Then he'd looked into her eyes and known there was no going back.

She owned him now.

Now, hours before dawn, he was hard again and couldn't sleep. Her hair had dried from their midnight shower, and the dark strands haloed around her head and covered both their pillows, enveloping him in the scent of the shampoo he'd lathered into the thick, silky strands. He'd developed a Pavlovian reaction to hairpins and knew it was fueled by her refusal to wear her hair down. He suspected for the rest of his life the mere glimpse of a bobby pin would give him a hard-on.

He climbed out of bed, careful not to disturb her. Time to check in with JT. After she woke, he wouldn't have a second alone. Not if he could help it, anyway.

He left the master suite, cell phone in hand. In the guest bathroom, he turned on the tap, sat on the closed toilet, and placed the call.

"This better be good." JT sounded half-asleep and three-quarters grouchy. Good.

"I think the artifacts Riversong procured for the Aztec Room were stolen from the shipwreck Novak's been excavating."

JT cursed, then said, "Cultural goods. No way would the Mexican government let Novak keep those. Can you prove this?"

"I think Erica can."

"Find out. Fast. You got this from Erica? You finally got into her pants?"

He bristled but answered, "Yes."

"Good work." JT let out a low whistle. "She thinks you're young, immature, and spoiled but still slept with you. You're a regular James Bond."

"Shut the fuck up, JT."

He laughed. "Have all the fun you want with her, but don't let your feelings screw up the investigation. You need to find out about the artifacts and how Novak is involved with the Iraq smuggling."

"First I need to take Erica shopping; she needs a dress for Saturday night. By the way—as punishment for the hell I went through lying to Joe and Erica at the same time, you're paying for the dress. Designer, per Joe's orders. She's going as both my date and employee-of-the-month."

JT was silent. Finally he said, "Shrewd of Dad, but it

could backfire. Too bad we can't tell him what she's involved in."

"She's innocent. She was caught in a bad situation by Novak and walked. She lost everything because she worked for him and got nothing in return."

"You may have been taken in by a sexy con."

"I'm a lowly intern. If she's a con artist, she'd be after you."

"At least I wouldn't let my emotions get involved."

"She worked for Novak, but she's not a part of the Iraq smuggling."

"I hope you're right. Listen, I figured it was time to share real info with the feds and spoke with an agent I know. The Iraqis didn't let the FBI near the place where Matt Weber was killed until after it had been cleaned up. They've got nothing to go on there, but the agent said they'll be ready to dive in once the artifacts reach American soil. He agreed with your buddy Curt—because I authorized your hacking into the Talon & Drake network, you don't need a warrant, but they would, so he's content to hang back and let you do your job. Legally, we're fine as long as the Feds don't get wind of the cell phone hacking you've been doing."

"What cell phone hacking?" Lee said innocently. But the cell phones were the least of it. He could go to jail for the hacking he'd done to gather information on Erica, Drake, Novak, and Riversong. At the very least, he'd lose his business license. Joe had no idea the lengths they were going to protect him.

"Yeah, that's what I thought." JT paused. "The feds will search SARAC when it arrives. Focus on Novak. See if you can get into his computer. If the guy is selling Aztec artifacts, he'd have no qualms selling Iraqi ones."

"I know."

"We need to nail this sonofabitch to the wall," JT said.

"I think Erica's got proof against Novak."

"Then convince her to hand it over."

"Her proof could implicate Riversong."

JT swore. "Dad won't like that."

Lee wondered if JT was considering a cover-up. The thought made him ill. "If Riversong knowingly bought stolen goods, he's going down along with Drake and Novak."

"Dad will never turn his back on the man who saved his life when he was thirteen years old," JT said and hung up.

Lee returned to his bedroom. He crawled into bed, pulled Erica into his arms without waking her, and asked himself why he was risking jail and his career and lying to Erica. Was he trying to find out who'd murdered Matt Weber? Was he trying to protect Joe and the campaign?

His answer neither surprised nor pleased him. Twenty years after the divorce that hurt the most and fifteen years after being the screwup Joe had to rescue time and again, Lee was still trying to prove himself.

If Erica could prove Riversong had purchased stolen goods, Lee would have to choose between a man he'd known and worshiped most of his life and the woman who'd stolen his heart.

Chapter Thirty-Six

$\mathcal{E}$rica came awake from a deep sleep with the suddenness of swimming and surfacing for air. She hadn't slept that deeply in over a year. The man sleeping next to her was the reason she'd been able to let her guard down.

What a night.

He looked heart-skippingly sexy with the sheets tangled around his hips, leaving his sculpted torso exposed to her avid gaze. His hair, damp when they'd gone to sleep, stuck out at odd angles, and dark stubble lined his handsome jaw.

Twelve hours ago, he'd ripped her heart out.

Jake had believed she was his for no other reason than he wanted her. He'd claimed he was her protector then had taken kisses and groped her. But her kisses, her body, those were for her to give. Not for Jake to take. Not even for Lee to take.

Lee might believe he made the first move that night at the FDR Memorial, but she'd known exactly what she was doing as she stood on that rock. She'd wanted him to kiss her. In that moment, she'd reclaimed a piece of herself that Jake had tried to steal. Her body. Her choice. Afterward, she'd scanned the crowd, looking for Jake, as she wondered what the price of reclaiming herself would be.

Last night, she'd slept with Lee because she wanted to. She'd wanted *him*. Again, her body, her choice. He'd taken nothing from her she hadn't wanted to give. Not even the story of her mother or the incomplete truth she'd told him about Jake. And afterward, she'd made the choice to stay. She'd wanted his tenderness, wanted his passion.

Did she regret sleeping with him? No.

Did she want to stick around and face him this morning? Also no.

She quietly slid to the edge of the bed. He caught her wrist, his reflexes surprisingly sharp for someone who'd appeared sound asleep. He pulled her back against him and rose on an elbow, a sleepy, sexy smile on his handsome face. "Where are you sneaking off to?"

"We're"—her voice cracked and she cleared her throat— "late for work."

He dropped kisses along her brow. "We're not going to work today."

"I can't take a day off."

He nibbled on her ear, and she wondered why she'd considered escaping. Last night, they'd had mind-blowing sex —repeatedly. She wouldn't mind experiencing that again.

He trailed his lips along her collarbone. "After everything that's happened, you need a mental-health day." His mouth found hers, and he kissed her soundly. "We're going dress shopping." He slid down and sucked her nipple into his mouth.

Oh Lord. She caught her breath. What were they talking about? Oh yeah. "You want to spend a girly day with me, shopping?" She tried to focus. "Should we get our hair done too?"

"No scissors are getting anywhere near your hair." He slid his fingers through the tangled mass.

She closed her eyes as he massaged her scalp.

"And we're going to buy you lots of sexy underwear." He pushed her onto her back and kissed her neck and breasts as he worked his way lower and lower. "Unless, of course, you want to go commando. That'd be fine with me." He traced her belly button with his tongue, then continued south.

She discovered she lacked the will to get up.

"Say you'll play hooky with me today." He reached the juncture of her thighs. His tongue found her clitoris, and he demonstrated exactly how much he'd learned about her body during their marathon sex night.

"Yes," she gasped.

"Yes, you'll play hooky with me? Or yes, as in, 'I like that, don't stop'?"

"Don't stop." She arched her back as he did that thing that made her stretch tighter than a violin string, already on the brink of orgasm.

He stopped.

"Okay! Okay! I'll take the day off." Her choice.

He slid his tongue across her clit, delivering the sweet sensation she needed more than air. She came to a shuddering climax, but before she finished coming, he donned a condom and entered her, and the feel of his thick length prolonged her orgasm, stretching it out until she thought she'd come apart with the intensity. He arched his back and let out a low, guttural sound as he came, and she loved the feeling of him losing control of his strong, powerful body inside her.

Afterward, she snuggled against him. "Damn, you're persuasive," she said.

"I was captain of the debate team in college."

"Was? Don't tell me, you got kicked off the team for seducing the professor."

He laughed. "No, he was—is—a tiny old man with a Napoleon complex."

"So why aren't you captain any longer?"

"I don't have time for it."

She rose up on an elbow and traced circles on his perfect chest with her fingertip. She was his supervisor but felt no more in control of her reaction to him than she did any other facet of her life. She knew so little about him. "Tell me what you do at school. What keeps you too busy for debate? Do you have a job?" She stopped and pulled her hand away as a sudden thought chilled her. "Do you have a girlfriend?"

He caught her hand, entwining her fingers through his. "No. I don't have a girlfriend. But I have someone in mind for the position." He brought her fingers to his lips and kissed them one by one.

"Forget it."

Hurt crossed his face. "Why?"

"In a few weeks, you'll return to school. We live in different worlds and are in different places in our lives." *I'm afraid to trust you.*

"So? I'm wild about you."

"This is just sex." *It has to be. I can't handle a broken heart on top of everything else.*

He sat up and looked down at her. "Don't give me that bull. If this was just sex, I'd have been finished after the first orgasm."

He towered over her, so she sat up. "College and long-distance relationships don't work."

"I'm not a freshman finally tasting freedom, and you certainly aren't a high school girl waiting for her college boy. I'm a man who knows what I want. And I want you."

"A man who needs to complete an internship so his parents will pay for school."

He stiffened and started to speak, then stopped. Finally, he said, "You can't get beyond that, can you? I'm sorry your mom was a shit. But I'm not going to apologize for the fact that my parents help me out with school."

Feeling struck, she climbed out of bed and headed toward the bathroom.

He followed and caught her around the waist, pulling her back against his naked body. "I'm sorry, Erica. I was out of line."

"No," she murmured. "You're very astute. You should change your major to psychology." She tried to pull away. "I'm going to take a shower."

"Don't do this. Don't build a wall between us."

She faced him. "I have to, Lee. In a few weeks, you'll be gone. Until then, there's nothing more between us than sex."

"You mean really great sex."

She let out a short, painful laugh. "Spectacular sex. But that's all this is. Hell, my biological clock will be going off soon. What would you do then?"

"Get rid of the condoms."

She couldn't give in to the pleasure his words caused. "Please. You're twenty-five and haven't yet started a career or your adult life. You don't want to be saddled with an older woman longing for babies while you take your first low-level, soul-sucking job."

He laughed. "You should be a recruiter for the business world. And don't tell me what I do or don't want. I know my own mind, and dammit, I'm falling in love with you."

Fear arced through her, and she pushed him away. "You can't be."

"There you go again, telling me what I want, how I feel. You're stubborn, hostile, secretive. Generally, a pain in the ass. But still, I'm madly, crazily falling for you."

She tried to ignore the flutter in her chest, the aching need for his words to be true. "As far as romantic declarations go, you could have done better."

"If I'd complimented you, you'd just argue and tell me how I feel. But notice you aren't arguing after hearing your faults. Now get over here and kiss me like a woman who's just been told the man of her dreams is falling in love with her."

He offered her what she wanted most, what she feared most. If she slipped and said the words back to him, then the pain and humiliation when he left would be so much worse.

When she didn't move, he took her hand and pulled until her palm rested against his chest. She could feel the even beating of his heart. "See. Just like I said. Stubborn." His voice dropped lower. "I'm only asking for today. Tomorrow we can negotiate all over again."

"Today. That's all you want?"

"I want a hell of a lot more. But I'll take today."

She was in way over her head, but later, when he was long gone and her life resumed its lonely course, she'd have the memories of today to sustain her.

Her choice. "You can have today."

Chapter Thirty-Seven

*D*ress shopping was sheer torture for Lee. Erica tried on sexy dress after sexy dress, and he was forced to behave in front of serious saleswomen hawking overpriced gowns.

She'd turned white when she saw the price tag of the first dress he wanted her to try on. She hissed at him when the saleslady was out of earshot. "This costs more than my rent. No way are we spending that much on a dress."

"It's not your money. It's Talon & Drake's."

"It's obscene. If we're going to waste money I'd rather eat steak."

"I'll buy you steak, but you're still trying on the dress." He'd pushed her toward the dressing room, but the gown wasn't right for her. Neither was the next one, or the next. Each time she stepped out of the dressing room wearing a different megapriced designer gown, his reaction was instantaneous. No. She needed to look like a starlet on Oscar night.

Saturday night she would stand by his side and be the recipient of a whirlwind of attention from the press, and he would make it blatantly clear she was his. When his relationship to Joe and his new position at the Bethesda office was announced, she'd never have to fear Novak again.

She'd be devastated by his lies, but she'd be safe.

Erica was determined to try on dull dresses guaranteed to grant anonymity. He took yet another gown from her hands and hung it on the rack. "Shortcake, you have terrible taste."

"I do not. I have practical taste."

"Same thing. You need a dress that's decadent, frothy. Gorgeous. Like you."

"I am *not* frothy."

He pulled her to him, and his lips hovered over hers as he murmured, "I was referring to the gorgeous part, but there were times last night when you were *very* frothy." He kissed her, a deep, leisurely exploration. She grasped the front of his shirt, and damn if she wasn't turning frothy right there in the upscale boutique.

He reluctantly broke the kiss. "We need a break. Let's get lunch."

He took her to a bistro, and they sat outside in the sultry summer heat. Erica ordered a steak sandwich, and the look of ecstasy on her face as she took her first bite caused a rush of feelings he didn't want to face.

Damn, but this was a rotten situation. He'd lied to her from the first moment they met, and come Saturday night, she would hate him. But he couldn't stop the coming storm by confessing now. She hadn't explained what happened with Novak or why she'd really warned Joe about stolen Aztec artifacts. What if she still worked for the treasure hunter? Fear of Novak didn't exonerate her; it just meant she wasn't a fool.

They drank wine and entwined fingers across the white tablecloth. Her eyes were a rich, warm gray, and she wore her hair down. Christ, he really was falling in love. "I need to call JT. He'll know where to find a dress."

"JT is an expert on women's fashion?"

"In the circles he moves in—both political and business—

he often needs a well-dressed companion on his arm." He pulled out his cell phone. When JT answered, he said, "I need to know where Alexandra buys her dresses when she accompanies you to political events."

"It's an exclusive shop—appointments by referral only. I'll call and get back to you."

"I can't believe JT's going along with this," Erica said after he hung up. "The idea of spending a thousand dollars on a dress is ridiculous."

"It's going to cost much more than a thousand bucks. Think of yourself as Cinderella."

"You and JT are my fairy godmothers?"

He laughed. "All I have to do is wave my magic credit card, and you can go to the ball." He lowered his voice. "Last night, instead of fairy *god*mother, you just called me God. Repeatedly." He kissed her fingers. He could see the arousal in her eyes as her pupils dilated and the gray took on more color.

She slipped a finger into his mouth. He caught it between his teeth and sucked on the tip. She shifted in her seat, crossed her legs, straightened her spine. She was as turned on as he was.

"I don't want to shop anymore," she murmured. "I have other entertainment in mind."

"We haven't found a dress yet."

She pressed her foot against his crotch. Bare toes explored his erection.

"Yes. I'm hard. I want you. But we still need to find you a dress." Oh God. If she did that thing with her big toe again, he might change his mind.

His cell phone rang. It was JT. "She's got an appointment in fifteen minutes."

He scooted his chair back, and her foot dropped away. He missed the heat of her against him as he wrote down the name and address of the shop. Minutes later, the bill was paid, and they were back on the street, heading to the exclusive boutique.

The proprietress greeted them like old friends. She scanned Erica from head to foot, then said, "I have just the thing," and disappeared into the back, leaving them alone.

Lee poured them both champagne from the ready ice bucket and passed a glass to Erica. Before she took a sip, he caught her around the waist, pulled her against him, and kissed her.

He leaned back and studied her flushed face and closed eyes. Her beauty stirred him, sure, but this went deeper than that. He was nearly undone by the look of relaxed happiness she wore and felt a rush of masculine pride. *He'd* put that smile on her face. *He'd* drawn out the sensual woman hidden inside the scared and tense shell.

He dropped small kisses along her jaw, ending at her ear, where he nipped the lobe. "After we find your dress, we're going underwear shopping," he whispered.

"I don't need underwear." She pulled at his shirt. "I just need you." Her lips were next to his ear, her words a low, breathy whisper. "Inside me."

Good Lord. He felt a painful ache as she again surprised him with her alluring, wanton nature. Perhaps she'd boxed herself up for so long and, now freed, was no longer containing her sexuality. Whatever the reason, he liked it. A lot.

The shop owner returned, and he reluctantly let her go. "This will look wonderful with Ms. Kesling's pale skin and dark hair." She held up a floor-length crimson silk evening gown. The shoulders were nothing more than thin straps of silver beads, and the low V-shaped bodice was entirely covered in red and silver beads. At the waist, the beading tapered into points that became thin strands of vertical silver that trailed down and disappeared in the uneven, frothy hem.

"It's...beautiful," Erica said, reverently running her

fingers over the dazzling beadwork. The look in her eye told him she wanted the dress, even though it wasn't practical, even though the cost was obscene. They'd finally found a dress frugal Erica couldn't resist.

"It's Escada," the saleswoman said. "A new design, destined to be knocked off, but this is an original."

Erica pulled her hand back. "No. I can't—"

Lee smiled. This was in all likelihood the only true example of a mouth saying no while eyes said yes. He placed a finger under her champagne glass and tilted it to her lips. "Relax. Drink your champagne. Try it on."

She took a large gulp and couldn't possibly have tasted the French vintage.

He took a seat while she slipped behind a curtained wall to don the gown. A few minutes later, she returned in glittering red and silver. Hit in the gut by how stunning she was, he choked on champagne and suffered a coughing fit, making his eyes water. The beaded bodice hugged her breasts and threatened to overflow, guaranteeing every heterosexual male eye would follow her all night long. The silk fabric draped over her hips; the lines of silver beads accentuated her natural curves.

The coughing eased. "I believe that's where the word 'breathtaking' comes from." He turned to the saleswoman. "She needs shoes."

The woman opened a box already in her hands. "How about these?" The high heels had thin straps of silver beading, and the red silk matched the dress.

"Perfect," he said. He touched the delicate glass beads and smiled at Erica. "Close enough to a glass slipper." But by midnight, his identity would be the one revealed.

After completing the purchase, they left the boutique. Lee held her hand as they headed for the lingerie shop up the street.

"How much was it?" she asked.

"You don't want to know." She'd freak out if she knew the dress, shoes, and evening bag had cost several thousand dollars. The price was excessive, but the dress was exactly what she needed for Saturday night. The party was important. More than she knew. Possibly even more than he realized. He just hoped the armor of an exceptional gown would protect her.

❋

*U*nderwear shopping was sheer torture for Erica. She wanted to buy the first items she could find, head home, and drag Lee into the bedroom. But he made her try on bras. And camisoles. And negligees.

"Lee, I don't need this much underwear. What I need is clothing for work."

His eyes turned liquid sexy. "You can wear these to work. I'll go insane knowing you're wearing a silk teddy under your shapeless, boring outfits."

She grabbed a thong off the nearest display table and shot it at him. He caught it and held it up. "Good idea. Grab five more of these."

Finally, she'd selected enough items to please him. She studied him as he signed the credit card slip. She'd never met a man so at ease with dressing a woman. How did he know so much about women's clothing? "Do you have sisters?" she asked as they left the shop.

"Sisters? No. Why?"

"You're awfully comfortable shopping for women's clothing. But you're too young to have had many long-term relationships."

"I started young."

"Hmmm… You're handsome enough, but you know computers too well, and you must have gone through a terrible awkward stage when you shot up to six-five. Then there's the debate team. Nope. I don't believe you. You were a high school geek."

He tried to look offended, but his eyes were laughing. "Not all programmers are geeks."

"No. But the really good ones are. Let's face it, if nerds could get laid, they wouldn't spend so much time playing computer games."

He chuckled. "I'm tempted to play *Tomb Raider* when we get home to prove you wrong."

"When you could have sex with a real archaeologist? I don't think so."

"True." He grabbed her hand and pulled. "Walk faster. I've had a hard-on for hours. I can't take it anymore."

She laughed. They began walking at a brisk pace, but by the time they were within a block of the Watergate, they'd worked their way up to a jog. Then he looked at her, a devilish glint in his eye and he took her hand and pulled her into a flat-out run. By the time they reached the elevator, she was winded and laughing hard.

The elevator doors opened onto their floor, and again they ran, racing each other to the apartment. Inside, Lee closed the door and leaned against the panel. "Get your panties off, woman." He undid his belt. "If I don't bury myself deep inside you soon, I'm going to make a mess and disappoint us both."

She laughed and helped free him from his pants. Her lips brushed against his. "Don't worry. I'm not wearing panties. The last time I was in the dressing room, I took them off. You wanted commando, you got it."

He pulled up her skirt and groaned when his hands touched bare skin. "You just ran through the streets of Georgetown in a short skirt without underwear?"

"Why do you think I was laughing so hard? One wrong step and people were going to get a show."

He slid his hands over her butt, pressing her against his erection. "Wall or floor?" he asked against her lips.

"Wall," she gasped as his fingers slid inside her.

He pulled a condom from his pocket just before his pants dropped to the ground. He ripped the foil package open, rolled the condom on, and entered her on the same forward thrust. "God, you're so wet," he murmured.

With her back braced against the wall, she wrapped her legs around his waist and tucked her head into his neck, fighting embarrassment. Was she too hot for him? Was it a sign of her neediness? She didn't want him to know how much she needed him. This.

He must have sensed her reaction, because he whispered in her ear, "Look at me."

She met his gaze. He thrust into her again. She closed her eyes.

His tongue slid into her mouth, copying the rhythm of his body. He lifted his lips. "Open your eyes."

She complied.

His eyes burned into hers. "You were hot and ready"—he slid deep inside her to punctuate his words—"and you feel… incredible. There's nothing sexier than having you ready— just from thinking about me—before I even touched you. I feel like a god right now." He slid into her again, closing his own eyes this time.

"You are a god right now," she said. *This is just sex. Hot, hard, incredible, but sex and nothing more.* Her legs tightened around him. "Oh God," she groaned as shock waves of pleasure spiraled through her.

He held her against the wall as his body shuddered with release. She cupped his face between her hands and kissed him, sucked on his tongue, breathed him in, enjoyed every bit of this perfect moment, this perfect man.

He lifted his mouth from hers and stared into her eyes. "I'm sorry, Erica. For how I questioned you last night." He was serious. She could see it in his eyes, in the sad twist of his mouth. "I really am falling in love with you."

Her heart thudded. She was so damn tempted to say the words back. She settled for what she could say. "I forgive you." She even meant it.

He smiled, but his eyes clouded over. Would her unwillingness to love him back drive him away?

She kissed him again. Forgiveness tasted savory, a sauce that intensified an already rich flavor.

The rest of the afternoon and evening was a sensuous blur. All she could give him, all she could take, was today. No one had ever stuck by her through rough times, and she knew come Saturday, she was in for very rough times.

❀

*I*n the early hours of the morning, she woke up alone in the bedroom. "Lee?" she called.

No answer. She tumbled out of bed. He couldn't be in the connecting bathroom; she'd have heard him. She made her way to the hallway, still more asleep than awake. He wasn't in the guest bathroom either.

The click of a computer keyboard gave her the first clue as to his whereabouts. She padded to the den, leaned against the doorjamb, then shut her eyes tight to block the bright overhead light. "You'd better not be playing *Tomb Raider*, or I'm going to feel insulted."

"I didn't mean to wake you." She heard him get up, then heard a soft click, and the red inside her eyelids turned black.

She dared to open her eyes. "Thanks," she muttered in the dark room. His arms slipped around her, and she pressed her face against his warm chest. "What are you doing at the computer? What time is it?"

"Four. I couldn't sleep and decided to work on JT's database. I'm behind."

"I knew you were a geek. Only a computer nerd turns to programming when he can't sleep." He smelled like Lee: a warm, rich, masculine scent that was both sexy and comforting.

His chest shook with laughter. "That's my Erica. Even half-asleep, she insults me. Is it any wonder I'm in love with her?"

She shook her head and pulled away from him. "This is just lust. But I'm too tired to argue. You coming back to bed?"

"No, but you should sleep. I'll wake you at five thirty so we can work out together." He kissed the top of her head, and she left, smiling at the thought of sparring with him.

She was drifting back to sleep when she sat bolt upright. An image from the computer monitor had seared into her brain, but it had been too brief a flash for her to register what she'd seen while she stood groggily in the hall.

Lee had been viewing a photograph of the Bassetki statue base of Naram-Sin of Akkad, which had been looted from the Iraq museum in 2003. The name of the piece of art was burned into her mind as indelibly as the image on the computer screen. She'd researched the artifact after finding a picture of it in Jake's cabin. The same picture Lee had been looking at a moment ago—the picture she had found with the envelope she'd taken from Jake's cabin.

The envelope she'd sent to a DNA lab on Wednesday.

Chapter Thirty-Eight

$\mathcal{L}$ ee heard the bedroom door slam against the wall. Alarm raced through him. Was Erica okay? He bolted to the hall and caught her as she flung herself from the bedroom and into his arms.

"Sweetheart, what happened?"

Her eyes were wide with fear. "What are you working on?"

A wave of cold dread ran through him. Had she seen the computer screen when she surprised him before? He'd hacked the cell phone that sent the message about SARAC and had recovered deleted photo files, which were year-old snapshots of Middle Eastern artifacts. Had she recognized a photo? Could she be in on the smuggling?

"What do you mean? What's wrong?"

She shook her head and seemed to recover herself. Some of the fear left her eyes. "I want to know what you're working on for JT." She took a breath. "I saw the photo on the screen of the statue base, and I'm wondering what Mesopotamian artifacts have to do with JT's database."

Relief swept through him. She was telling the truth. For once. Too bad he couldn't do the same. "I was taking a break.

I'd been thinking about the deck of cards you said Janice has
—the ones about looting in Iraq—so I googled the Iraq
museum."

She didn't believe him; he could see it in her eyes. What
he'd been dreading had finally happened: she was suspicious
of him. She pushed him aside and entered the den.
"Show me."

"Sure." Using the mouse, he accessed his browsing history
and returned to the web page he'd viewed *after* recovering the
cell phone photo. The screen showed the official museum
photograph of the Bassetki statue base and an article about
items looted from the museum. The statue was listed as still
missing.

"This is what you were looking at?" She looked confused,
like she didn't believe him yet wanted to.

"Yes. Why?"

"I thought I saw something else."

Dammit. She was still holding out on him. Had she
helped Novak with this deal? Was she the photographer? Was
the disposable cell phone hers? It had been used Tuesday
afternoon in Alexandria, Virginia—while she was clothes
shopping, alone. Once the phone was activated, he'd locked
on and snatched all the data he could download from the
memory card before it was shut off again. He was sorting
through the data now, in hopes of identifying the owner.

He stood and wrapped his arms around her. He was stiff
as anger coursed through him. She didn't trust him, which
was maddening enough. But worse, he couldn't trust her.

What do you do when you both know the other is lying? Keep up
the pretense.

He forced himself to drop the stiffness and tightened his
arms around her. He massaged her back and murmured,
"You were half-asleep. The light was bright. I'm surprised
you saw anything at all."

Slowly, very, very, slowly, she relaxed against him.

He reached down and cupped her butt. Maybe he could distract her with sex.

She didn't respond to his touch. This was a first. And a sign distrust still went both ways.

"You should sleep," he said.

She nodded and padded away on silent feet. He closed the den door and locked it. He had a hell of a lot to do and didn't have time for more interruptions, more questions, more lies.

Christ, he may have fallen for a thief.

❂

*T*hey rode the Metro to work, both silent. Erica was in turmoil, wondering who Lee was and if he worked for Jake.

Talon & Drake had a team of people working in Iraq, and those employees could have smuggled artifacts out of the country and passed them to Sam Riversong—or someone else within the tribe—who then contacted Jake and traded Iraqi artifacts they couldn't use in the Casino's museum displays for Aztec ones they could.

It was possible JT was involved. Soon, Jake would be working with Talon & Drake. Jake could have warned JT about the need to neutralize her. Was Lee nothing more than JT's method for dealing with her? Was his sham of an internship merely their attempt to control her?

Was their entire relationship a con?

She felt sick, realizing her apartment could have been trashed to force her to move in with Lee, to make his seduction that much easier.

She studied his square jaw, chiseled cheekbones, and sculpted muscles. He was…utterly gorgeous. A handsome, enticing man. Had JT spent a fortune hiring this male model to play intern and seducer?

If that was the case, at least she'd gotten JT's money's worth. The man was an amazing lover. And she'd been falling for him.

He smiled and dropped a hand to her knee, giving it a comforting squeeze. Or rather, it would be comforting if she didn't believe he was in league with the scumbag who'd destroyed her life.

She grabbed at the rush of anger and held it, massaged it, used it to squelch the river of pain that ran through her, threatening to sweep her overboard, beat her against the rocks, then spit out her lifeless body.

She didn't think she could survive another betrayal.

They arrived in Bethesda and in silence walked down Wisconsin Avenue to their high-rise office building, going straight to the lobby-level workout room, which was empty as usual at six thirty in the morning.

"Do you want to spar?" he asked.

She'd opened her body and mind to him and had been falling for him from the first moment she saw him in this very room. Her heart cracked a bit, and she said, "Yes."

She wanted to kick his ass.

With her first kick, she let him know this was no friendly sparring match. He barely blocked her follow-up punch in time. But then his eyes took on a steely glint that told her he knew exactly what she was doing.

In her haze of anger, she recognized he held back; he blocked and defended but never attacked. If he did fight back, she'd remain standing maybe ten seconds—if she were lucky.

Instead, he let her have her one-sided brawl, but finally, when she was winded, he took her down and pinned her to the mat. "What the fuck are you doing?" His face was red, furious.

"Did Jake hire you to screw me?" She hated the hurt in her voice.

His eyes narrowed. "Honey, I'm screwing you for free. Hell, I should pay *you*."

She punched him in the jaw and cursed the glove that softened the blow. It was the first hit to make it past his razor-sharp reflexes, and she had a feeling he'd allowed the punch, even goaded her into it.

"Care to tell me *why* you think I'm working for Novak?"

"You were looking at a picture I found in Jake's cabin on his boat. That photo is the reason I quit working for him."

Relief entered his eyes; then his whole demeanor changed. He sat up, pulling her upright along with him. "You're sure the photo is Jake's? I've been trying to figure out who took it. Why did that picture make you quit?"

She wanted to ask him a dozen questions, but knew she'd get more information if she answered his first. "He didn't take the photo; he received it—in hard copy. I found it in Jake's cabin and realized he was a high-end dealer in black market antiquities, so I fled his boat in the middle of the night."

He smiled a blinding, dazzling smile that had the power to alter the rotation of the earth. Her piece of it, anyway. "Shortcake, I wish you'd told me that before." He kissed her with an urgency, a passion that would have flattened her if she didn't have so many questions of her own.

Dammit, his kiss felt real. His fervor felt real. His intensity couldn't be feigned.

Could it?

Her lock on her emotions shattered and she kissed him back. She needed him to be real. If another person took a chunk from her soul without giving anything back, she'd cease to exist.

She ended the kiss. "Your turn. Why do you have a copy of Jake's photo?"

"He wants to team with Talon & Drake but could be bad for the company, and you're clearly terrified of him.

I'm certain he was behind you being trapped in the Thermo-Con house, even if he does have an alibi. So I hacked into his cell phone to see if I could find text messages that could have been the order to trap you in the basement or anything to show JT that would convince him to stop Drake from teaming with Novak. But his phone was empty. So I hacked into the phone he's received several text messages from."

She gasped. He'd been protecting her? She felt a painful ache in her chest. "I'm not surprised his phone was blank. Jake's very careful with technology. We weren't allowed internet or smartphones on his boat." She studied him. "How did you hack his phone?" Her mind began to race. This could be a very good lie to win back her trust. "Prove it. Show me."

"No."

The hope that had been building deflated. "Why not?"

"When I hacked into his phone, I was committing a crime. I won't have you party to that, and I won't do it here, using Talon & Drake's network."

She was about to argue the first point, but his second stopped her cold. The only thing she knew for certain about Lee was he had strong ties to JT and the senator; he wasn't likely to risk a lawsuit against the company.

But he could help me find the person who bought the Aztec artifacts.

"You did it from JT's condo."

His mouth hardened. "No."

"If you won't show me, how can I believe you?"

"You're just going to have to trust me."

"I ran out of trust a long time ago."

"Dammit, Erica, I love you, but I refuse to be held accountable for what others have done to you. You're just going to have to give me the benefit of the doubt on this." He turned and walked away from her, slamming the door to the men's locker room.

*L*ee was in a foul mood by the time he sat at his desk a half hour later. He wanted to go back to the workout room and beat on the bag, but he had work to do.

Yesterday afternoon, he'd looked into her eyes after hot, hard sex and felt a rush of pride and possession. She was everything he'd ever wanted, and he knew she was falling for him too.

The apology burst from him, unbidden and unwelcome —not when he couldn't back it up by coming clean with her —but he'd been sincere. The words had come from the depths of his heart. Then she'd done the unthinkable and accepted his impetuous words. She'd forgiven him.

The last thing he deserved from her was forgiveness.

Now today, he'd lied to her and demanded her trust in the same breath. When she learned who he was tomorrow, she'd feel betrayed in a way that could—would—make reconciliation impossible.

And there was nothing he could do to soften the coming blow.

Jesus, she messed with his mind. He'd fallen hard and fast, but she could be the very person he was spying and hacking to find. He wanted to believe she was innocent, but she hadn't told him everything—and he couldn't trust her until she did. Was he in love with a beautiful, sexy criminal?

He didn't believe it.

But was that simply because he didn't *want* to believe it?

She sat five feet away at her own desk, staring at him as if she searched for what to say, on the defensive now. But if she were truly innocent, then every apology from her would be another nail in his coffin when she learned the truth.

His cell phone rang. It was JT. "SARAC arrived in Norfolk early this morning on an aircraft carrier. I was notified in time to contact the FBI, who sent out a team to search the crane as soon as the carrier made port."

"And?" Lee said, feeling his stomach clench, knowing from JT's tone he wouldn't like what was coming.

"They didn't find a damn thing."

He swore. They were back to square one. "How is that possible?"

Erica glanced up from her computer.

"I was hoping you could tell me," JT said.

He got up and left the room. He'd only had three hours of sleep before he got up to comb through the phone's data, and his brain wasn't capable of maintaining his cover in front of Erica while talking to JT. He found an empty conference room and closed the door. "Okay, I'm alone now. What happened?"

"Exactly nothing. They searched the crane top to bottom. It was clean."

"Fuck. So where is the Bassetki statue?" He'd sent JT an email to let him know they might be looking for an extremely heavy statue base, which thieves had dragged across the marble steps at the Iraq Museum, breaking every one.

"The statue could have arrived in an earlier shipment. The photo was taken a year ago—which could be when the smuggling started." JT paused. "Erica worked for Novak a year ago and got a job at Talon & Drake not long after. She's the link."

He wanted to defend her. When she'd told him about the photo this morning, he'd seized on her story as a sign of her innocence and had kissed her in relief. In hope. But she knew more than she'd told him, a damning omission.

To hell with his feelings; he had a job to do. He reflected on their night together. The first crack in his cover had come when she saw the photo on his computer at four a.m. "What time was the search?"

"Six a.m."

Christ. She could have tipped off an accomplice. Another thought chilled him. "Does Drake know the crane was searched? Does he know you're aware of the smuggling?"

"The FBI kept it quiet. The search happened with only a few naval officers present. But if someone leaks, we're screwed."

Lee hung up and returned to the office he shared with Erica, more disturbed than before, but he needed to make peace with her if he was to have any hope of her spilling the truth before tomorrow night when his cover was likely to be blown.

She studied him warily.

Best go with offense. "You owe me an apology." He was driving in the coffin nails himself. Later he'd ask himself if it was worth it.

She flinched and bit her lip but said nothing.

He crossed the room and stood directly in front of her, then pulled her to her feet. "I've given you my home, my body, and my heart. What more do you need from me?" He winced at his mistake in referring to his home.

"I don't know." Her shoulders drooped. She leaned her forehead against his chest. "Every time I trust, I get burned. I'm afraid."

If he were a better man, he'd goad her into hitting him again. He deserved a solid punch to the jaw. Instead, he crushed his guilty conscience with the weight of her repeated lies.

She lifted her head. Her slate eyes were liquid. Tracing her lips with his thumb, he said, "I'm afraid too. I'm terrified every time I admit I'm falling in love with you. But I still say the words because I know you need to hear them."

This was true. Just like it was true that he'd given her his home, his body, and his heart. There was some solace in the fact that he was being honest about his feelings in this attempt to win her back. He wasn't lying, not in this.

He would be true to what was between them to the full extent that he was able.

He saw a brief flash of pain before she closed her eyes. "I'm sorry, Lee. So sorry."

He placed a finger beneath her chin, gently nudging her gaze upward. "Hey. Look at me. This is going to be okay. I'm not going anywhere."

She opened her eyes and met his gaze. "Maybe you should though."

"Face it, you're stuck with me. And I'm going to keep telling you I love you until you believe it."

She gave him a weak smile. "You're not going to give up on me?"

His heart ached at the pain in her words. "Oh, Erica. No. Never." He lowered his mouth to hers and kissed her, long and hard. When he let her go, she was unsteady on her feet. She dropped back into her chair, definitely dazed, probably confused. But his again.

For now.

Which had to be good enough, because he had a job to do, and precious little time. He settled in front of his laptop to finish going through the phone's data.

An hour later, his laptop let out a soft pinging sound. His heart rate kicked up. The sound he'd been waiting for, alerting him Novak was using his phone. He ran a program, which allowed him to see Novak's screen.

A series of text messages arrived. One after the other. They'd been sent hours before but only now had Novak turned on his phone to receive them.

The first one said: *a. 18 440703.* The second one: *a. 4091209.*

After viewing several texts, it appeared the messages were paired by letter. He opened a blank spreadsheet and organized the data. Fifty text messages, twenty-five pairs. Each pair started with the number eighteen followed by a six-digit

number. The second number of the pair was always seven
digits. The six-digit numbers ranged from 440703 to 462956
and the seven-digit numbers ranged from 4091209 to
4092208.

But what did the numbers mean?

He checked the sender. A new number, one he hadn't
come across before. It would take some hacking to determine
where the texts originated from.

Jake replied to the last text message: *729 / 0300 / dwarf.*
Then the signal was lost. Lee tapped a few keys and determined Jake hadn't just shut off his phone; he'd pulled the
battery. Yes, Jake Novak was very careful with technology.
Suspiciously so. Fortunately, at least one of his accomplices
hadn't been as careful—the person had used the same disposable phone for over a year and probably felt secure having
deleted incriminating photos. Whoever it was had no idea
they were under suspicion or they'd have ditched that phone
months ago.

Had that accomplice finally changed phones, or was this a
new conspirator?

He stared at the list of numbers and reread Jake's text.
Searching for a pattern, for an explanation. The text looked
easy. Today was July twenty-seventh. Could 729 mean July
twenty-ninth, and 0300 mean three a.m.? Could it really be
that simple? Was Novak giving his accomplice the meeting
time and place for the exchange of artifacts for cash? Was
dwarf the location? An autocorrect error on wharf?

Why use a fancy code when you had no reason to believe
anyone was on to you?

Jake's text reply didn't clear Erica. She knew the old
number was compromised and could have another phone he
didn't know about. But in that situation, surely Jake would
have used a more complex code.

Who was giving artifacts and who was receiving? The
Aztec Room was set to open tomorrow, on the twenty-eighth,

meaning the Aztec artifacts Erica didn't want to admit existed had to be in place at the casino already. Was Novak brokering a sale of Iraqi artifacts at three a.m. Sunday morning, just hours after the casino room opened?

Lee's gut told him one thing: something had arrived on SARAC and had somehow made it past the inspection and into Novak's possession.

Chapter Thirty-Nine

*E*rica woke early on Saturday, feeling anxious. She looked at Lee, lying next to her, still asleep. She'd been determined to keep her distance, to remain detached and rational. But last night they'd cooked dinner together, then eaten by candlelight as he seduced her again with words, laughter, and his intense masculine charm she couldn't resist. He then offered her the one thing she needed above all else: tenderness.

In short, the sonofabitch had breached her mental barriers and made love to her. She feared she'd never be the same.

Tonight she'd see the artifacts again, and tomorrow life as she knew it would be over. Her actions would harm the senator's campaign, and Lee would probably never speak to her again. She already felt the pain of the coming heartache. But revealing—and proving—the artifacts were stolen was the only way to protect herself from Jake.

She wanted to linger in bed but forced herself to take a shower. Hot water poured over her, clearing her mind as she closed her eyes and tried to focus on what she would do when she saw the artifacts tonight. She felt a draft and opened her eyes to see Lee stepping inside the shower.

She reached for him. He didn't work for Jake. He couldn't. And they still had today. Twelve hours until the party. Twelve hours she could hold forever in her heart. After they showered, he made breakfast and insisted on serving the meal in bed. But once they were in bed again, he distracted her until the food was cold and she needed another shower.

All in all, it was a damn good morning.

In the early afternoon, she settled in front of the desktop computer in the den to check email. A spreadsheet was open in full screen mode. "Lee?" she called to him in the other room, "Can I close this file?"

"What is it?"

"It looks like a list of UTMs."

He was by her side in seconds. "What are UTMs?"

"Universal Transverse Mercators—they're coordinates, the metric version of latitude and longitude. Maryland is in Zone 18, which is the first number in every column. The six-digit number is the Easting—coordinates on the east/west line—and the seven-digit number is the Northing."

"So those are Maryland coordinates?"

"Zone 18 is bigger than Maryland. Why do you have this file open if you didn't know what it is?"

"It's something I was trying to figure out for JT. So, where are those coordinates?"

"It's easy to look up." She copied the first set of digits then minimized the file and went to a mapping website she used for projects, where she pasted the numbers in the search boxes. In seconds, a map appeared. She zoomed out to see the full area. "These coordinates are in the Atlantic Ocean, eighteen miles east of Virginia Beach."

She could see a sudden intensity in Lee's gaze as he stared at the computer screen. "Near Norfolk but in the water," he murmured. "Try another set."

The next set of coordinates came up with a location slightly east of the first.

"Now try the last set."

The last coordinates were a location nearly ten miles east of the first set. He kissed her hard on the lips. "Thanks for your help."

She smiled. "You're welcome."

"You've just given me the last piece of a puzzle." He pulled her from the chair. "I feel the need to celebrate."

She pushed him away and laughed. "You're insatiable."

"You make me insatiable. I've never been this way before."

She felt a flutter and told herself not to give in to the emotions he stirred. "That's because you spent your high school years with cyberwomen. Real women are more fun."

He picked her up and tossed her over his shoulder with a gentle smack on her butt. "Woman, I'll make you pay for taunting me with my geek past."

She laughed as he carried her down the hall. "Past? Honey, I hate to break it to you, but your geek days aren't behind you."

In the master bedroom, he tossed her on the bed. "Then this geek is about to ruin you for cool guys forever."

She reached for his belt buckle, wondering if his words were pure bravado, but discovered he wasn't boasting. And she knew he spoke the truth: he had ruined her for other men.

※

*E*rica tucked two sets of the Aztec artifact photographs into her evening bag along with the doubloons. Her fingers shook. This was it.

She checked her appearance in the floor-length mirror in the master bedroom, then took a deep breath before stepping out to meet Lee in the living room. The silk skirt of the dress brushed against her thighs and ankles in a soft, sensuous sway. She had never in her life felt more feminine, more sexy, more beautiful. More terrified.

Lee looked her up and down, his eyes showing pure carnal approval. "Stunning. Perfectly, absolutely, breathlessly stunning." He took her hand and brought it to his lips.

"You look pretty damn hot too," she said. It was true. He looked heartachingly handsome in his single-breasted black tuxedo.

"Nobody will notice me with you by my side." He touched the silver and red beads she'd threaded through her hair before pulling it back in a loose twist at the nape of her neck. "I suppose you put the beads in so I'd leave your hair alone?"

She laughed. "Will it work?"

"Tonight? Yes. When we're alone? Never." He kissed the inside of her wrist. "JT will be here any second."

"Does he know about us?" she asked. The question had been nagging at her.

"Yes. He said he saw it coming a mile away."

"Was I that transparent?"

"No. I was."

The front door opened, and JT entered with a stunning blonde dressed with equal expense and care. Upon seeing Erica, JT let out a low whistle. "Spectacular, but you wasted time putting those beads in your hair. No man is going to look above your chest."

The woman at his side elbowed him in the ribs. "Jesus, JT, have you ever heard of sexual harassment?"

His eyes softened as he looked at the blonde. "I'm not hitting on her. I'm stating a fact." He turned back to Erica. "Erica Kesling, meet Alexandra Vargas, an old friend who has graciously agreed to decorate my arm this evening."

Alexandra batted JT's shoulder. "You'd better not introduce me to everyone that way, or I'll be sure to tell the press the Talon men are a bunch of sexist pigs."

"I'm sorry, I meant to say, 'This is Alexandra, who has agreed to fill my evening with witty banter and interesting observations on the arts, mathematics, and string theory. That she looks good while doing so is irrelevant.'"

The woman smiled. "Better. But it still needs work." She grasped Erica's hand. "It's nice to meet you." She turned to Lee and kissed him on the cheek. "Lee, it's been ages."

"You're gorgeous as ever. I feel I should remind you that you can do way better than JT."

She grinned. "I know. But he's rich. And his dad might be president one day, so I keep him around in case he becomes useful."

"God, I forgot what you two are like together. What was I thinking, having us share the limousine?" JT complained with good humor.

Alexandra knew Lee. Erica wondered what the woman could tell her about her enigmatic lover.

"Erica, JT asked me to bring earrings for you to wear tonight." From a small jewelry bag, she pulled out a pair of diamond studs that had to be at least a carat each.

"I couldn't possibly—I'd be terrified of losing them."

"You lose them, JT'll buy me a new pair. Won't you, pumpkin?" She said "pumpkin" with false sweetness, making the endearment ironic. Erica liked her more with each second.

"Absolutely, muffin." JT spoke in the same saccharine tone.

They headed to the limousine parked in front of the Watergate. The smell of hot asphalt hung in the humid air, and Erica felt the stares of total strangers as she climbed into the vehicle. With the stares came a strangely powerful feeling. As if she was someone important and not just in the company of important people. The feeling was a heady ego boost when she needed it most.

She clutched her evening bag which held the key to her salvation. Tonight, people would pay attention to her.

She supposed that's why Senator Talon had wanted her to sparkle tonight—to show that everyone associated with him and his company, even a lowly staff archaeologist, was special. It was too bad it would backfire on him when she revealed the truth about the artifacts.

Lee sat next to her and draped an arm around her shoulders. JT poured champagne and passed glasses around. They toasted to a successful evening for the senator and casino.

They'd driven only a few blocks when Alexandra snapped her fingers in front of Lee's face and said, "Yo, Lee, come up for air. You're going to get drool on that spectacular cleavage and discolor the silk."

Erica was astonished to see him turn red. "How embarrassing, I'm a spider caught in my own web. I wanted Erica to wear the most dazzling, eye-catching dress possible to turn men into blithering fools. But the only fool here is me."

"Don't worry. JT'd be drooling too, if he didn't know I'd kick his ass."

JT smiled and sipped his champagne. "You both look spectacular. We men are mere mortals and quiver in your glorious radiance."

"Please. Gag me," Alexandra said. "What you really mean is we look elegant yet fuckable, that perfect combination of sexy and class."

Erica laughed, feeling at ease, something she hadn't expected. "Alexandra, I must know, what is your day job?"

"You know that thing JT said about string theory? That was true. I'm a theoretical physicist. We work along the edges of known mathematics to describe nature, movement, time."

"She'd make an ideal trophy wife," JT said, "because she's brilliant and beautiful and outshines every man she's with. But also, she's too successful to be a mere trophy, making her the greatest prize of all."

"Which is why your proposals keep falling on deaf ears, pumpkin."

"I think your problem, JT," Lee said, "is that with a woman like Alexandra, you need to play hard to get. She spends her days around science geeks who turn into incoherent fools every time she walks into the room. She's tired of attention. She's craving indifference."

"Good advice. I'll give that a try." JT turned his sharp brown eyes to Erica. "So, you doing anything after the party tonight?"

She nearly spit out her champagne. "You're on your own, boss." Then she smiled, getting into the rhythm of the banter. "I don't date up the hierarchy. I prefer interns I can dominate."

"Ohh," Alexandra squealed. "Domination is such fun. Why this one time, I—" JT's hand covered her mouth.

"Muffin, you really shouldn't share that story." He shook his head at Erica and Lee. "Scientists. No social skills."

JT then kissed Alexandra as though they were alone, and Erica realized he was in love with her.

She wondered how much of the teasing was true. Had Alexandra really turned down several proposals? In that moment, JT became more human to her. Not an intimidating boss, not the son of a presidential contender, but a man hopelessly in love with a woman who refused him, and Erica felt sorry for him.

The ride continued, as did the laughter and banter. If JT was nervous about the coming announcement, he didn't show it. For her part, Erica grew increasingly anxious as they drew nearer the casino.

Lee's lips caressed her collarbone. "What are you thinking about?" he whispered.

"I'm nervous."

"Don't worry. The crowd will be friendly tonight—the senator's inner circle."

"And hundreds of reporters."

"Not hundreds. A dozen or more, maybe."

"Thanks. I feel so much better now." She studied him, her heart cracking as she absorbed his handsome face, his strong presence, his possessive smile and body language. Every motion, every look, proclaimed she was his. How would he look at her after the senator made his announcement in front of stolen artifacts? What would he think after she told that same dozen reporters that someone from the tribe had knowingly purchased stolen artifacts to decorate their casino?

A frontal assault tonight, while the room was filled with reporters, was her best hope. With reporters eating up the story, the FBI would be forced to listen. And Marco couldn't attack while cameras were fixed on her. Lee would know she could have prevented the coming scandal but instead chose to cause it.

They arrived at the casino. Looking out the tinted window, she was terrified by the sight of red carpet flanked by reporters. Lee had been wrong. There were at least two dozen.

JT emerged from the limousine first, turning to help Alexandra climb out. Lee followed and performed the same service for Erica.

Cameras flashed, and she focused on the strip of carpeting she needed to follow to get inside, away from the surreal sea of faces staring at them beyond the flashing lights, cameras, and microphones. Men and women shouted questions to JT. Thirty feet of cameras, then she'd be safely at the reception that was taking place in the Pueblo Room prior to the ribbon-cutting ceremony that would open the Aztec Room.

She slid her arm through Lee's, who whispered in her ear, "We're going to pause at the blue mark and smile for some pictures. JT and Alexandra will stay outside and work the press, but we're nobodies and get to go inside."

Reporters flocked to JT, the senator's only son. He smiled and joked with the reporters. When asked direct questions about the campaign, he said he would support his father in whatever announcement he planned to make that evening.

They stopped at their mark and smiled while a dozen flashes blinded them. Lee kissed her cheek and whispered, "You're doing great, sweetheart." She was surprised to hear her name called out by a reporter but didn't catch the question.

Lee stiffened when a female reporter called his name and asked something about the senator's son. He hurried Erica down the last feet of carpet and inside the vestibule. A security guard used a handheld metal detector, then waved them through. The doors closed behind them.

The abrupt silence was a relief. "How did they know my name?" she asked.

The set of Lee's jaw made her wonder what had upset him. "The senator released the guest list, and you were named as my date."

Am I missing something? He was just a well-connected intern, right? A cold wave of apprehension hit her. Why hadn't it occurred to her to google Lee Scott until this moment? "How did they know who you are?"

He shrugged. "The Talons and Scotts go way back. C'mon. Let's get a drink."

The tuxedoed bartender was one of several she'd flirted with for information over the last months. She thought of Tommy, and acid flooded her stomach. She wished there'd been room in her beaded bag for her ubiquitous bottle of antacids, but all she'd had room for was her lipstick, ID, phone, keys, and evidence of a crime that could destroy several people and a presidential campaign.

She took a glass from the laden bar with only a slight nod

of acknowledgment to the bartender, then skirted the center of the room, studying the rapidly growing crowd. "Do you know people here?" she asked Lee.

"The only person here who matters to me is you."

Why is he being so evasive?

"Lee, who *are* you?"

"Come with me," he said and pulled her into the empty corridor that led to the Great Basin Room. They stopped near the display where she'd waited for Tommy the night he was killed. She tried to wipe that thought from her mind and instead remembered the flutter she'd felt when she'd turned and realized Lee had been the man who'd kissed her. She'd been falling for him even then.

"You want to know who I am?" he asked. He took her champagne glass and set it on a windowsill next to his own. "I'm a man who's crazy about you."

"What are you to the senator?"

"I'm an old family friend, that's all." He kissed her, slowly, deeply.

She found the will to pull away. "You're what—twelve years younger than JT? Yet you talk to each other like you've been friends forever, like you're equals, not CEO and intern."

"You, my dear, are a snob if you think JT can't be friends with me because I'm an intern."

"That's not what I mean—"

He kissed her again. "I don't care. I love you even though you're a snob."

"I'm not—" But his mouth covered hers once more, distracting her with heat. She could no longer remember what she'd asked him. Seconds after that, she forgot where she was. She was dangerously close to forgetting her own name.

"Feel me, Erica," he murmured, pressing his hips against hers. "I've made love to you countless times in the last few days, and still I want you. I can't get enough of you."

"This is just lust," she said, hoping to convince herself.

"No. It's love."

She pressed her fingers against his lips. "That's not true." Every time he said he loved her, a piece of her broke. She wanted this to be real. She wanted to love him back. She wanted this to last. But it wasn't, she couldn't, and it wouldn't.

"It is. I love you. I'm crazy about you. Remember that." The last words sounded pained. "Always remember that." His lips traced her throat. "Everything I have, everything I am is yours. I only want one thing in return: tell me how you feel."

"No." But she kissed him, hoping her actions would suffice. Her kiss was hard, full of pent-up emotion and he responded in kind.

His lips left hers to explore the column of her throat, then moved lower to her overflowing cleavage. Heat slammed through her, overpowering her. She wished she could show him with her body how she felt, because she was afraid to say the words.

"Say it, Erica. Tell me."

She felt wild, ready to drag him farther into the darkened corner, to hell with her hair, to hell with her dress, to hell with the party going on in the next room.

"Say it."

His touch had become air, his kisses water. Her survival depended upon him. "I…"

"Say it. *Please.*"

And then the words broke free, as if of their own accord, "I love you, Lee."

And she did, dammit. She was mad for him.

His lips found hers again, a kiss of joy, satisfaction. Different from the kisses they'd shared before. He leaned his forehead against hers. "Thank you." He smiled with triumph.

She playfully pushed at his shoulders. "Don't let it go to your head."

He placed her hand on his crotch, holding her fingers against his erection. "Too late." She caressed him. His eyes closed, and he let out a groan of pleasure.

"Do we need to go back to the party?" She wanted to escape, and not just because she wanted to make love with him. If she left now, she wouldn't see the artifacts. She wouldn't have to ruin this perfect night with accusations that would make her a pariah.

He took her hand and led her farther down the corridor to a restroom. "You need to fix your lipstick."

Inside, she faced herself in the mirror. In her flushed face she saw a slight resemblance to her mother—not the woman she'd been in the last years of her life but the woman her mom had been before Erica's father died. Losing the love of her life had destroyed her mother. Erica had already lost everything that mattered to her. Could she survive losing Lee?

If she couldn't, she'd have to let Jake get away with his crime.

For the first time in a year, she didn't want to redeem herself. She didn't want revenge. Redemption and revenge would cost her the one thing she wanted more: a life, a future, a chance at happiness. Lee.

Chapter Forty

$\mathcal{B}$y the time they rejoined the party, Erica felt drunk, but not on champagne. She was giddy, happy. Crazy in love. Lee looked at her with fervent eyes, and the air between them crackled with electricity, the buzz of energy that came with intense feelings.

She'd made a decision. She wasn't going to give up her chance at happiness tonight. For once she'd take the safe route and wouldn't fight the lonely fight. She would remain silent.

After the party, she'd tell Lee everything, and together they'd find a way to keep her safe.

They circulated among the guests, talking with politicians, pundits, and celebrities. Lee introduced her to US Attorney Curt Dominick, whom he described as an old friend. Her mood was so high, not even Curt's speculative gaze could break through the warm cocoon that enveloped her.

The senator, already the front runner for his party's nomination, hadn't made his entrance yet, but the excitement in the room was a testament to the facts of his candidacy: he was a charismatic minority from a hardscrabble background with enough experience to make him the ideal candidate. His supporters considered him a shoo-in.

Edward Drake walked up and clasped her hands like they were longtime friends. "Erica Kesling," he said. "The senator told me he invited you. I wasn't aware you knew him."

"My work on the Thermo-Con project brought me to his attention."

Drake cocked his head. "Thermo-Con. Is that the concrete house on the reservation? I didn't know Joe was interested in that project." He looked at Lee and did a double take. "You look familiar. Do you work for Talon & Drake?"

She could think of at least two instances when Lee had stood right next to Drake in the office, yet he hadn't noticed the six-foot-five intern. Hard to imagine, but she was aware of Lee on a primal level and therefore wasn't a reliable judge of his impact on other people.

He held out his hand. "Lee Scott."

A look of surprise and recognition crossed Drake's face. "Oh. I get it now." He chuckled. "Joe's invitation didn't have to do with Thermo-Con, but you can tell people that, if it makes you feel better." He walked away, leaving Erica dumb-founded.

"What the hell did he mean by that?" she asked.

Lee snagged two fresh glasses of champagne from a passing waiter. "There's something I need to tell you."

No kidding.

A man approached and said, "Lee Scott, the senator needs to speak with you."

She stifled her groan of frustration. She had unlawful carnal knowledge of the man but had no idea how everyone here knew his name.

Lee kissed her cheek. "I'll be back in a minute." He followed the aide.

Dammit. What had he been about to say? She scanned the room for Alexandra, perhaps the one person who would tell her how Lee was connected to the Talon family. Given everyone's tight lips and vague statements, she'd assume he was the senator's illegitimate son, but Lee didn't look like he had an ounce of Talon in him.

She straightened her spine and began to circulate the room, then heard a low whistle behind her. "Cream Puff, you do clean up well."

She spun around to face Jake. He wasn't the sun-bleached, tanned treasure hunter she'd spent a summer with, but a polished, Armani-wearing businessman.

She smiled stiffly. "Jake. I'm surprised the senator would risk inviting you."

"You're finally getting your spine back. You know, I really hated breaking your spirit."

"You never broke my spirit. I'm just methodical. There is a phrase, 'revenge is a dish best served cold.'"

He grabbed her arm and squeezed her biceps. "Don't threaten me, Erica. You've never really understood the situation. I'm your only hope."

"Let go, or I'll scream."

He dropped her arm instantly. She felt a surge of power and silently thanked the gown and Lee for making sure people would notice her in this room full of important people.

"Screwing the senator's stepson has made you cocky. But soon you'll be dumped by both Scott and Talon & Drake. Then you'll need me."

He stalked off, and she stared after him, stunned. His insinuation was chilling, but it was nothing compared to the maelstrom he'd created in calling Lee the senator's stepson.

Erica had seen several profiles of the senator and his wife on TV, and every one of them mentioned the senator's current wife—his third—was childless. She wasn't Lee's mother. JT's mother was wife number one. Lee's mother had to be wife two. Her head began to throb. Why the hell hadn't he told her?

She saw Alexandra on the far side of the room. She headed toward the vivacious blonde, but before she'd taken three steps, the announcer asked everyone to move the party to the front room. The crowd shifted en masse. She had no choice but to follow.

Sam Riversong stepped onto the dais set up in front of the Aztec Room with a microphone in his hand. "Good evening," he said. "Welcome to the Menanichoch Nation."

The crowd applauded.

She took a shallow breath and tried to calm herself. Had Lee *lied* to her or just omitted the part about being Joseph Talon's stepson?

Was there a difference?

"We're all gathered here for a very special evening," Riversong continued, "and I know you didn't come here to listen to me, so I'm going skip the flowery words and just hand the mic over to the man we're all here to support tonight. It is my great pleasure to introduce to you my brother in spirit, fellow tribal member, and the best senator this country has ever seen, Joseph Talon."

The room broke out in ecstatic applause worthy of a sporting event, and Joseph Talon took the microphone. An arm slipped around Erica's waist, and she felt a light kiss on her neck. She glanced at Lee and felt choking anger.

"I need to tell you something," he murmured under the sound of the crowd. "Joe just told me he's going to introduce me—"

"Jake told me. How nice of your *stepdad* to include you," she said through gritted teeth. A pool of raw, burning, ferocious hurt simmered inside her.

His eyes changed from wary to urgent. "I love you, Erica. Remember that."

"Bullshit." If he loved her, he'd have told her who he was.

Her eyes blurred. She grasped at the anger. Heartache would break her, but anger would get her through the next three seconds, three minutes, three hours.

Back in control, she faced the senator, who waited for the crowd to quiet.

"Thank you," Joseph Talon said. "It is such a joy to be in this room tonight, as I see here family, friends, and colleagues who give my life and work meaning. I have a few words I wish to say before I cut the ribbon to open up the newest addition to the Menanichoch Casino."

An expectant hush fell over the crowd. Flashes went off from the press area at the side of the room. "As you all know by now, I came from nothing. A nobody orphan raised in an Indian boarding school. I didn't have a home, a family, or even hope. When my school burned down, I had nowhere to go. But my good friend Sam Riversong gave me a home, the people of the Menanichoch tribe became my family, and at long last I discovered hope. The Menanichoch sent me to college, where I met Edward Drake, a professor of engineering who took me under his wing and encouraged me. Later, Edward and I started a company, an engineering firm, Talon & Drake. I'm immensely proud of the company. It has grown over the years into a multimillion-dollar business with clients all over the world." He paused. "Not bad for a boy from nowhere. Not bad for 'a stupid Indian kid.' That's a quote, by the way, said often by the headmaster at the Indian school.

"When I joined the senate, I was pleased my son, JT, took over as CEO of Talon & Drake. JT has made me proud, and in the dozen years since he took over, he's doubled the size of the business. Now my good friend and mentor, Edward Drake, is retiring from his position as head of the Bethesda office."

Lee's lips brushed her ear as he whispered, "I'm sorry. I will explain later."

She jerked away from him and bumped against a woman to her right. Murmuring an apology, she stiffened her spine and listened to the senator.

"—as important to you as it is to me," he was saying, "but please indulge a proud father. Many years ago, I was married to a wonderful woman who brought to our union a son from a previous marriage. I am a flawed man and was even more so then. I was a lousy husband and worse father. I let Talon & Drake take all my time. The marriage ended because I failed to prioritize. But my stepson didn't leave my life when my marriage dissolved twenty years ago. He forgave my flaws, my ambition, and, even though I've had no legal ties to him since he was twelve years old, he has remained my son, my friend, my supporter, and a source of great pride. Tonight, I'm pleased to announce my stepson, Lee Scott, has agreed to take over management of the Bethesda office of Talon & Drake upon Ed's retirement. Lee, please, join us up here. I want my whole family with me as I embark upon this next great journey."

The attention of the audience shifted in their direction. Lee slipped an arm around her waist. She wanted to jerk away from him again, but everyone was watching. The sonofabitch had trapped her. Again.

Lee took a step forward, and she had to go with him or create a huge, awful, appalling scene. She plastered on a smile and walked toward the dais with Lee. Coldness swept through her. She was a glacier, moving relentlessly forward. Little did Lee know she would destroy everything in their path.

"With my stepson is his girlfriend, Erica Kesling," she heard the senator say. "An archaeologist who is as brilliant as she is lovely and the perfect addition to both the Talon and the Talon & Drake families."

Christ. Joseph Talon had just *claimed* her.

She was being manipulated by masters and now had to

stand and face the crowd while reeling from the blow of having the meager facts she'd known about Lee dissolve.

She felt the heat of the lights as she tallied what she knew about him to be true.

He was no intern. He was no career student.

His name. That was all she knew.

How old was he? He'd been twelve at the time of the divorce, which had happened twenty years ago, according to the senator. Lee was thirty-two. Older than her by three years.

She'd been such a fool. So easily duped. *Of course* he was older than her. He'd done a rotten job of playing the green intern. She'd just been too overwhelmed to see the truth. She'd been so absorbed in trying to corner Jake and Sam, she'd ignored every sign.

The senator had continued speaking, and his words finally penetrated her racing thoughts. "As I start this next great adventure, it's important to look at the foundation that made me who I am and to appreciate the gifts this life has given me. I'm proud of my sons and the business I created. Talon & Drake provides a vital service, here and around the globe. This is a great nation that gives a young orphan Indian —a stupid Indian kid—the opportunity to succeed and share that success with future generations. I got where I am not only because I am intelligent and driven. I got here because people believed in me, mentored me, and supported me.

"As a nation, we've become fractured. We're struggling as a world power and divided in our beliefs, our causes. That isn't the road to success. We need to come together and support each other. We need to offer aid to other countries, to help them find the tools to end their civil wars. We need to fight poverty with more than just platitudes…"

His words faded as Erica's concentration splintered into disjointed thoughts. Several times she'd asked about his past, his connection to JT, only to be distracted by roving hands or words of love. Tonight, when she'd asked him point-blank who he was, he'd responded by coercing her into saying she loved him.

Days ago, he'd been angry with *her* for using their attraction as a weapon, but she had nothing on him; his skill at deception outdistanced hers by miles.

Lee held her hand in a viselike grip. He brushed his lips against her temple. "Keep it together, Erica."

She tightened her smile and shifted so her pointed heel came down directly on his foot.

He didn't flinch. She dug in, shifting all her weight to her heel. He released her hand and moved his foot, causing her to teeter and clutch at him to stop her fall.

His caught her so smoothly she doubted anyone noticed their scuffle.

"…I have a plan." She tuned in to the senator's speech again. "And that is why I'm running for president!"

The crowd cheered. Cameras flashed. Lee looked down at her, beaming with enough warmth to fool the world. But not her. He would never fool her again. "Clap," he whispered.

She did as instructed. She'd been dressed up and set up. She may as well play her role until she got inside the Aztec Room and saw the artifacts.

Minutes, hours, it could have been years later, the senator finally cut the ribbon, and the gathering flowed into the room. Lee kept a firm hold on her as they followed the first visitors across the threshold.

She'd waited for this for a year, but a half hour ago, she'd decided to give up her plan for redemption because she was in love. No. Because she was a fool.

No more. She gripped her evening bag, which held the photographs she would use to convince the authorities the provenance for the artifacts was false, Jake was a thief, and Sam a buyer of black market antiquities. To hell with the senator. To hell with his campaign. She owed him nothing but a fancy dress.

She nearly stumbled as a wave of pain broke through her wall of anger. Lee had pushed her to admit she loved him. A last humiliation before the truth came out.

She felt a dull, cold ache and tried to pull away from him. He didn't let her go.

The chill inside radiated outward. She looked at Lee, not bothering to hide her hostility. Who cared if a reporter saw? She hadn't created this situation. He had. He could deal with the repercussions. "If you don't take your hand off me right now, I'll scream."

He let go.

"You and Jake are more alike than I ever imagined." She headed to one of the Aztec displays, near a roulette wheel. None of the artifacts were from the shipwreck. She approached another display, near the blackjack tables. Lee followed her.

"You won't find them," he said. "They aren't here."

She turned on her heel. "Won't find what?"

"The artifacts you and Jake recovered when you worked for him."

"I didn't recover the Aztec artifacts from the shipwreck. I refused. Don't group my morals with Jake's. Or yours, for that matter."

"I'm not the enemy, Erica." The hurt in his eyes was almost touching. If she didn't know better, she'd think he had feelings.

"Don't kid yourself, Lee." Her voice caught. She took a deep breath and continued. "You're worse than Jake ever was. Jake used my name and my reputation to get a permit from the Mexican government, then smeared both after they'd served their purpose. But you screwed me to distract me, so I wouldn't figure out who you are. You used *me*."

He headed toward a doorway labeled Employees Only

and pulled her with him. "I *made love* to you because I'm crazy about you. Keeping you from figuring out who I am was just a side benefit."

She searched his face, looking for some sign he told the truth. But all she saw were the same sincere green eyes that had sucked her in when he told her he was twenty-five. When he said he loved her.

"That's what I've been all along, isn't it? A side benefit. You cooked up your little scheme with JT to infiltrate the Bethesda office so you could scope things out before Drake quit and you were installed. Lucky you, you got to play spy and get laid at the same time."

"Keep your voice down."

"No."

"*Please*, Erica. We need to work this out. If not for other reasons, then consider the fact that I'm your boss now."

The sonofabitch was already pulling rank on her. "I quit."

For a second, she thought she saw fear in his eyes. "You can't. You need your job. You're stuck with me."

She sucked in a shallow breath. "I'll sleep in the street before I work for you."

"I'd rather have you sleep with me."

She wanted to slap him. What was stopping her? She raised her hand to strike.

He caught her wrist and pulled her through the employee door. Walking with purpose down a long corridor, he dragged her behind him until they reached an office door, where he punched a number into a keypad, opened the door, and pulled her inside with him.

He slammed the door closed and pulled her against him. "Okay. Hit me. We both know I deserve it."

She swung full force, but her fist only grazed his cheekbone. He held her too close. The angle wasn't right to actually *hurt* him. "Back up," she said. "I want another shot."

He cupped his cheek. "No. I think that's enough."

"It's nowhere close to enough." She aimed for his testicles with her knee, but he pushed her against the wall and forced his legs between her thighs. She couldn't knee him.

"We need to talk."

She tried to scratch him, but he caught her wrists and pinned them to the wall on either side of her face. His grip was loose enough to not be restraining, but she couldn't scratch him or knee him. "I'm sorry, Erica. I——"

"Don't you dare! Don't you *dare* claim to love me again."

"I do——"

"Everything you've told me is a lie."

"I lied. Yes. But I had a good reason."

"A good reason to use me?" Raw pain cut through the anger. He thought he could justify what he'd done. Just like her mother. Just like Jake.

Everyone saw her as a pawn, expendable.

"I had no choice."

"You always have a choice, Lee."

He released her wrists. "Dammit, Erica, I've done a pathetic job of pretending to be an ignorant kid with you. I couldn't be the character JT and I created, because I wanted you, and you'd never give that boy the time of day."

"So you're saying this is *my fault* for being a fool and failing to see through your farce. You don't need to rub my face in it. I figured that out while the senator droned on."

"No. I'm saying I'm crazy about you." He stepped away from her. "I'm sorry I hurt you."

She rubbed her wrists. "Was it fun lying to me? Seducing me?"

"I hated every lie." He looked earnest, sounded earnest.

But she wouldn't be taken in again. "Bullshit."

He cursed under his breath. "This isn't about you or me. Hasn't it occurred to you that I could have a very real reason for pretending to be something I'm not? Have you been so self-absorbed it hasn't crossed your mind I could be doing something more important here?"

She flinched. "Tell me."

"I can't. Not yet."

After everything he'd done, he still refused to tell her why. Cold hurt gripped her. "You won't get a chance later."

His eyes flashed with alarm. As if he was afraid she meant it. He took a deep breath. "We need to rejoin the party. If you have any respect for the senator, please go out there and smile and play your role."

"Arm candy to the senator's stepson."

"No. You aren't a decoration. You're everything I want."

"Are you so desperate you need to sink to this sort of deception just to get a date?"

He smiled, his mouth crooked and sad. "Only with you."

Her head pounded. She was sick with heartache and fear. "Where are the artifacts?"

"JT talked to Riversong, who, I assume, removed them."

"Where are they?"

"I don't know. Probably long gone—so they won't be able to hurt the campaign."

She hadn't told Lee the truth because she was afraid the artifacts would disappear—which was exactly what had happened. She had nothing on Jake. Nothing on Marco.

Nobody but herself and the people who illegally bought and sold them knew the artifacts even existed. That was why she'd never been able to go to the FBI. No artifacts, no crime.

The FBI wouldn't expend energy searching for items that had been stolen from a place where they lacked jurisdiction without solid proof the items actually existed.

She would never be rid of Jake or his threats.

Rage, hurt, and fear battled for primacy in her fractured mind. What the hell was she going to do?

Logic told her she was stuck with Lee for the next few hours. Jake was here. He couldn't touch her while she was

with Lee. She pushed off the wall. "I'll play your date; then
we're through. I never want to see you again." She turned
toward the door.

"I'm not giving you up without a fight, Erica." His voice
was low, husky. Full of pain.

No, that was probably wishful thinking on her part.

"You've already lost." And he'd taken her down with him.
Anger spiked anew, and she whirled to face him. "When you
told JT to have the Aztec artifacts removed, you chose a
campaign over me. Those artifacts were my only chance to
protect myself from Jake and Marco. *That's* why I didn't tell
you or the senator the truth. Marco was in the restaurant,
listening to every word I said."

He reached for her, but she backed away. "I'll protect
you."

The thought of depending on him, seeking solace in his
arms was tempting. But it was just another lie. "Earlier
tonight, I would have taken you up on that offer. But you
aren't who I thought you were. I'd rather face Jake alone than
be with you." She spun on her heel and left.

Alone again. Just as she'd always been.

Needing to regroup before returning to the party, she
found a restroom and collapsed onto a love seat in the
lounge area. A sob bubbled up from deep in her chest. She
couldn't cry. If she allowed one tear, it would be followed
by great, racking waves of grief. Over a year of pent-up
hurt and anger, starting with her mother's betrayal and
ending with Lee's, waited for release. She couldn't let it
out now.

Several minutes later, the door opened, and Alexandra
stepped inside. "Erica? Lee said you might need company."

"How much do you know?"

"Not much." Alexandra sat next to her on the sofa. "I
knew Lee was supposed to be your intern, and I wasn't
supposed to mention Lee and JT had been stepbrothers."

"Did it bother you?" Erica asked, resenting the woman's complicity.

"Yes."

"Then why did you go along with it?"

"I knew there would be a good reason. JT and Lee operate on a different level, Erica. Talon & Drake holds huge international contracts, and Joe is making his bid to be the most powerful man in the world. Something very important must be happening in the Bethesda office for Lee to pretend to be an intern."

"What is Lee? Besides the senator's stepson, I mean. Is he an engineer?"

"He's a computer and cell phone security specialist. One of his biggest clients is the Department of Defense. He's very, very good."

She closed her eyes. Lee was a successful businessman. That made so much more sense than his slacker intern persona. She was such a fool.

"He may not be an engineer, but he'll be an excellent manager for the Bethesda office," Alexandra continued. "Brilliant move to have him replace Drake. Keeps it all in the family until the election is over."

"I'm sick of games and strategies," Erica said. "I'm sick of being a pawn."

"Pawns are more powerful than you think. Pawns who cross the board safely become queen."

Her head throbbed. "I don't want to be queen. I only wanted a chance at redemption so I could look at my father's portrait without shame. So I could work without fear of being fired."

"Your boyfriend is head of your office. There isn't a chance in hell you'll be fired."

At last, an opportunity to benefit from nepotism. The thought made her ill. "He's not my boyfriend."

"Then you're a fool."

She grimaced. "That goes without saying."

"Why do you need to redeem yourself?"

Erica sighed. She felt strange, realizing she could talk freely about her past. "There's a man here tonight. His name is Jake Novak. Officially, he's an underwater salvage expert, but really he's a thief and a fence. I was blackballed from archaeology because I worked for him."

"I met him. He invited JT and me to a party he's having on his boat next weekend."

"His boat?" She felt a surge. "*Andvari* is here? Already?" Jake's business was based out of California. Sailing from Oaxaca to Maryland would have been hugely expensive. The navy project timeline allowed plenty of time to bring the boat around if Talon & Drake won the contract, so why had he moved the boat already?

"Yes, that's the name. I gather he's teaming with Talon & Drake on a proposal. He's planning a reception on *Andvari* for the team."

Erica's mind began to race. "Do you know where the boat is moored?"

"It's here—at the Menanichoch marina."

And suddenly, Erica knew.

Talon & Drake had a contract in Iraq, with shipments of supplies going back and forth. Over the water. The Menanichoch Nation had a casino with great money-laundering opportunities. Someone at Talon & Drake was shipping artifacts back from Iraq, selling them through Novak, and laundering the money through the casino.

Lee had a list of UTMs, and all the coordinates were in the Atlantic Ocean, near Norfolk. Someone had tossed artifacts overboard from a Talon & Drake shipment, then recorded the UTMs for the drop sites so Jake could use his treasure-hunting vessel loaded with side-scan sonar and dive equipment to pluck the goodies from the water.

Had Lee been sent in by JT to find the Talon & Drake

connection? With a sinking feeling, she understood her past with Jake made her the most likely suspect.

Then a worse thought occurred to her. Lee could have been placed in the office to facilitate—not stop—the smuggling. She stood up. "I have to go."

"Oh no, you don't," Alexandra said. "You're going back to the party. The senator introduced you as part of his family. Your absence has probably already been noticed."

The need to find Jake's boat overwhelmed her. Had he already used the UTMs to collect the artifacts? She had to search *Andvari*.

She had one last chance to save herself.

Chapter Forty-One

*R*elief filtered through Lee when Erica returned to the Aztec room. He'd begun to wonder if she'd managed to sneak out of the building. She made a beeline for him and deliberately took his arm. She'd decided to play along.

She smiled prettily and said the right things as they circulated among the guests, showing no sign of the tension that coursed through her, but Lee could feel anger in the fingers that gripped him. He could see hurt in her cold smile. She never once spoke directly to him.

He hated seeing the pain in her eyes and being the recipient of her frosty glare. If only he could tell her the truth. But he couldn't. Not yet. He had no choice but to endure her animosity.

He wanted to believe she was innocent, but she'd never really told him what had happened in Mexico. There were gaps in her story. As long as doubt remained, he couldn't tell her about the smuggling or the employee who'd been murdered in Baghdad.

He had a job to do. His cover was blown, but his position was improved. Now he would have access to every network file, every company email, no hacking or pretending required.

Thanks to Erica, he knew why SARAC had been empty when it was searched. He even knew how the artifacts were recovered, but he still had to figure out where the smugglers were meeting in just a few hours. He needed to know what "dwarf" meant.

"Give me money," Erica said in a cold voice. "I want to gamble."

Lee smiled. The woman he'd met two weeks ago would never, ever have demanded cash from him so she could gamble. He reached for his wallet and handed her three hundred dollars. "Do I get to keep your winnings?"

Her gaze raked him. "I don't intend to win."

She sat on a backless stool at the roulette table, her spine stiff. He longed to massage away her tension, her anger. He stood a few paces behind and watched her, content to appreciate the view of her bare skin. If this was all he could have of her, he'd take it.

Jake Novak approached the table. Lee moved forward but stopped and allowed Novak to take the seat beside Erica.

The man looked askance at her. His gaze settled on her cleavage. Lee's hands fisted.

Erica kept her gaze on the table. "Look what the cockroach dragged in."

"Tsk, tsk," Jake said. "Now that I'm teaming with Talon & Drake, we need to get along. As the only underwater archaeologist they've got on staff"—he turned his head, directing his words to Lee, obviously hoping Erica's background was news to him—"we're going to be working together. Close together."

Lee wanted to tell the prick that he'd never team with Talon & Drake but held back, curious to see where this conversation would go.

Erica continued to focus on the table, but Lee noticed her

finger nervously tapping the green baize. "I don't do under-water archaeology anymore, Jake. You made sure of that."

"You could always work for me." Jake took her hand and began massaging.

She turned to Novak with an alluring smile. Lee clenched his jaw so tight he expected to be in pain tomorrow. He couldn't believe she allowed the man to touch her, let alone pretend to enjoy it.

"I did love your boat," she purred. "Fire Marco, and I'll consider it."

"I wish I could." Jake pulled her hand to his lips. "It's not that simple."

Lee expected the man to lose an eye or other useful body part, but she continued her flirtatious game. She was playing the treasure hunter, but why? Was she trying to make Lee jealous? He hated the fact that it was working.

"I heard *Andvari* is here," she said idly, dropping several chips on the roulette table with casual indifference.

Lee itched to touch her back, to stake his claim.

Novak leaned toward her. "It is."

"That's quite a trip. You're done in Mexico?"

"For now."

"Why'd you bring her around?" Her finger tapping increased. It could be because she'd placed her largest bet so far, but Lee thought her anxiety was because she'd zeroed in on the information she wanted from Novak.

It also happened to be the information *he* wanted from Novak.

"I'm expanding my business to the Atlantic Coast. There are a lot of shipwrecks here."

"So you brought *Andvari* around before you even had a project lined up?"

Novak shrugged noncommittally.

Lee wanted to keep this conversation going. He moved to Erica's side. "*Andvari*. Is that your boat?"

Jake nodded with distraction, focused on Erica. He must have suddenly remembered Lee was now head of the Bethesda office, because he turned to him and said, "Next weekend I'm having a party on *Andvari* for the team Ed Drake and I put together for the navy contract. I'd like you to come."

"We'll plan on it." Unable to contain himself any longer, Lee ran a possessive hand across her back. "I'm curious, what does *Andvari* mean?"

She straightened her back in a clear attempt to shake off his touch. He squeezed her shoulder. No way was he letting Novak know things were less than perfect between them.

She stilled, accepting him, for now. "The name is Jake's idea of a treasure-hunter joke," she said. "In Norse mythology, Andvari was a dwarf who had the power to become a fish. Andvari also had a magical ring called Andvarinut, which helped him to become master of all the gold in the universe. Loki caught Andvari when he was in his fish form and forced him to give up his gold and Andvarinut, so Andvari cursed the ring to destroy whoever possessed it."

Andvari was a dwarf. Excitement coursed through Lee. The artifacts were still on the boat! The meeting was scheduled for three a.m. He needed to let his FBI contact know he had the location.

"I wasn't aware you knew the Andvari story," Jake said.

She gave him another falsely—at least he assumed it was false—sweet smile. "Googling Andvari was the second thing I did after I returned from Mexico. I realized then the name is your way of saying anyone who takes your treasure will suffer. *You* are Andvari."

"It's just a name, Cream Puff. I like Norse Mythology. I'm also a fan of Tolkien and Wagner, both of whom borrowed from the Andvari myth."

Erica placed another bet on the table; she'd already lost more than half the money Lee gave her.

"What was the first thing you did?" Lee asked.

"Excuse me?" she asked with an air of innocence that might have fooled Jake, but not Lee.

"When you returned from Mexico. You googled Andvari second. What was the first thing you did?"

Her eyes glittered. "What every tourist does when they get back to the States. I printed out all the photos I took on vacation."

"Really?" Novak's eyes narrowed. "I'd like to see your pictures."

"You certainly would. I've got some great shots of you and the rest of the crew." Now there was an edge to her voice. Lee sensed the game had escalated, and he wasn't sure he liked it.

Novak's face lost any hint of flirtation. "I never saw you taking pictures."

The croupier cleared the table, and Erica placed a new bet by tossing a chip over her shoulder without breaking eye contact with Novak. "Because I didn't want you to. You know, I think the senator will appreciate seeing them."

Beads of sweat broke out on Novak's brow.

Lee had to get her the hell out of here. The man was dangerous, and she was baiting him.

He ran his hand down her back and cupped her ass, then said in a voice just loud enough for Novak to hear, "Short-cake, place your last bet, and let's get out of here. I wanna celebrate my new job with you in private."

"Sure thing, honey bear." Her tone emulated Alexandra's ironic endearments for JT. She tilted her head for a kiss, and he got a glimpse of her cold eyes as his lips brushed against hers.

His heart lurched. She was beyond hurt, beyond anger. She *loathed* him.

She slipped off the stool, dropped a hundred dollars in

chips on the table, and walked away. "Jake, it's been as much fun as always."

Lee turned to follow, then stopped and faced Novak. "Stay away from her."

Novak's gaze tracked her as she left the room. "She and I have unfinished business."

"Your business ended a year ago."

The man's mouth curved in a crooked smile. "She may enjoy you now—she's always liked men with money and connections—but it won't last. Erica needs me. Now more than ever."

Bile rose in his throat. Lee itched to deck the man, but this was Joe's night, and he couldn't ruin it. Instead, he dropped his voice to a menacing whisper. "It eats you alive, doesn't it? You're obsessed with her, but she loathes you."

Novak's eyes narrowed. Hatred and jealousy burned in their depths.

Lee'd scored a direct hit. "If you go near her again, you'll regret it." He turned and left.

Novak would pay for what he'd done to Erica, but this wasn't the time or place. No, the time and place was in three hours on board *Andvari*.

He found JT and told him he was taking Erica home and would send the limousine back, then left the casino. Before climbing in the back with Erica, he told the limo driver to take the long way home. He needed as much time with Erica as he could get. They pulled away from the curb while she moved as far as she could from Lee. With her back to him, she stared out the window.

The silence built until it became intolerable. "What happened in Mexico?"

She studied him, then took a deep breath. "I tried to protect the artifacts and stole them in the middle of the night. I swam a mile and a half to shore, dragging a float bag that held heavy stone and gold artifacts. I was shot at but got to my car and drove thirty miles into the jungle before it broke down." Her voice was cold, distant, as though she recited a dry list of events that had happened to someone else. "I hid the artifacts in the jungle but then was arrested by a cop on Jake's payroll."

She lapsed into silence and returned to gazing out the window.

When he realized she didn't intend to continue, he prodded her. "Then what?"

She wouldn't look at him, but her tone carried the same impassivity. It scared him more than if she'd broken down. "They starved me. When that didn't work, they withheld water."

His hands curled into fists. Five minutes alone with Novak. That was all he wanted.

She faced him, chin up, fierce pride in her eyes. "But I still didn't tell them where the artifacts were."

But she must have, eventually. What in hell had they done to get her to talk? "Tell me."

Erica turned away again. "Then Jake ordered his crew to gang rape me."

A rush of anger, fear, and self-loathing socked him in the gut. He'd used sex to win her trust, then used what he'd learned against her. He was no better than Novak. Worse, actually.

But still, Novak was a dead man.

She kept her back to him, staring out the window. "I gave up the artifacts."

"Did they…?"

"No."

He wanted to hold her, but from the rigid set of her spine, he knew reaching for her would be a mistake. "Why didn't you tell me?"

"Because I knew if I told you…" Her voice cracked, and Lee nearly did too. "You'd tell JT. He'd be more worried about avoiding scandal than the theft and would make the artifacts disappear."

"I'm sorry." He was but didn't know if he would have, could have, done anything differently, not without knowing the full story. "Why did you need the artifacts? Aren't the photos you took enough?"

"Without the artifacts, without the false provenance the casino museum would have, the photos are useless. I needed concrete evidence. And now, thanks to you, I don't have it. I'll never be safe from Jake and Marco." She rolled down the window between the front seat and the passenger area and said to the chauffeur, "Take GW Parkway to 395. Maine Avenue Exit. I'll point out the building when we get there."

"Yes, ma'am."

She rolled the window up.

"Erica, I can help you. Protect you."

"I'll work for Talon & Drake until I find a new job. Maybe Janice'll give me a good recommendation. If not, I'll start over. Again."

"I'm worried about you being alone in your apartment. Stay at the Watergate. With me."

"I'm starting to believe you trashed my apartment to force me to move in with you. Hell, for all I know, you trapped me in that basement just so you could rescue me."

His blood pressure spiked. Jake had abused her, yet she accused *him* of trashing her apartment and trying to kill her? "I was with you when your stuff was destroyed."

"Then you paid someone else to do it."

He gripped the door handle to prevent himself from punching out the window. He deserved her anger. He deserved her distrust. He took a deep breath and calmed himself. He'd created this rotten mess; he'd lost even the feeble trust he'd earned when he let her learn who he was from Novak, of all people. And that happened right after pushing her to admit she loved him, for no better reason than he'd needed to hear the words.

"Is there anything you've told me in the last two weeks that's true?" she asked.

"Yes," he said softly. "One thing."

She stiffened, then slammed her fist on the button to lower the window and gave the driver the last instructions to her building. They rode in silence until they pulled up in front.

Maybe this was just as well. He had an appointment with an FBI agent. He climbed out, then helped her out of the limo.

She straightened her spine and took a step toward her building. "See you Monday."

He caught her arm and swung her around to face him. He looked down at her, aware his face revealed his heart, if she cared to look.

The beads in her hair sparkled in the streetlight, and her sad gray eyes tore at him. He was head over heels in love with her, yet every choice he'd made had hurt her. His heart beat heavily. This could be the most important moment of his life —his only chance to win her back. He cleared his throat. "We're not done."

"Yes. We are."

He let her go, despite every muscle in his body aching to stop her. She entered the building and crossed the lobby. He stood on the sidewalk for several minutes after she disappeared from view.

Chapter Forty-Two

The artifacts would have been in the casino if she'd done nothing. If she'd stuck with her stupid cell tower assessments and let Janice write the Thermo-Con EA, the artifacts would have been there. If she had never met with Sam Riversong, if she hadn't tried to get his DNA, if she hadn't chosen to meet the senator, Lee would never have suspected a thing, and the artifacts would have been there.

If she'd taken the job at Starbucks and never met Lee, JT, Joe, or Sam, the artifacts would have been there. And Starbucks would have given her better health insurance.

Every action she'd taken, every choice she'd made, had been a mistake.

Probably including this one.

She tucked her car up against a run-down fishing shack located a half mile up the road from the Menanichoch marina. It was two thirty in the morning. She needed to search *Andvari* to find what Jake had pulled from the Atlantic near Norfolk. She opened the hatchback and pulled out her dive gear; she would approach the boat from the water.

Her stomach knotted. Would Marco be on the boat?

After donning her dive gear, she entered the Chesapeake,

her breath catching as she sank into the dark, cold water. On a clear day at noon, she'd only be able to see five feet in front of her, but now her flashlight illuminated only two feet. The full moon would be up for hours, so she surfaced several times to check the shoreline until she reached the marina entrance. There she spotted Jake's boat tied to the end of the longest dock and took a compass reading. Until she reached the boat, she would stay underwater, using her flashlight and compass to navigate.

She surfaced in the shadows of *Andvari*'s dive platform. Holding the ladder rail, she listened for several minutes to determine if anyone was aboard. Sick with fear, she placed her foot on the first rung. Her wet, gloved hands slipped, and she gripped the bar tighter. Her whole body shook as she boarded the vessel. Ironically, it was just one week shy of a year since she'd escaped this boat by jumping from this very platform.

She pulled her mask down around her neck and left the heavy air tank and fins on the platform. She would confirm Jake had Iraqi artifacts, get the hell off the boat, then call the FBI.

She entered the below deck area through a rear hatch and listened for movement, hearing only her pounding heart and water lapping against the hull.

She paused outside Jake's cabin. Any valuables would be inside this room. With her ear to the door, she listened for several seconds, then took a deep breath and turned the knob. She used her flashlight to scan the room. Shock and surprise rippled through her. Dozens of bright blue waterproof dive bags filled the cabin.

She reached for the closest bag and opened it. *Holy shit.*

Inside were neatly stacked bundles of crisp, new one-hundred-dollar bills. She hesitated, then decided her dive gloves made it safe for her to touch the money. She lifted a bundle and fanned the bills. The money looked real, the numbers sequential. How much money was here?

One hundred bills in a bundle meant each bundle was worth ten thousand dollars. Ten bundles would equal a hundred thousand. The money was arranged in four rows by five rows: twenty bundles visible on the top layer. She was looking at two hundred thousand dollars per layer.

She ran her hand down the side of the bag, trying to estimate how many layers of bundles were stacked. Her hands shook, and she lost count. Better just guess. Each bundle was a little more than an inch thick; the contents of the bag were stacked about two feet high. Twenty layers? Two hundred thousand times twenty—

She dropped her flashlight, then held her breath, wondering if anyone was around to hear the soft thunk that echoed in her ears.

She looked at the other bags in the room and tried to count them, but she couldn't focus as adrenaline surged through her. The one bag she'd opened contained approximately four million dollars. And at least twenty bags were stacked on Jake's bed and floor.

She wasn't looking at the proceeds from artifact smuggling. This was so much bigger, so much worse than that. Jake was now smuggling cold, hard cash.

Where had the money come from?

All she knew was she had to get off this boat. Now.

She was back on deck, closing the hatch when she heard a voice from the dock. "They'll be here soon," Jake said. She wondered who he was talking to.

She couldn't get to the dive platform without crossing open space. She waited. Jake entered the hull from the sliding door on the side, but his companion remained outside.

She ducked behind a storage bench on the port side, hoping she'd have a chance to make a run for the dive platform.

Seconds later, she heard a yell, and Jake raced onto the deck. "Someone's been here. There's water in the hall and in my cabin."

"Feds?"

"Feds wouldn't drip everywhere. My money's on Erica. She was asking about the boat tonight."

"You should have killed her. But you were too fucking horny for the bitch." Erica recognized Marco's voice. *Oh God.* She should never have come here.

"We couldn't kill her, and you know it. If she turned up missing, we'd have been asked too many questions by the wrong people."

Marco called out from the stern, "She's still here. Stupid bitch left her dive gear."

She heard a splash over the sound of her frantic pulse.

"She won't be able to get away without her tank," Marco said. "We're in deep shit. She probably called the cops. Get in the Zodiac."

The boat rocked—Marco jumping into the smaller vessel? *Please let them leave.*

"Get the stern line," Jake said.

Suddenly, light washed over the deck. Spotlights, coming from the dock.

"Fuck!" Marco yelled.

"Jake Novak, this is the FBI—" The rest was drowned out by the sound of an outboard motor revving. The small Zodiac sped out into the Chesapeake.

Erica heard cursing from the dock. The spotlight shifted from *Andvari* and found the fleeing boat.

Shit. What should she do? Stay and answer questions? She had a history with Jake, a reputation for stealing artifacts, worked for Talon & Drake, and someone who worked for the company was involved with smuggling.

By stepping aboard *Andvari* tonight, she'd cast herself as scapegoat.

Footsteps sounded on the dock. She had one chance to get away. She hoped the FBI agents were too focused on the fleeing boat to notice her. She ran for the dive platform, took a deep breath, and dove straight down.

She kicked downward and pulled on her mask, using precious air to clear it. She estimated she'd descended about twenty feet and hoped the light from her flashlight wouldn't be visible at the surface. When she reached the murky bottom, she read her depth gauge: thirty-five feet. In a drop that deep, the current could have shifted her scuba tank several feet in any direction. She could see only two feet in front of her.

She felt the sea floor frantically. Her lungs ached. She wasn't wearing a weight belt and had to kick in a frenetic rhythm to keep from rising, fighting both buoyancy and her desperate need for air.

She couldn't panic.

She'd spent hundreds of hours underwater and was trained to search methodically. She tried not to think of what was happening on the boat above her and swam in a circle, widening the radius with each pass.

The burning in her lungs became unbearable.

❈

*L*ee had been at his post on a neighboring boat for half an hour when he saw a dark form climb onto the dive platform of *Andvari*. Even in a wet suit, her body was recognizable. He probably knew her shape better than his own and felt a jolt of disbelief and pain slice all the way to his core.

Erica is still working for Novak.

No. He didn't believe it. Couldn't believe it.

The agent with him quietly radioed the other agents stationed on vessels throughout the marina. Lee and the agent were probably the only ones who'd seen her, as the other agents faced the boat from different angles.

"You know the woman? Does she work for Talon & Drake?" the agent asked Lee.

He didn't hesitate. "I can't be sure; the mask and hood hid too much."

Erica's water entry onto the scene caused a flurry of conversation as the agents decided what to do. They agreed to wait. The woman was the first conspirator to arrive.

At nearly three in the morning, Erica appeared on deck just as Novak arrived with someone else. A minute later, the unidentified man dropped her tank into the water.

The radio crackled. "A suspect is untying the Zodiac at the end of the dock."

The agent in charge came over the radio. "Shit. They're gonna flee. Move in!"

"You stay here," the agent said to Lee and left.

Alone, he watched the scene play out. She dove into the water while the Feds raced to the end of the dock, intent on the fleeing boat. He needed to tell the agents. Instead, he held his breath, wondering what she'd do without her scuba tank.

He watched, reminding himself she was a diver and an archaeologist. If anyone could find a tank in the murky Chesapeake, it was Erica.

The agents argued over whether there were two or three people on the fleeing Zodiac. Another boat left in pursuit.

He found it impossible to hold air in his lungs any longer and took a great gasping breath.

Time to tell the FBI the scuba diver had gotten away.

He hoped he'd given her enough time to escape.

*E*rica had to surface. She needed air.

She planted a foot on the bottom to push off for a fast ascent. Pain shot up her leg.

Her ankle had hit something. It was metal.

Her scuba tank. A frantic second later, she had the regulator in her mouth and took a slow, deep breath. She fumbled with the straps as she forced herself to take even breaths.

She checked her compass, found her bearings, and hoped she had enough oxygen to swim back to her car.

Chapter Forty-Three

$\mathcal{E}$rica was sound asleep on a pile of blankets and towels when there was a loud banging on her apartment door. She glanced at the clock: six a.m. She'd slept for an hour. She didn't have to fake bleary-eyed confusion when she opened the door for the two FBI agents.

They questioned her for hours, asking about Novak, *Andvari*, and her whereabouts at three a.m. She claimed to have been sleeping from one on but was truthful about everything else. She gave them the camera disk and the prints that proved the Aztec artifacts had come from the shipwreck, and as she'd expected, they told her the photos alone proved nothing. They had no artifacts to compare them to. She told them about the DNA test she'd sent off and her hopes that the envelope contained Sam Riversong's DNA. The agents, one male, one female, rolled their eyes and told her the envelope was useless without proof of where it had come from.

They asked to see her scuba equipment. When she'd arrived home, she'd rinsed her wet suit and dried it in the dryer. She would have dumped the suit in the garbage on the way home, but the cleaning crew might have seen the suit, so she had to produce the items for the FBI. She showed them her tank and pointed out a hole in the regulator hose, damage she claimed came from Jake when he'd trashed her apartment. She didn't think they believed her, but she wasn't arrested, which was an improvement over the last time she'd fled Jake's boat in the middle of the night.

Finally, they left. She locked the door and leaned against it. Then she began to shake. She staggered to her bedroom, lay down on the pile of blankets, and rolled into a fetal position.

She wanted to be held.

Hell. She wanted Lee to hold her. He'd said he loved her. Had his words been just another manipulation? She wanted one person to care about what happened to her.

Somewhere along the line, she'd fallen desperately, hopelessly in love with him. She could probably forgive him for everything if he stood by her now. She picked up her cell phone and started to dial his number, then stopped.

He was the senator's stepson, and she was embroiled in a scandal. If he loved her, if he truly cared, he'd contact her. But if he didn't, he'd avoid her at all costs.

She snapped the phone closed and set it down as the tremors became convulsive spasms. Hugging a tattered blanket to her chest, she tried to stop the quaking, all while wishing, praying, hoping her phone would ring. The endless shaking loosened the block of ice she'd clung to since her mother betrayed her, and pent-up tears from that disaster began to fall like snowmelt, forming first a stream, then a river. She cried until she was empty, then drifted into an exhausted slumber.

She woke up in the early evening and forced herself to eat a few bites of dry cereal, but the meager meal threatened to come back up. She paced her empty living room, fighting nausea.

Her cell phone was a cheap pay-as-you go Blackberry-style phone that didn't have internet. She had no TV, no radio, no computer, no idea of what was going on in the world. She didn't know if Novak had been caught or even if the press had learned of the raid at the marina.

All day she'd clung to memories of whispered words and intimate kisses, touches that made her feel beautiful… worshiped…loved. The sun had risen and set without a phone call, confirming those declarations of love had been made by a man whose every word was a lie.

She doubled over, broken with pain.

Her deepest darkest shame slipped through the cracks in her heart: there was something so terribly wrong with her, even her own mother had hated her.

And now, Lee hadn't called because she was nothing more to him than a means to an end.

⚜

*L*ee stopped pacing and stared at the television, which had been tuned to the news all day to catch updates on the investigation at the Menanichoch marina. "I'm going to call her."

JT grabbed Lee's cell phone from the coffee table. "You know you can't. Face facts, Lee, she's been in on it from the start."

In spite of the evidence he'd seen with his own eyes the night before, he couldn't—wouldn't—believe Erica was guilty. "No." He held out his hand. "Don't make me beat the crap out of you, JT. I'd like to beat on someone right now, and you'll do."

JT swore and handed him the phone.

The words "Breaking News" flashed across the screen, and an anchorman oozing gravitas faced the camera. "We've received confirmation from an unnamed source that the FBI recovered over one hundred million dollars from the boat that was raided at the Menanichoch Tribal Marina last night. For those of you just joining us, we will again explain the connection between the boat, owned by treasure hunter Jake Novak, and Maryland Senator Joseph Talon, who announced last night his candidacy for president at a gala event that took place only a half a mile away from the marina where the money was found…"

The anchor went on to trace the connections Jake had to Talon & Drake, starting with the recent project proposal and ending with Erica, his former employee, who was rumored to be an artifact thief. They showed the same footage they'd aired all day long: Erica emerging with Lee's help from the limousine after JT and Alexandra; pictures of Erica and him on the red carpet—she glowed with radiance while he looked down at her with proprietary lust; both of them standing near the senator as he made his speech.

The fact Lee was nuts about her was plain on his face in every single frame, and the press made much of the senator's stepson's involvement with a "person of interest" in the smuggling.

"It appears," the anchor said, "based on the serial numbers of the bills recovered from Mr. Novak's boat, the money is a portion of the twelve billion dollars of American money shipped to Iraq in 2004 and then lost in the war zone. We have confirmation the FBI is investigating Talon & Drake employees working in Iraq, who may have found a large portion of the missing money and then smuggled the bills back to the states. An FBI spokesperson has released a statement saying: 'We have yet to determine how this money got into Mr. Novak's possession, but we have a theory, which we are investigating.'"

Lee knew exactly how those bags of money ended up on Novak's boat. They had been tossed with the last regular garbage dump from the aircraft carrier on Thursday afternoon. The dump had occurred within fifty miles of shore, which was closer than naval regulations allowed, and Lee suspected the seamen doing the drop had been paid-off. The seamen would have used a GPS device to record the location of each bag as it was dropped, then, after the carrier was in port and the men released from the vessel, one would have given the coordinates to someone at Talon & Drake—Lee suspected Ed Drake—who then transmitted the information to Jake in a series of text messages.

Lee wouldn't be surprised to learn each bag contained a sonar beacon, making it even easier for Novak's divers to find the money. On Friday afternoon, Novak and his crew took the *Andvari* out on what was probably the easiest, most fruitful treasure hunting trip ever recorded. One hundred million dollars for a day's work. The number floored Lee. It made the artifacts they thought Novak had been smuggling seem paltry in comparison.

Jake Novak's picture filled the TV screen. "Mr. Novak and two unknown accomplices are still at large."

Every time he thought about the fact Novak had escaped, he wanted to break something. After a thirty-minute chase, the Zodiac had been recovered, empty of passengers. Novak and his accomplice had jumped from the boat and presumably swam to shore.

"I hope the bastard was eaten by sharks," Lee spat.

"And I hope he's alive and kicking," JT said. "He needs to be caught and take the blame, or Talon & Drake will suffer. I never thought I'd see the day when Talon & Drake would make Halliburton look good."

One hundred million dollars. He remembered the news stories about the money, embarrassing at a time when Iraq teetered on the edge of civil war. Twelve billion US dollars, imported to Iraq by the American government, had been lost in that country and had probably funded the insurgency that killed so many American troops and Iraqi civilians.

Twelve billion dollars which could have been put to good use at home or abroad, but now it had come back to the U.S.

as contraband, ready to line the pockets of greedy men like Jake Novak and power-hungry men like Edward Drake. But the worst was the possibility the money had been destined for laundering through the Menanichoch casino. Had Sam Riversong intended to use the money for Joe's campaign?

The damage to Joe's reputation could be insurmountable. Lee hoped the FBI would act swiftly and find the guilty parties, but right now it seemed the only person they wanted to investigate was Erica.

He gripped his phone tighter. He was desperate to call her. But he shouldn't contact her while she was being investigated. Anything he told her would be suspect, could change the investigation, even make her appear guiltier. He was supposed to stay away even though it meant she would believe he'd abandoned her.

He started to dial her number.

A knock at the door interrupted. JT admitted FBI Agent Roger Pratt, the man who had agreed to keep them informed in exchange for their silence to the press. Lee glared at the man, unable to hide his anger.

"I take it you've seen the news," Pratt said.

"Nice to know Anderson Cooper knew what was on that boat before I did," Lee said through gritted teeth. "I'm the one who found the boat. I'm the one who handed you that arrest—which your team fucked up."

"I don't need your shit right now, Scott. I just spent the past four hours trying to convince my boss not to arrest your girlfriend. I'm probably the only person in the department who believes she's innocent, and if you want to keep her out of custody, I need your help."

He felt uneasy, wondering if this was a ploy to get him to admit he'd recognized the scuba diver was Erica. "What do you want?"

"Another agent and I interviewed Ms. Kesling this morning. She was talkative. She knows more about Novak's operation than anyone still alive." Lee didn't like the way he stressed that last point. "She even gave us photographs of his crew. The photos are a lucky break; they could save all our asses.

"We've suspected for a long time that Novak's underwater salvage business was little more than a cover for a drug smuggling operation. But the DEA came up empty each time they searched his boat—thanks to you, we now know how he pulled that off, dumping the drugs overboard for later pickup —and he did enough real treasure hunting to appear respectable. But the DEA was ready to pounce last summer when he hired Ms. Kesling and managed to produce a bona fide excavation permit."

No wonder Novak was so damn careful with the internet. He knew he was being monitored by the DEA. Then the horror of Erica's situation sank in. She had spent a summer on a boat with drug smugglers. Novak hadn't been interested in the Manila galleon excavation; it had all been a farce, Erica merely his cover, his legitimate reason to be in Mexican waters for an extended time. Then, when Erica found something worthwhile, the bastard got greedy and decided to take that too, destroying her in the process. "Erica's work was legitimate; she couldn't have had anything to do with the drug operation."

"I'm inclined to believe her, and my boss is coming around," Pratt said. "I don't think she has a clue about the drug smuggling. Listen, she said she told Novak about the photos when she saw him last night. Novak must have shit a brick."

"Why?" JT asked.

"One of his crew—Marco Garcia to her, but with her photo we've identified him as Marco Delgado—is the brother of a Mexican drug lord. Marco is a brutal killer, suspected in at least a dozen execution-style murders, but we've never had the proof to nail him.

"We believe Delgado fled with Novak this morning," Pratt continued. "We had no idea Delgado worked with Novak, or rather, Novak worked for Delgado—the Delgados work for no one—or that anyone from the Delgado cartel was even in the states. If we can catch Marco Delgado, it will be Al Capone-like ironic that Erica's photos and testimony can nail the bastard for artifact smuggling—especially given that treasure hunting was just a front to begin with."

Lee slammed his fist onto the table. "A Mexican drug cartel might be after her, and she's not in protective custody?"

"Her apartment is under surveillance, and we've got undercover security everywhere in her building. She's safe. What's important now is the artifacts. Ms. Kesling said she believed you had Sam Riversong remove the artifacts from the casino before the Aztec Room opened. We need the artifacts and fake provenance if we're going to prove Delgado and Novak stole them."

"Sam Riversong said he thought the paperwork was real," JT said. "He had no idea Jake stole them from a shipwreck."

"Where are the artifacts?"

"In a safe at tribal headquarters until we can authenticate the provenance."

"Good. Now here's what I need from the two of you. To Delgado, Kesling is a loose end. Right now, we can't connect him to the money, but Kesling and her photos can connect him to Novak. He's not the type to leave witnesses who can testify against him, but he won't approach her at home. They'll come after her in a public place, where they can hide in the crowd. I think they'll wait for her outside the office. Wisconsin Avenue is busy, difficult to secure—"

"That's why you haven't arrested her." Cold fear gripped Lee. "You want to use her as bait."

"Yes. And we need your help."

Chapter Forty-Four

*M*onday morning, Erica dressed in a dark pair of slacks streaked with red paint and a torn but mended top. All her undamaged clothes were still at the Watergate and had been paid for by either JT or Lee. She wouldn't touch them. Her current outfit would be part of her new homeless-but-clean look. She found a paint-splattered tote bag in a pile of salvageable items and dropped her cell phone, ID, keys, and a padded envelope inside. The paint stains matched her slacks. For once, her purse matched her ensemble.

On her way to the Metro, she received several curious stares and stared back without flinching. On the train, people chose to stand rather than sit next to her.

She arrived in Bethesda and walked down busy Wisconsin Avenue toward the office. The day looked like any other, yet nothing was the same. She berated herself for not getting up early to go to the workout room, but she felt listless, hollow. In the battle between the workout bag and herself, the bag would win.

She reached the elevator vestibule on the eighth floor and was met by a security guard. "Erica Kesling," he said.

"Yes."

"I've been instructed to give you this box, which contains your personal belongings. Your services are no longer needed by Talon & Drake."

"You mean I'm fired." *So much for nepotism.*

"Yes."

"Can you tell me why?"

"I wasn't told, but I've seen enough on the news to guess."

So there had been headlines. She should have at least picked up a newspaper to prepare herself. "What was on the news?"

The security guard shrugged uncomfortably and held out his hand. "Please turn in your ID card."

"Can I speak to my boss, Janice Rabinowitz?"

"I've been instructed to prevent you from entering the office.

The knot in her belly tightened. She had no choice. "I want to speak with Lee Scott."

"Mr. Scott gave the order to fire you."

The man's words hit her with the force of a fierce kick to the belly, and she staggered backward. The bastard had fired her and didn't even have the decency to face her himself.

She took several shallow breaths, acknowledging that deep down she'd expected this. But part of her had held out hope that he wouldn't prove to be so vile.

She gave the man her company ID and took the box containing her belongings. From the box she plucked out her gold pen—an engraved gift from her mother when she received her MA, paid for with the first credit card her mother had taken out in her name, and the only item Erica had to show for her massive debt. She used the pen to scribble a note on the padded envelope and handed the package to the security guard. "Please give this to Lee Scott."

She was about to drop the pen into her bag when she

paused. "Here," she said to the guard, holding out the expensive implement. "I don't want this anymore."

The man looked at her curiously.

"Melt it down, sell it, I don't care. Just take it."

"Thank you, Ms. Kesling." He slipped the pen into his pocket. "And good luck."

She hit the button for the elevator, and the doors slid open. She leaned against the wall, feeling sick to her stomach as she descended back to street level.

Outside, she found a bench and sat down. Gazing at the building, she counted the floors and stopped at nine. The corner office was Drake's. Now Lee's? She wondered if he was in there now, making himself at home in his new digs, enjoying the power of his new position.

She remembered the joke he'd made on his first day, that he'd be her boss in two weeks, and she felt a laugh strangle in her throat. Today was two weeks to the day. Well, what do you know? There really was one thing he'd told her that was true.

The security guard must have given him the envelope by now. She wondered if he suffered any pang of regret. No, he'd have to be human to feel regret.

She glanced into the box which represented her six months at Talon & Drake and catalogued the contents: a bottle of antacids, a Metro SmarTrip card with a few bucks on it, a dollar seventy-three in change, a smooth heart-shaped rock she'd found on survey and used as a paperweight, her radio with headphones, and her favorite Marshalltown trowel.

She'd brought her gym bag to the Watergate on Friday. Somehow she'd have to get that and her purse back. Stupid decision number 963: placing her copy of the key to JT's—but now she suspected it was Lee's—condo in the envelope for Lee before claiming the items that belonged to her.

She popped an antacid in her mouth and turned on the

radio, hearing familiar top-of-the-hour music on the local NPR station. The reporter ran through the major headlines. While she listened, she slipped the flat, sharp-edged trowel in her back pocket and transferred everything else into the tote bag.

She ate another antacid tablet, but the medicine couldn't keep up with the burn in her stomach as she listened to the news.

✦

*L*ee stood in the window and looked down at Erica, alone on a bench. He turned to Agent Pratt. "Promise me she's protected."

The agent pointed to a woman window-shopping across the street, pushing a baby stroller. "There's no baby in that stroller. There are other agents on Wisconsin, ready to follow her wherever she goes. If Delgado is watching, he'll know she's been cut loose from Talon & Drake."

Lee pressed his hand against the glass and watched her put the headphones on. Her computer, TV, and radio had been destroyed. Her cell phone didn't have internet. The agents watching her hadn't seen her buy a newspaper in the last twenty-four hours, and his hacking had shown she hadn't used her cell phone to make a call or text since Friday. Was she only just now learning what was being said about her on the news?

"We should have told her what's going on and faked the firing. She'd still be bait, but she'd know what she's facing." He hated everything about this, starting with Agent Prick, who had insisted a security guard fire her to make sure Lee didn't screw up by telling her the truth.

Which, of course, he would have done.

"Until we know for certain she's in the clear, we can't risk it," the agent said. "If she's innocent, Delgado will come after her. If she's guilty, now that she's without you for support, she'll contact Novak and flee with him. Either way, we get them."

He couldn't tear his eyes away from her. "She's innocent. And if anything happens to her, Pratt, I'll—" He wasn't stupid enough to threaten a federal agent, not in front of witnesses, anyway.

"She'll be fine," JT said. "Erica's smart."

"Dammit, how would you feel if Alexandra was bait for a drug-dealing murderer?"

"I'd be ready to strangle someone. But we have to do it this way. We don't have any evidence she's not in it with Novak. I don't care what you claim; she was on the boat Sunday morning."

He flinched at the reminder he hadn't told JT the truth. Everyone knew he was lying, risking his integrity, his self-respect, to protect her.

All of Talon & Drake's employees currently working in Iraq were now on military transport, heading back to the United States for questioning. If all went well, the guilty party would cut a deal and identify the individuals they shipped the cash to stateside. Erica would be cleared then.

But eleven billion nine hundred million dollars were still unaccounted for, and if the senator's political opponents had their way, they'd pin it all on Talon & Drake.

He glanced at the front page of the *Washington Post*, which ran a photo of them on the red carpet as he kissed her cheek. The headline said, SENATOR'S STEPSON INVOLVED WITH SUSPECTED TALON & DRAKE CONSPIRATOR.

Minutes after the photo was taken, he'd surprised himself by coercing her into saying she loved him. The need to hear her say the words before everything exploded had come from some unknown part of his soul.

When he watched her climb aboard the *Andvari*, he'd

thought she was involved with the artifact smuggling, but only because she believed she was protecting artifacts destined to be stolen or destroyed in the war zone. Now, knowing Novak was a drug smuggler, he was convinced of her innocence. "She's not money driven beyond wanting a secure job and a steady paycheck. She would never touch drug money or the money from Iraq. She's not greedy; she craves security."

"Money is security," JT said.

"She values her reputation more than money. She wanted her name cleared."

"Lee, for all we know, her next stop is a pawnshop to hock Alexandra's earrings so she can join Novak. She could have several million waiting in a Swiss bank and was just sticking around for one last score."

The office door opened, and Agent Marie Silver stepped inside. "Ms. Kesling gave this to the security guard, instructing him to give it to Mr. Scott." She held up a padded envelope.

Pratt was immediately on his feet, reaching for the package.

Silver ignored Pratt and handed Lee the envelope. "I've checked the contents."

Lee tossed Agent Pratt a glare, then saw the writing on the outside of the envelope. Her usually neat handwriting was choppy; the words looked angry, rushed. He read the opening line and didn't know if he should laugh or cry. "You're sure this is for me?"

Agent Silver nodded, sympathy in her eyes.

Congratulations on finding a whole new low—just when I thought it would be impossible for you to sink further.

Inside this envelope are copies of the photos I took while working for Jake. I had hoped you'd help me get the artifacts from Riversong before they're lost forever on the black market, but since you're a selfish pig, I give up. Frame the photos or burn them, I don't give a damn.

The doubloons are the only payment I ever received from Jake. Having them made me feel sick and ashamed but selling them would have been worse. Since you are a conscienceless bastard, it is only fitting you have them. You should be able to get about $9000 on eBay for them—use the money to buy your next victim a dress.

—Erica

He opened the flap. In addition to the stack of photos and gold coins, he pulled out a key to his apartment and a pair of perfectly matched large diamond earrings. He handed Alexandra's earrings to JT.

"I think I misjudged her," JT said. He held the earrings up. They caught the light and sparkled and flashed. "Guess how much these are worth."

Lee shrugged, more interested in the gold doubloons than the earrings. "A few thousand."

"Fifteen thousand, to be exact. I think lending them to Erica—a woman she'd never met and was told not to trust with the truth—was a game for Alexandra, letting me know how little my expensive gifts mean to her."

"Alexandra's never been interested in money. It's always pissed her off you couldn't see that." The gold warmed in his hand. Clean, smooth edges bit into his palm as he squeezed.

"I'm stupid when it comes to women."

"I've been telling you that for years." Lee held up the doubloons. "She's so broke, she skips meals, yet she's had these all along. She wouldn't hock them because selling arti-facts violated her ethics."

"I was wrong about her." JT set the earrings on Lee's desk and picked up the stack of photos. "Which one is Delgado?" he asked Pratt.

"That's him, holding up a necklace."

JT paused, studied the picture, then began flipping through the photos, slowly at first, then again, more rapidly. Lee watched his usual olive complexion turn pasty white.

"What's wrong?" he asked.

"These aren't the artifacts in the tribe's safe. You've got Erica out there playing bait to a killer for no fucking reason. You can't prove shit with these photographs."

Chapter Forty-Five

*E*rica used the Metro card to go through the faregate. She heard a train coming, and, even though she wasn't in a hurry, habit made her run down the escalator to the platform, dodging slow-moving tourists. She raced into the car, and the doors whooshed closed behind her. She took a seat at the back and wondered why she'd bothered. She didn't even know where she was going.

The morning rush had ended, and only five other people shared the car. She usually loved riding the Metro. Surrounded by solitary people commuting together, she lost her feeling of loneliness. The subway was one place she belonged. But now she wondered if the other passengers would recognize her and tried to keep her head down.

She'd used the change from her personal belongings to buy a newspaper and studied the picture of Lee and herself on the front page. He was a damn good actor. Even knowing it had all been an act for him, she would swear the besotted look on his face was real.

She'd heard on the radio Jake was still at large. The article said his accomplices remained unknown. She wondered if the

FBI guessed Marco was the man who'd fled with Jake. Yesterday she'd told the agents Marco Garcia was Jake's first mate, but because she didn't admit to being on the boat, she couldn't identify him beyond that. She wondered for the thousandth time if she'd made the right choice in fleeing. She'd be in jail right now, but at least she could tell the truth.

A young African-American girl in a pretty sundress decorated with embroidered daisies sat with her mother facing Erica. The girl made faces at her reflection in the window as the train sped through the dark tunnel. Erica watched her play, wondering if this would ever blow over.

She couldn't imagine a time when this would just be an event from her past. Over and done with. Would she ever again be just another anonymous rider on the Metro? Could she someday take a daughter or a son to visit the White House or one of the Smithsonian museums? She couldn't imagine how she'd get through today, let alone believe she had a future.

The train stopped, and a man boarded. Holding a newspaper in front of his face, he made his way down the empty aisle and chose a seat that blocked her view of the girl. She dropped her gaze to her own paper and studied the picture of Lee and herself, heartache welling up again.

"How old is your daughter?" she heard the man say, and she looked up sharply. "She sure is pretty." That voice had haunted her nightmares. Marco.

"Six," the mother said, and Erica gave the woman credit for her wary tone.

"You in first grade, *chica bonita*?" Marco said. His eyes flicked in Erica's direction, and fear surged through her.

The girl looked in confusion from her mother to Marco. The mother gave her daughter a protective squeeze. "I've taught my daughter not to talk to strangers. I'm sure you understand."

"Good call. She could talk to some psycho who'll slit her pretty little throat."

The woman jumped up, grabbed her daughter, and tried to pull her into the aisle, away from Marco, but he moved quickly and blocked their escape. He looked directly at Erica and spoke in Spanish. "You hit the button, the little girl gets hurt."

She dropped her hand from the emergency call button and said, "Leave them alone."

"Cooperate and I won't hurt them." He spoke English now.

"What do you want?"

Marco's smile gave her the creeps. It always had. "You fucked things up in Mexico, and you've fucked them up here. Now it's time for you to disappear." Without warning, he lunged and grabbed the girl by the throat. The mother screamed.

Two of the other passengers—a man sitting alone reading a newspaper at the opposite end of the car and a woman in a middle row—looked to see what was going on.

"Nobody move," Marco said, "or I hurt the girl."

A Black teenager wearing headphones and sitting with his back to the unfolding drama moved his head in time to music only he could hear. Marco must have decided the young man wasn't a threat, because he turned to the girl and caressed her chin. "*¿Cómo te llamas, chica?*"

The girl's eyes were wide with fear.

"What's your name?" He was angry now; his fingers tightened on her chin.

The girl's mouth opened, but she made no sound.

"Daisy," the mother said. "Her name is Daisy."

The train operator announced the next stop.

"Stand and grab the upper railing," Marco announced. "No one gets off, or Daisy dies."

The mother let out a sob.

Erica slipped her arm through her tote strap and gripped the overhead handrail. The man, woman, and Daisy's mother did the same. The teenager continued to keep time with the music. Marco tightened his grip on the girl and dragged her down the aisle until he could reach the teen. He lashed out with one arm, whacking the young man on the back of the head.

"Hold the rail so I can see your hands!" He pulled a gun and aimed it at the boy.

The teenager's eyes widened. He pulled his headphones off and said, "What the fuck, man?" But he stood and grabbed the overhead railing like everyone else, convincing her he'd heard every word Marco had said. "This is AU. My stop. I wanna get off."

"No one gets off here. Hold the rail and do as I say." Marco slipped his gun back into his pocket. He pulled Daisy onto his lap and sat down. Daisy's mother held the rail while silent tears trailed down her cheeks.

The train stopped. Nobody moved. Nobody said a word.

Jake Novak stepped into the car.

Chapter Forty-Six

*L*ee ran to the window and scanned the street below. Erica was gone. "Where is she?"

Agents Pratt and Silver both talked softly into their headsets.

"Where is she, dammit?"

"She's entering the Metro station," Pratt finally answered.

"Call it off. There's no reason to use her as bait!"

"She was on the boat Sunday morning. She can identify Marco, place him on the boat, and testify he fled with Novak."

He was frantic. His claim he hadn't recognized the scuba diver wouldn't protect her anymore. "But she never admitted to being on the boat. She lied, so her testimony won't be worth shit. Call it off. Take her into protective custody."

Pratt's eyes narrowed. "I knew you lied to protect her. This is our one chance to nail a key member of the Delgado family. I'm not screwing it up now."

Lee took a swing at the agent, but JT caught him and pulled him back before his fist connected. "That won't help Erica."

"Let me go after her." He started for the door, but Agent Silver blocked his way.

"Don't be stupid. Delgado won't go near her if you're there," she said.

Pratt held up a hand, indicating he was getting information from his headset. "She's on a train. Damn. The agent following her hung back too far, and Kesling ran for the train."

Lee felt sick. "The agent missed the train."

Agent Silver's eyes were devoid of expression. "Yes."

He wanted to break something. "She's on her own."

"She'll be okay," Silver said. "We know where she is and can get an agent on board down the line. As long as she's not approached while she's on the train, we've got her covered."

Agent Pratt continued listening, his eyes suddenly flashed with alarm. "Another agent got a visual on Marco Delgado. In Bethesda, he boarded a different car in the same train as Ms. Kesling. At the next stop, he stepped onto the platform then boarded the car Kesling is in."

❦

*E*rica hands were slick and sweaty on the overhead rail. Jake approached her. She gripped the bar tighter until her knuckles ached. He stopped only inches in front of her and stood with his back to the rest of the passengers. He spoke in a low voice that wouldn't carry beyond her ears. "You stupid girl. You just had to take pictures, didn't you? You may as well have put a gun to your head. You have no idea who you're dealing with."

"Siccing Marco on a little girl is vile." Her voice shook with fear and anger.

"I didn't," he whispered. "He's done listening to me. He's a sadistic bastard who feeds on fear, and right now he wants to hurt *you*." Jake caressed her cheek. "I warned you. I tried to protect you, but you had to fuck it up by looking for the artifacts."

"Protection. Right. You trashed my apartment and tried to kill me in the Thermo-Con house."

Jake shook his head. "That wasn't me. I protected you on *Andvari* because it was my fault you were there in the first place. But the situation got out of my control the moment Marco saw you with Tommy Riversong." He glanced at Marco, then back at her. "Sorry, but I've got to make this look good." Jake raised a hand and slapped her across the cheek.

Her head snapped back and she tasted blood, but she didn't lose her grip on the overhead rail. She remained on her feet. Barely.

"Again," Marco said.

Jake's blow was harder the second time. Her fingers slipped from the bar, and she fell backward, into the rear door of the car. Her ears rang as she slid down the panel.

Jake loomed over her. "He's the boss, Erica. He's always been the boss." He crouched down, bringing his face level with hers.

She pressed the back of her hand to her throbbing mouth and asked, "Why?"

His voice was low. For Marco and the other passengers, his words would be lost to the motion of the train. "The DEA was closing in. I needed an archaeologist and a permit, so I hired you. In the end, Marco agreed to let you go because the DEA would pounce if you went missing. But then he saw you with Tommy and figured you'd zeroed in on him because the fool had blabbed about his involvement with our organization. He killed Tommy to shut him up."

"Jake!" Marco barked. "Grab the bitch and let's go."

Jake yanked her arm, pulling her to her feet. She struggled to break his hold; then she saw Marco stroke Daisy's cheek. "Don't fight Jake."

She wanted to puke. "Let Daisy go. I'll cooperate."

"We don't trust you, Cream Puff." Jake took her cell phone from her bag and shoved it in his pocket; then he pushed Erica toward the exit nearest where Marco sat with Daisy on his lap.

Marco wrapped one of the girl's many braids around his fingers, much as he'd done to Erica a year ago. He held her gaze as he twisted the dark strands tighter and tighter. "You will do everything I say."

The train operator announced the next station. She felt Jake's gun press into her spine.

"This is our stop," Jake said.

She wondered if others on the train saw the gun and knew she was being coerced. They must have seen Jake hit her, but that didn't prove she wasn't an accomplice. She hoped someone would tell Lee, and he'd understand she was innocent. She didn't want to die with him believing she was guilty.

Jake pushed her toward the doorway.

"You're getting off?" the teenager asked. "I want to get off at Vann Ness too. You already made me miss my stop."

"Shut the fuck up," Marco said. "The girl and Erica get off with us. The rest of you stay on the train. Anyone talks, anyone comes after us, and Daisy is one dead *chica*."

Erica caught the teenager's intense gaze. He wanted her to know something. His lips moved, almost imperceptibly. She realized he was whispering. Talking to himself?

Understanding dawned. She saw exactly what she'd failed to notice in Lee: the man wasn't as young as he appeared. He had to be FBI.

He'd twice said the name of the station as the train neared a platform. Was he broadcasting the information to other agents?

Marco stood with Daisy in his arms and waited for the door to open.

"You don't need the girl. I'll do whatever you want if you leave Daisy here," Erica said.

"She stays with us," Marco said.

No matter what awaited them in the station, her life was forfeit. Marco intended to kill her, she had no doubt about that. If it wasn't for Daisy, she'd make a stand here, now. But she couldn't risk the girl's life. She met the mother's gaze. "I'll protect her. I promise."

"Don't hurt my baby!" the woman wailed.

The doors slid open, and Jake pushed her onto the platform. Seeing it was empty, she wondered if the FBI had enough time to clear the station. She glanced over her shoulder. The doors of the train slid shut. Through the window, she saw the Black man with the headphones run to Daisy's mother. He spoke urgently into his collar as the train pulled into the dark mouth of the tunnel.

Jake, Marco, Daisy, and Erica were alone in the cavernous train station.

Chapter Forty-Seven

"*A*n agent was positioned at Medical Center station," Pratt said. "As soon as he heard Kesling was moving toward the Bethesda station, he took a chance and caught the next train. He was in the end car, and we caught a lucky break—Kesling jumped in the last car—the same one the agent was already on. When Delgado switched cars and made contact, the agent couldn't radio without blowing cover, so he opened his mic."

Lee was at the keyboard, frantically trying to hack into the Metro security-camera system. "Is Erica okay?" he asked.

"Delgado and Novak took a girl hostage and are using the girl to control Kesling." He held up a hand as he received more information. "They're getting off at Van Ness."

His fingers flew over the keyboard. In seconds, he opened the Van Ness camera feed.

"I'm going to pretend I didn't see you do this, Scott."

He ignored the agent and watched as a train pulled into the station. Only the doors on the rear car opened, telling him the FBI was in contact with the train operator. Three people stepped onto the platform, one of them carrying a small girl.

"He's got a gun to her back," he said, pointing to the grainy scene as Novak pushed Erica toward the escalator.

"The agent on board said both men have guns."

The escalator was broken. Sweat broke out on Lee's brow as he watched the foursome slowly climb the stairs. They paused, and Jake pulled something out of his pocket and handed it to Erica. A phone? They spoke for a moment; then she held the item to her ear.

His stomach dropped when his cell suddenly rang.

*D*aisy cried for her mother, and Marco shook her. "Shut up."

Erica reached for her. "Please, let me carry Daisy."

"No," Jake said, pressing the gun into her spine. "Get moving."

She approached the escalator to the mezzanine level, which was broken and wondered if it had been shut down to slow their progress out of the station. Was the FBI on the next level?

Jake held out her cell phone. "Call your boyfriend. Tell him to meet you at the DuPont Circle Starbucks in twenty minutes with cash and a car."

"He won't do it. He thinks I'm working for you."

"He'll do it."

"How are we going to get to DuPont Circle in twenty minutes?"

"Call."

She dialed while Jake prodded her up the stairs. If the mezzanine was also empty, Marco would realize the station had been evacuated because the FBI knew they had taken Daisy hostage.

"Erica?" Lee said, his voice an urgent plea.

She stopped and closed her eyes, the sound of his voice ripping through her. "Lee."

"Move," Jake said.

She didn't dare take another step. She was terrified of what Marco would do when he discovered the next level was empty. "I'm innocent," she said into the phone.

"I know," Lee said. "I'm so sorry. I—" He cleared his throat. "Listen, the FBI has snipers at the top of the street-level escalators. If you can, get yourself and the girl out of the way."

How did he know what was going on?

Jake reached for the phone, "Put it on speaker."

She jerked away from him and said into the phone, "I love y—"

Marco ripped the phone from her hands and spoke to Lee. "We need a car, and we need money. Meet us in front of the DuPont Circle Starbucks in twenty minutes. For every minute you're late, Erica loses a finger. Tell anyone and she's dead." He tossed the phone onto the empty train tracks below. "That should keep him and the FBI busy. Stupid fucks."

"We aren't going to DuPont Circle?" Erica asked, stalling.

Jake shoved her up the stairs. "Hell no."

The station was eerily quiet. The mezzanine level was empty. All the faregates were wide open.

"What the fuck?" Marco said, looking around. "Where is everyone?"

Jake grabbed her hair and pulled her head backward. Her scalp burned with pain. "How the fuck did you do it?" He ripped open her shirt, then twisted her arm behind her back. "Are you wearing a wire?"

"No." She couldn't help it, she whimpered in pain.

Daisy began to scream, her yells echoing in the vast empty space.

"You stupid fuckwit," Marco snarled at Jake. "She set us up."

"How did they know to evacuate the station?" Jake asked as he twisted the bun at the nape of her neck and tightened his grip on her arm, ratcheting up the pain by slow, intense degrees.

She sucked a breath and managed to say, "The kid with the headphones. On the train. I think he's FBI."

He threw her down.

Her chin hit the floor, and she tasted blood.

"The punk must've already been on the train when she boarded," Jake said.

"Fuck. We're trapped down here."

Jake and Marco couldn't see her hands as she climbed on all fours to get up. She pulled the heart-shaped rock from her bag and held it in her palm so it wouldn't be obvious to either man. Her middle finger fit within the V of the heart, giving her a firm grip on the smooth stone.

Jake yanked her to her feet, then pulled her back against his chest. Pressing the gun to her temple, he bit her earlobe.

She took shallow breaths as they inched toward the long escalator to street level. They passed through the open fare-gates and reached the bank of escalators, all of which were stopped.

A voice came over the public-address system: "Jake Novak, Marco Delgado, Erica Kesling, release the girl and climb the escalator with your hands up. Every exit is blocked, and armed agents are in the tunnels."

Jake tightened his grip around her waist. "They think you're one of us, Cream Puff. Your only hope now is to flee with Marco and me to Mexico."

She jerked away from him. "No!"

He slapped her across the cheek so hard she spun in a circle and nearly dropped the rock.

Marco tucked his gun in his waistband and held Daisy

against his chest in a two-handed grip. "We'll go up single file, the *chica* in the lead."

The bastard intended to use Daisy as a shield.

Jake took his position behind her. He groped her breasts, then ran the barrel of the gun across her temple. He slipped the weapon into her mouth. "This is what I wanted to do to you when I realized you were screwing Scott. I saved your life in Mexico, but you fucked *him*."

The gun tasted like blood and fear, and a strange acceptance settled over her. The nightmare was over. Her breathing slowed, evened out. She closed her eyes and waited for Jake to squeeze the trigger.

She hoped Lee had heard her say she loved him, and wished she'd said the words more—to him, to her mother. Had she ever told her mother she loved her? Needed her? Or had she locked that part of her away when her father died? Another regret. One among thousands.

Daisy screamed, a loud shriek that echoed throughout the empty station, and Erica's eyes flew open. Marco held the girl high in a rough grip, blocking his head, preventing a clear line of sight from above as he stepped onto the escalator.

Almost without thought, she jerked her head backward, dislodging the barrel from her mouth and head butting Jake in the nose. She pulled her trowel from her back pocket and sliced behind her, catching Jake across his thigh; then she shifted forward and slammed the heart-shaped rock into the base of Marco's skull.

Jake yanked her arm, whirling her around. She jabbed the trowel deep into his belly. He took a step backward, shock on his face, and she twisted toward Marco, who had staggered forward and dropped Daisy. He swung around to face her. She kicked him in the head and used the momentum of the spin to smash the rock into Jake's jaw. He teetered but managed to stay on his feet.

Her head jerked back. Marco's fingers had slithered into

her bun. He twisted the knot of hair. She yanked the trowel from Jake's belly and stabbed backward over her shoulder toward Marco's head while shifting her weight and kicking Jake in his wounded gut. Trowel and foot met their targets at the same moment.

Pained yells eclipsed Daisy's hysterical cries.

Jake doubled over. Erica turned to see she'd opened Marco's face from eye to chin. Blood seeped between his fingers. She slammed the rock into his neck, trying to shove him aside so she could get to Daisy, who lay at the bottom of the escalator, screaming.

He didn't budge. Instead, his fist caught her ear. She rocked backward as pain exploded in her skull.

He reached for the gun at his waistband.

She kicked out and dislodged the weapon, which clattered to the floor. The force of her blow sent him backward. Daisy screamed louder as he wobbled above her.

Erica dropped the trowel and grabbed his shirt, catching him just before he fell. She pulled him closer and rammed her knee into his crotch, then shoved him away from the escalator, away from Daisy.

Daisy's eyes widened as they fixed on something over Erica's shoulder. Erica turned. Jake's face was ashen. With one hand, he held his stomach; the other still held the gun, which he slowly lifted.

She stood directly in front of Daisy. One shot could kill them both. She flung herself to the side to draw the gun away. The barrel followed the arc of her body.

A shot exploded through the hollow station. The sound reverberated for several long moments, then faded into utter silence.

Both men crumpled to the ground.

It took her a moment to realize two simultaneous shots had come from above.

She crawled toward Daisy as men and women in flak

jackets flooded the top of the escalator. She hugged the little girl, whose screams had given her strength to take on Jake and Marco. "You were so brave. So brave," she murmured to the girl. "Your mommy will be here soon. She'll be so proud of you."

In moments, an FBI agent stood above her. The woman tried to take Daisy from her arms, but the girl clung to her and cried harder.

"Can't we wait for her mother?" Erica asked.

The agent nodded.

Several minutes later, Daisy's mother arrived. She dropped to her knees and hugged both Daisy and Erica at the same time. "Thank you. Thank you. Thank you for saving my baby."

She passed Daisy into her mother's fierce grip, then faced the undercover FBI agent who had been on the train. She held out her hands, and, as she expected, he cuffed her.

Chapter Forty-Eight

$\mathcal{L}$ ee watched the aftermath at the Metro station in shock. He was winded, drained; his body ached as though he'd fought the armed drug dealers along with her. "I need to be there."

"You can't talk to her until she's been debriefed," Agent Prick said.

"Sonofabitch!" JT said, pointing to the monitor. "She's been cuffed."

"We have a warrant for her arrest. We were waiting until after Novak and Delgado contacted her to serve it."

Lee didn't hesitate. He spun and punched the agent with a hook to the cheek, dropping the man to the floor.

A look passed between agents Pratt and Silver. Then Pratt smiled, obviously pleased he had a witness on his side. "Stupid move, Scott."

"So sue me. Just know that if you do, I will make sure everyone—especially the girl's mother—knows your methods risked the lives of everyone on that train just because you wanted to beat the DEA and collar Novak and Delgado yourself."

Pratt got back on his feet, rubbing his cheek. "If she

hadn't lost her tail, she'd have had two agents with her on the train."

So the fiasco in the station was Erica's fault? He wanted to punch the man again. When Novak put his gun in her mouth, Lee had nearly lost his mind with rage and fear.

"I'll forget you hit me. I'm even going to forget about all the illegal hacking you've been doing, because you've been such a good sport to help us with this investigation." The man's smile was slick, smarmy. "Don't worry about Ms. Kesling. She probably won't be charged. She'll spend a night in custody answering questions. No big deal."

"As long as she has a lawyer present."

"Not if she doesn't lawyer up." He left with Agent Silver in tow.

Dammit. She was broke. She'd be terrified of what a lawyer would cost her and wasn't likely to request a public defender. He could hire fifty lawyers to defend her, but if she didn't say the magic words, they'd all be stuck waiting outside the door. She'd never even know they were there.

JT picked up the earrings again and studied them. "You really do love her, don't you?"

"You're just figuring that out?"

"No. I knew it the first time I saw you two together, in the copy room. You couldn't take your eyes off her. But I thought it was just lust."

His laugh held a harsh edge. "So did Erica."

"I have an idea. A way we can turn public opinion in her favor. But I'll only tell you on one condition."

"What's that?"

"I wanna be best man."

He smiled. "Deal."

Chapter Forty-Nine

The FBI held Erica for twenty-four hours. She was released without pending charges late Tuesday morning. US Attorney Curt Dominick and Agent Roger Pratt escorted her through the parking garage to a less visible exit while the FBI Director held a press conference inside.

"You sure you don't want a ride home?" Dominick asked.

She scanned the slow-moving traffic, took in the scent of hot asphalt, and smiled. Baking pavement, the smell of freedom. Her ordeal was really over. "I'd rather walk."

"Watch out for reporters. They haven't staked out your building yet, but they'll probably show up after the press conference." Dominick smiled. "You're big news."

Someone had tapped into the Metro's security cameras and posted the clip of what happened in the Van Ness station on YouTube. The video had millions of hits before it had been pulled from the site. In spite of the violent content, several news networks had aired the footage. According to Dominick, the press had embraced her as a hero.

Some hero. She should have acted sooner, before sicko Marco had a chance to harm Daisy's young psyche.

She said good-bye to the FBI agent who wouldn't explain

his bruised cheek or say who had posted the clip, and the man turned back to the building.

Agent Pratt had told her much about Lee and why he had been working undercover, filling in the last pieces of the puzzle. The FBI had threatened to charge her along with Jake and Marco if Lee didn't cooperate. He'd been forced to fire her.

Curt Dominick remained with her in the garage. "Dominick, can we talk off the record?"

He raised an eyebrow.

"You know Lee. You're friends, right?"

"I've known him since he was fourteen."

"Yet you forced him to set me up as bait."

He shook his head. "No. That was the FBI. I didn't know about the raid on the boat, and I didn't know about Novak and Delgado. I wasn't brought in until after you were in custody. It was my job to decide if we had enough to charge you." He ran his fingers through his hair. "I knew Lee and JT were investigating something in the Bethesda office—but Lee indicated it was internal embezzling, and he wanted to know what type of evidence he needed that would be usable in court. If he'd told me he was investigating Novak, I'd have told him about the drug investigation. He would have been warned about who he was dealing with."

"How did you know? About the drugs?"

He grimaced. "After you arrived in DC, I received a briefing from the DEA—they were tracking you because of your association with Novak. Then, when your name turned up on the witness list when Tommy Riversong—a known dealer—was murdered, I received another briefing."

She frowned. "That's why you studied me so suspiciously at the party."

His mouth curved in a faint smile. "I look at everyone that way. But yes. I was concerned. Especially since it was clear Lee was ass over teakettle."

She turned away. She wasn't about to discuss Lee with this man.

"Erica, you should know, if I had any inkling Delgado was involved and that you could connect him to Novak, I'd have put security on you 24/7."

"And now? Am I in danger from the rest of the Delgados?"

"No. You were a threat to Marco because you could testify against him. But he's dead. No trial. No testimony. And you don't know anything about the Delgado cartel. You aren't a threat to them. You're a free woman."

She thanked him and left the parking garage. She walked slowly, gawking like a tourist as she passed world-famous landmarks and museums. She had moved to DC out of necessity but now realized she wanted to stay. She liked the city with the low skyline, whose only industry was politics. She liked the stately, self-important architecture. She was free of her past now. She could make friends. Build a life.

She desperately hoped Lee would be part of that life.

A half hour later, she entered her building. The concierge came to attention when he saw her, and called across the lobby, "Miss Kesling! You're back! Welcome home." His voice was filled with new friendliness. "We've been watching you on the news. You…you…" he stuttered. "You were amazing."

The building manager rushed out from the back office. "We've been receiving calls and deliveries for you all morning." She switched to her firm manager voice. "I allowed the furniture movers into your apartment even though you hadn't reserved the elevator for the delivery. I could make an exception today, but please schedule future deliveries with the office."

Hope blossomed in her chest. She could think of only one person who would buy furniture for her empty apartment. "Thanks," she said and hurried to the elevator.

She reached her floor and stood outside her apartment

door. She took a deep breath before stepping inside. Her heart began to race when she saw the couch she had hoped to purchase from the same store where she bought her original dining set. *How did he know?* She whirled around and gasped when her eyes fell on the dining set, a replica of the one destroyed by Jake.

In her bedroom, she found a king-size bed. A note and a red rose lay on a pillow.

Erica,

I love you. I love you. I love you.

I hope by now you understand why I pretended to be someone I'm not and can forgive me for lying to you. I never wanted to hurt you.

As much as I want you with me, sharing my home and my life, I also wanted to make sure you have a choice. I bought furniture so you can stay in your apartment and hired a lawyer to handle your fight with the credit bureaus. Your credit should be reinstated soon. If you can't stand the idea of working for me at Talon & Drake, you should know that job offers, even book deals, are pouring in. You won't have trouble supporting yourself.

I'm at the office, hoping, praying, waiting for your call.

I love you. - Lee

She picked up the rose. The delicate scent washed over her. He wanted her. During the last twenty-four miserable hours, she'd battled the treacherous hope he really did care for her, afraid if he didn't, she'd fall apart.

She had to see him. The clothes she'd left at the Watergate were hanging in her bedroom closet. She showered and dressed, excitement and fear coursing through her in equal amounts.

Traffic made the normally thirty-minute drive take an agonizing forty-five, but finally, she pulled up behind the office high-rise and parked. Seeing a few reporters staking out the front of the building, she slipped in through the parking garage and convinced a security guard who recognized her to let her through the secured entrance. She took the elevator to the ninth floor, assuming Lee'd taken over Drake's office. In the elevator vestibule, she paused, surprised to see the chaos in the reception area on the other side of the double glass doors. The area was crowded, dozens of people packed into a space designed to hold ten. No one looked in her direction, and she was content to watch the mayhem from outside.

Lee entered from the hallway that led to the executive offices. He wore a tailored suit that projected style, class, and authority. He must have met with JT's barber, because even his hair was executive perfect. "Okay," she heard him say through the glass, "they're ready to interview Arnie Ross in the north conference room."

Several people groaned as they let Arnie pass.

"I know you've been waiting all morning," Lee said, "but the FBI needs to interview everyone separately."

"I need a file from my office," Lily Davenport said.

"No one gets access to their office or computers until they've been searched and cleared."

Erica studied him. Handsome, polished, as intimidating now as JT. How had he ever convinced her he was a young intern? Was she completely *blind*? He was a natural leader. He'd already earned the respect of half the employees, and when the furor died down, he'd have the rest in the palm of his hand. And she would be right there with them.

She opened the door. First one person noticed her, then another. In seconds, silence filled the packed lobby, and a path cleared between her and Lee. Her stomach did flip-flops.

He smiled slowly, warmly. His chiseled features went from handsome to devastating. "I like your hair."

She'd worn her hair down, knowing that would please him. "Thanks." Her gaze locked with his. "Yesterday, you fired me."

"That wasn't my choice."

"I want my job back."

"It's yours."

She walked toward him, oblivious of the coworkers who lined her path. "With a raise."

"No problem."

She stopped directly in front of him. "I have other demands."

He grinned. "We can negotiate in my office."

He led her to Edward Drake's large corner office. Once inside, he closed the door and dropped to his knees in front of her.

Her heart lurched.

"I'm so sorry, Erica. Sorry I lied about who I am and why I was here. Sorry I didn't trust you. Sorry I manipulated you for information. Sorry I didn't protect you from Jake."

She took in the moment. Lee, on his knees, saying the words she'd needed to hear from his lip as she looked into his eyes. He meant it. Down to his very soul.

They had a lot to work through, but this confirmed her hope that forgiveness was possible.

She tugged on his hand until he stood again. He wrapped her in his arms. She pressed her face against his chest. "I'm sorry too. I wish I'd trusted you with the full truth."

He stroked her hair. "You had no reason to. I was a shit." He tilted her head back until he could look into her eyes. "Yesterday, watching you fight Novak and Delgado was—" His voice cut out. He cleared his throat. "*Hell* doesn't begin to describe it."

His arms circled her again, pressing her snug against his chest. She'd wanted someone to hold her from the second the violence had ended. Instead, she'd been interrogated. "What was the one thing you told me that was true?"

"I love you, Erica. I'm totally, completely in love with you."

"Hm. Then I guess you're *not* a fifth-degree black belt?"

He laughed. "Okay, I told you two true things."

She smiled, then pulled his face to hers and kissed him. "It was true for me too. I'm crazy in love with you."

His kiss was fierce, passionate. Different. He pulled back and studied her with sad eyes. "I wanted to tell you. I almost did several times."

"We will talk about this." She smiled up at him. "But right this moment, I'd rather plan our future."

"I'll do anything, go anywhere, as long as I'm with you. I told Joe I'd stay on through the campaign, but, given what's happened, if you want to leave DC, we'll go."

He was choosing her over Joe. Over JT. A joyful ache cascaded through her.

"I like DC." She pulled away from him and circled the office, trailing her fingers across the mahogany desk. She didn't think the office furnishings were Lee's style, but then again, there was so much about him she didn't know. "Will this work? Me working for you?"

He crossed the room and slid his hands around her waist. "If it doesn't, you can quit. I make more than enough to support us both."

She closed her eyes and breathed deeply. He was offering her security.

"The Watergate condo is mine. We can live there, or your place. I don't care. I just want to be with you."

She leaned her forehead against his chest. Breathed him in. Relished this moment. "I'm supposed to start classes in a few weeks at American University. Since I can't use my underwater archaeology Master's, I'd decided to study Environmental Science."

"I know. I hacked into your application before we met."

She stiffened, then relaxed. "You know more about me than you ever let on."

"I needed to know who I'd be working with, but nothing prepared me for you."

JT entered. "I heard you were here, Erica."

Lee's gaze narrowed. "Then why didn't you knock?"

She slipped out of Lee's arms and faced JT.

"I didn't want Erica to run and hide from me." JT then surprised her by wrapping her in a warm bear hug. "Welcome back. I was worried about you."

She was stiff but then relaxed into the unexpected embrace. He kissed her forehead in a brotherly fashion and released her. "Now, if I'm going to give you custody of Lee, you're going to have to promise to take good care of him."

She laughed. "So Lee is a puppy now?"

JT ruffled Lee's hair, undaunted he had to reach well above his own head to do so. "I'm going to miss having Skippy around."

Lee gave his stepbrother a good-natured glare.

"We can negotiate visitation privileges," she said.

"Cute," Lee said and kissed her nose. "I've got to get back to work. The FBI is gutting the computer system, and I need to do what I can to contain the damage. You," he said firmly to Erica, "are taking the week off. Go home. Go furniture shopping, clothes shopping. Whatever you want." He handed her a credit card.

She studied the card. Her name was embossed on the surface. "When did you get this?"

"I had you added to my account the day after you told me about your mother."

Tears welled just beneath the surface. She heard the door click shut and knew JT had left them alone. Lee pulled her to him and rained kisses on her face. She breathed deeply and tried not to break down.

"I'm looking forward to making love to you tonight," he murmured. "We've never been together without lies." His smile was crooked. "Tonight I get to be me, all me, only me."

Heat replaced the threatening tears. His method was effective. She slid fingers through his expensive new haircut and kissed him. "Hurry home," she said against his lips.

"You can count on it."

She turned to the door, then stopped. "Lee, the FBI told me what you were doing, but I don't understand who else was involved. Who was working with Jake?"

"At least one person in the office worked with Novak. We suspect Ed Drake. He hasn't been arrested because the FBI doesn't have anything concrete. The FBI recovered a cell phone from Novak—the one he used to communicate with his Talon & Drake contact. They traced the number to a prepaid cell phone." Lee paused and winked at her, and she knew this must be the phone he'd recovered the photos from. "But a search warrant of Drake's belongings hasn't turned up the phone. He probably ditched it in the Chesapeake the moment he saw the raid on *Andvari*. At this point, the FBI is hoping they'll find evidence in the computer system—Drake wasn't nearly as careful as Novak. In the meantime, the senator is distancing himself from Drake, hoping to limit the damage to his reputation. If Riversong ends up being involved, it'll get dicey, but so far, it looks like Riversong is in the clear. It's more likely Tommy was the one who hooked up someone in the casino's museum office with Jake and Marco."

She nodded. "Tommy knew all about collection management. He was going to help me get a job when the current manager went on maternity leave." She cocked her head. "But what you said about Drake and the senator...the campaign isn't dead?"

"No. Joe hasn't done anything wrong. Right now it looks like a few bad apples who worked for the company." He grinned. "The press spent so much time tying you to me and Joe that yesterday, when you became a hero, you boosted Joe's image by ten percentage points."

She cringed every time someone called her a hero. The fight had been brutal, violent, and ended with the death of two men and lifelong mental trauma for a sweet young child. "I'm afraid the FBI still suspects me. With Jake and Marco dead, I'm scared they'll rush to round up conspirators and come back to me."

He slid his fingers through her hair. "You know, I miss the hairpins in the weirdest way." He played with the long strands for a moment. "Have you been honest with the FBI? Did you tell them you were on the boat Sunday morning?"

"You knew I was there?"

"I helped set up the raid. I saw you."

"They know everything. I don't have any more secrets."

There was a knock on the door, then JT said, "Lee, we need you. Now."

"Am I allowed to return to my office?" she asked.

"It's been searched, and your computer's been confiscated. You've been questioned. You're cleared." He handed her her company ID card.

She kissed him, slipping her tongue into his mouth for a brief but deep caress. "I'll see you tonight."

She left him with JT and used the stairs to reach her office. In the last days, her emotions had been on a wild roller-coaster ride. She needed to catch her breath. Get her equilibrium back. She pushed open her office door and flopped down in her chair, feeling exhausted and drained but happy.

She stared off into space for several minutes, absorbing the unusual quiet. Most employees must not have been cleared yet, because the floor was empty. After a few minutes of meditative silence, she noticed the FedEx envelopes on her desk. From the broken seal, she knew the FBI had searched the contents.

The first envelope had to be the DNA test results. The second one surprised her—she'd forgotten all about her request for information on Thermo-Con from the law offices of Morton, Fairfield, and Lawson.

She decided to save the best for last and put the DNA test results aside and opened the packet from the law office. She flipped through the pages, most containing information she'd already copied at the patent office. In the file, she found a better copy of the article published in the army post newspaper, and a January 1953 article published in the *Baltimore Sun,* which contained the same text as the *Citadel* article but included a photo of the house being poured. Several ERDL engineers who worked with Higgins employees stood in the foreground and were named in the caption. Surprise spread through her as she recognized a very young Edward Drake's eyes staring back at her from the old photograph.

*a*fter everything Edward Drake had done for Joseph Talon, the man had dumped him at the first sign of trouble. To think he'd ever felt guilty for what he'd done to Ricky Guerrero all those years ago. And look how little Ricky had turned out. The boy would take his so-called Indian heritage all the way to the White House, never knowing Ed was the one who made his rise to power possible. But Ed could also take it away.

Joe didn't know he was Ricky. He knew nothing about his past or who his parents really were. The man had no idea how badly he'd fucked up in letting Erica Kesling send off his DNA to be compared to the DNA from the bones found under the Thermo-Con sump. Christ, of all people to provide a comparative sample, she got one from *Joe.*

Her research could uncover Ed's work on the Thermo-Con house all those years ago. Would she then realize he'd denied knowledge of Thermo-Con because he didn't want anyone to connect him to the house, to the bones, to Regina?

He remembered his horror that November day in 1952, when the senior engineer placed the sump in the northeast corner, not the southwest one, as indicated on the plans. He'd dug only a shallow grave, expecting the concrete pour to hide her forever. He'd had to go back in the night, after the cement set, to undermine the concrete surrounding the sump and push her body into the soil under the slab. It was the best he could do.

At first, Regina and Ricky Guerrero's disappearance caused hardly a ripple. One person raised an alarm, but people knew Regina had planned to take Ricky to Montreal to live with her parents. She was a flake and didn't say good-bye. Problem solved.

But six weeks after she disappeared, Claudio Guerrero died in Korea. The colonel tried to contact her through her parents, and they discovered no one knew where she and Ricky were.

Another soldier's wife had known about his affair with Gina, and he was questioned. Fortunately, the MPs believed Regina had left her husband. Years passed, and Ed stopped worrying. But sometimes, in the dead of night, he remembered what he'd done. He remembered Ricky's eyes as he left him on the front steps of the school.

He made a choice to make up for his mistakes and tracked the kid down. He learned Joe was living with the Menanichoch and attending community college. At the time, Ed was a college professor at a Maryland university. A man, shaping the lives of other men.

He started a program to recruit Indian kids into the engineering program and arranged for a full scholarship for Joseph Talon if the boy would study engineering. The boy was smart and had great potential. From there Ed became Joe's mentor and eventual business partner.

But Ed never gave Joe a hint of their shared past.

Talon & Drake had started as an equal partnership, but early on, to Ed's great amusement, Joe wanted to use his Indian heritage to win contracts. To receive minority-owned-business status, Ed couldn't own fifty percent of the business, so his ownership was reduced to a third. Ed didn't mind. He preferred to work behind the scenes and let Joe be the face of the business. Ed's backseat role to Joe had worked well over the years, as Joe gained power but Ed was the force behind the man, the puppet master.

Until yesterday, when Ed had been locked out of his own company by Joe's son and then, even more insulting, been replaced by Joe's stepson—a kid who knew nothing about engineering. As if Ed's vital role could be replaced by just anybody.

But Joe had no idea how deeply embedded the strings were; he thought he could make Ed the scapegoat and save his campaign. He was wrong. The senator had made a huge mistake.

Now he had to deal with the slut who was screwing the upstart who'd replaced him. If only he'd managed to kill her when he'd trapped her in the Thermo-Con basement.

But nothing had gone right. He'd destroyed the electrical system at the house so the plumbers would remove the sump and give him the opportunity to dig out the rest of Regina's bones. But the bitch had shown up and nearly caught him in the basement. On impulse, he'd trapped her there. If Erica had died, no one would have pursued the bones—they'd have been written off as an old burial and ignored, as he'd been urging Sam Riversong to do.

But Scott had saved her. Another reason to hate the bastard.

He hadn't known then that she'd worked for Novak, or that Novak had let such a dangerous loose end escape. Novak must have known she was after the artifacts, but he didn't tell his partners who she was, what she was doing. He'd had some sort of sick obsession with her. Novak had gotten what he deserved.

But Erica was still a problem. He'd trashed her office in a rage after searching for the Thermo-Con project file and coming up empty. Afterward, he'd had to destroy other offices so no one would guess which was the real target. Then she'd gone searching for the patent, and he'd methodically vandalized her apartment to cover his search for the file there. He'd hoped the destruction would distract her, but the woman had gone after the project with the intensity of a bitch in heat.

He hadn't been able to read the file until she finally left it in her office on Friday, when, to his horror, he read the article about the missing mother and son published on the same page as the Thermo-Con article. Even worse, he found her notes and learned she'd mailed the DNA test, with results expected on Monday.

The fix was simple. He would intercept the DNA results and destroy them. But before FedEx arrived, she'd become a hero and the FBI had evacuated all Talon & Drake employees from the office. Only now were they letting employees in, but Ed wasn't one of them. He'd been publicly named a suspect and wasn't allowed to enter.

He knew damn well the FBI had nothing to link him to the smuggling. He'd been careful. If Scott had hacked the disposable cell, anything he'd found couldn't be used against him. All evidence there was tainted by the illegal methods Scott had used.

No. His primary concern was the damn DNA test. Thirty minutes ago, he'd watched Erica enter the building through the garage. She could be reading the test results now. She needed to be silenced. There was no statute of limitations on murder. He would not spend his retirement years in prison because that lying bitch Regina couldn't keep her footing after receiving a well-deserved punch.

He didn't have to do the dirty job himself, though. No. Joseph Talon had more to fear from Erica's revelations than anyone.

He intended to tell the senator everything. Even after the man discovered his business partner had killed his mother, he wouldn't do a thing about it, because Joseph Talon would be ruined if the world learned he was really Ricky Guerrero.

Ricky had been born in Canada. His father was Cuban and his mother French Canadian. Ricky wasn't a natural-born American. Hell, he wasn't even an American citizen.

By constitutional law Ricky Guerrero couldn't be President of the United States of America.

Chapter Fifty-One

*E*rica looked at the picture of Edward Drake in shock. He should have told her he'd worked on the Thermo-Con project. He could have saved her hours and hours of fruitless research. She considered bringing the photo to Lee but stopped herself. Here it was, only his second day as top man in the office and the FBI was wreaking havoc. This could wait.

She reached for the second envelope. Funny, but the results of the DNA test hardly mattered now. The FBI was collecting their own evidence and had already told her they weren't interested in this because the results wouldn't be admissible in a court of law. Regardless, she would now find out if a Menanichoch tribal member had licked the envelope she'd found on Jake's boat.

She broke the seal and carefully read the cover letter. The lab technician explained an abnormality in the results. While they were looking for genetic markers of the same heritage, they'd noticed substantial overlap, to the degree that they'd run a second test. The second test was conclusive: Sample A, the bone found in the Thermo-Con basement, was a matrilineal match with the DNA of Sample B. She felt lightheaded and oddly afraid as she understood Sample A was Joseph Talon's mother.

Sample C was even more disturbing. Sample C was an exact match of Sample B. Sample C, taken from the envelope she'd recovered in Jake's cabin, was none other than Senator Joseph Talon.

Chapter Fifty-Two

$\mathcal{L}$ee sat in a conference room with two FBI agents, watching as they dissected the network. He pointed to a section of code and told the agent to stop. "That line is broken. Ninety-nine percent of the time it wouldn't matter, because the line isn't usually run at startup, but when a user forces the program to run that bit of code, the program must skip this whole sequence." He pointed to hundreds of lines of code that followed.

"What's the sequence that's skipped?"

He studied the following lines of code. "Network Log-in," he said after a long pause. "If a hacker can access that line, they can bypass security and enter the network without anyone knowing they'd been there."

The younger agent looked at him with suspicion.

"I'm good at what I do," he said.

He glanced up to see Erica waving to him from the window next to the door. He got up and met her in the hallway, closing the door behind him. "You going home?"

"Yeah. The Thermo-Con research arrived, but it can wait."

She looked upset but given everything that had transpired

in the last few days, he couldn't blame her. He pulled her against him and held her for a long moment. He couldn't quite believe how crazy he was about this woman. "I love you. I'll be home as soon as I can."

"Good," she said. "I need you."

This was real. The lies were behind them.

"Thank you," she murmured against his lips. "For everything you've done for me."

"For us."

She looked unsure but repeated, "For us."

"Sweetheart, what's wrong?"

She gave him a melancholy smile. "I'm still figuring things out, I guess. It's going to take some time for me to process all that's happened." She paused. "Lee, I'm curious, did the senator know you were pretending to be an intern?"

"No. He didn't know a thing. I nearly had a heart attack when you showed up at the restaurant where Joe and I were having lunch. I was worried you'd call me your intern and introduced you as my girlfriend because he thought we'd met through JT, not the office."

"Why didn't you tell him the truth?"

"We didn't want his opponents to claim he had anything to do with the business or investigation. The last thing Joe needs is to be accused of being part of a nonexistent cover-up."

"You were protecting him." She flashed a wry smile, then shook her head.

"It's over now."

"But no one from the company has been arrested."

"When the employees in Iraq start talking, we'll know who was involved."

"Lee, have you considered the possibility *Joe* is involved?"

Her words hit him like a lightning rod, and he dropped his arms, releasing her. Alarm crossed her face, followed by hurt, and worst of all, fear.

"I'm sorry," she said. "I guess I'm tired. I should go."

"No, I'm sorry. You just surprised me, that's all." He reached for her, but she was stiff, tense, and didn't relax against him. "The answer is no. I've never considered Joe a suspect. He wouldn't be involved in something like this."

"But if you thought Sam Riversong could be involved, why not Joe?"

He shrugged. "I know Joe. He's a man of integrity. But I didn't know Sam." He saw the shuttered look in her gray eyes, and a disturbing thought occurred to him. "Erica, you need to be careful who you say things like this to. It's okay to talk to me, of course, but every reporter in the country wants to interview you. Anything you say—to anyone—could be quoted to a reporter. You can't say you suspect Joe. He's innocent, but your suspicion could kill the campaign."

She cupped his face between her hands. "I should go. I love you, Lee." She kissed him with surprising urgency. "Remember that I love you."

He watched her leave, feeling troubled. She sounded like she didn't expect to see him again.

⚜

*E*rica slipped through the parking garage and made it to her car without any of the reporters noticing her. She supposed wearing her hair down was a disguise of sorts. On the drive home, she considered what she would do, reeling from what she'd discovered.

Before talking to Lee, she'd gone through the Thermo-Con file and read every article she could find about the missing boy and his mother. She'd come to one inescapable conclusion: Joseph Talon was Ricky Guerrero. He and his mother disappeared from Fort Belmont in November 1952 and were reported missing one day before the Thermo-Con house was poured. She knew from the senator's biography that was around the time the orphaned Joseph Talon arrived at the Indian boarding school. No one knew the exact date because when the school burned, all the records were lost.

But more important than his false background was the fact that Joseph Talon was behind the smuggling. There could be no other explanation. At first she'd worried Lee was involved, but logic ruled him out. Without Lee, they wouldn't have raided Novak's boat and found the money. And JT would never have set Lee on the task of finding the smugglers if he were involved. He'd have sent in someone incompetent, someone to perform a token effort to allay suspicion. JT was also clear.

She'd wanted to tell Lee everything, but his reaction to her question was sharp, vehement. He wouldn't believe Joe was guilty without concrete evidence.

The envelope wouldn't convince him any more than it would convince the FBI or a jury. Only she had seen the envelope in Jake's cabin; only she knew the photos of artifacts from the Iraq museum had been inside. If she told Lee what she knew without solid proof, he'd be angry. Her accusations could be a fatal blow to their nascent relationship. And Lee was the only person in the world she had.

She could see the satellite trucks parked in front of her building from the 395 exit ramp. The press had arrived. She passed her building as she tried to decide what to do and ended up pulling up to the curb three blocks away.

She could probably get into her building through the parking garage without being seen. Or she could go straight to the front door and stop and make a statement. Maybe then they'd go away. But what would she say? What sort of horrid questions would the reporters ask? *How does it feel to fight two armed men and then watch sniper bullets blow out their brains?*

She stared at the tall antennas on the vans parked in front of her building and wondered why anyone would crave media attention. She didn't want her fifteen minutes. She didn't want fifteen seconds.

But the YouTube clip of her fight with Jake and Marco had convinced the world she wasn't the drug smugglers' accomplice, and she was grateful for that, because while the FBI might have eventually been convinced of her innocence, the rest of the world, not having access to the evidence, would not have been so forgiving.

People could review the same evidence and form conflicting opinions, but they trusted what they saw with their own eyes. Just as she trusted what she knew, because she'd found the envelope.

An idea struck her with the force of a blow. She might not want her new fame—notoriety, really—but she could use the media attention to trap the senator.

❂

*T*he reporter took Erica's call immediately and accepted her offer of a private interview with gushing excitement. Erica met the woman in front of the fish market a few blocks from her apartment. The ambitious newswoman was even more eager than she'd been last Wednesday morning, when she stood in front of the casino and spoke of the Aztec Room and Joseph Talon.

Erica outlined what she wanted. The reporter called her producers, and within minutes, they acquiesced fully to every condition, causing Erica to marvel at her change in circumstances.

Erica Kesling wanted a camera hidden in her apartment with a live broadcast feed?

No problem.

She promised a scoop the networks would kill for?

Excellent.

How about three hidden cameras?

In the end, they agreed on two.

Thirty minutes later, Erica, the reporter, and a cameraman drove into the underground garage and parked in her usual space. She led them up to her eighth-floor apartment. The cameraman hid one camera inside a throw pillow on the sofa and the other in the living room curtains.

Everything was perfect. The reporter and cameraman left for the remote-operations van already parked in front of the building. They'd begin broadcasting when Erica gave a prearranged hand signal.

She stood in her living room for several minutes, trying to find the courage for the next part of her plan. Finally, she pulled out her cell phone and dialed the senator's office. "This is Erica Kesling. I need to speak with Senator Talon."

"Prove you're Ms. Kesling," the aide said.

"Last week the senator gave me a DNA sample. No one else knows about the sample."

"I'll confirm this with the senator." She was put on hold.

A minute later, the phone was picked up. "Erica, dear, I'm glad you called."

"Senator," she said, "we need to talk."

"Is Lee okay?" He sounded genuinely concerned.

"He's fine. Listen, I've learned something you need to know about. About you and your parents. It's vital."

"Come to my office, and we'll talk."

"Reporters are lined up in front of my building. Come here and you'll get good press for visiting me personally after what happened. Then we can talk. Alone." She held her breath.

"I'll be there in twenty minutes," he finally said.

"I'll be waiting."

Would Lee hate her for what she was about to do? If what she suspected was true, then the senator was guilty as sin. No matter what had happened to him as a child, he'd made his own choices.

Chapter Fifty-Three

*R*icky hung up the phone and stared at Ed with hard, angry eyes.

Strange, after all these years, I still think of him as Ricky.

"She knows, doesn't she?" Ed asked.

He'd just finished telling Ricky the sordid truth when Erica called. The senator sat behind his impressive desk, looking much like the lost four-year-old Ed had left on the steps of the school all those years ago.

Slowly, as if in a daze, Ricky nodded.

"Did she mention the name Ricky Guerrero?" Ed asked.

"No. She hinted." His voice strengthened, then solidified as Ricky sat straighter in his chair. "She wants to speak with me. Alone. I'll explain to her that Ricky can't be president. She'll agree to keep my identity secret, if not for me, then for Lee." He again pierced Ed with a glare. "After all, it's not my fault. I didn't even know."

If the truth could come out without ruining his shot at the presidency, Ed knew Ricky would have called the police already. He smiled. He'd killed Ricky's mother, but now Ricky would help cover up the crime. "She could change her mind. She could destroy everything."

"It's a chance I'll have to take," Ricky said.

"No. I've been preparing for this ever since she found the bones and started researching Thermo-Con." He pulled out a keychain. "Using a false name, I rented a parking space from a resident of her building. This electronic tag will get you into the garage and inside the building."

He enjoyed the look of surprise on Ricky's face. The man had no idea how thoroughly he'd been running things for the last dozen years, because, like any good puppet master, Ed had been invisible.

No more. Senator Joseph Talon had just found out who the real boss was.

"The key is for a Zipcar parked two blocks away. You're going to drive to Erica's building and enter the south garage and park in space 231. Using the stairs, you can get to her floor without being seen." He pulled on a pair of gloves, then lifted a gun equipped with a suppressor from the satchel at his feet. "Use this, then drop it down the garbage chute, across the hall from her apartment, and get the hell out of the building."

※

*L*ee couldn't sit in the office for another minute. The FBI might be gutting the network, but Erica had been through hell and needed him. He was demonstrating the same screwed-up priorities Joe had exhibited twenty years ago, which had precipitated yet another divorce. He wouldn't mess up his relationship with Erica in the same way.

He left the office without a word to JT or the FBI agents he'd been working with all day. Traffic was heavy, and with each minute, he felt apprehension build. He never should have let Erica leave the office alone, especially when she seemed so upset.

He saw the reporters lined up outside her building and made a choice. He found a parking spot on the street, tucked a newspaper under his arm, and boldly approached the door.

The reporters surged forward. "Mr. Scott, what can you tell us about the investigation?"

"Mr. Scott, where is Ms. Kesling?"

"Mr. Scott, does the senator approve of your relationship with Erica Kesling?"

The questions all came on top of each other, but he had to smile when he heard the last one. He turned to face the crowd and several microphones were thrust in his face. "I am not at liberty to discuss the investigation. If Erica wanted you to know where she is, she would have told you herself. And I haven't asked Joe if he approves, because his opinion is irrelevant."

"But what is your relationship with Ms. Kesling?"

He smiled. "Don't you people read the papers?" He held up yesterday's *Post* with its full-color picture of him ogling his own date. "I'm crazy about her." He entered the building as more questions were called out, making him wonder how long the press would camp on her doorstep. He made a beeline for the elevator, his heart picking up speed. He felt like he'd been waiting for this homecoming forever. At last he reached the apartment door and knocked.

She opened the door immediately, then looked stunned— no, crestfallen—to see him. "You're not supposed to be here."

Her words cut unfathomably deep. "Why not, Short-cake?" He heard the edge in his voice and cursed. He was always showing her anger instead of the hurt that churned inside him.

She grabbed his arm and yanked him inside, slamming the door behind him. "I can't explain. He's going to be here any second."

Her words rocked him on his heels. "Who is *he*? What the hell is going on?"

"You shouldn't be here." She ran into the living room, her face pale, stricken. "This won't work." She paced the room in circles, then stopped and tilted her head toward the curtains in an odd way. "Lee's not supposed to be here. This isn't what I planned. It's not what I want."

He felt the blood rush from his body and wanted to punch something. "What the hell do you mean this isn't what you want?"

There was a knock at the front door.

If possible, she turned even paler. "You've got to hide. Now," she whispered urgently. "Go. Out on the balcony. With the curtains closed and the door ajar, you can listen."

He stayed rooted to the spot.

"Please, Lee. You've got to hide. I don't want you hurt."

Too late, but he did as she bade.

The curtains were still swaying when she opened the front door. "Thank you for coming," he heard her say.

"What's going on, Erica?"

Lee recognized Joe's voice, and his world tilted. What the hell was he doing here?

He heard footsteps, which he thought were Erica's. She stopped just on the other side of the curtain. Her voice was crisp and clear. "I got the results today from the DNA tests I sent off last week. For starters, I learned you aren't Joseph Talon or a Menanichoch Indian. You're Ricky Guerrero, the son of a Cuban man who was trying to earn citizenship by serving in the army." She paused for breath. "But more important, I learned you were the person who traded Iraqi artifacts with Jake Novak for Aztec ones." Her voice hardened. "You've been in on the smuggling from the start."

In an instant, Lee split the curtain and surged into the room.

Joe looked stunned to see him, but no more stunned than Lee was to see Joe reach into his satchel, pull out a pistol with a suppressor, and point it at Erica.

Lee dove for her and shoved her behind him. "Put the gun down, Joe."

Joe stared at him, pain in his eyes. The muzzle lowered, then wavered, not quite down.

"Why the fuck are you holding a gun?" If Joe flinched, Lee would lose a kneecap.

"I came here to convince her to be silent about Ricky —me."

"You knew?" he asked, still trying to put the pieces together. He remembered the name from the old newspaper article. How the hell had Erica connected Joe to that story?

"No. I didn't know. I learned the truth an hour ago."

"Drake must have told him," Erica said from behind him. "I think Edward Drake killed Regina Guerrero, then dumped Ricky at the Indian boarding school."

"Actually, he said he dumped me first, then killed my mother." Joe sighed but still didn't quite drop the gun. "Erica, Lee, you can't tell anyone. Ricky Guerrero was born in Canada. His parents weren't Americans. He can't be president, but Joseph Talon can."

"Joseph Talon doesn't deserve to be president," Erica said. "Joseph Talon is a thief who worked with drug smugglers to launder billions of dollars from Iraq through his tribal casino. Riversong wasn't involved at all, was he? It was all you."

The gun rose again. Joe angled to the side, trying to get a fix on her. Lee locked his hands on her hips and pivoted, keeping himself between Erica and the gun.

"You can't prove anything," Joe said.

Erica tried to move out from behind Lee. "You mailed photographs of Iraqi artifacts to Jake. You licked the envelope."

"An envelope proves nothing."

"Erica, stay behind me! Joe won't shoot me."

"The envelope was addressed to Marco. Tell me, Senator,

why were you sending mail to a member of a Mexican drug cartel?"

"The envelope was addressed to Marco Garcia. I didn't know he was Marco Delgado."

The man had just admitted he'd mailed the envelope. *Christ, Erica was telling the truth.*

He'd wanted to believe the gun was the result of Joe suffering some sort of temporary madness upon learning his whole life was a lie, but the man he'd worshipped for most of his life was a fraud. Anger and horror flooded him. "You intended for Erica to take the fall with Novak, didn't you?"

Joe studied him, and Lee looked into the same sharp, clear brown eyes he'd known since he was six years old. The man wasn't crazy, and he wasn't stupid. "I didn't know she'd worked for Novak. Novak kept us all in the dark."

Everything he'd achieved had been driven by the desire to earn Joe's respect. "Why?" He nearly choked on the word.

"The money was wasted in Iraq. It was stupid to give them so much cash. I found a way to put it to use that would be good for everyone."

"To buy the presidency."

"We need a good president. I'm doing the world a favor."

"You've always been good at justifying your actions." Lee heard the bitterness in his voice and realized some resentments never faded.

"I believe in what I'm doing," Joe said. "It's necessary. And no matter how much Erica believes her pitiful envelope is proof, there's no evidence I was part of the smuggling, and there never will be. You and JT have done an excellent job insulating me. No one will ever find a dime of the money in my campaign funds. But I can't let anyone find out about Ricky Guerrero." He pointed the gun at Lee's heart. "I'm sorry, son."

Adrenaline and fear shot through him. He tightened his grip on Erica.

She spoke in a rush. "There are TV cameras hidden in the room. You're being broadcast right now on the national feed."

Joe paused. "Nice try."

"I mean it! Check the couch and the curtains. I set this up so that no matter how many millions you funnel into your campaign, no one will vote for you."

Lee heard sirens in the distance, getting louder. The gun wavered in Joe's hand.

"The reporter probably called the police as soon as you pulled the gun," she said.

She was brilliant. Magnificent. If Joe didn't have a gun pointing straight at them, Lee would kiss the hell out of her. "Drop the gun, Joe."

Joe moved, trying to get a clear shot at Erica. Lee shifted, preventing him.

The sirens came to a halt right outside the building. Erica threaded her fingers through his and squeezed. "Pull that trigger and you're going down for murder, you lying, cheating, thieving, sonofabitch," she said.

Joe looked stunned. "Christ! This is all Drake's fault. He set me up."

The whirr of a helicopter grew louder and louder, until it sounded as if it hovered above the building. An amplified voice said, "Senator Talon, drop the gun. The building is surrounded."

Lee knew the exact moment when Joe's grip on the gun tightened. The man had nothing left to lose and was going to pull the trigger. The gun shifted, but before Joe could take aim at his own head or Erica's, Lee kicked, connecting with the weapon.

A loud thump came from the balcony.

The gun went flying at the same moment the windows behind them exploded inward. He used his grip on Erica's fingers to yank her to the couch, where he fell on top of her, shielding her as glass rained down.

He felt a stabbing pain in his arm, while sharp, needle-like jabs pricked his back and legs. He held her close, taking comfort from the feel of her warm body beneath his. Behind him, he heard men shouting orders to Joe.

"Mr. Scott, are you okay?" a man asked.

He lifted his head and took in the scene. A half-dozen SWAT officers had entered from the balcony. Joe was on his knees on the floor, holding his wrist, which was bent at an odd angle. Three officers had guns trained on him. He howled in pain as a fourth cuffed his broken and bleeding wrist.

Lee gingerly moved his arms and legs. He stood up. He'd been cut by several shards of glass, but that was all. He took Erica's hand and pulled her to her feet. She was okay.

He held her and whispered in her ear, "It's over, honey. It's over."

She met his gaze with a weak smile; then her eyes widened, and she gasped.

The world went black.

Chapter Fifty-Four

*B*lood seeped between Erica's fingers as she tried to staunch the spurting wound in Lee's arm. Paramedics arrived seconds later and pushed her out of the way. She stood nearby, frantic with worry.

"His brachial artery's been nicked," one said, applying pressure to the wound.

She felt lightheaded. She was going to be sick. "Is he going to be okay?"

The bleeding stopped, and the medic wrapped Lee's arm in gauze. "He'll be fine. We'll get him on an IV to get his fluids up. He'll probably wake then. We'll take him to the hospital for monitoring."

They took pity on her and let her ride along in the ambulance. Some part of her registered the sea of reporters who followed their progress from the building to the ambulance, but the rest of her was focused on Lee's pale face.

He woke before they turned off Seventh Avenue. He saw the bandage on his upper arm and tried to sit up. "Was I shot?"

"A shard of glass cut your brachial artery," the paramedic said.

"I passed out because of a shard of glass?" He lay back down and closed his eyes. "That isn't the least bit manly. JT will never let me live it down."

The paramedic chuckled, and even Erica found a small laugh inside her.

He opened his eyes and squeezed her hand, then brought her fingers to his lips. "You have the most beautiful smile. I want to see it more."

She burst into tears.

"Hey, Shortcake, I said I want you to smile. You have to do what I say; I'm the injured one."

"Because of me. My stupid plan to trap the senator could have killed you," she said.

"It could have killed *you*. Why didn't you tell me?"

"Everything you've done has been for Joe."

"I was wrong about him." His voice dropped as he squeezed her hand again.

She kissed him, telling him without words she'd be there for him as he dealt with Joe's betrayal. This wound, she knew from personal experience, might never heal.

The ambulance arrived at the hospital. Erica was told to wait while Lee was examined. An hour later, they finally let her inside the treatment room.

He lay on the bed, shirtless. She took in his sculpted biceps, his handsome face, his crooked, sexy smile, and for the first time since he'd passed out, she was able to take a deep breath.

"Come here," he said.

As soon as she was within reach, he grabbed her with his unbandaged arm and pulled her onto the mattress alongside him.

She squealed. "I don't want to hurt you!"

"It's just a nick. I'm fine. They're going to release me soon." He snuggled her against his side. "I need to hold you."

She settled her check against his chest, listening to his

strong heartbeat. "I've been watching the news in the waiting room. The FBI arrested Drake."

"Good."

"And you bled all over the new sofa."

"Damned inconsiderate of me." She felt his chuckle against her cheek. He played with her hair, his nails grazing her scalp.

She let out an exaggerated purr, and he laughed aloud.

"I wish we'd met at a different time," he said, turning serious. "Different place. I'd have treated you so much better than I did as your lying, manipulative intern."

She traced circles on his chest. "I'm not complaining. You saved my life. Twice."

He flashed a cocky grin. "Well, you have a nice ass. It's a shame to see you fall on it."

She nipped his smooth skin with a chuckle, then settled back on his chest. "Lee, tell me something about yourself."

"What?"

"Anything. I know almost nothing about you."

"I guess we've never been properly introduced." He stroked her hair. "My name is Lee Scott. I'm thirty-two, I'm a computer and cell phone security consultant, and I love you. Those are the most important points."

She smiled. "I'm Erica Kesling. I'm twenty-nine. I used to be an underwater archaeologist before I destroyed my reputation by working for a treasure hunter who turned out to be a drug smuggler. I'm deeply in debt, have a bad credit rating, and just destroyed the man who owns the company I work for. I don't know what the hell I'm going to do with my life, but whatever it is, I hope I'm with you, because I love you."

"That's all that matters," he said. "For now."

Epilogue

One Month Later
San Diego, California

*A*n alarm shrieked, yanking Erica from sleep. She bolted upright, her hands feeling for the clock on the nightstand. It wasn't there. The furniture didn't feel right. She had a moment of panicked disorientation. Even the blare of the alarm was unfamiliar.

Where am I?

Beside her, Lee cursed, the sound pulling her back to her senses. Grounding her.

Oh yeah. San Diego. Vacation condo.

Apparently the previous renters had set the alarm for—she cracked open one eye and located the clock on Lee's nightstand—three a.m.

"Sorry, Shortcake, I've got to turn on a light to figure out how to turn the damn thing off," Lee said.

"I don't care about the light. Just make it stop." It was the worst sort of alarm, a high-pitched shriek, designed to drive everyone within earshot insane.

The lights flicked on and a moment later there was

blessed silence. She let out a sigh of relief and settled back into the bedding with closed eyes.

"Don't get too comfortable, that was just the snooze button."

She grinned. "Is the clock too much for my tech geek?"

"Whoever designs these things are sadists. They're so complicated now and they still don't work."

"Clearly, this one does."

"It won't when I'm done with it." The bed shifted as he left her side. She heard him moving furniture to get to the outlet so he could unplug the clock.

"Don't forget the backup battery," she said.

"I'm on it. Just need a screwdriver."

She opened her eyes. Sure enough, he was digging around in his suitcase and pulled out a case that held a half dozen tiny screwdrivers for opening electronic devices. "You are such a nerd. You packed your screwdriver kit?"

He flashed a grin. "You never know when these things will come in handy. Like at three in the morning when my sweetheart needs me to rescue her from a vicious alarm."

"Touché."

"Actually, I brought them in case we find a computer I need to pull apart in the storage unit."

That made sense, but she didn't think her mother had a computer.

He removed the battery then flicked off the light and crawled back into bed. He pulled her against him and she smiled as she felt his growing erection.

"Someone is awake."

"It's six a.m. in DC. We're usually getting up now."

Their flight had been late and they didn't check into the condo until nearly eleven p.m. local time. They'd had three hours sleep at most…but now she was awake too. She slipped a hand between their bodies and stroked his erection, smiling as he grew thicker in her hand.

He made a guttural sound in the back of his throat and pressed his mouth to her neck. He cupped her breast, rolling her nipple between his fingers. His hand slid lower, to the juncture of her thighs. He slipped two fingers inside her slick opening and groaned again. "I'm not the only one who's awake."

She didn't waste time with words and shifted position, directing him inside her. In one smooth motion he rolled her to her belly and slid deep. His big hands cupped her hips—God, she loved when he touched her like that—and lifted her ass, urging her to her knees.

Zero to a hundred in three seconds flat. Or maybe his first swing was a home run...

All she knew was making love with him was just the escape she needed from the anxieties that had accompanied her on this rushed trip.

For the thousandth time she reminded herself she would be happy in any job, as long as she was with Lee, but the prospect of being able to recapture the career that had been lost to her...

Lee stroked her clit as he thrust inside her. He teased her, bringing her close to the brink then backing off. She pressed her face into the pillow and luxuriated in the feel of him. The slide of him inside her. The slap of his hips against her skin.

Lee. Her Lee.

Inside her. Possessing her. Loving her.

It was hard to believe they'd only been together for a little over a month. Hard to believe the intensity even when it was middle of the night, jet-lagged sex. The act was straight up physical, and yet...not. It was never just physical with Lee.

These moments of connection bound them closer together while also providing escape from an ongoing emotional minefield. They could get through anything as long as they had each other.

If Lee could accept the dissolution of his relationship

with the man who'd been his father far more than his biological father had ever been, she could certainly face sorting through the storage unit with her mother's belongings.

Lee's fingers stroked without letting up, again pulling her back into her body, back into the moment. Her orgasm came hard and intense. She cried out into the pillow as she clenched around him.

He thrust faster, issuing endearments as he came.

He collapsed on her, careful, even in his post-orgasm bliss not to put his full weight on her, even though she loved the feeling of his body pressed to hers. Loved knowing he was depleted and satisfied.

He rolled to his side, pulling her with him. He nuzzled her neck. "I love you," he said against her skin.

She turned in his arms and faced him. "I love you too. That you're here with me for this…it means the world to me. Especially after I—"

He placed a finger over her lips. "I'd never let you face this ordeal alone."

She brushed a lock of hair away from his forehead. His brow was damp with sweat. "How did you ever convince me you were a twenty-five-year-old slacker?"

"You were too blinded by my body to delve deep."

She laughed, although he did have a point. The attraction between them had thrown her off-balance from the start, and he'd admitted to using that to his advantage.

Any residual anger she might have felt over that disappeared when she understood the stakes. His reason for lying was greater than the two of them, and most of the time they'd been together he'd had no way of knowing if she was innocent or complicit. She'd forgiven him but knew he felt guilty anyway. It didn't help that she hadn't pounced on his proposal.

But she'd denied him for a different reason.

She snuggled against him and closed her eyes. "I suppose

it's too early to go to the storage unit." A year ago, she'd rented the cheapest unit she could find in the aftermath of fleeing Mexico. Cheap meant no twenty-four hour access, which she'd never thought would be a problem. "What if my thesis isn't there?"

"Then we'll fly to Hawaii and make the school find a copy," he said. "They awarded you the M.A. They'll have it on file somewhere. Every single copy can't have been destroyed."

A job had opened up in the Underwater Archaeology Branch at Naval History and Heritage Command. She was beside herself with the idea of being able to use her expensive MA again and work in the field she'd lost.

A job, doing underwater archaeology, in DC. It would be the ultimate redemption.

The only catch was, Secretary of the Interior qualifications for professional archaeologists required the Office of Personnel Management to have a copy of her Master's thesis. It was doubly important in her case because her graduate school refused to provide her with a reference.

It should have been a simple request from the university, but apparently, around the time the school was supposed to scan the document and add it to their online library, it had disappeared.

Erica had no doubt one of her former friends had destroyed the print version along with all digital copies. Her peers had felt so betrayed, and more than a few of them had the computer savvy to seek and destroy.

She'd been blackballed on every level.

It didn't help that Edward Drake had ruined her computer when he trashed her apartment, and she hadn't dared copy the file onto her computer at work, because she'd hidden her degree from Janice, fearing her boss would ask why she'd never mentioned her MA and experience.

Janice might have fired her, just as Erica's employers on the West Coast had.

So now here she was, back in San Diego. The storage unit in which she'd crammed her mother's belongings was her only hope for laying hands on the thesis that could bring her redemption full-circle and land her her dream job.

In all likelihood, she'd end up working with some of the very people who'd tried to erase her from the profession.

"I'll get it for you, sweetheart. I'll find a copy somewhere in the University of Hawaii computer system."

She shook her head and pressed her lips to his throat. "No hacking. This isn't worth you losing your business license or landing in jail."

He shrugged. "I don't get caught. And what was done to you was wrong."

She leaned back and met his gaze. "I wish that were true, but it's not. I did it to me. I'm the one who accepted the job from Jake. I knew the consequences. Jake and Marco did a lot of horrible things, but the first step, that was on me. They couldn't have hurt me if I'd turned down Jake's offer." She pressed her fingers to his lips. "But I appreciate your support —emotional, not the hacking kind. Instead of freaking out over the damn thesis, I need to take stock of just how lucky I am."

"I'm the lucky one." He nipped at her fingers. "Now, try to sleep. If your thesis isn't in the storage unit, we'll figure something out."

❖

*H*er thesis wasn't there. After hours of sorting through boxes, Lee could tell Erica was barely holding herself together in the face of utter disappointment.

They'd taken the trip on ridiculously short notice—he'd surprised her with it as soon as it became clear obtaining her thesis wasn't going to be easy. They'd decided to spend a few days sorting through her parents' belongings and arrange to have the items she wanted to keep shipped to DC, disposing or donating the rest.

He'd hoped they'd have time to play once they were done. He'd never been to San Diego, while Erica had moved here when she was twelve. He wanted to see her favorite places, eat at her favorite restaurants, to get a glimpse of the woman she'd been before Jake and Marco had sabotaged her world.

But now he'd just give anything to see her smile. Looking through her mother's belongings only made her bleak mood worse.

"Forget sorting through this stuff," he said. "We'll pay for a few more months of storage and deal with it later."

"There are a few more boxes in the back—"

"We'll check them. Tomorrow. It's hot. We're jet-lagged and I'm starving. Let's take a break. Regroup. I can make some calls to the university."

Erica's advisor had been ducking her calls. Just because she'd been redeemed in the eyes of the media—and the law —didn't mean her alma mater was ready to welcome her back into the fold. But Lee had friends in government, and not just his disgraced stepdad. The US Attorney for the District of Columbia might be willing to lean on the professor.

Her advisor was bound to have a hard copy somewhere in his office or in the department. And Lee would do just about anything to get that dejected look in her eyes to go away.

He'd hoped she'd change her mind about his proposal on this trip, but the way things were going, it didn't seem likely.

She plastered on a smile and nodded.

He wrapped an arm around her. "You don't have to fake it. I know what this means to you."

"I just—I shouldn't have let myself hope."

"I'll do whatever it takes to track down your thesis. If you don't get the job, it won't be due to a technicality like this." He slid his fingers through hers. "No matter what happens, you aren't alone anymore."

A smile lit her eyes. This one was the real deal. Her gray eyes went soft and she looked at him like he was the center of her universe. "How can I be unhappy when the man of my dreams has my back?"

He laughed. "Damn right. And I love your smile. If it weren't ninety degrees in this tin-can, I'd show you just how much."

She glanced around the full storage unit. "If we clear off the sofa…" Her long lashes hooded her eyes and her lips curved in a sexy smile.

He laughed. Her mood had lightened, but it wouldn't last if they stayed here much longer, even if they fooled around. "No way. Sex in a storage unit isn't my idea of a vacation. It sounds more like high school."

"You didn't—"

He shrugged. "Well, maybe college. As you've kindly pointed out, I was something of a nerd in high school and only hung out with cyber women."

"*Was?*" she teased.

That was his Erica, through and through. He kissed her, long and deep, loving the way she melted against him. Just when she was hot, ready, and eager, he released her and said, "Let's get out of here."

She gave him a playful pout, all worry gone from her eyes. "A girl has needs, Lee."

He winked at her. "But she won't buy the cow if the milk is free."

She laughed. "You did *not* just say that."

He flashed a grin as he stepped back and reached for the handle to pull down the garage-style door. "I'll put out for you anytime, anywhere…except here."

He drove their rental car, with no destination in mind. On

the right there was a picture of a baby elephant on a sign for San Diego's Wildlife Park, which was just a block away. Damn, that baby elephant was cute. It was hard to feel down while looking at baby animals. He changed lanes and turned into the parking lot for the Wildlife Park.

⁂

"*I* can't remember the last time I was here," Erica said as they held hands and strolled down the paved, shaded paths. It smelled just like she remembered. Dirt, flowers, the earthy scent of furred mammals in this section of the park, and under it all a mild layer of dung.

Not unpleasant like a privy, but more like being in the woods for an archaeological survey, only slightly more concentrated.

Lee led her to see the baby elephant. Signs indicated Mbali had been born at the Wildlife Park nearly seven months ago as part of an endangered species breeding program.

"I think that baby elephant is the cutest thing I've ever seen in my life," she said. She sat down on an open bench with a view into the elephant enclosure. Mbali flopped down in a large puddle of mud that had to be cool on the hot day.

"While you watch the elephant. I'm going to get us some ice cream." He leaned down and kissed her, then left her side.

His confident stride was probably the only thing that could draw her eyes away from the insanely adorable elephant. It was surreal to be in San Diego with Lee. Home. Sort of. Really DC was home now. Her life was with Lee, to hell with underwater archaeology.

In the grand scheme of things, getting to work in the field again didn't matter, not when she had so many other things to be thankful for, starting with the man who was getting her ice cream.

Her cell phone rang and she checked caller ID. Janice.

She answered, feeling bad she hadn't been able to reach Janice and tell her about the trip before boarding the flight.

Janice had been on vacation and probably wasn't happy to return to the office only to discover that her assistant had taken off for a week.

Until Rob Anderson officially accepted the position, Lee was the general manager of the Bethesda office of Talon & Drake, so she had zero chance of being fired for taking unauthorized leave—thank you, nepotism—but she didn't like disappointing Janice. The woman had given her a chance when no one else would, and Erica had prided herself on working her butt off as a thank you.

"Erica, I just got off the phone with the hiring manager for Naval History and Heritage Command—"

"She called you already? I'm sorry, Janice, I wanted to talk to you about the job opening first—"

"I was on vacation. You couldn't. No problem. I'm delighted to give you a reference, but—"

"I know. We haven't talked about Jake Novak." Erica had taken a week off after Joseph Talon was arrested. She couldn't face the office right away. It was only with Lee's encouragement that she'd gone back at all. By then, a family emergency had Janice's attention, and they'd only spoken in passing and always about business. Then Janice had taken off for a scheduled vacation. They'd promised to sit down for lunch and really talk when she got back.

Janice laughed. "No more interrupting, my dear."

"Sorry," she said, wincing. She clearly wasn't employee of the month material.

Janice's voice was warm as she continued, "The personnel manager said they're having trouble tracking down your thesis. I wanted to ask you if I should make a copy of the one I have before I have it couriered over to them."

Erica bolted to her feet even as her stomach dropped. "You have a copy of my thesis?"

"Of course I do, my dear. When I first hired you for the field job, one of the crew told me all about your sordid history. She was upset I made you crew chief and was hoping I would fire you."

Erica rocked on her heels. *Janice had known the entire time?*

"I'm not one to take rumors as fact," Janice said, "but I was concerned to learn you had an MA from UH that you hadn't mentioned, especially when that would have bumped up your salary considerably. No one would give you a reference, so I contacted the school and requested a copy of your transcript and thesis."

Janice's request might've been what triggered someone to destroy all copies at the university, but they hadn't been able to stop the copy from being mailed.

"Your thesis was solid," Janice continued, "so I decided to offer you the office job."

Erica's heart pounded. "You never said a word."

"I was waiting for you to tell me."

"So all those times you mentioned that I didn't have enough experience…you were trying to nudge me into confessing?" Her legs wobbled and she felt somewhat light-headed. "And that conversation with Ed Drake about Jake… you knew, even then?"

"Yes. I knew. I'd hoped you'd give me a reason to force Ed to drop the proposal—although now it's obvious nothing would have swayed him."

"You even helped me get my apartment. Without your reference, I never would have found a decent place to live. I'm stunned you'd do that for me, given the rumors."

"My dear, I've been an archaeologist for thirty-five years," Janice's voice held the affectionate tone she'd often used with Erica. "I've known academics who would eat their young. I couldn't sit back and let them devour you. You made a mistake and took a job for a treasure hunter. That wasn't criminal. The job you were hired for was perfectly legal. And once I got to know you, I had no doubt the rumors about you stealing artifacts were lies. Many times these last months I've wanted to take your hand and tell you that you had a friend."

Erica swiped away a tear. "And a thousand times I wanted to tell you everything, but I was so afraid." Lee approached, holding two ice cream cones. "I don't know how to thank you, Janice."

"Sweetie, I'm thrilled to see you landing on your feet. I'm going to miss you though, when you take the job at NHHC. I've never had a harder working assistant."

"Well, the job isn't a sure thing," she said, forcing her voice past the emotion that clogged her throat.

Lee reached her side and looked at her questioningly.

She flashed a wide smile.

"Actually," Janice said, "It is. They told me that if your thesis checks out, they're going to make the offer."

Erica squealed, the sound rivaling that of the elephants twenty feet away.

Janice laughed. "I asked them to let me be the one to tell you."

"Thank you so much, Janice."

"You're welcome. Now enjoy your week in San Diego with Lee, because when you get back, we have a lot of work to do before you abandon me for NHHC."

She laughed. "I will."

Janice hung up and Erica tucked away her phone then she threw her arms around Lee, who did his best to hug her without using his forearms or hands, which were full of ice cream cones.

"Janice had a copy all along!" She ran kisses over his face, frenetic in her joy.

He planted his mouth on hers, stilling her. His kiss was

hot, deep, and centering. When he raised his head she was lightheaded again, but for an entirely different reason.

"Okay. Slow down and tell me everything," he said.

He released her and she took her ice cream. She faced the world's most adorable pachyderm as she relayed her conversation with Janice, her head spinning with the change in fortune.

He smiled and ate his ice cream. "I guess we could've skipped the trip to San Diego."

She licked her own cone. The cold, creamy texture was heavenly on her throat in the afternoon heat. "If you're eager to get back, we could catch a flight tonight."

"Hell no. This is our first vacation together." He draped an arm around her shoulders, his half-eaten cone in his other hand as he led her down the path. "And now we can enjoy it. I seem to remember someone talking about having needs earlier."

"You're going to put out?" she asked with a laugh. She eyed the tram ride that crossed over the park. "Anytime, anywhere?"

"Excluding hot storage units and places that will get us arrested. Let's go back to the condo."

The moment they were inside the vacation rental, Erica started stripping Lee. Unable to make it to the bedroom, they made love on the couch.

Afterward, she snuggled against his side. The wide front window faced the water. "How is this different from what we'd be doing in DC?" she asked.

He rolled over, pinning her into the cushions. "We can't look at the ocean when we make love in DC."

"From my apartment we can see the Potomac."

"Not the same." His lips trailed along her neck. "I've been thinking about your apartment. I'd like to move my office there."

She threaded her fingers through his hair. "Are you

worried I'm going to move out because I didn't accept your proposal?"

"No. You're too crazy about me to ever leave."

She laughed. "True." He knew she hadn't said yes because he wanted children. What if she was like her mother, and lacked the maternal instinct?

"My reason is straightforward, your apartment is cheaper than my current office space." He met her gaze, his eyes serious. "You know, if you decide you don't want children, I can accept that. I want you. Period. From now until the end of time."

She loved the fact that he never attempted to brush off her concern about being a lousy mother. He didn't minimize or offer false reassurances. He just accepted. "We don't have to rush that decision," she said. "If you're willing to give me time."

"Sweetheart, you can have all the time in the world."

She pushed at his chest, and he released her so she could sit up. "Ask me again," she said.

He laughed. "You want me to propose now, while we're naked in the living room?"

"Actually, I have a better idea." She slid off the couch and positioned herself in front of him on one knee.

His eyes widened, then he settled back against the cushion with a broad smile.

"Lee Scott, from the moment you invaded my morning workout, you've taken over my world. I'm crazy in love with you"—her voice broke as emotion swamped her—"and I want nothing more than to spend the rest of my life with you." She cleared her throat. "Will you do me the honor of becoming my husband?"

He slid off the couch, took her in his arms, and kissed her. "I thought you'd never ask."

Author's Note

Several real events inspired parts of this book. Some may be familiar to readers, some probably aren't. Many readers will likely remember the looting of the National Museum of Iraq in 2003 but may not recall the twelve billion US dollars that went missing in Iraq in 2004. In 2007, the US Department of Defense created a deck of cards to educate troops about protecting cultural resources in the Middle East. For links to articles about these cards, please visit my website at www.Rachel-Grant.net.

I drew upon a sad chapter in our nation's history in placing Joseph Talon in an Indian boarding school. Starting in the 1870s, the US government forced hundreds of thousands of Native American children to attend off-reservation Indian boarding schools with the purpose of erasing the cultural identity from the students.

Something that will be familiar but which did not inspire this story are the politically motivated lies spread about President Barack Obama's birth certificate. The first draft of this story was finished in 2007—before the first ballots were cast in the 2008 campaign and before (to the best of my knowledge) the media began repeating the false assertions. I was never quite sure how to handle that development and need to thank my clever editor for suggesting a way to address the issue in this story.

Last but most important on the list of real inspirations for *Concrete Evidence*: Thermo-Con is real. In 1998 the engineering firm I worked for was contracted by US Army Garrison Fort Belvoir to write an environmental assessment of a house made out of a strange, yeasty concrete. They didn't know who had built the house on the post or why, and wanted a detailed history as part of the EA. As in the story, I went to the National Archives and found a journal entry that gave me the date the house was built and the name Higgins. Three days later, after rereading a 1949 article in the army post's newspaper, *Belvoir Castle*, I was inspired to try to track down the patent.

For story-line reasons, I changed both the year Thermo-Con was developed and the location of the house. But the information about Thermo-Con's relationship to Andrew Jackson Higgins is accurate, and the newspaper article Erica reads is nearly a word-for-word duplication of the *Belvoir Castle* article (Vol. VIII, No. 43, Friday, April 22, 1949). The bones in the basement, of course, are pure fabrication.

When I researched Thermo-Con in 1998, information for older patents could only be found in card-catalog file drawers located in an old storage room. The patent office has moved now, and much of the information has been scanned into an online database, but I took fictional license and kept the old patent office and research methods, preferring the way it really happened to how it could happen now.

Lastly, as in the story, the day before the Thermo-Con EA was due, I ran a simple internet people search on the inventors listed on the patent card and ended up on the phone with Andrew Jackson Higgins's great-grandson. He gave me his father's number, who in turn put me in contact with the wife of the man who ran the Thermo-Con development team. The Higgins family members' names were purposely left out of this story, and I wish to thank them for their help and enthusiasm back in 1998 and hope they appreciate this fictionalized account.

About the Author

USA Today bestselling author Rachel Grant also writes thrillers as R.S. Grant. She worked for over a decade as a professional archaeologist and mines her experiences for storylines and settings, which are as diverse as excavating a cemetery underneath an historic art museum in San Francisco, survey and excavation of many prehistoric Native American sites in the Pacific Northwest, researching an historic concrete house in Virginia (inspiration for her debut novel, CONCRETE EVIDENCE), and mapping a seventeenth century Spanish and Dutch fort on the island of Sint Maarten in the Caribbean (which provided inspiration for the island and fort described in CRASH SITE).

She lives in the Pacific Northwest with her husband and children.

For more information:
www.Rachel-Grant.net
contact@rachel-grant.net

Printed in Great Britain
by Amazon

57835777R00239